ONLY THE WHORES WORE WATCHES

Frank
10/05/2012
Falkland Arms .

ONLY THE WHORES WORE WATCHES

AS TOLD TO FRANK

Matador
5 Weir Road
Kibworth Beauchamp
Leicester LE8 0LQ, UK
Tel: (+44) 116 279 2299
Fax: (+44) 116 279 2277
Email: books@troubador.co.uk
Web: www.troubador.co.uk/matador

ISBN 978 1848764 491

British Library Cataloguing in Publication Data.
A catalogue record for this book is available from the British Library.

Typeset in 11pt Sabon MT by Troubador Publishing Ltd, Leicester, UK
Printed and bound in Great Britain by TJI Digital, Padstow, Cornwall

Matador is an imprint of Troubador Publishing Ltd

ACKNOWLEDGEMENTS

This story first stuttered into life during a brainstorming session some years ago with my brother Roger. I have incorporated some of his ideas. I would also like to thank my sister Janet who proofread the first draft and offered some valid criticisms. James Ferguson of Signal Books was in on the ground floor too. He sent me a copy of Blood & Silver by Kris E Lane, a history of Caribbean piracy which I strongly recommend, and provided an introduction to Hugh O'Shaughnessy. Hugh's excellent 1984 work Grenada: Revolution, Invasion and Aftermath complemented my personal experiences.

This novel is dedicated to Elda Cherie.

Puerto Príncipe 1668

The Welshman's Savages

The Cimarron shuffled his feet, uncomfortable in reluctant sandals. He tried to ignore the stampeding mob, the screams, the smoke, the severed body parts. He sniffed, briefly, the air. An appetising barbecue aroma of burning wood and scorched bodies was slowly dispersing at last with the acrid fumes as they slowly surrendered to the pungent stench of rotting flesh.

All his life he had been familiar with the cocktail of odours produced by human bodies. Heat made smells worse. He'd heard men speak of extreme cold of course, but he'd never experienced it. Not even at sea.

At sea. Yes. Sweat, shit and piss mingled with the stench of death on that voyage. A voyage he thought would never end. A third of the cargo died and were tossed overboard to feed the sharks. Now he had been offered the opportunity of returning to sea, this time as an equal. An equal of the Welshman's savages that is – not of the Welshman. Who stood alongside him now impassively surveying the rampaging horde to his right.

Much of yesterday's battle was fought in this plaza, formerly the pride of Puerto Príncipe. Already it had been disfigured, vandalized, the homes and shops ransacked. Charred yellow-ochre and once-whitewashed buildings gaped hopelessly, ashamed of their failure to protect their owners. Blackened skeletal woodwork, still smoking, almost

1

charcoal now, loitered in the gaps where sturdy doors and window shutters had promised security. Broken flagstones, abandoned weapons, dead horses and assorted human body parts littered the ground. That looks like a hand. Difficult to be sure with all that blood and the torn flesh but it does look like all four fingers and the thumb are intact. If that belonged to one of ours he'll be needing a hook now. If he survived. Smashed carts and broken furniture, the remnants of the barricades, cluttered the entrances to the plaza and the narrow alleys beyond. A gust of wind, contemptuous of the slaughter, whipped through the shattered streets, collected a spiral of smoke and wrenched it away into the upper air.

There were still a couple of corpses which had been robbed but not yet flung aside. Both Spanish judging by their bloodstained clothing. Probably killed defending their town but, then again, they may have been hacked down for sport when pleading for mercy. Maybe they would remain there until the pirates left and the survivors could bury them. Before they stank too much or were eaten by the dogs. In one corner injured invaders were still being patched up whilst some of their comrades were noisily quaffing from flagons and sorting through loot.

The Cimarron ceased speculating on the smells and opened his ears to the noise. On the east side of the plaza stood the church, now a prison. Here an unwashed rabble thrashed at the remaining townspeople with cutlasses and cudgels as they herded them inside. Curses mingled with screams as the blows landed. A few of the victims were men of fighting age. Survivors of the battle were they, or too afraid to fight? Maybe they had fought then surrendered. The rest were old men, women and children. Added to those already imprisoned they would number hundreds. Maybe they would be starved for days inside the church or perhaps the building would be set afire with them all locked inside it. Nobody knew yet.

The Welshman had threatened to burn the entire town

to the ground. First his desperadoes would herd the terrified survivors into the church. Next those prisoners would hear the screams of the unfortunates dragged outside to endure torture or rape. Or both. Their nostrils would twitch to the acrid smoke of buildings burning. Unable to see what was happening in the town and to their friends and families outside their imaginations would run riot, fearing the worst.

These townspeople reminded the Cimarron of cattle. Many loped forward eagerly into the church as though it was a place of safety, rather as some cows might hurry into an abattoir. Others glanced behind and to their sides, searching for an escape route or trying to determine their attackers' intentions. Some, mainly women and children, had fallen or had been pushed to the ground and were trampled underfoot. Many screamed or begged for mercy but most realised the hopelessness of their position. They allowed themselves to be herded inside, resigned to their fate. They expected to be kept in custody, starved and tortured, until this drunken rabble were sated. Which, probably, would take several days.

The Cimarron had no pity for them. These were precisely the people who exploited and tortured his own kind.

The richest families were interrogated first. Probably they would be persuaded to surrender their wealth instead of their lives. Those joining them in the church were the last of the survivors. Most of those who had fought or were unable to withstand torture were already dead. The Welshman had tasked search parties to scour every building in the town from attic to cellar. They were searching for loot and Spaniards. Once every building was cleared marauding bands would extend their reach into the surrounding countryside, thrashing through the cane fields in their hunt for fugitives and hidden treasure.

These pirates were not the lovable rogues of the popular imagination. The main man didn't boast a parrot perched on his shoulder and you wouldn't hear jocular shouts of "Yo ho ho."

The Welshman's savages, that rabble herding the terrified townspeople into their church, prodding them forward with pikes, swords and musket butts, were a bunch of psychopaths and ne'er-do-wells led by a man whose name would be whispered hoarsely by Spanish mothers to terrorize their children. Most were drunk, or getting there. Some were bare-chested and bare-headed, some wore rough clothing they had lived in for weeks, others flaunted stolen silks. Most heads sported unwashed greasy hair tarred or tied behind and faces obscured by unkempt beards. Many suffered scarred skin and some carried recent wounds.

Should I join this rabble? That was the Cimarron's question.

He and the Welshman had led them here from the coast yet, though grubby from their overland trek, neither was as slovenly as his unwashed comrades. The broad-backed Welshman's flowing locks, temporarily tied behind his head by a blue bandana, showed signs of occasional grooming whilst his curved moustache obviously received attention daily. His open-necked shirt and leather jerkin were well-tailored. Voluminous dark blue pantaloons were tucked into close-fitting boots. Even the leather belts and straps which held his pistols, daggers and sword proclaimed quality.

The Cimarron, wiry yet muscular, was dressed simply and appropriately for the climate. The tight curls of his hair were cropped short to the scalp. An oversized smock flapped loosely around his torso partly obscuring his belt and the machete in its crude scabbard. A rough pair of calico trousers were cut off just below the knee. His feet were offered the protection of sandals. Now he drew his hand across his face, wiping away much of the sweat. There were no flies on him. There was plenty of fresh meat for them to feed on.

Chapter One

"Café Colon Very Good"

At last, I felt free. I couldn't stretch, there was no room, and I'd resolved not to take a deep breath until we were well out into the country. Perhaps not even then. But at least I felt free. Alone, that kind of free.

I'm not antisocial you understand. I enjoy company. But I felt hemmed in by Jean-Pierre and Colleen. It was tiring speaking with Jean-Pierre, translating the occasional French phrases, unscrambling his heavily-accented, fractured English and coping with his unpredictability. Colleen was very nice but I had to be constantly on my guard to avoid giving away my secrets. It didn't help that she was a nervous passenger and a Know-All.

Fortunately, as I'd hoped, she preferred to stay overnight at the Hotel Jacmelienne whilst Jean-Pierre and I continued to Les Cayes. We endured a very long drive on appalling roads and darkness had engulfed us by the time we arrived at that dilapidated hostelry on the coast opposite the late Henry Morgan's hideaway island.

Ile-à-Vache was a disappointment. Not as a candidate for our new tour programme - there are two fine beaches and a magnificent resort, Port Morgan, which would be perfect. OK, it's difficult to get there. But that could be an advantage when you consider our innovative, hopefully exclusive, concept. It is precisely the sort of location I'd been despatched to discover. Good food, excellent accommodation, a great setting and genuine pirate connections.

This island was a regular rendezvous of the pirates in the final decades of the 17th century. Where they assembled vast fleets before launching major assaults on The Spanish Main. Then the survivors would regroup here to divide up the loot before returning to Port Royal or Tortuga. Ile-à-Vache was a particular favourite with Henry Morgan who enjoyed riotous drunken parties offshore. During one, in 1669, his flagship exploded killing 350 men. Morgan was one of the lucky few who were catapulted skywards and spewed into the sea stirred but not shaken. The following year he returned and mustered the multinational armada he needed to attack the Spanish at Panama.

Sometimes these buccaneers were licensed privateers - in fact the ship which exploded, HMS Oxford, had been loaned by the English Crown. So the Governor in Port Royal and his French counterpart in Tortuga expected a cut of the winnings when the ships returned laden with loot from their rape and pillage. The more booty the buccaneers brought home the higher the Governor's cut. Therefore I reckoned Morgan and others must have buried some of their plunder here. Perhaps I would strike gold.

My first problem was the size of the island, around twelve miles long with a population of maybe 5,000. So even if I identified the exact bay used by Morgan and his pals I could assume any treasure might well be buried miles away. It was not in the nature of freebooters to trust each other.

The charming French couple who manage the resort offered no encouragement either. They exchanged glances when I gave my name.

"Morgan? You are related?"

We got past that one, but it gave me a perfect excuse to ask about the notorious criminal and the possibility that he hadn't returned to retrieve all his buried booty. They were dismissive.

"Do you mean he never buried any, or that it has already been found?" I asked.

Just a Gallic shrug and a polite but discouraging reply. "Who knows? For sure it is possible. But long time ago, I can tell you, every square metre of the island was digged. Soon divers will come to look for, aah, the remains of that ship. She which exploded. Maybe there is treasure on the bottom of the sea."

We collected Colleen and returned to Port-au-Prince. Again it was dark by the time we completed our journey and perhaps Jean-Pierre was tired from the driving. Anyway he failed to respond with alacrity when a lunatic driver hurtled out of the anarchic traffic into the side of our VW giving us a hefty clout and another dent. Perhaps some nutter who wanted to squash a Beetle. Colleen stifled a scream. Jean-Pierre and the other idiot leapt from their vehicles and squared up to each other hurling threats and curses. I wearily intervened.

"No problem" I said. "We go police."

Jean-Pierre got the message. He told the other driver, in Creole, that we would let the police sort it out. The guilty party took one look at Colleen and me and grasped the implications. He decided he was in a hurry and couldn't spare the time for arguments or the police. He turned and strode quickly back to his car waving his arms and muttering incoherent threats.

When we rented the car the manager encouraged me to pay extra for Collision Damage Waiver. In those days CDW covered all accidental damage with no excess, as he was keen to emphasise. But when we returned he seemed to regret his persuasiveness. He stomped around the vehicle pointing to the damage suffered since he had last seen it and remonstrating with the driver. Jean-Pierre waved at the original dents as if they excused later collisions. I strolled outside to have a puff of my pipe and let them get on with it. Eventually a chastened Jean-Pierre emerged and we set off for the *Gare Du Nord*.

Please don't confuse this terminus with its namesake in Paris. There are no trains, platforms or even buildings. It is just a grandiose title for an uneven patch of littered muddy ground near the market. This is where you go to catch a *tap-tap*. That's not an exotic animal. It's what they call the elderly substitutes for buses. Large truck chassis mounted with gaudily-painted wooden bodies hand-built to transport upwards of fifty people in discomfort for several hours. They congregate here like elephants gathered around a jungle watering hole.

After wandering among these behemoths for a few minutes I selected *Pan Am Clipper*. Maybe it would fly. I climbed up into the cab to negotiate the price with the driver. Following the advice in the book I reserved a window seat at the very back and paid the four dollars requested. I calmly rejected all Jean-Pierre's entreaties.

"I'm sorry Jean-Pierre. I have to go alone. I'll see you when I get back."

I was also free of Colleen. We separated when I dropped her off at the guest house before returning the car and I hadn't seen her since. I wasn't avoiding her on purpose but for now I just wanted to be alone.

Well I was free, but hardly alone. I'd boarded early as advised but soon *Pan Am Clipper's* wooden superstructure was heaving with Haitian humanity. Women mainly, all ages, all sizes, garbed in rough colourful cottons and encumbered with baskets. The bench seating stretched from side to side, no aisle, so to get to the back latecomers needed to climb over the benches and other passengers. I watched them as they clambered to their designated seats, hauling themselves front to rear, squeezing their bums onto the wooden boards and bickering over space with their neighbours. I suspected that this would be the most uncomfortable journey of my life so far. At least it would offer me a taste of the real Haiti.

Eventually *Pan Am Clipper* was chock-a-block with chattering Haitians and their hand baggage. We lumbered, rocking gently, over the muddy hillocks and out of the *Gare Du Nord* like an energised elephant departing the watering hole having drunk his fill. We heaved our way into the traffic flow with a staccato crunching of gears and turned north.

I was glad to be leaving the smoggy and smelly mayhem of Port-au-Prince and looking forward to enjoying more of the dramatic mountainous landscape. And I was to find that the grass really was greener on the other side of the hill.

At first we trundled through the northern outskirts of the city. That was of no interest to me. The run-down concrete buildings gave way to wood-and-tin shacks and the crowds thinned out. They lost their downtown urgency, replacing it with a hopeless lassitude. Slowly the smell from the open sewers and refuse piles dissipated. Once clear of the capital I scanned the scenery. The disadvantage of being crammed against the window - which was, of course, unglazed - was dust. I would be breathing in and choking on road dust and diesel fumes, but I didn't mind. I would have the benefit of the breeze. Better than being squashed and clambered over on an overcrowded plank in the airless centre. And after the night's rain there would be little dust anyway. Now I witnessed the effects of the defoliation of the coastal plain. When Columbus arrived Haiti was both mountainous and thickly forested. It is still mountainous but over the last three centuries the lowland trees have been culled so drastically that the subsequent soil erosion has prevented the forests regenerating themselves. Still, today, the poorest rural people are chopping down trees and burning them to produce charcoal. Now the coastal plain is arid with no obvious signs of agriculture. Occasionally we passed small villages of African-style mud huts, circular with conical roofs. Brown rondavels clustered in the beige dirt.

At independence in 1804 most of the former slaves were first generation Haitians and even among those born here African traditions were entrenched. So after Toussaint

L'Ouverture's abduction they abandoned the plantation system, in spite of its economic advantages, and returned to their traditional lifestyle. Where the land retains its fertility subsistence farming in small communities continues today. I marvelled at the contrast with Jamaica. Two countries so close yet so different.

Apparently our *tap-tap* had departed the *Gare Du Nord* with some empty seats. Looking towards the front I couldn't imagine where these could be and several other passengers shared my opinion. Obviously the driver knew something we didn't. Early in the journey he eased off the gas, crashed down through his gears and pulled over to take on extra bodies. He did this eight times. At first just a few of my crushed fellow passengers complained but their numbers increased and their yelling became more vociferous on each subsequent occasion until eventually almost everyone was hurling abuse at him. Every time we stopped bags and boxes were tossed up to the two crew members who travelled on the roof and the new arrivals forced their way through the packed masses dodging curses and muttering.

Whenever we halted to set down and collect passengers we were surrounded by vendors. Hordes of them. They clustered around both sides of the *tap-tap* hustling cold drinks, fruit, bread, biscuits, nuts and cigarettes. In this cacophony of noise, movement and colour I was always quickly spotted and selected as the main target. *"Blanc! Noix de coco?"* or *"Blanc! Pain?"* or even *"Monsieur! Banane?"* They called up to me in turn, elbowing a passage to my window.

Gonaives, the third largest town, was our main stop en route. Here quite a few of my fellow passengers disembarked. And around a dozen were set to join us.

I spotted her amongst that crowd as I gazed out. She stood proud, almost as if she was illuminated by spotlights. A complete contrast to the others. Elegant, stately of gait, dressed in smart-casual and confident of manner, she mounted the few steps at the front as though she was a film star or royalty gracing a luxury yacht with her presence. I noticed jeans. I never saw another black person wearing jeans. Normally fashion items were only flaunted by the mulattos of Petionville. I fancied her straightaway. But. Knowing my luck, I mused, no chance. She disappeared from my view inside the vehicle. I withdrew my head and glanced towards the front expecting, hoping, to see her clambering through the masses. There was no sign of her. She must have found a seat near the door. Unless she was a mirage.

After Gonaives the road swings inland, not to brave the coast again until it reaches Le Cap. The countryside was still wet after the night's downpour. The road dust had been churned to a fine mud, rich red in parts and creamy beige elsewhere. Up here peasants still farm the land and the forests have yet to be felled. Lush foliage glistened in the sun's rays which now bathed the dramatic hillsides with flickering colour. Spectacular mountains which had so impressed the Spaniards five hundred years ago plunged into each other in seemingly endless rows, almost as if the earth had crumpled itself like a piece of paper in its anger. The road was a twisting ribbon of tarmac laid into the mountainsides, snaking up and down at a rate which reduced our *tap-tap* to a speed of 10 mph, sometimes less. At times the snake coiled back on itself and I observed other vehicles straining uphill or tackling the descent in bottom gear. This imposition of man was set against a backdrop of every shade of green from emerald to olive as the emergent sun speckled the hillsides like a patchwork quilt. I wondered how long it would be before this beauty disappeared for ever, when even these forests would be chopped down and burnt.

Here in the mountains and at the beginning and end of my journey the road was satisfactory. Potholed of course, but surfaced at least. Elsewhere it degenerated into little more than a track covered with loose gravel. I did see roadworks but whether these were attempts at road building or just emergency repairs I couldn't tell. At these places *Pan Am Clipper* would lurch off the track and trundle across earth or field until we could again use the highway. We came to a river, wide but shallow. Fast-flowing waters rushing over rocks and gravel. As we plunged into the riverbed I could see a bridge to our right. A minibus was traversing it. *Ebenezer?* Presumably this bridge was too flimsy to be trusted with our weight and bulk so we roared and bumped through the river at barely reduced speed.

Eventually, after a long day on the road, we pulled into the bus station at Cap Haitien. Although merely a passenger, and occupying one of the best seats, I was tired from the journey and worn out by the constant demands of vendors. As the only white passenger I expected to be the centre of attention again but now I would have to get off. The best policy, I decided, was to ignore the mayhem that would soon be raging around me.

Sure enough a swarm of upturned faces located me immediately. I faced stonily forward, ignoring them and adopting the aspect of a deaf mute. Entreaties supported by a forest of waving arms were pitched in my direction. Shouts of *"Blanc! Taxi!"* were interspersed with names of hotels. As I watched my fellow passengers eagerly evacuating *Pan Am Clipper* I tried to ignore the bedlam. Out of the corner of my eye I saw baggage being tossed down from the roof.

Suddenly I panicked. Hang on! What if I did sit here, as intended, until everyone had gone? My baggage would have been thrown down and someone might run off with it. Yelling out the window "No thank you, I go Café Colon" I stood up and started towards the front, hunched under the low roof as I clambered across the benches.

I heard a female voice call.

"Yes. Café Colon very good. I take you."

I halted my crouched forward progress and peered out. There, unbelievably, was my girl. She of the regal manner and blue jeans. In amongst the crowd but they'd given her room. Nobody was elbowing her. Maybe my luck was changing. I hurried off the bus and let her take charge.

Inside the taxi, luggage safely stowed, she introduced herself.

"My name is Veronique but you can call me Vera."

"I prefer Veronique. More exotic" I ventured. "Vera sounds too English."

"Sound English is bad? No, no. Is good. England great country."

At Café Colon Veronique located the owner and arranged something in Creole. She was obviously accustomed to taking charge. We deposited my bags in the room and were soon downstairs in the bar, the only customers. In this relaxed atmosphere, isolated from the maelstrom of Haitian life, I could sip my drink and appraise Veronique in more detail.

She was a smidgen shorter than me, of average build with rounded features. She covered her hair with a scarlet and ultramarine patterned headscarf. A well-tailored pale blue blouse of a lightweight material, perhaps chiffon, fitted neatly. And those blue jeans, which I now noticed were embroidered.

"A nice pair of jeans" I commented. "Very unusual to see in Haiti. And the first I've seen embroidered."

She beamed with pride at the restrained compliment. "I make them myself. A friend get the material, then I make them. And the - what did you call it? I stitch the pattern. And this shirt" she leant back, placing her hands each side of her bust, thus drawing my attention to it "I make this too."

I was impressed. Not just a pretty face then. We chatted for a few minutes, polished off our drinks and agreed to meet back here in two hours.

Veronique returned a few minutes early. Hmmm, keen I thought, particularly in respect of her appearance. She had tarted herself up for me. Her hair was styled in cornrows and lightly gelled. She'd applied make-up and lipstick and was probably wearing her smartest clothes. Warpaint! Why do women always do that? I preferred the natural girl I'd spotted in Gonaives wearing jeans, blouse and headscarf. Never mind. I'm sure there's a real person behind the disguise.

"We go?" she asked without sitting.

"Sure."

I rose and followed her into the street. She led me away from the centre of town into a residential quarter where, after a few minutes, we reached an off-white bungalow. The door was ajar so we entered without knocking. Immediately inside I saw a tallish woman ironing with her tits hanging out of an unbuttoned blouse. She and Veronique exchanged a few words then I was introduced. Veronique ushered me to a chair whilst the woman continued her ironing. She didn't consider it necessary to cover her tits now a strange male had joined the company and, anyway, I thought, it's not sexy for some reason. Veronique sat down and the ladies chatted.

Presently a very thin – perhaps anorexic – and obviously highly-strung girl in her twenties rushed in. First she gabbled at the woman with the tits, shaking a piece of paper at her, then turned and hastened over to Veronique, gabbling and shaking again. Veronique calmly took the sheet of paper and perused it. It looked like a bank statement. The new girl animatedly stabbed a finger at a recent entry and gabbled louder now, first at Veronique then, flicking her head back and turning, at the tall lady with the tits. Which, I now noticed, had disappeared within her blouse. The thin girl seemed very happy – maybe she'd received an unexpected windfall – but I was a mite concerned for her health. Both physical and mental.

Also I was becoming increasingly concerned about my own position. I'd foolishly assumed that Veronique fancied me for myself. OK, I'm not the first guy to kid himself about that and I realised that as a rare white visitor to Haiti, and especially Le Cap, I would be singled out as a meal ticket. Like Jean-Pierre and the other guides she could be hoping to make an honest dollar from the tourist industry, such as it was. But I'd become a little nervous. If this is the company she keeps perhaps she's a prostitute. A new experience for me. I'd never paid for sex. I like sex to be part of a relationship. Not that I have to be in love you understand, but I want more than a Wham-Bang-Thank-You-Mam or whatever they call it. How could I find out without causing offence?

I cleared my throat and began nervously "I, erm, there may be a misunderstanding. Not that I want to suggest, er, anything untoward, but I'm not sure . . ."

Veronique turned to face me. She was impassive, waiting.

"Well, when we met. Today. I think you're very nice. But maybe I didn't realise."

She continued to watch me impassively and patiently.

"Well, the thing is, I've never paid for sex." I'd got it out but if I was wrong I would cause offence. Presumably to all three ladies.

Veronique sat sharply upright. "You pay, we stay here. You no pay, we go." She held my eyes in a steely gaze.

The other ladies were not offended, just interested and perhaps mildly amused. Veronique was giving me a simple choice. Well, no choice really if I was genuine. I stood up. Veronique also rose, took my arm, said goodbye to her friends and led me outside.

First we went to the movies. That's been a regular excursion for a first date since way back before I was born. We watched a third-rate Western dubbed into Creole with French subtitles. Pointless really as very few Haitians speak French – still the official language then – and even fewer can read it. Ever seen All-American rough-tough cowboys arguing in Creole? John Wayne-type characters cursing each other in an alien tongue as they work themselves up to a gunfight, their lips totally out of sync with the soundtrack? Surreal. Much funnier even than a Spaghetti Western and, it occurred to me, part of the magic which is Haiti. Most of the audience, and occasionally Veronique, joined in with the movie cast as if they could be heard, yelling encouragement to the Goodies and hurling abuse at the Baddies. Interactive entertainment - the Haitians had it first. I don't think this audience participation had any effect on the course of the movie but in the land of voodoo and black magic you can never be sure.

The crowd left the cinema chattering and laughing. Now we visited a restaurant. It was here, halfway through our meal, that I suddenly felt an overwhelming desire for a gallon of milk.

"Milk" I said. "I need milk. *Lait. Leche.*"

Veronique called the waiter over. After a few words were exchanged in Creole she turned back to me. "They have no milk."

"Can they get some?"

Another brief exchange with the waiter then she replied "Not here. Not at this time."

But I needed something. It wasn't thirst as such. It was my body issuing very clear instructions. No milk available, so maybe a substitute. "Water. Ask them for some water."

I knew I was taking a risk. You don't drink the tap water in Haiti. But I was desperate. My body was crying out for something to drink urgently. The waiter brought a jug of water and a glass. I knocked that back very fast. More was brought. Altogether I must have swallowed a litre. I didn't know what was wrong with me - in fact I never found out - but I felt better. We finished our meal without further drama.

"Now we go Café Colon" said Veronique.

"OK."

I paid and we left the restaurant arm-in-arm, presumably headed for my guest house. We'd strolled through the dark night for about two minutes up a slight gradient when I was overcome by acute nausea. My head was swirling around and felt like it might twist off. Something was banging about inside it. I staggered off the path to my left and vomited against a tree. I threw up so suddenly that I was still upright. I hoped my dinner had missed my shoes.

Veronique was displeased and unsympathetic. "Why you drink all that water? You want make yourself sick?"

I could only flap an arm in her direction before throwing up again. This time I managed to lean forward first. I staggered upright. My head was still whirling. I reached out for the tree and slapped my palm against it with my arm at full stretch. It was the only way I could remain standing. I tried to take a deep breath before replying.

"No. Not that. There's something wrong with me. Just came on. Maybe something I ate. In Port-au-Prince or Jacmel." That was all I could manage before vomiting for a third time.

"You say food not good here?" she demanded.

"I'm not saying that" I protested, taking deep breaths. "It could happen anywhere." Another deep breath. "Any country."

It was too dark to examine the contents of my stomach, now deposited somewhere at the base of the tree, but this mysterious sudden sickness must have been caused by something I ate.

Veronique changed tack. "You not like me" she said. "You drink water to make you sick because you not like me."

In spite of my splitting and spinning head and my, now diminishing, nausea I just had to laugh. It was so ridiculous I couldn't believe it. She obviously thought that for some obscure reason I was trying to avoid sleeping with her.

"Not like you? You must be joking." I removed my arm from the tree and discovered I was able to stand shakily upright without assistance. I turned around to face her and took a rapid succession of deep breaths before continuing. "You're the best girl I've seen since I left England." Another couple of breaths. "Everywhere, Jamaica, the guide in Port-au-Prince, everywhere, people offering me women." I leant my left arm back against the tree and took some more deep breaths. I was beginning to feel better. "I told them I find my own women. When I saw you get on the *tap-tap* at Gonaives" more deep breaths "I could see you were special. I couldn't believe my luck when you called to me at the bus station."

Wow, that was a lot to get out in my state. But I meant it. Every word. I couldn't have her thinking that I didn't fancy her, perhaps because she was black, although what I would be able to do about it in my current condition was another question. I took some more deep breaths then staggered along to the next tree and sat down there.

During my speech Veronique had been studying me. Now she became most solicitous. She produced a handkerchief from somewhere and mopped my brow. Then she supported my head with her left hand and wiped around my mouth. Obviously my explanation rang true. At the very least she must have realised that I wasn't trying to avoid sleeping with her. She helped me get to my feet.

"I'm feeling much better now" I said.

"I'll look after you" she promised.

Although my legs had apparently turned to jelly and I needed Veronique's willing support we arrived back at Café Colon with no further drama. We took turns to use the bathroom then sat together on the bed. My head had cleared almost completely by now. Perhaps to prove my desire I leaned sideways and kissed her. She seemed to like that. She wrapped both her arms around me and pulled me close. Neither of us were spontaneous but, well, you know.

A movement in my trousers suggested that this mystery illness was having no effect on my libido. Well, ill or not, I'll give it my best shot. I ran my right hand through her hair and with my left I started unbuttoning her blouse. It fell open to reveal a bra. Well, no problem. I've done this before. Gently, and I hope sensually, I moved my hands around her back to the clasp. OOH that skin. I had never felt skin so smooth. Like velvet. No, better. Chocolate Cream. The clasp came apart in my hands almost as if I'd broken it. Her bra fell forward. I eased it off, hooked one end around my index finger and swung it across the room.

Veronique was not idle either. She was running her fingers through my hair, gently massaging my scalp and the back of my neck. She resumed command.

"Now we get undressed" she said. "Then we make love."

She stood up, unfastened her skirt and let it fall to the floor. She picked it up and folded it carefully but sensually. Whilst watching her I unbuttoned my shirt and tossed it on a nearby chair.

We hadn't turned on the light after returning from the bathroom. There was sufficient illumination from the street – whether from moonlight or street lights I was not inclined to check - to see what we were doing. And the subdued glow was far more romantic than the harsh artificial light in the room. Not only that. Aware of the limitations of my physique I was too shy to expose my body to a thorough visual examination.

As I bent to remove my shoes Veronique was silhouetted against the window. She straightened up from folding her skirt, her breasts apparently having a life of their own. She slipped her hands inside her knickers along her thighs and gently eased them down. I could do that. Maybe tomorrow. Now this wonderfully curvaceous silhouette eased out one leg, then the other, then bent to her side and laid the knickers on her skirt. She straightened up again and put her hands on her hips. Now she was ready for action.

Enthralled by this beautiful vision I'd fallen behind in the Undressing Stakes. I pulled my shoes off quickly and tossed them to one side. Socks were next. Off they came and were flicked in the general direction of the shoes. I stood to remove my trousers. Not, for once, shorts. These I needed to fold as they were my only pair of smart long pants. Normally this is not a difficult undertaking but tonight I was all fingers and thumbs. Concentrate. That done I was down to my underpants. I looked across to the window and saw that Veronique had gone.

There she was on my left, on the bed, the subdued light from the window flattering this gorgeous example of woman. She was lying half on her side coquettishly massaging her left calf with the sole of her right foot. Her right hand was extended towards me.

I needed no second invitation. I slid alongside and planted another gentle kiss. My hands found that wonderful silky skin and caressed her neck and torso.

My underpants were giving me grief. Too tight. I was still wearing them and the contents was pushing hard. Feeling a little embarrassed I slipped them off then continued with the job in hand. As it were. Why did I think of such silly things a these times? Surely sex was meant to be taken seriously. No wonder I didn't get much.

Now I moved my hands to those pendulous breasts. They were not firm, presumably having been fondled often, but I liked them. Soft. Except for the nipples. My mouth found the left nipple whilst my hands moved downwards, gently caressing that wonderful body. Down further, tickling the erogenous zones.

Now. Now's the time I realised. Gently I slipped my penis home.

"Hmmmm. Good" Veronique murmured softly as she eased her head back and her torso forward. "I like small ones."

Chapter Two

That Beautiful Skin

Next morning I awoke reasonably clear-headed. Immediately, perhaps because of the unfamiliar surroundings, I remembered the night's events. I turned my head to the left. Venus was still there, beside me, lying face down. She appeared to be sleeping. I leaned over and kissed her right buttock. It wasn't quite like waking a sleeping princess but in response I felt her hand on my head. Then it glided down to my neck. She gave a little squeeze then released me and rolled over.

"Ah, Morgan" she said.

I reached across and held her hand. We remained like that for a minute or two. Then she stirred, sat up and slid across me off the bed to get her clothes.

"I go now. You like *petit déjeuner,* breakfast?"

Yuk. No. I couldn't face breakfast, or any food. I was still not well. The thought of fried eggs was turning my stomach. Not that eggs and bacon would be on the menu, more like fish and rice. But I didn't feel like eating.

"No" I said. "I'm still not well. Maybe it's food poisoning. If it is I shouldn't eat anything even if I wanted to."

Veronique was starting to dress. "OK. I go home have *douche*. I come see you later."

I lay there and watched her dress, which she did very quickly and precisely with the occasional glance and smile in my direction.

"You give me five dollar" she said. "I go hairdresser, get my hair nice for you. Also maybe I get food in case you well later. You not eat here. Better I cook for you. Then you not ill. My kitchen very clean."

This sounded like a very fair proposition. Even if I didn't feel like eating later, what was five dollars? I sat up and cast around the room to see where I'd flung my trousers. Good God. I hadn't flung them anywhere. I had folded them neatly and placed them on a chair. I reached over, rummaged in the pocket and pulled out some dollar bills. I peeled off a five and handed it to Veronique. She was fully dressed by now.

"*Merci*" she said. She stepped the few paces over to me, bent slightly and gave me a kiss on the forehead. Then she was gone.

I rolled around in the bed for a while, maybe half an hour. Then I decided that I'd better get up and visit the bathroom. I eased myself off the bed. As I did I noticed some dollars protruding from my trouser pocket. Obviously when I gave Veronique that five I didn't put the rest back properly.

I pulled out the folded bundle, checked that no notes had become separated in the pocket, then confirmed that all the bills were in the proper order. That was just force of habit. I would have been surprised if they'd been jumbled up. Large notes, twenties to the back, ones at the front, tens and fives in between. 20, 10, 5, 1. National heroes' heads all the same way, heads up. Jackson, Hamilton, Lincoln and Washington. They don't have one with Nixon on yet. *In God We Trust* emblazoned on the back. That always reminds me of a sign I once saw in an American bar – *In God We Trust. All others pay cash.*

Whilst my mind was wandering in this half-awake state I instinctively counted it. Probably some subconscious concern. Suddenly I noticed something was wrong. I sat up with a jerk and counted it again. $102. That's not right. I was sure I had $127 when we left the restaurant. That was before I was overcome with the nausea. I'd automatically checked it when I paid the bill. Well, I've just given five to Vera so that should leave $122. Have I bought something and forgotten about it?

I knew how much was there when I left Port-au-Prince – $174. I spent nothing on the journey. Then on arrival I gave the taxi driver $2 as Vera suggested. Café Colon got another thirty for three nights accommodation, again as per Vera's instructions. Hang on. Why am I now calling her Vera? Have I fallen out with her already? It's Veronique. Our drinks in the café downstairs cost a dollar, two dollars for the cinema tickets and twelve dollars for dinner. That leaves $127. Did I spend money on something else and forget about it? In my semi-comatose state that was possible but I would think about that later. In the meantime let's work on the assumption that I haven't. I lay down again, closed my eyes and did some mental arithmetic. It always worked out at $127 before the five I'd just given Veronique. So I should definitely have $122 now but I only held $102 in my hand. Well, bathroom first, worry about it later.

In my weakened state it was easy for me to fall asleep when I returned to the room. I awoke to see Veronique sitting by the bed with a bowl of soup and a spoon. She was back in mothering mode, or was it the Florence Nightingale option? I struggled up straight. She moved her chair close to my new position by wiggling her arse and shuffling her feet. She scooped up a spoonful of soup and offered it to me. Dutifully I opened my mouth and she gently poured in the warm liquid.

"Hmmm. Fish soup" I said.

"Yes" agreed Veronique, spooning up some more "I make special."

"There's no need to do that" I told her, reaching for the spoon. "I'm not dying. I can feed myself." I took the spoon and dish from her. She seemed happy enough to relinquish them. She sat and watched as I polished off the soup.

"You're very clever" I said. "You speak English and French as well as Creole, you make your own clothes and now this delicious soup."

That pleased her. "Also Spanish and some Dutch" she beamed. "And Papiamento, a little. I have a friend from Aruba. He rich. Plenty money. He give me this watch." She leaned forward and thrust out her left wrist. She proudly touched a gold Omega with her index finger.

That's strange, I thought, I never noticed that yesterday. I should have done. If there's one thing that typifies Haiti – well, actually there's so many things that you can't count them, but anyway – one thing I'd noticed in Haiti was the absence of working clocks. When I did see a clock – I couldn't be sure but I seemed to recall spotting one on the Iron Market – invariably they had ceased functioning. Sometimes the hands were missing. This watch of Veronique's was the first I remembered seeing. Presumably the rich mulattos of Petionville possess watches and clocks but timepieces obviously are a luxury among the black majority. It is tempting to suggest, and the ignorant would claim, that there is no need for watches or clocks as the Haitians have no concept of the passage of time. But that is simply not true. *Tap-taps* leave the *Gare Du Nord* promptly at 0600. Planes run to schedules.

"I didn't notice that yesterday" I said.

"No, I not wearing. Not necessary for *tap-tap* to Gonaives. But today I wear to look nice for new boyfriend." She flashed me another of her lovely smiles. There was a gold tooth at the back there somewhere.

Suddenly I felt very tired. I lay down again. Veronique picked up the dish and spoon and stood. "I go now. Let you sleep. I come back tonight." She paused at the door for a quick wave and smile then disappeared.

It was dark when she returned. I'd been asleep most of the afternoon and awoke shortly before her arrival. She'd brought a plate of food, a knife, a fork and a napkin. "You like this?" she asked.

I leant over for a closer look. A steaming chunk of fish, some white rice and mashed plantain. I could probably manage that.

"I'll give it a go" I said.

There was a makeshift table in the room so I leant across and moved my trousers from the chair and laid them on an item which was probably intended as a bedside console. Slipping completely out of the bed I picked up the chair and moved it over to the 'dining table'. Veronique placed the cutlery and food in front of me. It was delicious, in its way the best meal I'd enjoyed in Haiti. I managed to eat all of it though I wondered if that was wise. I still felt tired but at least I didn't feel nauseous.

Meanwhile Veronique undressed completely, flashing me coquettish glances when my attention wasn't concentrated on the food. Tonight she was back to her 'smart casual' look – for me far sexier – although she was still wearing the watch.

She'd obviously decided on an early night. She lay languidly on the bed, inviting but not overly provocative.

"Come." She patted the sheet beside her.

I needed no second invitation. I slipped off my underpants, which I must have put back on for some reason. Maybe when I visited the bathroom. It reminded me of some Hollywood movies where two lovers are wearing underwear in bed at the end of a sex scene. If they've just made love, I always think, how can they still be wearing their underpants and knickers? Sometimes the lady has still got her bra on.

I lay down beside Veronique. No mad hurry for sex. We've got all night. Let's just have some cuddles for the time being.

I kissed her whilst I caressed that unbelievably silky chocolate cream skin, starting at the neck and slowly, smoothly, working my right hand down. I'll give my left a rest for the moment. Down to her belly. Gentle circular motions, then back up to her breast. At this point I allowed my left hand to do some work as I softly fondled both her breasts, those jellyish globes which were not textbook standard but were fine by me. I felt her nipples harden and moved my mouth down to her left nipple. Now I moved my right hand down to her buttock, smoothly drawing it along her leg and to the inside of her thigh.

Hang on, wasn't I getting carried away here? This was supposed to be cuddles. And there was the concern that had nagged at me occasionally all day. When I was awake. I'd packed something in my luggage in preparation for this very eventuality. Quite apart from the pregnancy question there was the matter of protection from disease. I separated my body from hers as carefully as I could and sat up.

"Hmmm. Don't go" she murmured.

I laughed. "Don't worry. I'm not going anywhere. I'm just getting something."

I slid off the bed and shuffled over to my bag. I unzipped it and rummaged around for a square packet containing the products of The London Rubber Company. Ah yes, here they are. I opened it, extracted one of the little foil packages, dropped the packet back into my bag and eased myself on to the bed. Lying on my back I tore open the package. How best to explain this?

"Er, last night Veronique" I began.

She glanced over at me, curious. Then she saw what I was holding. She sat up abruptly and giggled. Snatching the condom from me she knelt on the bed, legs apart for support – ooooh – and put it to her lips like a balloon. Taking deep breaths she blew into it until it reached quite an impressive size. She leant back for one last good blow, probably hoping to burst it, when it slipped from her fingers and shot across the room in a sinuous streak, expelling air as it went and letting loose a sound somewhere between a whoosh!! and a gigantic fart. It died by the window.

Veronique clapped her hands together, giggled uproariously and bounced up and down on the bed. Well, she's made her views clear on that subject then.

The next morning I again woke before Veronique. Or so I thought. When I looked her over she appeared to be asleep but as I sat up a little voice asked "How you feeling?"

Maybe she never sleeps. I'm not one of those ten-minute merchants who turns over and falls asleep after sexual intercourse. I'm rather fond of post-coital cuddles so I was awake for at least an hour after our latest sexual bout. I'd thought she'd fallen asleep before me but now a vague sixth sense was telling me this was not so.

"Weak. But OK. Not nauseous."

"Not sick then? Not ill?"

"No. OK."

"You see, that food I bring you make you well. You see. You not have breakfast" she rolled over to the side of the bed and straightened up. "I come back. I make *déjeuner* for you for middle of day."

She slid easily off the bed, stood and turned towards me, stretched her legs apart, arched her body, rolled her head around her neck and extended her arms. "You give me ten dollars."

Do that again and I'll give you twenty dollars. I reached over to my trousers and pulled out my dollar wad. Finding a ten I handed it to her.

"You still weak" she said. "But if you rest now, after you eat, later, maybe you well again. Maybe you can see Le Cap. I take you to meet people."

Again she was quickly dressed and gone.

Although I felt a bit mean doing it, I felt I had to. But not immediately. Just in case she returned suddenly. I waited about twenty minutes once she'd gone then reached over for my trousers. The banknotes were still folded in order. I counted them. There should be $92 now.

It was only $72. So I didn't make a mistake yesterday. I'd counted it correctly and accurately remembered what I'd spent. I hadn't bought something and forgotten. Either she fell asleep after me or woke before me. Probably both. Perhaps she never sleeps when she's working. Does that make her a Twenty Dollar Whore?

Strangely I didn't feel any resentment. She has to make a living and in this country prostitution is a popular and legitimate profession. If I'd agreed to pay her twenty dollars a night right up front then she wouldn't need to rob me, would she? But she probably would anyway so I was ahead. In fact I was way ahead. With my sickness I hadn't been spending money on food and travel and under Veronique's care I was recovering from whatever bug I'd harboured.

Unfortunately the sickness was preventing me from doing my job properly. Yesterday was a total washout from the viewpoint of my responsibilities to Sunstroke Holidays. They weren't paying me to shag prostitutes. They were paying me to research Cap Haitien, check out the hotels and beaches and evaluate the downsides. There are two good beaches with resorts on them a little way out of town. I should be checking those out. Then The Citadelle, which the Haitians claim is The Eighth Wonder Of The World and a compulsory excursion for visitors to the north. And Sans Souci of course. Not to mention Tortuga, or Ile de la Tortue to give it its current, French, name.

The thought of all this made me feel weak again. Even if I did feel well enough to go these journeys in the hot sun would be taxing. Particularly the final steep climb up the mountain to The Citadelle which was tackled astride a mule. The beach resorts I could leave to the contracting department. Just give them the details and let them get on with it. But I should really visit Ile de la Tortue.

With nothing else to do I could allow my brain to mull over the history of these parts.

Way back in the 16th Century Spain claimed the whole of Hispaniola, the island which comprises Haiti and The Dominican Republic. They introduced cattle and pigs and attempted to establish sugar plantations. But Hispaniola was no match for those Spanish possessions where the colonisers looted gold and silver, or those suitable for its transhipment, so it became a colony of secondary importance.

Over the following decades many of the pigs and cattle escaped and bred rapidly in the fertile conditions. Then during the 17th Century an assorted rabble of shipwrecked sailors, deserters and even some escaped slaves established themselves on the offshore island of Tortuga.

Many of this motley crew would spend several months each year hunting feral cattle, operating in pairs. After skinning the animals for their hides they would cut the flesh into strips and dry it over a wooden frame the natives called a *boucan* – hence *boucaniers*. They sold their produce to passing ships, operating from Tortuga or the northwest coast of Hispaniola in dugout canoes. As their number increased supply exceeded demand so they turned to piracy.

They carried out their raids against Spanish ships and settlements. Spain was the major European power with the largest fleets and greatest wealth. And contemporary politics gave these pirates an excuse, a fig leaf of legality. Spain was at war with England, France and Holland for much of the 17th Century – though not necessarily with all at the same time – so frequently these raids were justified as 'acts of war'. Local governors commissioned pirates to carry out attacks so licensing these buccaneers as privateers. State-sponsored terrorism if you like.

Then politics changed. At the end of the century England made peace with Spain and the government decided that buccaneers were becoming a damned nuisance. New governors were despatched to the Caribbean colonies, particularly Jamaica and The Bahamas, with instructions to wipe out piracy.

This truce didn't include the French. In 1697 Western Hispaniola was ceded to France and became Saint Domingue. Tortuga was renamed Ile de la Tortue and was now officially French. The governor continued to commission his pirates and the island became the pre-eminent buccaneer stronghold. So Ile de la Tortue was even more important than Port Royal and, I realised, I should visit it if I could. It is only forty miles from Cap Haitien. I just felt so weak.

This time it was some sort of meat. Ah, pork probably. In a kind of sauce. And she'd found some green vegetables somewhere, and potato. Potato! It was almost like being at home. Except that there was no Veronique at home and I'm quite sure my mother wouldn't let her in the house if she knew her line of work. This was good too. A woman of many talents that Veronique.

She was watching me as I ate.

"Hmmm. Great" I said between mouthfuls. "This pork" pointing with the knife "so tender".

"I'm glad you like. This food make you better."

She was dolled up a little this evening, but not tarted up like on our first night. She'd styled her hair but dispensed with the make-up. Thank God I thought. Black people don't need make-up anyway. And it'll ruin that beautiful skin. She was wearing a different pair of blue jeans, a yellow blouse, the watch and a gold chain with a crucifix around her neck.

As I gulped the last mouthful she said "Now we go. Leave plate to later. Now you get dressed and I show you Le Cap."

I thought I'd better make an effort as Veronique so obviously had done so I pulled on my long pants and a shirt which wasn't really creased. We set off into the early evening.

The town was quiet compared to Port-au-Prince. Certainly busier than Jacmel, but that was a ghost town. Here the traffic was fairly orderly and pedestrians could venture into the streets without fearing for their lives. The buildings seemed less French, probably the consequence of three major fires and an earthquake, but a few were attractive in a Spanish sort of way, painted in pastel colours with shuttered windows and terracotta-tiled roofs. I did spot a gingerbread-adorned building way above us on a hillside.

"That one is hotel" said Veronique "but we not go there

today. Perhaps tomorrow" she promised. Yeah, right. I suspected that she had no intention of carrying out that promise. I'd already noted the endearing habit of lying which many Haitians employed. They would tell you any tale they thought would make you happy.

Veronique took my arm as we left Café Colon and we were strolling as a couple. I noticed other strolling couples and family groups and guessed that this was the promenading hour. Occasionally she would hail someone or, usually, they would hail her and brief pleasantries would be exchanged. I see. She's showing off her new boyfriend. This isn't a customer, this is my new *blanc* boyfriend. Well that's fine by me.

After about thirty minutes we arrived at a small hotel. It described itself as a guest house, The Sea Breeze, but it was far superior to any guest house I'd so far seen in Haiti. Its clientele would be exclusively foreign and mainly American. All the signs were in English including its name, its slogan – 'The Best According To The Guest' – and the highlighted use of purified water. Veronique introduced me to the American owner. He invited her to sit with him and summoned someone to escort me on a tour of the property.

I liked it. The rooms seemed comfortable, all had *en suite* bathroom and the premises were immaculately clean throughout. It was also close to the sea. The rates were extremely reasonable too. I would certainly recommend the Sea Breeze to the appropriate people at Sunstroke. This visit also ensured that I'd done some work today after all.

I was led back downstairs to find the owner and Veronique deep in joyous conversation. She was holding a drink, some sort of cocktail. Now this was a surprise. None of the tourist hotels and few of the guest houses in Port-au-Prince would allow a black guide through their doors, or sometimes even within the gates. Yet here Veronique was respected as an honoured guest. I joined them and was handed a drink.

"Well, what d'ya think?" asked the American.

"I like it" I told him truthfully. "Of course I'm just here for research purposes. I'm too junior for contracting. But I'll definitely be recommending this hotel."

"You Brits are always so modest. If you were junior they wouldn't send you out here. How many Brits ever been to Haiti? But I'm glad you like the place."

Veronique finished her drink. She turned to the owner. "Thank you. We go now. I am show Le Cap to Morgan."

I felt that my return from the inspection tour was breaking up the party. Never mind. They both live in the town and will have ample opportunity to see each other socially again. Obediently I knocked back my drink, which was a rum punch, and stood up.

Our tour of the town was nearing its end. Within ten minutes Veronique was leading me aboard a ship about the size of a coastal freighter, black-hulled and moored fast to the careenage. A gate had been cut into its side so that a wide gangplank gave easy access up a slight incline. It appeared guests were welcome although there were no exterior lights showing and no clue to what awaited within. A dimly-lit interior beckoned half-heartedly. As we strode up the gangplank a shape moved out of the shadows to meet us. Another American. Introductions were made.

"Hi. You caught me just in time. I gotta leave tomorrow."

"Tomorrow you go?" asked Veronique.

"Yeah."

He ushered us inside. Now I could see that it was some sort of casino.

"They don't want me no more. Your authorities" the American continued. He turned to me. "I'd fix you a drink but it's all locked away now."

"That's OK" I assured him, peering into the dim interior "we've just had one." I could see blackjack tables, at least one roulette wheel, card tables – probably for poker – and some apparatus set up for a game that was alien to me. Maybe something from Nevada. Why would an American want to operate a floating casino in Haiti? And who were his customers? Visitors or locals? There's hardly any tourists in Haiti and very few locals could afford to gamble. And why were they kicking him out? Perhaps his bribes were not big enough. After a quick scan of his catchpenny casino I asked "Did you do something to upset them?"

He shrugged. "I guess so. But you never know with these people." He turned to Veronique. "Ask Vera. They're a law unto themselves."

Veronique was staying out of it. "Time to go home" she said.

Chapter Three

My Hand Started Wandering

I awoke and glanced around the room. I noticed that the plate and cutlery were still sitting on the table. No surprise there. That's where we left them last night. There was a difference in Veronique though.

She was more businesslike this morning. Bossy even. She hopped out of bed immediately she realised I was awake. She started dressing briskly. I rolled over and surveyed her.

"What's the hurry Veronique?"

"I not happy. Tomorrow you go and leave me."

"I have to Veronique. I'm working. My company is paying me to do work for them. I can't stay here for ever."

"You ill. You not work when you ill. I make you better. Now you better you leave me."

Good God, I thought, this is like being married. Women. "Maybe I can come back later" I offered. "Or I come back for holiday. We could go Citadelle and other places together." I was speaking in broken English again. Apparently, subconsciously, I thought I could communicate better that way.

"If you love me you would not go. Stay here. Be boyfriend."

"Veronique." I beckoned her back to the bed. She came, a little petulantly, and sat beside me. I put my hand behind her head and gave her a little kiss. "You are a fine woman and very clever. But I really have to leave tomorrow."

"OK." She stood. "But you have to go from here today. I take you better place for today."

"You mean leave Café Colon?"

"*Oui*. We go better place for you last day."

Well, if this is the price I need to pay for domestic peace then it's no big deal. "OK" I agreed.

"You pack bag. Get ready for when I come back." She flashed me a forgiving smile, picked up the crockery and cutlery and left.

About an hour later she was back. "We go now."

I shouldered my holdall while she picked up my red Moroccan leather shoulder bag and camera. Once in the street she transferred them to her other hand and with her right felt for my left. We strolled down the street like two lovers which, I mused, we were really. Neither of us felt it necessary to speak.

Before long we reached a gated enclosure. An old man loitering just inside the open gateway gave Veronique a little bow as we entered. She led me into a two storey building, up the stairs, along a corridor, into a room and dropped my red bag and camera on the bed.

"Give me ten dollar. I pay for room."

I rifled in my pocket for my depleted wad of cash, separated the last $10 bill and handed it to her. She left and I surveyed my new surroundings. On this floor there were about a dozen rooms which could all be accessed from a communal balcony. There was a door but no lock on it. I checked the door to the corridor and couldn't find a lock on that either. Not that I was worried. Veronique wouldn't bring me to an unsafe place and, anyway, if I was with her people would know and leave me alone. This room was slightly smaller than my accommodation at Café Colon but here the double bed was protected by a mosquito net, there was a fairly solid chest of drawers, a rudimentary wardrobe and a rickety chair. And bathroom *en suite*. Sort of.

I wandered in there. Well. The toilet was a bucket with a

crude wooden seat. There was a washbasin, towel rail – wow, luxury – and a primitive shower. I turned it on. A dribble of water reluctantly trickled out of the crude head, a thin circular metal disc with tiny holes irregularly drilled into it. I turned the tap up full and now the water made a half-hearted attempt at forming itself into a spray. Still more of a dribble than a drizzle. Well it's only for one night.

At this point Veronique returned. "It's better, no?"

I wasn't sure about that, but there was no need to disappoint her. Not after her fit of pique this morning. I don't like domestic arguments. "It's OK."

"OK? It's good." She half turned and flourished with her left arm. "Now you have your own bathroom!"

"Yes" I conceded "and balcony" motioning outside with a nod.

She smiled. "I'm glad you like. I go now. Come back later."

I removed my red bag from the bed and lay down, feeling tired again. If I rest now I will be well enough later to have a proper look at the town, maybe take some photos, and stroll down to the *tap-tap* terminal to buy a ticket for the morrow. Money. Of course I haven't checked yet. Arching my back slightly I extracted the folded bills from my pocket and spread them out. After the $10 I'd just given Veronique there should be $62 left. There wasn't.

Two creased portraits of President Jackson smiled enigmatically up at me as if he was party to the joke. Washington peered myopically in duplicate. $42. This set me thinking. If today is Saturday then tomorrow is Sunday and the banks will be closed. If another Jackson disappears tonight then I will be left with the change from $22 after I've paid for my bus ticket. $16 if that bus in the guide book is still serviceable or $18 if I return by *tap-tap*. Not really sufficient for my expenses in Port-au-Prince. I will need that extra twenty. What should I do? Well two can play that game. I'll pinch $20. But where should I hide it? Oh yes, that's best I thought, secreting a Jackson and returning the rest to my pocket. After the bus ticket that'll be down to $16 and no-one's going to steal that.

By the time Veronique returned, around noon, I'd moved to the rickety chair.

"You OK?" Have good rest?"

"Yes, I'm fine."

"Good. You give me maybe five dollar for hair?"

This was unexpected. Obviously she was hoping to maximise her winnings. I hesitated, then turned a steady gaze on her.

"I can't Veronique" I lied. "I've only got twenty two dollars left. Out of that I have to buy a bus ticket today and then my expenses in Port-au-Prince tomorrow. You know, taxi, hotel and so on."

She stiffened, thrust her right hand on to her hip and glared at me.

"No!" she exclaimed. "You have forty two dollar!"

I nearly burst out laughing. That's given the game away hasn't it? I managed to stay relaxed. I leant back in the chair and affected surprise.

"I know. You're right. I should have. More in fact. It's strange isn't it? Where's the money gone?"

"Look in your pocket."

Obediently I stood and slowly emptied my pockets. The left contained those twenty two dollars just mentioned. I laid these on the bed. She picked up the three notes, checked that two were not stuck together, then tossed them down. My right hand pocket delivered up a handkerchief.

Obviously impatient with the tardiness of my search she stomped over to me and felt inside both pockets, then turned them inside out. Nothing. She swept around to my back pocket and fished out my wallet. As usual that was empty apart from business cards. She felt inside my shirt then my shorts. That was nice. She sat back on the bed and stared at me in exasperation.

"You have forty two dollars!"

"I know I should have Veronique. More, like I said. But where is it?"

She leapt up off the bed and set about the room like a whirlwind. I hadn't unpacked my holdall – after all, I was leaving in the morning – so she rummaged through that then emptied the contents. Now she scanned the room wildly. On top of the chest of drawers she spotted my red leather shoulder bag. Triumphantly she lunged over there, snatched it up and swivelled round, showering its contents on the bed. My passport, driving licence, credit cards, air tickets, tourist information, scribbled notes, pens, exposed and unexposed camera film, telephoto lens, spare notebook and a packet of nuts tumbled out. But no money. She looked under the mattress, in all the drawers, through all my spare clothes and even checked the bathroom. Finally she slumped back on the bed with questioning defeat in her eyes.

"It's odd isn't it Veronique? Now I know why you brought me here. Every night at the other place some money disappeared from my pocket. Regular as clockwork. Somebody must have got in the room whilst we were sleeping."

She looked up sharply and stared at me, momentarily disconcerted. Then, abruptly, she swivelled round and jumped on the bed so that she was on all fours like a recalcitrant child, scattering my belongings. She pounded the mattress with her little fists.

"You fuck me too much! You fuck me too much!"

During this excitable performance she was observing me slyly through the corner of her eye. I sat there, motionless, unperturbed, still leaning back in the chair, successfully suppressing a grin. Another bout of flailing the sheets.

"Me no *voleuse*. You fuck me too much!"

Ah, I thought, *voleuse* must be French for thief. She's probably expecting trouble. Perhaps she thinks I'm going to make a scene, call the police, beat her or something. I suppose normally, if she makes a habit of helping herself during the night, her customers would not notice any missing money. Frequently they would be drunk I expect. But if they did notice, or catch her stealing, then they would very likely give her a beating.

I laughed. "Oh come on Veronique. What are you getting upset about? It's me who should be upset."

"You fuck me too much. You fuck me too much. Me no *voleuse*."

"I'd like to fuck you some more" I admitted, grinning "but I have to leave tomorrow."

That stopped her. She squirmed around and stared at me, sitting there in the wooden chair with the wobbly leg, laughing. Obviously I wasn't going to hit her or go to the police. Either I knew what she had done and was being cool about it or I didn't suspect. She slid off the bed and stood up.

"OK. You go, get *tap-tap* ticket" she said, heading for the door in graceful defeat. "When you back later I have dinner for you."

I found my shoes – at opposite ends of the room where the hurricane had flung them – and slipped them on. I shoved all the clobber on the bed back into its respective bags and stuffed the $22 in my pocket. Picking up my camera and telephoto lens I set off to roam around Le Cap.

Outside it was sunny and hot. The streets were quiet with hardly any traffic and very few pedestrians. Maybe that was because of the heat and time of day. "Mad dogs and Englishmen go out in the midday sun" I mused. Now I noticed, because I was concentrating, that the architecture was almost entirely Spanish. There seemed to be nothing of the French heritage remaining. I took some shots using my telephoto lens, mainly architectural studies. Parts of buildings where I liked the shapes, colours and textures, but I had to be careful. In the tropics the light is so intense that shadowed areas which appear grey to the naked eye become an impenetrable black in the finished photograph.

After about half an hour I was ready to wander down to the bus station when a rangy and dishevelled girl sidled up to me. She smiled.

"You take photo."

You don't need the brains of Einstein to work that out I thought. "Yes."

"I am friend of Vera."

Now she got my attention. Slim, but not too skinny, aged about twenty, she wore very short navy blue shorts, a much faded and stained lime green T-shirt and a slightly sly expression. That's all. Her hair was disarrayed. She didn't possess the charisma of Veronique or, indeed, any charisma at all.

"You are Morkan?"

"Yes."

"I am Cheryl." She thrust out her hand. I shook it. Cheryl? What kind of Haitian name is that?

"What you do now?" she asked.

"Well, I'm on my way to the bus station. For *tap-tap*. I have to buy ticket for tomorrow."

"I come with you?"

I regarded her doubtfully. "You'll need to put some shoes on."

She beamed with pleasure. "You wait. I get shoes." She ran off like a small child, skipping with joy.

Within five minutes she was back, wearing black sandals. She stood with her feet together and directed my gaze to them. "You like?"

"Ah yes, very good."

She took my hand. "Now we go *tap-tap gare*. But they not here now."

Yes, of course, the buses won't arrive from Port-au-Prince until later in the afternoon. So plenty of time to wander through the town to the bus station, which is to the very south, and get a good feel for the place. Cheryl strolled and skipped happily by my side.

"You take plenty photos Morkan?"

"A few. But now I just want to see Le Cap."

"I show you."

All was well for twenty minutes but then my hand started wandering. Not my fault. It was not under my control you understand. Cheryl still gripped my right hand in her left. She moved it onto her body, under the T-shirt.

"What are you doing Cheryl?"

"Oh. Just. Nothing." She didn't drop my hand though. Now it wandered up to the underside of her breast. I dragged it away.

"What *are* you doing?"

"It nice. Like boyfriend."

"I am *not* your boyfriend Cheryl. And, anyway, if I was, I wouldn't be doing these things in the street."

"I know. You Vera boyfriend. Vera very lucky."

Christ! What has Veronique been telling her?

My hand had moved back on to her body again, this time around her waist.

"Cheryl" I said in my best warning tone.

"This OK. We do this in Haiti."

"I'm quite sure you do. I'm quite sure you do lots of things that wouldn't go down well in Eastbourne."

But I didn't resist this time. It seemed harmless enough.

I was wrong. Five minutes later my hand reached her breast again. Now normally I'm quite keen on fondling breasts but there's a time and place for everything. There were few witnesses on the streets but I had no way of knowing how many pairs of eyes were trained on us from the darkened windows of the surrounding buildings. I was a little embarrassed. I withdrew my hand sharply.

"You're at it again." I shoved my hand into my pocket.

She pouted. "Let me hold hand."

"No. You can't be trusted."

"I can. Just hold hand."

I must be soft in the head. I relented, although for the

moment I kept my hand in its temporary refuge. "OK" I informed her with mock strictness "but if you do it again I will fuck you right here in the street. Do you understand?"

She smiled and nodded. Oh my God, I thought, I've done it now.

I took a deep breath. "Cheryl" I said. "You must understand that I'm English. In England we don't walk around fondling each other in the street even if it is normal in Haiti." Which, frankly, I doubted.

"OK. I be good girl. If I bad again you fuck me in street."

Well hopefully that's clear then.

Unfortunately it was too clear, even if a mischievous hooker needed to spend some minutes thinking about it. Once my hand departed its sanctuary – well, it was a hot day – she took it in hers. No resistance and no problem. Then, before I realised it, I was fondling her left breast.

"Right! I warned you" I blurted, reclaiming control of my hand.

If you issue a threat you must carry it out. I whipped around in front of her and stopped her in her tracks. Simultaneously I swung her arms above her head and gripped the hem of her T-shirt. I pulled it up to expose her tits. She started squealing, attracting the attention of a strolling couple on the other side of the street. I released her and stood back, wagging my finger in her face.

"I told you what would happen and you said you understood. Right?" She stopped screaming and started grinning at me, wondering what I would do next. "I am English" I continued. "We don't do this in the street. I told you what would happen if you did it again."

The couple across the road lost interest, apart from a private giggle, when they realised there wasn't a rape in progress. Cheryl remained standing there with her breasts proudly exposed, T-shirt around her neck, arms raised above her head. She flashed me a wicked grin.

"So, in England" she asked "you fuck people in the street?"

"Not personally. Are you going to walk to the *gare* like that?"

"*Peut-être*. You put it like that, not me. So you not fuck me then?"

"Not if you start screaming. The police will come. I'll be arrested."

"No is OK. I tell them you my boyfriend."

"I am *NOT* your boyfriend Cheryl, as I keep saying. I am Veronique's boyfriend. What would she say if I fucked you in the street?"

She pouted again then with both hands reluctantly pulled her T-shirt back down to restore a semblance of decency.

"We go. I take you to meet some friends."

Chapter Four

Only The Whores Wear Watches

The first few of these friends presumably inhabited tumbledown shacks in the poorest part of town for that is where she took me. Whilst I casually surveyed the streams of sewage slowly trickling past us Cheryl spoke animatedly to two ladies, occasionally gesturing towards me. They nodded politely and I gave a little bow in return. As they chatted, Cheryl feeding them some fiction in which I no doubt featured strongly, I contemplated my surroundings.

We were perched on a tiny earth hillock. I was loath to move in case I stepped into the sewage. The water – or, anyway, liquid – coursed gently along snaking gutters formed naturally through the undulating street. Some children were enjoying a 'boat race' in the main channel. They threw sticks into the meandering brook and each excitedly urged on his own. They rapidly disappeared behind a shack, deftly jumping from mound to mound to avoid slipping into the foul-smelling streams, yelling at each other and their sticks.

I was curious but reluctant to scrutinise the nearby buildings closely, particularly as I still carried my camera, because I felt that would be rude somehow. These people had little enough privacy without some foreigner sticking his nose in.

Eventually Cheryl finished her social chit-chat and adroitly led me away, stepping over the dribbling detritus, until we were well clear of the shanty town. We were still not back on a major thoroughfare though. This was an unsurfaced track which I assumed would lead to the main road.

We soon approached a greyish-white six foot high wall which had black wooden double gates set in it. The top hinge on one gate was broken. It stood open at right angles to the wall, its leading edge stuck firmly in the mud. Where I reckoned it had been for some time. Cheryl pushed open the other gate, we stepped around a puddle and entered a muddy stable yard. That's what it looked like to me. Around three sides were stalls, each big enough for a horse, but I could see no other evidence of livestock. Without hesitation Cheryl headed straight for the middle stall of the bank on our left. As we approached it I could see that there were no exterior bolts on the chest-high stable doors so presumably horses were no longer housed here. Cheryl called out to someone inside, pushed through the swinging jaws of the cell and beckoned me to follow.

I'd made the mistake of thinking nothing else in Haiti would shock me. But this shocked me, though I hoped it didn't show. Across the far end of the stall I saw a double bed with disarranged sheets which, from where I was standing, didn't look too clean. Lying across the bed on her side, her head supported by her crooked left arm, wearing only a very brief pair of knickers, I saw an extremely fat mulatta woman with pendulous breasts.

She beamed at me as introductions were made. I didn't catch her name.

Fortunately in this cramped space, which also housed a washbasin, were two chairs. I collapsed into one whilst Cheryl moved towels from the other and settled onto it. Yes, that's right, English. No, I don't have a cigarette. Sorry. I just smoke this pipe. Sometimes. Yes, sure you can have some tobacco. Here you are. But it might be too strong for a cigarette. Oh, you smoke a pipe sometimes too?

Whilst Cheryl and the mulatta chatted, and the latter fondled her fanny through the knickers, my mind whirled. The Jamaican in Port-au-Prince, the same guy who recommended Café Colon, yes he, told me about the whores from The Dominican Republic. They come in on nine month visas. But why? Surely there's enough whores in Haiti to satisfy demand. Yeh man, but some o' dem dey need a break from de black woman, or mebbe dem prefer de whiter skin. I was disconcerted. Quite a few of the black whores were not unattractive, obviously not in the class of Veronique, who was special, not just to me, but also to everybody, hotel owners included, but some of the others were not bad, even Cheryl if you were feeling really horny, but what kind of depravity was this? What kind of man, presumably after a good night out on the town, would come back to this? Very drunk and very desperate presumably. And what kind of life was it for the woman? She seemed to live here, in this stall, judging by a few garments I could see scattered around and the fact that Cheryl could just turn up unannounced and find her here. Absolutely no privacy at any time. And the nocturnal noise. Grunts and squeals and curses spreading like an epidemic through those cells.

I was in a semi-dazed state when we left. I don't know how long we sat there and I didn't pay much attention as Cheryl led me to the bus depot. Which I was glad to reach. Normality had returned. Here were the *tap-taps* lined up, some of the drivers selling tickets to tomorrow's passengers. Cheryl led me to *Pan Am Clipper*.

"No" I said. "I came in this one. I want to go back in another."

Traversing the country on a wooden bench in the back of a converted truck was fine once, an interesting experience, but I fancied a bit more comfort for the return trip. I scanned the bus park hoping to see *Ebenezer*. Sure enough it was there and exactly as described in the guide book. A small red-and-white bus designed and built in an industrialised country for the specific purpose of conveying passengers. It even boasted glazed windows. No matter that the seats had been renumbered by an inexpert hand in crude white brushstrokes to carry 39 people instead of the 27 for whom it was originally intended.

I sauntered over and booked seat number 34 much to Cheryl's displeasure. Presumably she was hoping for commission from the driver of *Pan Am Clipper*. I paid the six dollars asked and we set off back to town.

We'd strolled less than a hundred yards when we were halted by a whistle from behind us. Cheryl's name was called. She swivelled round and saw the driver with his arm raised beckoning to her. She cast an insecure glance at me then trotted quickly back to *Ebenezer*. I waited, watching. Almost as soon as she reached the driver she took something, turned around and ran back, her little girl excitement returned. She was waving money.

"Three gourde." So she got her commission anyway.

In the centre of town the streets were still quiet. Cheryl took me inside a corner building and led the way past a few unoccupied tables to the counter. We were the only customers. As we parked ourselves on stools she said something to the attendant and two ice creams quickly appeared. Cheryl handed over two-thirds of her commission, passed one of the ices to me and sat back to lick the other. Immediate needs settled, she looked across. By interpreting the glint in her eyes I fancied I could read her mind.

It had been a good day. She'd had some fun escorting me around town – especially that episode where I'd pulled up her T-shirt – she'd introduced me as her boyfriend to some of her pals and now we were finishing up with an ice cream apiece.

"Come" she said, sliding off her stool and taking my hand "we go Vera's house."

Veronique was not pleased to see us. Firstly, I was late. Dusk had arrived before we did. She'd expected me back before now and cooked something special. Secondly I was accompanied by Cheryl. This was not in the script. Veronique glared at me then fired a torrent of Creole at Cheryl who, far from being humbled or scared, seemed to be giving cocky replies. And probably lying. Veronique turned to me, quite furious, face alive with anger and hurt. She wasn't acting this time.

"Me jealous! Me jealous!" she screamed.

I was amused but tried not to show it. I spread my arms in my best gesture of innocence. "We only went to the bus station. Nothing happened. Then she bought me an ice cream."

"Why you go *tap-tap gare* with her?" The anger was unabated.

"She met me in the street. Told me she was your friend and asked to walk with me."

Veronique returned her attentions to Cheryl. She spat more fierce questions at the slimmer girl but the answers were less cocky now. Cheryl was becoming less sure of herself by the minute, perhaps because a small crowd had gathered, amused by our domestic squabble. Veronique turned back to me.

"You ask her to go *gare*? Who ask who?"

Well, just tell the truth. "Like I said, I was standing in the street taking photographs. Down there. Cheryl came. Said she was a friend of yours. Then asked to come with me. I said 'Get some shoes and you can come.' She got shoes and we walked to the bus station." To reinforce my case I adopted my most innocent expression, widening my eyes, raising my eyebrows and shrugging my shoulders.

She stared intently at me, presumably trying to decide whether I was telling the truth. Obviously I'd lied about the missing $20 bill. But this time? Why should I lie? Why would I want to bother with Cheryl when I had her? Cheryl, on the other hand, was known for it. She turned again to Cheryl who was standing there casting me anxious looks and intimidated by the watching crowd. There was now some gesticulation as

Veronique delivered a final rebuke accompanied by what I guessed were dire threats and warnings. Then Cheryl was dismissed. Veronique turned back to me.

"I still jealous. I very jealous. She bad girl, not like me. Now you go back hotel and I bring dinner."

And it was a good dinner too, fish again with rice. She had an odd expression in her eyes as she watched me eat. A little sad, a little uncertain.

"Morgan, I can't stay with you tonight."

Of course. It was Saturday. Probably Saturday was The Big Night Out here like the rest of the world. "I understand" I replied. "You have to work for a living."

She ignored that remark though it was not intended to be offensive. "I come in the morning early" she promised. "To wake you, so you not sleep and miss *tap-tap*."

"Sure. I'll see you then."

She left with the plate and cutlery. I felt tired again but this time it was a good tired, a productive tired. Today I'd achieved something, even if it was only seeing the town and buying a bus ticket. Slipping under the mosquito net I lay on the bed and allowed my thoughts to wander.

Even without seeing everything I felt I'd gathered enough research material on Haiti. Someone, perhaps one of the Americans if not Veronique, had advised me to avoid Ile de la Tortue. The island was controlled now by a French – no, not French, a Canadian – priest who also supervised the only accommodation suitable for visitors to the island. And apparently, although I had no way of determining the truth of the contention, this priest was not favourably disposed towards people researching the evil deeds of pirates. By now I'd given up the idea of discovering buried treasure there. As a location it was less promising even than Ile-à-Vache. Firstly there was no reason for pirates to bury it at their base, particularly as the French governor was resident there, and secondly the island now harboured a population of two thousand. If they hadn't unearthed pirate booty no one else was likely to. Maybe the priest has squads of them digging on a regular schedule.

I mused within a blanket of night. Obviously it was not yet late as the only sounds I heard were from the corridor outside my room. Night-time ladies passing, greeting each other, perhaps exchanging confidences. No noise yet from the streets. I lay there some time.

Suddenly a surreptitious movement from the balcony alerted me to someone entering the room. Maybe there was a slight change in the light quality as the door was opened. Peering through the mosquito net and the darkness I could just discern two figures entering, apparently a man and a woman. The man moved quickly and stealthily to my red leather bag on the dresser.

"Hey! What's going on? What's happening?" I shouted.

The woman whispered something to the man. He dropped the bag and disappeared abruptly through the other door into the corridor. I quickly sat up and pulled the net aside to find myself a few inches from Cheryl.

"Cheryl! What's going on?"

"I just come to see you."

"Who was that guy?"

She shrugged her shoulders. "Just a friend."

"What was he doing here?"

No answer was forthcoming. She just shrugged again and started to climb onto the bed.

"Cheryl, what are you doing?"

"I just sleep with you. We have nice time. No?"

"No."

"You not like? I see, you afraid of Vera."

I sighed deeply. Was she trying to provoke me or just stupid? Or perhaps the plan was for her friend to return when I was otherwise engaged or sleeping.

"Cheryl, I am leaving tomorrow. Veronique can't do anything to me. But if she finds out – when she finds out – she'll kill you."

Cheryl reflected on this and evidently decided I was right. "OK, I come back in the morning and wake you for bus." She left by the same door as her friend.

Gggrrreat I thought. I'm going to have two hookers wake me in the morning. It will be a great send-off if they don't scratch each other's eyes out. I eased completely through the net and stepped over to the dresser. I checked my red bag. Passport, driving licence, credit cards and air tickets still there. That bloke hadn't stolen anything then. I checked my trouser pocket. Still $16.

I'm not in the habit of going to sleep wearing my socks so I'd discarded them as I hauled myself onto the bed. Now I located them and looked inside. From the second one I retrieved a crumpled and sweaty $20 bill. I seemed to have wiped the smirk from Jackson's now-wrinkled face but bearing in mind I'd been trampling him underfoot all day his condition didn't seem too bad. I folded him amongst his fellows. Now I felt strangely confident that they would all still be there in the morning. A brief shower and I was ready for bed.

The noise started just as I sank back on the mattress. Latin rock music, mainly Santana, wafted through the night from a couple of blocks distant. Surely Santana couldn't be in Le Cap? I wouldn't want to miss that. But very unlikely. Must be records. Noise was also building up in the corridor. First just girls' and women's voices, then later a few men's, then later still men and women in equal measure. Ah yes, just as I suspected. This is a whorehouse.

I couldn't sleep. Whether it was the noise, the anticipation of the journey tomorrow or the feeling that this marked the end of, shall we say, an interesting chapter in my life, I don't know. Maybe I was afraid of another unscheduled visit. But whatever it was I lay there listening to faraway music, still recognisably Santana for the most part, disparate but gradually subsiding corridor sounds, thinking of Veronique whilst musing on islands to come. For sure this was the end of any excitement.

Eventually, in the early hours, silence settled over the town. I lay there for quite some time, still unable to sleep, until I needed to visit the toilet. Sitting on the makeshift seat over the bucket I spied the first glimmers of dawn. Dawn. Dawn was usually around six wasn't it? And the bus would leave at 0630. From the other end of town. There was no way of checking the time as my watch, a Longines, had stopped, probably with an exhausted battery, in Port-au-Prince. And I was certainly not going to allow anyone in Haiti to repair that watch or even examine it. Damn. I knew there wouldn't be a clock anywhere. In this country, I reflected, only the whores wear watches. And they were all asleep.

I couldn't take the chance of missing the bus. As soon as I finished in the bathroom I checked that I'd packed everything, grabbed my bags and rushed downstairs. The corridor was deserted but the stairs were crammed with bodies. Whether they'd been too drunk to ascend to their quarters, too eager to commence copulation or too poor to afford a room I didn't know, but I needed to squeeze past three interlocked couples in varying states of undress. Once outside in the yard the path was clear to the gate. But it was locked. What do I do now? Climb over the wall?

It was too high. Don't panic. I returned to the hotel building and woke the couple on the bottom steps. I tried to explain my predicament.

"I need to go out." I waved an arm at the gate. "Gate locked."

They understood completely. The woman pointed to a recumbent form a few feet away. "*Concierge.*"

Concierge? I strode over there and woke him. It was the old man who'd been standing by the gate when we arrived yesterday. He fully understood what I required. He stood up, fished a bunch of keys out of his pocket and ambled over to the gate. Fumbling a bit at first, he found the correct key and opened up. Very relieved, I thanked him.

Out in the street I could see that the glow was brighter

now. Good. If that way is east then this must be south. I headed off in that direction earnestly hoping that I would be in time. The narrow streets were dark, illuminated only by the weak rays of the rising sun bathing the tops of the buildings, and completely deserted. Suddenly a prowling taxi appeared. I hailed it and a few minutes later I was deposited at my destination. The cabbie charged the correct fare too.

I stood alone with my bags in the silent and deserted bus depot. Empty. Empty of people that is. The *tap-taps* and *Ebenezer* were all there, ready and waiting for their day's work, but I was the first passenger to arrive. I need not have panicked.

Within half an hour the scene was transformed. The sun rose to bathe a teeming throng within its warming glow. *Ebenezer* was filling up nicely. Of course I was first on the bus. Peering out the window I could see the activity surrounding the other vehicles. Luggage was being thrown on to roofs and passengers were arriving in taxis, by cart and on foot. I closed the window and rested my head on the seat back. Now perhaps I could get some sleep.

After a few minutes I was startled by a tap on the glass. I opened my eyes, jerked upright and looked out. It was Veronique. Now dressed in casual-casual but still looking good – to me in fact looking beautiful. She appeared to have enjoyed a full night's sleep. I slid the window open.

"I wanted to say goodbye to you" she said with her best smile, as if this was the beginning of a romance, not the end "and I know you have not much money."

She reached into her purse. Pulling out some US dollar bills she continued "This is for the taxi in Port-au-Prince. And the hotel." Again her hand went to her purse. "And money for the taxi to the airport. And Santo Domingo." I wondered where she'd picked up that idea. My next stop would be Grenada and I intended getting there as quickly as possible. "And you will not have me to cook for you. So here is money for restaurants." She handed me some more bills.

I didn't need to count it. I knew it would be the exact amount she'd stolen, $60.

We just smiled at each other for a few moments. I couldn't get my head through the window, it was too small, and the bus was about to leave, so I couldn't get out. I reached for her hand and kissed it.

"Send me a postcard" she said.

"I need your address."

"I have written it down for you." She handed me a piece of paper. "Goodbye Morgan. Don't forget me."

I felt like crying. This was the most beautiful thing that had ever happened to me.

Chapter Five

"It's From A Madman"

Jerry had hustled as an ice cream salesman, a minicab driver and God knows what else before joining the board of Sunstroke Holidays. He slotted in well with the other spivs. His salesmanship was legendary. Or so I was told by some of the Reservations staff who enjoyed telling tales, sometimes embellished, about the nefarious activities of our bosses in their previous lives. Like Jerry that time at Hyde Park Corner – itself a dubious location in my view – on a rare beautiful summer's day.

A group of French youngsters – probably vacationing students – were lounging on the grass, sunbathing. A girl left her pals and approached Jerry's van.

"Please, you make for me one of zat" she said, pointing to something advertised on the outside of the vehicle. Jerry obligingly leant over the counter and craned his neck to identify the object of her desire. As if he didn't know.

"That?" he enquired pleasantly, bending his left arm back to stab the illustration of a 99.

"*Oui*. Please."

He took a cone, squirted a liberal portion of the soft ice cream into it, inserted a chocolate flake, leant down and handed it to the girl with a flourish and his insincere but charming smile. She offered him a fiver. He turned around and bustled for a bit, as cynical ice cream salesmen and taxi drivers do, pretending to search for change. After a couple of minutes he straightened up and turned back empty-handed but ready with his "Oh sorry, of course" should it be needed. The girl was gone.

She was back with her friends already, showing them the 99. Together the others rose to their feet and headed towards Jerry. All five of them. This looked like trouble but he could handle it. Look, I've got the change but she rushed off.

Surprisingly they seemed friendly not hostile as they approached him. The leader pointed back at the girl, now lying on the grass licking her cone, then the ad for the 99 and proffered a £5 note. Jerry now noticed that each of the others was flashing a fiver. A good bit of business.

And a good story if it was true.

I was remembering this tale as the crowded escalator bore me and the other commuters up to the street. Past the pictures of attractive ladies modelling skimpy underwear and the occasional Smirnoff ad. Which none of us even glanced at. Seen it all before. Daily. A line of hurrying people, either late for work or over-anxious to get there, pushed past on my left.

Yesterday Jerry held an emergency sales meeting to which the Reservations staff were summoned for a pep talk. The new brochure had been distributed a few weeks ago but sales were still sluggish.

Jerry liked to present himself as avuncular but thinking back now to those days I have to say he brings John Prescott to mind. Although, unlike Mr Prescott, he could charm a rattlesnake with his insincere smile and patter. Yesterday he was as expansive as ever, smiling to encourage us. He directed his attention at my department.

"Wally" he began. They all called me Wally. To them it was some sort of joke. Not Walter, my Christian name as used by my mother, or my preferred name, Morgan. That's what my university friends knew me as. But some gossipy and malicious person had seen my file which gave my full name, Walter Morgan Fairchild. That intelligence was swiftly passed around and soon everyone addressed me as Wally.

"Wally" Jerry continued. Maybe he enjoyed saying it twice. "Golden Sands. It's a great hotel. Brand new. Just built. As you know. Push it. I've seen it myself. We're already getting great reports. We've got most of the beds there. Push it."

I hoped that I didn't sound exasperated in my reply. "Jerry. It's all I can do to push people on to planes at the moment." The room erupted into laughter. As I rose slowly upwards I was still wondering why. I hadn't intended to make a joke.

Before I could think that one through I reached the top of the escalator, passed through the barrier and emerged on the Tottenham Court Road. Without enthusiasm I followed my daily routine. Turn right, right again into Goodge Street and the zone popular with advertising agencies, media companies and the trendy restaurants and pubs essential to that way of life. Those glamour professions had injected a little – but only a little – colour into a few of London's dreary streets. In the gloomy morning haze buildings stood dejected like elderly people in a bus queue. Dressed in greys, browns and the occasional off-white they accepted that their best years were behind them. Some boasted brightly-hued Perspex fascias at their ground level, a liveliness which reminded me of small children fidgeting and chattering in front of their sombre grandparents.

My workplace was close to one of the capital's seedier districts. Fortunately the sleaze and tourist tat of Soho rarely migrates north of Oxford Street. Foreign tourists and frustrated provincial businessmen hunting for cheap thrills will only stray here in error. So we hardly ever saw them on our little patch where on a pleasant sunny day a stroll is enjoyable. Unfortunately London is blessed with few sunny days and fewer still are pleasant. The continual traffic flow harasses drivers and pedestrians alike and noxious exhaust fumes taint the air. Most of the buildings are as unwelcoming, unfriendly and anonymous as the offices of Sunstroke Holidays. The exterior of that four storey building looked as though it had never been cleaned and the interior was hardly more inviting. I use the past tense because although, to the best of my knowledge, the building still stands Sunstroke are no longer with us.

I have a habit of arriving slightly late so I entered at 0915 with a silent sigh and trod the threadbare carpeting from the grimy glass front door to a large room buzzing with responsive voices. These belonged to the Reservations Clerks, all tethered to their desks by the umbilical cord of their telephone headsets. From the hubbub I could distinguish individual young Cockney voices repeating credit card numbers, spelling out reference codes or just quoting prices and availability.

The noise, bustle and litter of files and reservation cards might give the visitor the illusion of a booming enterprise but we all knew that business could be much better. Some of the accounts staff – those who had the wit to notice – were aware of the depressing details but it was senior management on the top floor who needed to tackle the problem. That collection of spivs and third-raters was continually dreaming up brilliant schemes to make the reservation hall hum more insistently. Or so they liked to think.

The directors were desperately searching for a new gimmick. They knew that as a medium-sized company they were vulnerable in the modern marketplace. In the near future Sunstroke Holidays would be marginalised with its standard 'bucket and spade' holidays. The company would be starved of retail outlets and forced to pay over the odds for airplane seats.

What did they need? Me.

Stuart 'Stew' Arrowsmith, the Operations Director, persuaded his colleagues that the solution was a specialist department. They were all smart enough to realise that this wouldn't work with the existing staff so they needed to recruit a few people of a higher calibre to research and run it. Finding them was proving difficult with the poor salaries they were offering.

Margaret Thatcher came to their rescue. The year was 1983 and the government's strategy of creating mass unemployment in order to castrate the unions was proving more successful than in their wildest dreams. I think at one stage there were three or four million on the dole, including university graduates. I held an honours degree in Mediaeval History but no realistic hope that this would assist me in finding a job. Not that I really wanted a job. A lifetime spent studying history would be heaven but I needed a job because I needed a salary. So a few months earlier I was hired by Sunstroke, initially as a Reservations Clerk.

Quite soon they realised that they'd hooked a useful employee so I was promoted quickly. As a Section Leader I was thorough, conscientious and paid attention to detail. Of course this set me apart from my colleagues, most of whom had left school at the earliest opportunity. The chaps there, the majority anyway, were Millwall fans (that sounds like a cheap shot but actually it's true. Probably because they hailed from The Isle of Dogs or Bermondsey). The girls were obsessed with TV soaps and celebrities.

I struggled with my staff until they dumped Patel on me. Nobody could pronounce his first name – and I can't remember it now – so we all called him Patel. He was conscientious and intelligent but somehow he managed to create major cock-ups in every position they put him. Department after department rejected him until he wound up in Ticketing. Here a solid skinhead from Greenwich ruled his manor with a rod of iron. Nobody ever suggested that Mick was a racist and I never heard him mouth a racist remark. Not even when some of the others complained that the Accounts Department staff were "stinking out the basement with their chapattis" at lunchtime. But he did seem obsessively strict with Patel. Wandering up there one afternoon I witnessed Mick at his most bullying. He was towering over a hunched Patel and lambasting him with obscenities.

Patel retaliated in his own way. Sunstroke Holidays were operating Boeing 737s in the charter configuration of 130 seats and writing tickets by hand. So when Patel wrote out four entire flights incorrectly he wasted around 500 tickets. Not to mention the problem that someone else had to rewrite them in double-quick time. 'Stew' Arrowsmith brought him down to me.

"He fucks up every job he's given so this is his last chance."

Arrowsmith glared sideways at him as if he wanted to cuff him about the ear. "If you don't take him he'll be sacked."

I was pleased to take him. He would be additional to the four morons who'd just been dumped on me and who I was struggling to convert to useful employees. And I suspected that he might be more efficient – certainly more willing – than them. I was right. He became the most competent member of the team. Was that because he was being treated with some respect?

Patel's quick wit would often give me a laugh. He was handy with a catch phrase, a humorous snippet and an occasional swipe at our employer's cynical attitude to our customers. Whilst engaged one afternoon on a raft of 'consolidations' – the company's policy of arbitrarily shifting clients from the flight they'd booked to another, often on a different day or from a different airport – he looked up brightly, smiled sweetly and suggested a new company motto.

"We leave no holiday unchanged."

With Patel's more serious help the section was ticking over more or less smoothly when my brilliant idea hit me. The one prompted by the letter.

I regularly provided the management with innovative ideas. Most were rejected out of hand but this, I thought, could propel us out ahead of the pack. I brought it up with 'Stew' at a flight check meeting one day.

"Why not combine the two?" I suggested.

Arrowsmith leaned back and adopted a world-weary

expression intended to suggest that he would like me out of his office as soon as possible.

"Combine what two?" he responded, as if he'd already forgotten what we'd just been discussing. His speech resonated with a nasal twang. It always reminded me of a dirty old man, a telephone heavy breather. Although I never saw him with a soiled raincoat.

"Well" I continued, encouraged "if the Caribbean holidays are not selling because our competitors can do them a lot cheaper, and the cultural holidays are a flop because we don't have the reputation or the best lecturers, why not combine the two?"

"Cultural holidays in The Caribbean Wally? You're joking aren't you? There is no culture in The Caribbean."

I persevered. "Well, what about Haiti?"

Arrowsmith sighed deeply. A sigh that suggested that he had, at least, heard of Haiti. "What about Haiti? We are not going to get rich selling holidays to Haiti Wally. What's their culture anyway?"

"They've been called 'West Africa in The Caribbean' and its also where Caribbean piracy started. The word 'buccaneer' was invented there."

"Pirates Wally?" he snorted. "Pirates? You must be joking!" He sneered at me, obviously calculating how he could make a joke out of my suggestion.

All of them, except the MD, felt free to take the piss out of me because I didn't fit into their shallow world. 'Stew' Arrowsmith was typical. He liked to spend long lunches in the little Italian round the corner where he sampled the wine copiously. So his afternoons were a washout. But he did have the knack of getting other people to do his work for him so he was prepared to tolerate me if he thought I could be useful. A few times I rescued him from impending cock-ups or pointed out operational problems which he'd overlooked. One time, an occasion which still gives me a laugh, I saved him from appearing a totally ignorant prat.

"Wally" he instructed me one afternoon "can you send this telex to Manuel in Palma?" Briefly leaning forward from his customary slouched position he rudely thrust a sheet of paper across the desk at me.

Mallorca was never my department but I didn't mind. My own work was done for the day and my section was beginning to tick along nicely. I took the proffered paper and read the scribbled message slowly and carefully even though it was obvious he wanted me out of his office as soon as possible. So that he could reach for that bottle of whisky in his desk drawer probably.

"I don't understand Stew."

"What don't you understand Wally?" he rasped wearily. "It's quite simple. We have a situation."

That last phrase was a cliché, a standing joke amongst the Reservations staff as Operations under Arrowsmith's stewardship lurched from drama to crisis. Anecdotes were invariably prefaced by "We have a situation" delivered in an imitation of Arrowsmith's nasal tones.

"A minor operational problem" he continued. "So we need to get tomorrow's Palma people up to Barcelona. We have enough seats on the Barcelona flight. Just send the telex" he finished, impatiently waving his arm in the direction of the telex room.

"You won't be able to get them to Barcelona in time."

"For fuck's *sake*. Why not Wally? The flight's not until tomorrow."

"The ferries are not daily and they take about a day anyway. Manuel will never be able to arrange it."

Now he sat up straight. "Ferries, Wally? Ferries? Who said anything about ferries? You can read, can't you? That telex says coaches. I want Manuel to arrange *coaches* from Mallorca to Barcelona. There should be plenty of time for that. What's the big problem?"

I was successfully keeping a straight face. I could see that Arrowsmith was dying for that drink now. And I could guess what he was thinking. That bloody Wally could be tiresome sometimes. A bloody perfectionist too. God knows what could be bugging him this time.

I executed an exaggerated glance behind me, ostensibly to confirm that the office door was shut, then leant over the desk and spoke quietly.

"Stew. Mallorca's an island."

Sorry about that. I go off at a tangent sometimes. Back to the story.

As I said, Arrowsmith had a talent for getting other people to do his job for him and pinching their ideas. He could grasp the potential of pirate-themed holidays so he pressed me further.

"What makes you think anyone would want to go to Haiti? Or be interested in pirates' lairs Wally?"

"We got a letter" I told him. "It's from a madman. When we check the address we'll probably find it's a lunatic asylum but it gave me the idea. People are fascinated by pirates. You've got that *Jolly Roger* excursion boat in Barbados and we could organise treasure hunts."

"Local reps already have treasure hunts."

"These would be different. There's lots of islands where the pirates operated. If we research it properly we could have hunts for real treasure. Buried loot. It would give us something the other companies don't have, especially if the clients found some. Think of the publicity."

"What happened to the letter?"

"I've got it here."

I handed him a scrap of poor quality lined paper, about five inches by seven, apparently ripped from a notebook. Both sides were covered in scribble jotted in blue ballpoint pen ink.

"FIRST:
ACOMPLAINT - SMALL PRINT ON Pages

Just inside Brochure too small & almost unReadable againt that Brown/Orange background.

2ND

I CANT AFFORD THE HOLIDAY JUST AT THIS MOMENT, BUT I *would like to know how much it would* cost, FOR 1 OR 2 WEEKS PLEASE QUOTE FOR BOTH (NON EXPENSIVE HOTELS)

DESTINATION: –

HAITI: HOTEL, OR DOMINICAN REPUBLIC:– HOTEL.

SINGLE ROOM WITH BATH/SHOWER &W.C. HALF OR FULL BOARD, (& PACKED LUNCHES, ON REQUEST

(VISAS?) *Language:– DO they speak English?*

I DONT SPEAK FRENCH.

OBJECT:– TO VISIT & EXPLORE EX–PIRATE STRONGHOLD OF TORTUGA (OFF HAITI.)

TRANSPORTATION TO & FROM TORTUGA PER DAY & PER WEEK? (HOW BIG TORTUGA?)

:– cost of Flight From either Gatwick OR HeathRow to & From The Carribean? TOTAL COST?

Hearing about the unrest on Haiti (ie. PAPA DOC) A SHORT WHILE BACK, WOULD IT BE WISER TO *Stay in Dominican Republic?*

I have always been interested in Stories and Films of Pirates & wanted to visit The Island Of TORTUGA.

I did read in one travel Book that it was overgrown with vegetation; & was a good place for Scuba Diving, which is no good to me as I can't swim.

The time I maybe able to take the Holiday would be either in the Last half OR ³/₄ of this year, or sometime Next year.

Please can you help me with any suggestions?

TAKE YOUR TIME. NO HURRY. *Any Information on* TORTUGA WELCOME"

I could see that Arrowsmith was struggling to read the letter.

Eventually, presumably having finished, he leant back in his chair and sneered. He waved the paper at me.

"Forget it" he rasped. "The guy's a madman, like you said. I don't know why you waste your time reading this crap."

"OK Stew."

"He's never going to book it. No-one else is going to book it either. Who wants to go with this" he peered at the letter "Papa Doc there?"

"Papa Doc's dead" I told him. "It's his son now, Baby Doc."

"Big deal! Who cares?"

"OK" I said as I turned and left his office "It was just an idea."

Chapter Six

Thinking Pirates

Board meetings at Sunstroke Holidays were held weekly in the Managing Director's office on the top floor. There was no boardroom, just this office, furnished barely better than the other rooms throughout the building. Its main concession to the MD's status was a well-stocked bar. The five directors, each with a drink to hand, were clustered around the sole desk in an assortment of ill-matched chairs and dispositions of nervous informality. Once the agenda had been despatched and the latest sales figures gloomily discussed the MD asked if anyone could contribute any bright ideas. Stew, suitably fortified, spoke up.

"Er, well Jim, The Caribbean" he began. "You know we've been getting complaints about some of the cheap hotels we use in Barbados." He paused and tried to ignore the MD's critical stare. Continuing hastily, before anyone should castigate him for his choice of hotels, he added "Those in the Rockley area. But we can't match the big boys on price."

Tell us something we don't know, the sullen stares said.

"But I was thinking. If we had a Unique Selling Proposition then price would be less of a factor."

Sure Stew, we all know that. They waited.

"So, what about theme holidays? I was thinking pirates. You know how people get excited about swashbuckling adventures. *Treasure Island* and all that." He glanced around the room at the other faces. Nobody seemed set to shoot him down just yet. He enlarged on his theme. "There's already a pirate ship in Barbados. People get drunk on rum punch and walk the plank. Well, we could go one step further. Send people to actual pirate hideouts – where there's a decent beach of course – and they could dig for buried loot."

The Managing Director nodded, perhaps to himself. He was pondering.

"Where are these hideouts?" he asked.

"Well, you know, Jamaica I'm pretty sure. And a few other places."

"If we had exclusive resorts" the MD mused "and exclusive hotels, and an angle no-one else has thought of, price wouldn't be such a factor."

"And if some punter managed to dig up some treasure, can you imagine the publicity?" said Stew.

The atmosphere was positive and the MD seemed in favour so Sally Perkins, Finance Director, chipped in. "The clients could be encouraged to dress up as pirates and so on."

"And the women could be serving wenches" suggested Fat Freddie. He'd taken the low-slung armchair, designed to put its occupant at a psychological disadvantage to the MD towering above behind the desk. It was a bit of a struggle to climb out of but the seat was wide enough to accommodate his fat arse and it was the most comfortable chair in the room. Freddie always arrived first for these board meetings. He thought of them as 'bored meetings'. As usual he hadn't really grasped the concept of the matter under discussion so to allay suspicion he flashed his broad smile around the room.

All was going well, Stew realised. After a few more inane suggestions they got down to brass tacks.

"We'll need someone who knows what he's doing to research it all" said the Managing Director.

Stew suggested me.

"Wally? I thought you were going to send him to Egypt before transferring him to that section" said the MD, somewhat surprised. "And he's too junior for any hotel contracting."

That got them all grinning. A snigger from Fat Freddie. The thought of me, Chief Tosser, negotiating with hard-nosed hotel owners.

"No contracting" Stew assured them. "Just research. Don't forget he's got a history degree."

Chapter Seven

An Increasingly Unsafe Situation

"Hey man!"

I was grabbed from behind. A strong arm gripped my left shoulder and hauled me back on to the kerb, my left heel dragging against the stone as it retreated and my right foot pivoting on the edge. I almost toppled backwards. Only the vice-tight grip saved me from death. Or serious injury anyway.

I'd been about to step under the wheels of a fully-loaded minibus. I heard a screech of tyres and a blast of horn. The driver's face, a few inches from mine, broadcast a speechless message. You wanna die man?

I answered in the negative with a rueful grin, flapped a hand in apology and turned to the man still gripping my shoulder.

"Thanks. I wasn't thinking."

Trouble was, I was. Which is why I'd almost become a road accident statistic. Daydreaming about Henry Morgan's campaigns, my current project and my secret plan – or, anyway, hope – to get rich. So I shook my head to allow those thoughts to escape from my ears and concentrated on my tasks for today.

I stepped back two paces, well away from the kerb, dropped the map and brochures into my red Moroccan leather shoulder bag and gazed around Sam Sharpe Square.

People who needed to be somewhere fairly soon sauntered with a languorous bustle, in deference to the heat, along the cracked and crowded pavements here in the spiritual centre of Mo'Bay. A few forsook the sidewalk to casually weave their way through the traffic – exercising more care than I'd done. Some others just stood. Talking, sussing the scene or waiting. All were dressed for the climate in loose-fitting clothes. Cotton shirts, T-shirts and flowing wraps mainly, as I would have expected, but surprisingly some wore synthetic fibres. Bright colours and pastels predominated but a few boasted black.

In contrast to the continual movement in the square I spotted a gang of youths lounging in the shade of the fire-damaged Court House on the west side, a symbol, it seemed to me, of the slow death of the colonial heritage. The damage, that is, being the symbol. A nearby sun-baked memorial played host to a few of the younger ones not bothered by the blazing heat and The Cage, in the same corner of the square behind me, had attracted hustlers like flies to dogshit.

The Cage, an ugly, squat, grey stone building, was originally built to temporarily house recaptured runaway slaves. Lock 'em up before they become maroons. Hence the name. Now it functions as a tourist information centre. Two friendly ladies chat to the few holidaymakers brave enough to venture downtown and hand them the slickly-produced promotional literature. The lucky ones, like me, might also get a copy of the detailed road map which includes excellent street plans of Kingston and Montego Bay.

Now I noticed the traffic. Everyone had rolled down their windows, most vehicles were crammed with people and a few were blasting out the latest reggae. Some of the cars reflected Jamaica's colonial past. Cars I would rarely see back home, reminding me of my schooldays. Legends of the British motor industry – cars designed and built in the 50s and 60s – rumbled into view. Stylish anachronisms circulating amongst the continuous stream of bland modern saloons invading the square from Fort Street. Most were merely old and tired, just motor vehicles as far as their owners were concerned, but a few were showing the love and care lavished on a proud possession. There was a beautifully customised metallic-blue mini, a smart green and white two-tone Triumph Herald convertible, complete with whitewall tyres, and even an early 70s Ford Capri. This growled aggressively into the square thrusting its matt black bonnet, go-faster side stripes and rear spoiler into the mêlée. Or is that a luggage rack?

There were only a few of those lovingly customised cars. The most common British saloons were the sturdy Austin Cambridge and Morris Oxford, large enough to carry the family and strong enough to survive the country roads. Although perhaps mechanically sound their bodywork was usually rust-speckled and they were approaching their use-by date. Their exhausts belched the more obnoxious of the fumes that dissipated slowly in the still air. Soon these dinosaurs would die. They are of no interest to the automobile aficionado.

A grey Austin Cambridge ground to a halt close to me. As the doors were flung open and the passengers evacuated the vehicle the driver, a soberly dressed middle-aged man, also left his seat and strode to the front. He opened and lifted the bonnet, holding it with his left hand, and peered inside. He wiggled something with his right then slammed the lid shut. Roughly brushing his hands together, presumably to remove any dust or rust, he straightened up. Then he noticed me watching. We exchanged nods.

"They don't make them like they used to" I suggested.

At this the driver nodded reflectively and commented dryly "Yeah man, tank de Lord. Now dem mek Toyotas."

There were a few of those. I'd already noticed that none of the newer vehicles were British. New cars are expensive in Jamaica and so the more modern vehicles were, as elsewhere in the emerging world, mainly Japanese. Good, strong, reliable Toyotas and Datsuns. Most were cars but there were a few 12-seater vans and small trucks. All were vying for space in the narrow streets and trying to make progress without glancing pedestrians or another vehicle.

Time for me to be getting on. I noticed that although most of the traffic continued through the square and out on to St. James Street some would stop to disgorge passengers whilst a few would turn up one of the side roads. I decided to do likewise, but on foot. I set off up Market Street.

At first the bustle seeped up the street with me as I walked. Reggae music escaped from open windows and shop fronts, injecting a skip into my stride, but soon faded behind. As I reached King Street I found myself in an oasis of relative calm. The hum of the square and faint strains of music could still be heard, if I bothered to listen, but now there were few pedestrians and just the odd car. I stopped to check the map. That was when I noticed someone following me.

About fifty yards to my rear, on the same side of the street, I spotted a tallish, thinnish, shabbily-dressed man who seemed to stop at the same time as me. He suddenly found something very interesting in a shop window. Hmmm. He doesn't look like he can afford to buy anything. I continued up the street, slowly now, on my guard. Without, I hoped, appearing to, I kept this man in the periphery of my vision. Yep. Sure enough he lost interest in the shop window and ambled up the street matching my speed.

I'd already noticed in the square that people here did one of three things. Some loitered, either alone or in small groups, others were obviously heading for a destination, whilst the remainder chatted to friends and acquaintances. This man did not fit into any of those categories. If he had an interest in anything at all it was me. Was he one of those hustlers I'd spotted hanging about outside The Cage? I couldn't be sure.

I noticed a uniformed policeman strolling up the other side of the street, further behind. He seemed to be tailing both of us. Was he watching out for me? Well, let's find out. I sauntered a further hundred yards up the street then stopped again to consult my map. As if he was on tow my stalker also stopped. The copper continued on his beat.

I was curious to see what would happen if I loitered here for a few minutes. Would this officer continue to pace up the street? Would he find an excuse to stop, speak to me or perhaps approach my stalker? If he proceeded on his way the shabbily-dressed man would have a clear shot at his target and would probably make himself known.

The policeman plodded effortlessly up the hill, crossed over to my side of the street ahead of me and turned left at the junction. Out of the corner of my eye I saw my tail resume his walk.

Now I set off again up the incline. I planned to make a right at East Street, left at Church Street then right again at the T-junction of Dome Street. I was heading for the YMCA on Humber Avenue. I wanted to check this place out as it would be even cheaper than the recommended guest house where I was staying.

As I turned right and crossed over I glanced behind as if making sure I wasn't about to be mown down by a speeding car. Yep, this fellow was still behind, but closer now. Up here the streets were almost completely deserted, the buildings were silent and only the occasional vehicle wheezed past. What to do? I knew I was venturing into an increasingly unsafe situation so I stopped at the Dome Street junction and casually looked around, map in hand. My shadow continued his journey and halted next to me.

A grinning face disfigured by knife scars beamed down. Tall, lean and fit but dressed in shabby and ill-fitting clothes, its owner was evidently from the margins of society.

"Wha' appun' mon?"

I looked up and returned the smile. "Oh, jus' lookin' around Montego Bay."

"See you gotta camera mon. You journalis'?"

"No" I hurriedly replied.

I'd already discovered that journalism is a profession loathed by the Jamaican man in the street. Journalists were blamed for the declining numbers of tourists. The lack of visitors was not caused by the violent crime, endemic in parts of the country, but was the consequence of potential visitors being told about it. Jamaicans didn't feel that the notorious gun battles between supporters of rival political parties at election time was sufficient reason for tourists to vacation elsewhere. Though casualties were counted in the hundreds tourists were unaffected. Those gun battles were mostly confined to the slum districts of West Kingston. Also most crime against the person, even bag snatching, was committed in Kingston. Murders were a purely local affair too. Tourists didn't visit Kingston – or, anyway, very very few ventured there – and they were hardly ever victims of crime. No, the problem – this dearth of big-spending tourists – was caused by journalists. Interfering busybodies informing people about matters which did not concern them. It was sensational newspaper stories and TV footage of gunfights among the shacks which scared off the tourists.

Yesterday I spotted a milling throng clustered near a concrete building on the fringe of a poor residential area. I decided to take a picture using my telephoto lens. Just as I was focussing I was disturbed by a shout.

"Hey man! What you doin'?"

I lowered the camera and turned towards the voice. A large man was striding angrily towards me.

"Why you wan' tek picture o' dese people? Dem collectin' dere govmen' money? You journalis'?"

This outburst took me unawares. "No" I murmured apprehensively. This man was obviously volatile. His eyes were blazing as though he'd just been the victim of some great indignity or grave insult. "I just thought it would be a nice picture" I told him, as calmly as possible. "I didn't know why they were queuing." I flapped an arm vaguely in the direction of the multicoloured throng. "All their bright colours."

There was a barely discernible slackening of tension in the big man.

"You 'merican?" he asked.

"No, English."

A visible relaxation.

"Yo' on vacation?"

"No. Working. I'm a travel agent."

Wow! The man was transformed. You'd have thought I'd intoned "abracadabra" and waved a magic wand. All anger and tension evaporated from his body. Now he relaxed and a touch of enthusiasm shone from his eyes. A broad smile spread across his face. He leant forward and thrust out his hand. I shook it.

"Yeh man!" he enthused. "We need travel agen'. You tek all de pictures you wan' man!"

A few minutes later I'd resumed work when another guy approached me. This fellow was waving an arm and shouting, aggressive yet less assertive than the first man. Perhaps because he was smaller. Again I lowered my camera, ready to respond to questioning. Immediately I heard a shout from about a hundred yards up the road and saw the first man running down the slope towards us.

"Hey man! He OK man! Him travel agent!"

So now, remembering yesterday's altercation, I favoured my stalker with a friendly grin. I uttered the magic words. "I'm a travel agent."

"Travellin' agen'! You welcome mon! You send we plenty touris' mon. De country need bizniss. Which hotel you at?"

"Ocean View Guest House."

"It a good lickle place mon. I come tonight an' tek you roun' dis town."

With a goodbye flap of the hand he turned away then loped left up Dome Street towards the north.

The brevity of our meeting surprised me. I'd expected an extended conversation at least. Perhaps a request for a handout or an offer to supply drugs or change money. He'd been following me for some time, at least from Sam Sharpe Square if not before, yet he hadn't hustled me or approached me in a threatening manner. Then he departed as soon as we'd met. Perhaps, I thought, being of a suspicious turn of mind at times, he was concerned that the policeman might reappear. Or maybe there were plainclothes officers loitering in the area out of sight.

Tourists were rarely seen in this part of town so the few people I saw were locals going about their business. I wasn't approached again. Soon I located the YMCA and gave it a cursory inspection. It was very cheap alright, but also very basic. Rooms were private – some even had locks on the doors – but bathroom facilities were communal like a youth hostel. The very fat lady who guarded the establishment from her wooden chair by the door, and who had encouraged me to inspect inside, was anxious for me to stay there. Perhaps guessing from my body language as I re-emerged into the daylight that I wasn't impressed with her domain she offered me an inducement.

"It not like America here you know. If you need to bring a lady back wid you dat not a problem."

I decided that the saving wasn't worth the inconvenience. And I was planning to spend just a couple more days in Mo'Bay.

I wandered back to Sam Sharpe Square the way I'd come, cautiously treading the cracked pavement and skirting irregular kerbs. From there it's about two miles to my guest house. I decided to walk. All right, I would ooze sweat in this hot sun but I could do with losing some weight.

I arrived at the roundabout which gave me a clear choice of the coast road, Gloucester Avenue, or an ascent along the hillside. That was a slightly shorter route. The old folk song came to mind. "*You take the low road and I'll take the high road and I'll be in Scotland afore ye.*" As I wasn't headed for Scotland I chose Gloucester Avenue.

Beaches, including the famous Doctor's Cave,

restaurants, some small hotels, bars and shops line this stretch. So I saw a few tourists and a smattering of vendors and touts. I knew I would be hustled but I didn't care. I was sure I could handle any hustlers and, anyway, it might be fun. Drivers honked their horns at me as they slowed alongside and yelled "Taxi!". Some of them were taxis.

I spotted a group of three powerfully-built guys up ahead, all with their arms casually crossed. They were holding up a low wall by leaning their backsides on it. They weighed me up as I approached. As I reached them one spoke.

"You need some smoke man?"

I halted and turned to them. "They tell me it's illegal."

"You doan' need to worry yourself bout it man" advised the one in the middle. "It not like your countree. Po-lice 'ere cool man."

"Well I don't use it thanks."

"So how bout some Charlie?" one of the others asked.

"No thanks."

"So how you getting high man?"

"Jamaican rum and ginger."

All three guys wore dark coloured slacks and white trainers. One wore a green and blue hooped T-shirt, one a plain red T and the third a pale blue number with a tourist slogan emblazoned across it. Now they became slightly animated but in a good-natured way. Two unfolded their arms. They exchanged smirks at my last answer and something unintelligible to me was uttered with a laugh. Probably patois. I say unintelligible, but from their body language I could guess what they were saying. What kinda ting was dis? Of course ever'one like a lickle rum. Dey needs rum jus' to survive. But to get high, man, you needs sumting else. Stronger. They looked back at me. See dis English guy. Jus' off de plane obviously, his chubby face beginning to turn pink, dress up for some reason in safari gear. He tink he gonna see elephant an' tiger in Jamaica?

The guy in the middle, he with the blue and green hoops,

turned to the guy on his right and said something else in patois. He got a ribald answer and some laughter from the other two.

"I wish there was time for you to teach me Jamaican" I said.

Hooped T-shirt didn't like the sound of this. I was answering back. He moved his arse off the wall, attaining his full height, uncrossed his arms and glared down at me.

"What you say man?"

"I've only got a few days in Jamaica. Working. For my company. Travel agent. So I won't have time to learn Jamaican, but I would like to."

Hooped T-shirt was not mollified by this answer. Quite the reverse.

"What you mean man? I speak de Queen English."

I've never heard the Queen speak like him. As I remember she speaks in a quite refined manner. But better not to labour that point. I'd obviously upset the chap so now, somehow, I needed to calm him down.

"Just now, when you spoke to your colleagues" I began "I couldn't understand what you said."

Well, of course, I wasn't supposed to. And as it had not been complimentary they weren't about to repeat it. Though obviously they understood my point. After all, that was one of the advantages of speaking in patois. They were not about to concede anything but, probably because I was being polite and respectful, they decided to give me an easy ride.

"It jus' Henglish man, but we speak more quick is all. An' jus' accent, like you have in Englan' dere."

I persisted. Of course it was substantially different to English. "No, you have different words. We have Jamaicans in England you know." A silly thing to say really, as these guys probably have friends and relatives over there, but I wanted to ease out of this situation without leaving any bad feeling. And to score a draw at least.

"What words man?"

"Well, like rasclat for example."

The best thing I could have said. I must have been inspired. This is a subject of great embarrassment to the Jamaican male, even more than to men generally. Not a subject for discussion. Which is why it is their most commonly used swear word.

The three guys exchanged glances as Hooped T-shirt sank back on to the wall. One of the others, the guy on my right wearing the pale blue T boasting *I Slept On A Virgin*, chipped in.

"It just like bloodclat man. De same ting."

I spread my arms, innocently I hoped, and asked like a wally "What's bloodclat?" I was beginning to enjoy this.

Some muttering. Then Red T-shirt terminated the conversation.

"Well man, mebbe you right. Mebbe hard for you."

This group now lost interest in me. They were not going to sell me anything and they were not guaranteed to have fun at my expense. I assumed I was free to go.

As I continued up Gloucester Avenue I was offered carvings, taxis and women. But I just wanted to get back to my guest house and take a shower.

Chapter Eight

Jamaican Rum and Ginger

The Ocean View Guest House is more or less opposite the airport, just a few hundred yards from the terminal buildings. You can walk there, even in the hot sun and burdened with baggage. On arrival I'd tried to. Shouldering my bags I strode out into the late afternoon sunshine a little tired but pleasurably excited at the start of my great adventure.

I was confronted by an oversized unsmiling brute clad in a green uniform. At around my eye level a tape stitched to the left breast of his tunic identified him as a representative of the *Courtesy Corps*. Courtesy was not noticeable in his demeanour. Presumably he was some sort of tourist policeman but whether he was employed to protect or police tourists wasn't made clear by his actions. He spoke down to me.

"Taxi sir?"

Without waiting for an answer he indicated a battered vehicle resting a few yards away. "Over here sir."

From my researches I knew the location of the guest house. It was just beyond the roundabout on the main road. I also knew that the minimum taxi fare was $5, a hefty sum for a two minute ride.

"No thank you" I answered with a smile. "I can walk. I'm going to the Ocean View. Across the road there." I waved my arm vaguely in a westerly direction.

Now the officer's demeanour evolved from brusque to bossy.

"Everyone need to take a taxi sir." He stiffened and drew himself up to his full height. Extending his left arm he ushered me towards the waiting vehicle. I laughed.

"Look. I can walk. It's less than a quarter of a mile."

"It not safe." Obviously, surveying my unfit semi-rotund form, he'd decided that I could be easily intimidated. Logically as a lone traveller I should be more self-sufficient than a package holidaymaker travelling in a group but I suppose that thought hadn't occurred to him. Or he had dismissed it. He'd assumed that I could be dragooned into complying with his orders like the average tourist.

Right then and there he was correct. Anyone who has just stepped off a crowded plane after a ten hour flight, suffered the tedious queuing for Immigration, endured the crude baggage search of a Customs official then entered an alien environment is at his most vulnerable. Unless he's James Bond of course and I'm definitely not. As the officer shepherded me into the taxi he reinforced his warning.

"You could be robbed man. Walking."

Great. What an introduction to a country desperate for tourism. I slid my baggage along the back seat and followed it inside. The Courtesy cop shut the door.

My driver spent the next two minutes complaining over his shoulder about his passenger to his passenger. He hopin' to get a fare to Runaway Bay or mebbe down to Negril or at least someting into Mo'Bay. What he get? Just a lickle trip across de road. Some udder guy gonna score.

"Don't complain to me" I said. "I didn't want to get in your car. I wanted to walk. Have a go at that copper when you get back. Anyway the plane was full. You'll get another fare in a few minutes. You've just earned $5 for nothing."

The driver remained in his seat, engine running, whilst I trotted up the steps to reception. There was a room available and at a satisfactory price. When I returned to the car he was still slumped in his seat. He honoured me with an insolent stare. I leant in, hauled my luggage out, then paid him.

"What? No tip for me?"

"Sure, I've got a tip for you" I grinned. "Get that bloody chip off your shoulder."

I'd selected the Ocean View because of its location and price. It was strongly recommended by the guide book. I always call it the 'Airport View' but it is conveniently situated and in those days represented very good value. You could argue too, if anyone cared, that there is an ocean view. Ragged lines of almost vertical telephone poles strung together with sagging wire direct the eye across the road to a relay station. Cables feed into this forest of fencing, masts and spars then lead away in every direction. It brought to mind a long-legged spider brooding in the centre of his web.

If I sat at any of the four tables on the terrace above the car port and looked seaward across the road, past the two unhappy palm trees, through the web of wires, past the bushes before and beyond the runway, then I could just view the ocean. Sure it's over half a mile away and merely a narrow strip of ultramarine between land and sky but it was undeniably part of the view.

Nevertheless I hadn't selected this establishment for its vista. No-one did. According to the guide book it was '*the cheapest accommodation listed by the tourist board in Montego Bay.*' And, someone told me, they sold the cheapest beer in town. Not that I intended to spend much time drinking beer, but you get the general drift.

If I turned around in my seat on the terrace and faced the hotel I would see a solidly-built off-white single-storey structure merging with the hillside behind. Between the terrace and the hotel were those steps up from the drive. Up these and make a right, as I did on arrival, and you would be in the reception area which doubles as a tiny guests' lounge. Although I never saw any guests lounging there. The TV was usually blazing a blurred and frequently flickering message in gaudy colours sometimes accompanied by a scratchy soundtrack but there was never an audience. To the left were perhaps a dozen sea-facing rooms. Pass through the lounge and you'll enter a yard with more rooms along two sides of it. All accommodation has bathroom *en suite*, air-conditioning and bars on the windows. Quite adequate for my purposes. I didn't mind walking or taking a bus into town.

But why was I in Montego Bay at all? There is no history of piracy here. The town was established by sugar plantation profiteers. Well, I worked for a tour operator. Their *raison d'être* was to sell holidays and hopefully make a profit doing so (although one of Patel's favourite quips was his description of Sunstroke Holidays as "a non-profit making organisation"). Our theme holiday project would be doomed to failure if we restricted ourselves to featuring only the known buccaneers' hideaways. Many – if not most – pirate haunts are either difficult to get to, unsuitable for modern tourism or both. Just like the island of Tortuga in that madman's letter.

In life the perception is often more important than the truth, isn't it? So I needed to cheat a bit. Here in Jamaica we would combine visits to the sunken site of that most notorious of pirate havens with the wonderful beaches and breathtaking scenery of Negril and Port Antonio. And the modern tourist pleasures of Montego Bay.

I was scribbling notes about this last of Jamaica's inducements when I was interrupted. The light was failing so I couldn't have written much more, but it was still a shock to see a shadow move from my peripheral vision and stop in front of me, slightly to my left, obscuring my view of the setting sun. Presumably it had ascended the steps behind me silently.

This was my acquaintance from earlier in the day making his promised appearance. "You ready to go mon?"

He was just a silhouette but obviously the same chap. "Where?" I asked.

"Back downtown mon. I show you de night-time Mo'Bay."

Well, yeah, I supposed I should go, if only for research. I closed my notebook, leaned back in my chair and looked up at my prospective guide. He had the advantage of me. The last rays of the day illuminated my face but he was just a shadow. I deliberated, hoping he wouldn't guess what I was thinking. This could be expensive. How much could I afford to lose?

Rising from my seat I nodded vaguely and said "I'll just go to my room to get some money."

Back in my room I discovered $60 in my pocket. I separated twenty five, returned that, then stuffed the rest under the mattress. I could afford to lose $25.

I had difficulty seeing anything in the dark as I re-emerged from the brightly-lit lounge. Night falls quickly in the tropics so a black carpet now spread to infinity, relieved only by a flicker of grey in the sky and the artificial light leaking from the lounge behind me. Straining my eyes I could see no tall shape, moving or otherwise. The terrace now appeared deserted. I strained my ears, attempting to pick out any unusual sounds among the rustle of palm fronds and the chirping of cicadas. I was rewarded by the tinkle of a jet of water, rather like the splash from a fountain in an ornamental garden, coming from below. I peered down into the drive. I could just discern my new friend pissing against a tree.

The bus emptied in the centre of town. I was led away from the lights and crowds into dark and empty side streets. We turned left and right until I was sure we were lost, occasionally passing and being passed by shapes I barely noticed in the gloom, until we reached a building which was pumping loud reggae from an upstairs floor. Open windows allowed the insistent rhythm to blast into the alleyway and bounce off the walls.

We clambered up an unlit narrow and twisting staircase and emerged in a largish darkened room. By a subdued flickering light, probably candles, unevenly placed throughout, I could see people dancing. Along one of the shorter sides I spotted a bar. We squeezed through the crowds over there and were soon in possession of a quarter bottle of rum, a small bottle of ginger ale and two ice-filled glasses. We were obviously VIPs. Though some of the other rum drinkers imbibed from glasses none, as far as I could see, rattled with ice cubes and the beer drinkers were expected to swig straight from the neck of the bottle.

My new pal mixed the drinks and handed one to me. I took a generous gulp, enjoyed a shiver as the cocktail slipped down my throat, then turned around with my back to the bar. I propped my elbows on it, leant back and surveyed the scene. I liked this. The raw energy of it. Not like a tourist place full of people trying to impress each other flashing their shallow style, spouting fashionable slang and flaunting the latest fashions. For me that would be a non-starter. This joint was much cheaper too.

It didn't take long for the rum to warm me up – we were being miserly with the ginger – and the insistent reggae beat was drumming itself into my head. Without making any conscious decision, as far as I recall, I found myself among the dancers. I was slightly surprised to find I was welcomed. Then I attracted a partner. An alluring and feisty girl. I followed her movements as best I could and was just getting the hang of it when a rather excitable chap joined us. Briefly. He dragged the girl away and seemed to be giving her a bollocking.

"Come here mon."

It was my scar-faced guide. He led me back to the bar. Perhaps because the rum was finished. I ordered another quarter bottle and, though I was not sure we'd need it, more ginger. Casting my eye along the bar I spotted a new arrival hunched over the counter lighting a cigarette. A suntanned Caucasian face was framed by abundant blondish long hair held in check by a badly-folded bandana. By the brief light of his struck match that appeared to be dark red with light-coloured spots. In spite of the murk and my alcoholic haze I noticed that his left ear was pierced by a large ring. Was I seeing things? Was this one of Henry Morgan's pirates risen from the dead? Or just a hippy on holiday? Beneath the head I glimpsed a T-shirt of a lightish colour I was unable to identify.

The owner of this head had obviously been befriended by my guide judging by some discreet mutterings between them. I couldn't understand what they were discussing as their sparse exchanges didn't reach me through the bedlam of over-amplified music, laughter and shouts, but it did seem that some form of negotiation was being conducted. Fag lit, the hippy took a deep drag then pulled himself upright and tossed his head back. The cigarette looked both large and misshapen to me. As he exhaled I caught a whiff, faint but unmistakable, of something that could have been French. *Gauloise* or *Gitanes* possibly. Definitely not *Benson & Hedges*.

Now I fancied a puff of my pipe. I pulled it out, filled it from my pouch and after the usual preparations lit up. The new face glanced in my direction so I nodded to him but he didn't seem eager for conversation. He was more interested in talking to my guide. That's OK. With the loud music, darkened room, smoky atmosphere and effects of the rum I didn't feel like standing and chatting either.

I did feel like more dancing. Noticing my pipe had gone out already I dropped it on the counter next to my tobacco pouch. The other two would keep an eye on it. That's when I noticed another pouch lying there.

I rejoined the dancers. Now there were more of them, though no sign of my pretty partner from earlier, so I kept bumping into people. Nobody seemed to mind. After a time I realised it wasn't the crowds, it was me. Unsteady on my feet, probably because of the rum. About fifteen minutes later I called it a day.

I'd just reclaimed my position at the bar and raised my glass when I heard a commotion on the stairs. Someone near the door yelled "Police!" and sure enough four uniformed officers burst into the room. Simultaneously the lights over that side flickered into life. One officer remained by the door whilst the sergeant barged his way towards the bar shouting something as he came. The rest of the lights flashed on and the music died. Now I spotted surreptitious movement and excitable chattering among the dancers and drinkers, but no panic. Many were beginning to line up against the walls, without haste, and I saw a couple disappear in the direction of the toilets.

Presumably this was a fairly normal drugs raid judging by the relative calm with which the patrons accepted this disruption of their night's pleasures. I remembered what I'd been told earlier today on the street. "Po-lice here cool man. It not like your countree." Let's see.

As an innocent bystander I could afford to lean back against the bar and watch. One officer came around behind the counter and searched there whilst the sergeant and the fourth policeman insinuated themselves among the crowd, perfunctorily searching. Behind my back and to my right I heard my guide and the hippy exchanging mutterings. That hippy, I thought, might have a problem.

Once the sergeant finished frisking those customers milling around and lined up against the wall he left his accompanying officers to deal with the few caught in possession and bustled over to us. He was tall and broad, heavy-browed with eyes buried deep in their sockets, close-cropped hair and the manner of a bully. He spat sharp words of patois at my guide who replied in semi-reverential tones. He made the man raise his arms then roughly patted him down. He searched all the pockets but found nothing of interest there. Disappointed, he turned to the hippy.

"Where you drugs man?"

"No, no man. Peace and love" the hippy drawled, raising his hands in an unconvincing gesture of innocence. "I don't do drugs man. Search me."

The sergeant made a show of sniffing the air then accepted the invitation. He frisked the hippy, though not as roughly as he had Scarface, then went through his pockets. Nothing of interest. Then he picked up the pouch lying next to the hippy's elbow. With the lights on it looked rather like mine.

"What you ave here man?" he asked, opening it and sniffing the tobacco.

"Jus' tobacco for my cigarettes. Roll-ups" was the drawled answer. To prove his point the hippy picked up a packet of *Rizla* and flashed it at his inquisitor.

"We know what you have dey for man. Where you keep you smoke?"

"Honestly man, I have none. You can search me again."

The sergeant decided not to bother. Better not push too hard. After all, the country needs tourists. In fact they were so desperate they were even welcoming the hippies. He turned to me.

He was not impressed. It was only a couple of days since my arrival so I was beginning to turn pink and hadn't lost any weight yet. The spectacles would make me look less like a drug addict presumably, bookish if anything and not the type to be of interest to the police. My polyester shirt was sweat-soaked by now, with the dancing and the torrid temperature in this room, and he might have deemed my baggy beige shorts to be inappropriate evening wear. I'm guessing of course but evidently the sergeant did not expect to discover any *ganja* on my person. With a dismissive sneer he turned back to my guide.

"I know you man. Anyting appen to dis touris'" he flicked his head in my direction "an' I lookin' for you man." Presumably this warning was delivered in English rather than patois for my benefit.

The police now left with a little something to show for their efforts. A few small bags of *ganja* and four suspects. They'd put a dampener on the party though. Sure, the lights were extinguished and the reggae resumed, but no-one felt like dancing. Everybody needed a drink so the crowd around the bar became a crush. Suddenly I felt dizzy. Probably as a result of the heady mixture of rum, stifling heat and the toxic atmosphere. I grabbed my tobacco pouch and pipe off the bar and made for the door. The plan was to get out into the fresh air before I was sick. I tumbled down the stairs barely able to keep my footing. Out in the street I stood for a few minutes gratefully gulping down lungfuls of fresh air. It was cooler here too, probably only in the 80s. Maybe even 70s. I was joined by my guide, now police-appointed protector.

"You OK mon?"

"Sure" I told him. "I just need a walk."

The night felt deliciously cool. I could sniff a freshness in the air, a resurrecting tonic after the fug of that crowded upstairs room. My head cleared quickly as we strolled out of the narrow streets and turned west, towards the sea. It didn't take us long to reach the main road and on the other side of that I could just discern a moonlit park overlooking the bay. I spotted a bench positioned to offer a panoramic sea view. I wandered over to it and sat down. Leaning back against the wooden frame, my arms spread horizontally along the top edge, I took in deep, rhythmic lungfuls of the night air. Soon my head had cleared completely and I felt almost sober. I pulled out my pipe and tobacco pouch and prepared for a reflective smoke.

Scarface had disappeared. No matter. He would return.

Now, this might sound stupid. I'm sure that if I'd been home in my mother's house I would have realised immediately. But presumably the effects of the rum, my frenzied dancing and the totally alien surroundings – not to mention a few hours of oxygen starvation – must have dulled the edge of my senses. Certainly my sight and touch must have been deficient. I relaxed there puffing away contently totally oblivious to a different taste and scent. Soon I found myself light-headed and slightly nauseous. Again no surprise.

I remember that I started giggling when I recalled the night's events. Gyrating to the over-amplified reggae – thumping sound waves heavy enough to feel if I held my hand close to the speakers – too much rum and a police raid that now seemed like an episode from the Keystone Cops. Even the most mundane events seemed hilarious. Suddenly I realised that I loved everyone. Must be the effects of the rum.

I was seduced by the cool offshore breeze washing over me. I rose to my feet and meandered over to the seafront. This park was positioned at sea level so the sand began as soon as the grass finished.

A midnight swim might be fun. It occurred to me, briefly, that a dip could be dangerous. I was unused to this beach, I had no clue as to the water's depth or the sea currents and there might be jellyfish out there. I dismissed such thoughts. I can't go through life worrying about danger all the time.

I slumped down onto the grass and removed my shoes. The laces gave me more trouble than usual but I persevered and finally got them off. Socks were easy. Just yank. Then I stood and started to stumble towards the sand, unbuttoning and removing my shirt as I progressed. Mind you, by now it needed a good wash so it might have been more sensible to keep it on. I dropped it on the grass, took a few more steps, then stopped again to slip off my shorts. As I stepped out of them I overbalanced, fell, rolled over and laughed. The beach was now just a stride away. I kicked my shorts aside, stood up again, then jogged across the sand to the water's edge. Barely pausing I waded in.

The water was cool but not cold. It never is here. As I advanced it slowly enveloped me, cosseting me in its liquid embrace. Soon it flowed up to my waist, then my chest. Suddenly I lost my footing. The bottom had shelved away steeply. I tumbled below the surface, conscious that I was falling and striking out for a firm base. I was completely underwater and I hadn't taken a deep breath. Instinctively I threw my hands forward, as if to break my fall, and realised that I was on all fours. Don't breathe. Get up. I struggled to my feet but realised that I was still completely underwater. Must be at least six feet deep here. The current, though gentle, was trying to coax me out to sea. I bent my legs and kicked myself upwards. As soon as I broke the surface I greedily gasped for air but found myself choking. There was seawater mixed in with it. I tried to swim to shore but found that I was thrashing about in my panic. And, in the darkness, I wasn't totally sure in which direction the shore was. Look for lights. I must have stopped swimming – or thrashing – because my feet sought the bottom again. Perhaps I was hoping to stride to safety. My head went under and my feet struck the sandy bottom. Perhaps it was pure reaction, as I wasn't thinking clearly in my panic, but fortunately I kicked myself back up to the surface. I coughed up some of the seawater as my head broke the surface. I took a breath but was starting to go under again when I felt strong arms grab me and haul me back on to the beach. Someone pushed me face down on the sand and pummelled my back. I coughed up more seawater. As I started to recover, my mouth tasting of salt, that hoarse sensation at the back of the throat, eyes and nose watery, I registered voices. One phrase uttered, I realised, by my protector, was clear enough.

"Erryting cool mon."

I spat out what I hoped was the last of the seawater, rolled over and then, groaning, using my arms for leverage, sat up. I took a few measured, deep, breaths. Almost immediately I felt an arm around my shoulder and looked up to see the bandana-swathed long-haired Caucasian face from the nightclub, complete with earring. I spluttered a bit, tried to grin, probably giggled, and spoke. "Hi."

"Hey man. You OK? You're lucky we seen your clothes man. Looks like we hauled you out just in time."

They were both leaning over me now. I studied their concerned faces. "Thanks. I was doin' all right but the ground gave way."

"Not a smart idea to take a midnight swim alone. You could drown man. An' then there's the jellyfish." The hippy straightened up. "I think you took my tobacco."

I had trouble assimilating this new development. What's tobacco got to do with it? My brain was whirling around in my head. It stopped for a few seconds and presented me with a clear image of a tobacco pouch on a bar counter. The hippy's. The one that looked like mine when the police sergeant picked it up to sniff at its contents. Had this chap mislaid it? Did he think I'd picked it up?

"No" I said. "I've got my own tobacco. You must have left yours in the club."

"No man. Look" the hippy said. He pulled a pouch from a trouser pocket. "This is yours."

I staggered to my feet, a little concerned that the ground might give way again, took a step towards my rescuer and reached for the pouch. I missed. I straightened up, took a deep breath, and tried again. This time I was successful. In the dim light and without my spectacles I had trouble seeing clearly. Drawing the pouch close to my face I established that it was a familiar brand. I handed it back.

"You smoke the same tobacco as me!" I exclaimed.

The hippy seemed to be keeping himself under control for some reason. "No man. This is yours. Check the one you got."

Well, why not. No big deal. I started back up the beach to my trail of clothes. First I located my shorts. I stepped into those without overbalancing, but that might have had something to do with the firm hand gripping my shoulder. Then on to my shirt, my rescuers flanking me. The tobacco pouch was still in the pocket. I extracted it and made a careful examination. It wasn't mine. Perhaps, I was thinking through the cotton wool in my head, in my rush to get out into the fresh night air I'd grabbed the wrong pouch.

"You're right" I admitted. "Sorry. Can we do a swap?"

My rescuers huddled together in conversation as I

inserted myself into my shirt and set off for my socks. I'd pulled these on and discovered my shoes when my protector appeared beside me. I looked around for the hippy and spotted him trudging away shaking his head.

"Now I tek you for a good time" my guide promised.

I looked up at him. "But I've been havin' a good time. Except for nearly drowning."

"Come wid me mon."

"OK. Jus' let me get my shoes back on."

He led me back into the narrow streets. This was obviously a poor residential area, mainly shacks. Few taller buildings. After the maze of twists and turns we emerged in a dimly-lit plaza. He directed me towards a low wall. "Sit here mon."

He strolled over to a well-built lady of indeterminate age standing outside a house about twenty yards away. He spoke to her briefly then returned to me. "How much you got lef' mon?"

I stood up and searched my pockets. From the left I pulled out two crumpled dollar bills. Nothing in the others.

"Dis all you got left mon?"

"Yes. We mus' have spend the rest. In the club."

"OK mon. I buy some coke for the woman wi' dis." He waved the two notes. Then he turned and loped off the way we'd come. I never saw him again. Some coke for the woman? That woman I suppose. Why buy her some coke? I soon found out.

She waddled over and sat next to me. She took my right hand. "We go down de beach an' I give you good time."

I must have realised, subconsciously at least, by now, but I was still confused. The drink, the drowning. All I could think was People Very Nice Here. Everybody wants me to have a good time.

"I've jus' been to the beach. I've jus' come from the beach" I beamed.

"No, now we go for a good time together." To make her

intentions clear she rubbed her two index fingers together. This confirmed my sneaking suspicions. I laughed.

"I'm drunk" I said. "I would be no use to you."

"Doan' worry yoursel'. How much money you got?"

"I gave my last two dollars to that guy. He said he was gonna buy you a Coke with it."

She cast me a knowing look – sympathetic even – and stood. "Where you stayin'?"

"Ocean View Guest House."

"You get back OK?"

"Sure, no problem" I answered, getting to my feet.

"I'll jus' tek you to the main road" she said.

Chapter Nine

A Nasty Piece Of Work

I alighted in the Half Way Tree area of New Kingston. Beautiful sunshine illuminated a drab semi-suburban area. This time there was no *Courtesy Corps* officer waiting to prevent me strolling to my chosen hostelry. Just two teenagers at the intersection selling newspapers. One thrust the *Gleaner* at car windows as they slowed or stopped whilst the other solicited pedestrians. They noticed me immediately. They suspended their work, exchanged glances and strolled over.

Tourists are a rarity in Kingston. There is hardly anything here worth visiting. Only Devon House and the Bob Marley Museum – which in those days was still Tuff Gong Studios. Businessmen were sometimes seen but they didn't arrive by overstuffed Kamikaze minibus, did not haul their baggage around the streets and certainly did not dress as if they were about to hunt tiger. So to those lads I was a curiosity.

"Wha' appen' man?" the taller of the two enquired.

"Oh, I'm just here to look around for a few days. I'm hoping to stay at the Indies Hotel." I nodded down the street towards it.

This answer left them no wiser. They knew most tourists had been scared away from Jamaica. Even from the resorts, which were quite safe. The few who continued to come favoured the All-Inclusive hotels where the guests would 'Never need to leave the hotel compound'. Safe inside they would be insulated from all risks. Foreigners avoided Kingston. OK, some of the less wealthy businessmen stay at the Indies. But me? What was I? And didn't I realise that Kingston was dangerous?

"You do Kung Fu man?" the second youth asked.

I needed to think quickly. If I answered No they might take me for a soft touch. Relieve me of my possessions perhaps. If I said Yes they might regard it as a challenge. Or sense that I was lying. So I treated the question as a friendly joke, not requiring a literal answer.

"Well" I laughed, preparing to move on "there's one way to find out. But the answer is Not Today. I'm not in the mood." I favoured them with my best smile and shouldered my bag. They shrugged and returned to selling newspapers.

The following afternoon I took a bus downtown. Then another out to the eight miles of skinny, snaking spit of land they call The Palisadoes. After three miles of causeway barely wider than the road I encountered a tract of reclaimed land bordered by a few islands. On the map it looks like a foetus attached halfway along an umbilical cord. This is home to Norman Manley International Airport, the yacht club, Palisadoes Park and Gunboat Beach. My destination, the remains of Port Royal – that tiny smidgen not submerged by the earthquake – is right at the head of the snake. Just before you reach it you pass Morgan's Harbour Hotel and at the very end you encounter a vestige of Fort Charles.

I was here for the history. Kingston barely existed when Port Royal was The Wickedest City On Earth. Warehouses crammed with looted goods shared the murky streets with whorehouses crowded with wretched prostitutes. By the 1660s an estimated one-third of the population were pirates. This was the base for their attacks on Spanish shipping and coastal settlements from around 1660 to 1692. Along with Tortuga it was the most important pirate haven and a magnet for adventurers and rogues. The jails and taverns of England were quickly emptied of their villains and riffraff to populate the town and man the ships.

As I stood there peering into the sea, where I imagined great treasures still lay undiscovered among the underwater ruins, I did not realise how my namesake, Henry, would change my life.

Henry Morgan was a juvenile delinquent from South Wales. He was shipped to Barbados – considered a punishment in those days – as an indentured labourer to atone for his crimes. He would be no better than a white slave for a few years. This was too much like hard work for Henry so he escaped his indenture and Barbados by joining a pirate ship bound for Port Royal. After two or three years spent plundering Spanish settlements his knack for survival and skills elevated him to Captain. Soon he was elected Admiral and handed commissions by the Jamaican authorities.

Henry Morgan was the right man in the right place at the right time. He was a thoroughly nasty piece of work. He instructed or allowed his thugs to perpetrate some truly dreadful tortures in order to ascertain the location of hidden valuables and devised devilish schemes during his raids. Back in England he became a folk hero. He is justly famous for some particularly well-planned and brilliantly-executed adventures which struck the fear of his name into the Spanish. After his destruction of Puerto Príncipe in Cuba, for example, he launched successful attacks at Portobelo and Maracaibo on the Spanish Main.

But the assault of most interest to me was his infamous sacking of Panama.

Back in the 17th Century there was no Panama Canal. So a ship destined for Spain but sailing from Peru or Ecuador heavily laden with gold and silver looted from the Incas and other native tribes was faced with a long and perilous voyage. Just take a look at your atlas. Weeks of sailing down the Pacific flank of South America, around the storm-whipped Cape Horn or through the perilous Magellan Straits, then further weeks of travel up the Atlantic coast. With frequent stops for victualling and careening it could take months just to reach The Caribbean. These were fragile wooden ships remember, dependent on benign winds and prey to storms. Many would be lost before they reached the North Atlantic.

In order to considerably shorten the sea journey and so reduce losses the Spanish founded the city of Panama at the narrowest point on the Central American isthmus, very close to the southern end of the present day Panama Canal. Gold and other loot was shipped here from South America, transhipped by mule train and river across the jungle-clad mountains to Nombre de Dios or Portobelo on the Caribbean coast, then loaded on to galleons bound for Spain.

Now fabulous wealth was within striking distance of The Caribbean Sea. A great temptation for seagoing adventurers subject to little international control. At the end of the 16th Century Sir Francis Drake, with help from local *cimarrones*, had successfully raided a mule train laden with silver bullion. Not content with that he also attacked the settlement of Nombre de Dios. A century later Henry Morgan was determined to go one better.

The Cimarron became a regular member of Henry Morgan's expeditions. He was useful as an interpreter with the Spanish, slaves and other cimarrones. Also he seemed to have a natural talent as a scout in unfamiliar terrain.

Port Royal was an eye-opener for him. Its squalor and the licentiousness of its residents appalled and intrigued him. He was particularly astounded by the behaviour of his former comrades. He'd seen them experience great hardships and danger, suffer wounds and, in some cases, amputations, for what? Loot. Each man received his share of plunder earned, usually, over a period of weeks or months. Yet he saw most of them fritter it away in days. Permanently drunk, they were cheated in their gambling and robbed by their prostitutes. Some would end up living on the streets and most resorted to muggings and burglaries until it was time to return to sea. He, a wiser man, had lodged comfortably for over a year on his share simply by avoiding riotous living. Then he accompanied Henry Morgan on the Admiral's final escapade.

The pirate fleet was huge, a small navy. It comprised 37 ships from Port Royal and Tortuga manned by a multinational force of 2,000 combatants – British, French, Dutch, escaped slaves and renegade Spanish and Portuguese. First they captured the fort of San Lorenzo on the Caribbean coast. Morgan left a garrison there to guard the ships and sculled up the River Chagres with 1,200 men in small boats. They took only meagre provisions, expecting to find supplies on the route. Unfortunately the Spanish were forewarned and so destroyed or poisoned all food supplies during their retreat. The pirates were forced to survive on leaves, berries and even grass for several days. At one point they found some abandoned leather bags. In their desperation they boiled them until soft, barbecued them and finally ate them.

They fought their way upriver on empty stomachs for a week. Gratefully they then encountered some escaped cattle and mules. The boucaniers, those French sharpshooters who'd hunted cattle in Hispaniola, shot as many of the fleeing animals as possible. Other men made fires to barbecue the coming feast. Many of Morgan's troops were so hungry they didn't wait for the beef to be cooked. They ate it raw. According to a contemporary account 'the blood ran down into their beards and stained their clothes.'

The Cimarron too had starved for several days, surviving on berries, nuts and leaves, but he'd done that previously when he escaped from his plantation in Cuba. It was a character-building experience but hardly worse than his mistreatment as a slave and nowhere near as horrific as his nightmare imprisonment aboard ship on The Middle Passage. There, on the long journey from West Africa, he's been one of 200 crammed in rows like books on library shelves. Unlike books they were chained together. For almost the entire journey they suffered below decks, covered in sores, barely able to breathe the foul air through the stink of urine, sweat and shit. Of the 200 who'd started the journey weeks before only 124 survived to be landed in The Caribbean and sold into slavery. Compared with this the trials of the last few days were just a temporary inconvenience.

Eventually, on the ninth day, the pirates saw Panama ahead. On the tenth day they attacked.

The Spanish considerably outnumbered their weakened attackers. They faced the pirates with the elite of their forces, some 600 cavalry supported by over 2,000 infantry. In addition they boasted a secret weapon. They had assembled a herd of 1,500 wild bulls which they intended to stampede around the pirates' flank and rear.

Morgan divided his troops into three battalions. Observing that the defenders had stationed their cavalry in the front rank he decided to commence the attack with his boucaniers. And he'd chosen his battle site well. Marshy ground separated his men from the Spanish forces. When the boucaniers advanced to within firing range the cavalry charged forward but were slowed considerably by the soft going. They thrashed around in some disorder, the horses struggling to maintain a firm footing. The sharpshooters were kneeling and firing with military precision and inflicted tremendous losses. In desperation the defenders stampeded their bulls early towards the serried ranks of marksmen but without the desired result. Most of the bulls, frightened by the gunfire, ran off wildly whilst the few which charged the pirate fusiliers were gunned down by men who years before had done just that for a living. Some animals even careered into the ranks of the floundering cavalry.

Seeing how the battle was progressing Morgan moved his second battalion round in a flanking move. For some reason the Spanish infantry, well positioned on a small hill, mistook this for a retreat and forsook their strategic positions.

They charged into a gully where they were mown down by
pirate crossfire.

That first battle accounted for 600 Spanish soldiers,
cavalry and infantry combined, and gave encouragement to
the attackers for their assault on the town itself.

I was ruminating on all this as I teetered at the water's edge
and stared into the sea which now envelops the ruins of The
Wickedest City On Earth. I couldn't see anything.

Probably it seems strange that I should develop an interest
in such aggressive and antisocial types as Caribbean
cutthroats, but such was my fascination with history. Not to
mention my secret agenda. I was beginning to immerse
myself in my subject. Obviously I was not inclined to go
diving into the now-tranquil waters off Port Royal but I did
wonder if any of that fabulous looted wealth was still down
there. I was startled by a voice behind me.

"You too layet man."

I turned around and saw a middle-aged black man, wiry
with tough, wizened skin and clad in undervest and loose-
fitting trousers. Probably a fishermen from the small
settlement there.

"How do you know what I was thinking?" I asked.

"Ever'one de same man. Dem all tink mebbe dey go divin'
an' fine someting ever'one else not see. Go head man. De
'otel dere" he pointed to his right "dem ave de divin'."

"This is the spot though, isn't it?" I said. "Port Royal is
under all this water?"

"Yeh man. But people been lookin' for near tree 'undred
year now man. You too layet."

With that he turned and strolled on his way leaving me
musing. OK, maybe there was nothing left here. But there
was something strange about that Panama raid.

After a brief respite Henry Morgan led his forces in a
final assault on Panama itself, breaking through the

unfortified side. Hastily thrown up barricades and defeatist defenders were unable to stop him. In less than three hours of savage fighting the invaders controlled the town. A great prize in itself. This metropolis boasted a cathedral, eight convents with churches attached, 200 warehouses, a treasury and mint, a fort, a hospital, royal stables, a slave market and everything you would expect in an important maritime city. There were over 5,000 dwellings ranging from 200 stone mansions through wooden houses of varying status down to thatched hovels made from reeds. In fact there was an abundance of combustible material so it's not surprising that a raging fire took hold after Morgan's men gained entry. Opinions differ as to the perpetrators. The Spanish and today's Panamanians prefer to believe that the pirates set the city aflame. Henry Morgan claimed the inhabitants torched their town as a continuation of their scorched earth policy once they'd accepted defeat.

The pirates were not in a merciful mood. They'd endured a long sea voyage via Ile-à-Vache and Santa Catalina, a fierce battle at San Lorenzo, an arduous river journey during which they starved and were constantly ambushed by a Spanish rear guard and indigenous tribes and an exhausting trek through the jungle. Finally they'd fought two bloody battles against overwhelming odds. Now their sadistic instincts would be released. Morgan did not allow them to drink on the grounds that the wine was probably poisoned but he didn't halt the looting, murders and dreadful tortures now perpetrated in one of the world's worst atrocities.

A Dutch surgeon travelling with the pirates wrote an eye-witness account of the raid. In one of his horrifying anecdotes he recorded the torture of a man in detail. ' . . . . they first put him on the rack, wherewith they inhumanly disjointed his arms. After this they twisted a cord about his forehead, which they wrung so hard that his eyes appeared as big as eggs, and they were ready to fall out of his skull. But neither with these torments could they obtain any positive answer to their demands. Wherewith they soon after hung him up by the testicles, giving him infinite blows and stripes, while he was under that intolerable pain and posture of body. Afterwards they cut off his nose and ears and singed his face with burning straw till he could speak nor lament his misery no longer.'

According to historical accounts the Spanish received timely warning of Morgan's approach. They stuffed every seaworthy ship in the harbour full of treasures from the town and despatched them back to South America. Other valuables were buried outside the city and more were destroyed in the fire. Most historians therefore suggest that Morgan's gains were less than he expected. But I realised these historians are wrong. The notorious pirate retired after this raid and lived in great luxury on his Jamaican plantations. It is even suggested that he founded his own rum distillery. Where did the funds come from?

Many writers claim that somehow Henry Morgan and his closest cronies had secreted loot and after their return to the Caribbean coast departed separately for Port Royal at night whilst their surviving colleagues were drinking and gambling. If they did, maybe some others did too. There is a story that one group had boarded an abandoned galleon in the harbour. They were attempting to make it seaworthy with the intention of pursuing Spaniards in the Pacific when Morgan ordered the ship scuttled.

Another story which raises questions is the fate of The Golden Altar. According to legend this *Alter de Oro* from the *Iglesia de San José* was disguised by a priest and therefore escaped the clutches of the pirates. One account claims that it was whitewashed, another version that it was covered in pitch, and a third that it was coated with mud. Officially this glittering altar now takes pride of place in the replacement *Iglesia de San José* in the Casco Viejo quarter of the modern Panama City. But I had my doubts even then. Surely in a stay of four weeks the pirates would have discovered the deception? In any case it was their habit to destroy religious artefacts of no commercial value. Of course I know all the answers to these questions now. But I didn't then and neither did anyone else.

I will confess to mercenary motives for my interest in Henry's exploits. I felt trapped at Sunstroke Holidays. This nine-to-five, Monday-to-Friday, badly-paid job was just a means of survival. Five days a week, sometimes six, I tramped down to Gravesend Station, found a gap on the narrow platform and forced my way into a dirty and overcrowded carriage when the train arrived. I hardly ever found a seat. In fact, thinking about it, I never found a seat except on Saturdays. Then at Charing Cross the transfer to an equally overcrowded and dirty tube train. I couldn't live in London because of the extortionate rents yet the high fares and low wages made it impossible to save anything and forced me to live with my mother.

And at work? There I had nothing in common with my colleagues and little respect for the management. The dark grey world of central London, exemplified by the littered, bustling streets and perennial leaden skies and drizzle, seemed set to imprison me for the rest of my life. Sometimes I felt that only sudden riches could release me. I'd even considered trying the football pools, but then how many people who religiously complete their coupons every week have still not broken free?

So I harboured a dream that somewhere on my travels I would discover pirate treasure. You might laugh. Even I knew it was a longshot. But if I could pull it off I would become a man of independent means. No longer would I need to work at Sunstroke Holidays and suffer the jibes and incompetence.

Jamaica was a fine introduction to The Caribbean and its way of life. I felt comfortable with the rhythms and the people I met. Unfortunately there are few echoes remaining of that notorious pirate era and no chance of discovering ill-gotten gains there. I would need to travel onwards to the blood-soaked land of voodoo, the land of graveyards patrolled at night by Baron Samedi and his legions of enslaved zombies. A country controlled by a repressive government and sadistic secret police, the poorest country in the western world, Haiti.

Chapter Ten

Not Tonight Josephine

I was ensconced amidships, just behind the wing in my favoured window seat, so I felt the slight klunk as the undercarriage was released from its imprisonment and locked into place. Flaps shuddered then latched into their landing positions. I could see erect air brakes vibrating as the aircraft fought conflicting demands. Reduced power and increased drag forced her to slow and drop a little inelegantly, not unlike a duck skimming to a stop in the bayous, towards the mile-long ribbon of concrete.

Peering out along and under the wing I spotted lines of shacks speeding past cheek-by-jowl below us, slumped against each other as if each needed its neighbours for support. Perhaps they did. This, I presumed, was one of Port-au-Prince's forsaken shanty towns.

As it flashed by it looked like a child's model junked together from old cardboard boxes on a mud patch in the garden. Her inexpert use of scissors ensured that frequently the edges of walls, corners and roofs were not quite straight and some parts, where she had torn the sheets of corrugated cardboard, were quite ragged. The pieces were randomly butted together and the whole appeared as delicately balanced as a house of cards – no, a whole town of cards – that would be flattened by the first strong wind. Rivulets of water trickled through the toy streets.

If only it was a model. The reality of this degradation was the first evidence of the destitution to which the previous President's policies had reduced most of his people. Everything was coloured in variegated shades of brown or beige, even the corrugated iron roofs which were almost completely corroded by rust. Drab lines of washing barely stirred in the insufficient breeze which fumbled along the narrow, muddy streets. Human figures moved disconsolately, taking care not to step in the puddles or open sewers, those 'rivulets of water'.

My plane hit the deck and taxied over to its appointed stand. A large sign dominating the terminal building proudly announced that I'd arrived at the Aeroport Francois Duvalier, named after Jean-Claude's feared and loathed father.

In due course we all alighted and entered the arrivals hall where I spotted a group of Americans chatting nervously. They stood slightly aside, allowing plenty of room for our slow-moving line of newcomers to pass. There were six of them – Americans that is. Probably three couples, huddled together in their summer lightweights. Empty space surrounded them as arriving passengers kept well clear, granting them their privacy. Ages seemed to be in the range of late thirties to early fifties. From snatches of their timorous conversation which wafted my way as I dawdled into their vicinity I deduced that they were in transit for The Dominican Republic.

I was halted close to this group as the head of the arrivals line reached the Immigration desk. I eavesdropped on their whisperings, amused by their concerns. After all, I thought, a couple of hours here would be their only experience of this cursed yet magic land.

They didn't want to be in Haiti at all. The smokers were taking anxious deep drags on their *Camels* and *Kents*. All of them kept a tight grip on their hand baggage. Did they really think that this orderly line of arriving passengers would include bag-snatchers? Couldn't they conceive of the dire future – short as it would be – that awaited anyone fool enough to try? Perhaps this was just an unconscious expression of their nervousness.

Without obviously eavesdropping I attempted to unscramble a whispered warning urgently conveyed by a thin, earnest middle-aged man to the woman next to him, presumably his wife. "Papa Doc" were the only words I could make out. Some of the other Americans seemed to think that every Haitian wearing dark glasses was a member of the sadistic *Tontons Macoutes*, judging by suddenly lowered heads inclined towards a companion and urgent whisperings. Perhaps they were, but I thought it more likely that the secret police would be in the Departures Terminal. It also occurred to me that the background broadcasting of insistent voodoo drums was hardly calculated to put these tourists at their ease. One man nodded towards me and hissed portentously to his companion.

"He won't last long."

Immigration and Customs were very thorough but also very polite. Always a good idea to scribble 'travel agent' on the forms. As usual I passed through much more quickly than those who preceded me. The search of my baggage was cursory and I wasn't asked for a bribe. Once released into the smoky sunlight I found myself the target of a pulsating human wave of taxi drivers and touts.

A clamouring mob more like. Some thirty men of all ages, all humbly dressed, were pushing forwards, excitedly offering me everything from taxi rides to women. They came at me like a *tsunami*, halting a few feet away to form a squirming but impenetrable wall. I selected a middle-aged chap who seemed less shabby and pushy than the rest, handed him my holdall and followed him to a beat-up car, the two of us shouldering a weaving passage through a chaos of hustle and bustle which made Jamaica seem sleepy by comparison.

My Doctor Jekyll quickly degenerated into Mr Hyde. No

potion necessary. Once behind the wheel this mild-mannered man transformed himself into a belligerent demon as he powered his elderly vehicle, impatiently pounding the horn, first through the milling crowds and sloppily-parked cars and trucks, then past lumbering *tap-taps*, out to the open road.

When I write 'open road' I use the term relatively. Although the main highway was less chaotic than the immediate airport environs I could sense hazards arriving from every direction.

Driving standards in and around Port-au-Prince are best described as a discretionary mayhem. Where possible everyone will drive down the centre of the road. Fine, probably, out in the country or at three in the morning, but perhaps not wise during an average afternoon in the capital. When faced with the inevitable oncoming traffic all vehicles swerve over to their right at the last second, horns blaring, flinging their passengers across the seats and scattering unfortunate pedestrians. Pedestrians who are forced to walk on the highway as many of the pavements are crammed with vendors' stalls. Generally the leap for the sidewalk involved a vault over an open sewer and a sideways squirm on landing to avoid a stall and its customers. Some seemed quite practised at it. And dawdling pedestrians were not the only hazard facing the impatient driver. Animals, either disconsolately pulling carts or meandering aimlessly, slowed our progress. Hard on the brakes, a screech of tyres then accelerate towards the next danger.

In spite of all these obstacles straying into our path and the poor condition of the roads I was delivered safely to my desired destination within fifteen minutes.

The Santos Pacot Guest House was another choice selected from the guide book. At first I thought I'd blown it. This hostelry is not in the centre of town. But I soon realised that its hillside location was a boon. Not only did I enjoy atmospheric views of the city through the haze but I was able to appreciate the benefits of a cooling breeze. The rooms are comfortable, though gloomy due to furnishings of natural dark woods. My bathroom was shared but at the price I was paying I decided this was a minor inconvenience.

I'd heard that most European and North American visitors suffer from culture shock when they first arrive in Haiti so I decided to spend my first afternoon on the terrace with a beer and the guide book. That way, I figured, when I ventured on to the streets I would be in control.

'*There can be no place like Port-au-Prince*' I read. '*It has echoes of the east, undercurrents of West Africa, a little French chic, a Caribbean climate and friendliness.*' Apparently the downtown area was dominated by an Iron Market '*painted a flamboyant red and green and with a tin roof that gleams in the sun. It boasts minaret-cupolas that could be straight from Agra or Fatehpur Sikri in India.*'

I stood up and strolled to the end of the terrace. I could just make out a building answering to that description.

I knew something of the architecture and cultures of India. Before I suggested my bright idea to Arrowsmith he'd notified me of my impending transfer to Sunstroke's 'Discover The Exotic' programme. I'd researched the countries which might well be featured. So I was intrigued. Why would the capital of a Caribbean country, a former colony of France, feature an oriental market? Maybe it was just part of the enigma which embraces Haiti.

About an hour after dark, refreshed and enjoying the cool evening, I decided that a short stroll might be in order. The street lights weren't working but there was sufficient moonlight for me to take a stroll around the neighbourhood. I had the sidewalks to myself so presumably the local residents were indoors dining with their families. After ten minutes or so I noticed a shadowy shape drifting towards me. It spoke.

"*Bonsoir Blanc.*"

My French is hopeless. No 'O' Level. I dug into the recesses of my brain to extract a sentence. "*Bonjour. Mon français est un petit peu. Avez vous anglais?*"

"*Ah oui*. I can be your guide. Show you Port-au-Prince. Come."

Not again I thought. But then, why not? I'd had a good time last time.

The shadow thrust out a hand. "*Je suis Jean-Pierre.*"

I shook it. "Hi. I'm Morgan."

"Come. *Nous allons.*"

He hustled me at some speed through the moonlit streets, left here, right there, continually downhill until we came to a wide road where we halted. Fairly quiet now, this was obviously a major artery during the day. "We get *tap-tap.*"

Sure enough a brightly painted vehicle, mainly red with generous swirls of green and blue and even splashes of silver, soon appeared out of the gloom heralded by its one functioning headlight like a motorised Cyclops. It had started life as a Toyota pickup but now a handbuilt wooden cabin enclosed the cargo space. The legend '*God Is My Saviour*' was emblazoned across the bonnet. I was surprised to see this written in English but perhaps they'd borrowed the idea from The Philippines. I decided to trust in God and Jean-Pierre and joined the four passengers already seated on the wooden benches. Two nodded a salutation. Jean-Pierre said something to the driver then climbed in beside us.

Even downtown there were no functioning streetlights. Peering out through the back of the vehicle into the moonlit gloom I could learn little about the town or where we were heading. When the pickup veered sharply from the centre of the road to the right I could see the open sewers, occasional lonely pedestrians and greyish buildings and much of the time my nostrils were filled with the malodorous stench of decaying vegetable matter and sewage. But these glimpses offered no clue to where we were or where we were going. Jean-Pierre hadn't told me and I hadn't asked. After about ten minutes we hit the seafront and five minutes later we stopped.

"We are here" said Jean-Pierre and climbed out. I

followed and looked up. This seemed to be some sort of nightclub. Above the door I noted an array of different coloured bare light bulbs some of which were illuminated in an irregular pattern. Not by design obviously. Many had expired and not been replaced. Jean-Pierre ushered me into a gloomy interior and to an unoccupied table. I glanced around as we entered. This joint was having a quiet night. As far as I could see and hear there were few other customers and our table seemed to be positioned in a prime spot.

A few feet away a murky and foul-smelling sea slopped against a shoulder-high concrete wall. The space above it was unglazed so I could clearly see a scattering of lights in the harbour and a host of stars in the sky. No rain tonight then. As soon as we were seated a dishevelled waiter approached bearing a tray with a champagne bottle and two glasses. Obviously this was some sort of clip joint so I was certain that the contents of the bottle would not be Champagne but would be very expensive. I waved him away.

"No no" I said. "Bring two beers."

Jean-Pierre spoke to the waiter then turned back to me. "I not drink beer. I am Baptist. I have Coke."

Oh that's just great. He brings me to a clip joint then says he can't indulge because of his religion. Does his religion allow him to lead others into temptation then? *Wunderbar.*

Suddenly I identified raised American voices. I peered into the shadows behind. At a nearby table I saw three heavyset middle-aged Caucasians clutching beer bottles and leaning back in their seats. Their table was strewn with empties. Their laughter increased as three young women joined them. I guessed that this was just a normal night out for them. Are they hell raisers? They showed no interest in me which was just fine.

As the beer and Coke arrived on a battered metal tray and with some ceremony I asked Jean-Pierre "Why did you bring me here?"

Jean-Pierre seemed a little surprised by the question. He spread his hands. "This is where tourists come" he suggested, waving his right vaguely in the direction of the Americans. "It is not good?"

"Ah" I began. "I'm not a tourist. I am working. I am a travel agent."

"Working is good. Foreigners who work come here too."

I didn't want to get involved in an argument or an explanation so I sat back, sipped my beer and gazed towards the sea. This is where tourists come? What tourists? Haven't Papa Doc and Graham Greene frightened them all away? No, the only tourists likely to venture here would be the backpacking variety or intrepid culture-vultures. Those raucous Yanks behind can't be tourists. More likely roughnecks working on some construction project.

Then, not wishing to be rude, I turned back to Jean-Pierre and raised my glass. We sipped our beverages thoughtfully. In the sparse light I could see that he was fairly well dressed in sombre clothing, of medium height and slim.

I was just leaning forward to ask him to tell me something about himself when I noticed two lasses approaching. They were aged between 18 and 20. One was quite attractive. She sauntered up to my right side. Close up I could see that she was wearing a black cotton miniskirt and a loose-fitting pinky-red T-shirt, no shoes and apparently nothing under the T-shirt. She smiled sweetly.

"You like fuck?" she enquired.

I almost choked on my drink. Her sweet smile morphed into a cheeky grin as I studied her more closely. Well, for sure she was extremely attractive with a fine body, about half the age of the Jamaican woman and a thousand times more alluring. But I had no experience of black women, nor of hookers, and I was sure this was neither the time or place to start.

"What, here?" I gasped.

"Up there" she answered, indicating an open door in the wall to my left with a flick of her head. I leaned forward across the table and peered through the doorway to see a barely illuminated rickety wooden staircase leading to what must be very squalid rooms. Well, I couldn't confirm that they were squalid from where I was sitting but I assumed they would be quite grotty. This was a dilapidated clip joint in a poverty-stricken and corrupt country so I wouldn't expect anything else. I didn't fancy it.

"*Aujourd'hui non*" I said. "*Peut-être demain.*"

The girl giggled. "No. Today" she exclaimed, leaning forward with enough animation to prove that her breasts were indeed unsupported within the T-shirt. I was getting excited but I'd decided Not Tonight Josephine. I grinned and took a sip of my beer, inches away from temptation. The other girl made a suggestion in Creole. At this the first girl giggled again, straightened up and pulled her T-shirt over her head to reveal a truly fine pair of breasts.

I was impressed. They were just how I like breasts. *Playboy* centrefold. They were full, firm and the nipples were beginning to harden. Or was that just my imagination?

I suppose I was stunned. Before I could say anything, or, in an attempt to appear super cool, sip my beer, she leaned forward and plucked off my glasses. Clasping the back of my head, just above the neck, she sandwiched my face between those breasts. Gently she massaged my face with them, side to side then up and down. Lovely. Then she stepped back and pointed through the open door.

"Now we go?"

Oh God. Why not? I was sorely tempted, but remembered the inevitable seediness of those rooms, the fact that I didn't know where I was – only that I was in a clip joint – the risk of contracting AIDS and every other conceivable excuse. I could be robbed. It was my first evening here and everyone, as I'd discovered in Montego Bay, is most vulnerable on his first day. No. I'd better not.

"Not tonight" I repeated. "Maybe tomorrow."

The girls surprisingly accepted this dismissal with a good grace and left with a smile, a wave and a giggle.

Chapter Eleven

Every Day's A Challenge

Breakfast at the Santos Pacot is American-style rather than authentically Haitian. Thankfully. I was tucking into a plate of pancakes when a blond-haired youth in a check seersucker shirt sat down opposite. We exchanged nods.

"Been here long?" he asked.

"Yesterday" I told him.

"Me too. This your first time?"

"Yes. What about you?"

"I was born here. Haiti I mean." He spoke with an American accent but I couldn't quite place it. Yankee rather than Deep South though. "I'm at college in The States" he continued "but I come back here every chance I get."

"Why?"

He turned this over in his mind for a minute or two. Either he wasn't sure himself or there was some secret he didn't want to divulge.

"I guess" he eventually ventured "I guess it's because every day's a challenge."

So here was somebody who relished a challenge. I wasn't sure what challenges awaited me – perhaps something involving voodoo and zombies – but this youth seemed to have survived them.

"I take it you don't wander through graveyards at night" I asked through a smile.

He grinned. "OOOH The Baron." He waved his hands in the air. "Zombies do exist you know. It's done with drugs. But I've never seen one. Far as I know. You're going to ask me about the voodoo."

"Um, yeah. A guy I met last night suggested I might like to go to a ceremony."

"Don't. Unless you want to sit in a semi-circle with other tourists watching people tramping through red-hot coals and wailing. Genuine ceremonies are rare nowadays. They're held in isolated shacks miles away in the hills. Where the *Tontons Macoutes* can't find them. You'll only get to one of those if you've lived here for years so everyone knows you."

I nodded. That's what I'd heard already. We continued with our breakfasts in silence for a few minutes. Then our thoughts were interrupted by the scrape of a chair. A young fair-haired woman joined us. She ordered without looking at the menu and turned to me.

"You're the travel agent from England." Her tone was accusatory. Apparently in her opinion travel agents are A Bad Thing. Polluting the world's beaches with roasting bodies. Perhaps on a par with estate agents and journalists.

"That's right" I confirmed. I gave her a more thorough inspection. Maybe she was psychic. "How do you know?"

"I saw it in the register. You think tourists will want to come to Haiti?"

A clear implication that I was wasting my time. She was obviously somebody who would avoid tourists and the countries they infested. She probably called herself A Traveller. Her accent carried a strong antipodean twang so more likely a Kiwi than an Aussie. She was sensibly attired in lightweight jeans and a white cotton blouse, about five foot six and not unattractive. Obviously a little on the serious side.

Kiwis do not like to be mistaken for Aussies but Australians are cool if you accuse them of being Kiwis. I chose the cowardly option.

"Are you from New Zealand?"

"Yes. Hamilton. Why do you think tourists would come here?"

Before answering I speculated on the source of her intelligence. If she could label me so precisely then presumably the American youth and I were the only new arrivals. Still, it did mean that she was nosey. Most people don't bother flicking through hotel registers do they? I should be careful with my reply.

"Well, we're going to start doing theme holidays" I answered, hoping that was a vague enough description "and we will combine Haiti with normal holiday islands like Jamaica and Barbados."

"What sort of theme?" she asked as a bowl of fruit was placed before her.

"Well, er, combining culture and beaches." The title of the guide book came to my rescue. "And, you know, island hopping."

"Make sure you see the Iron Market here, The Oloffson Hotel, the Cathedral and the Presidential Palace" she advised. "And go to Le Cap" she added before concentrating on her fruit.

If I was a typical travel agent, as she supposed, I wouldn't have researched my subject. She would assume that my knowledge of Port-au-Prince and its attractions would be zilch. No need to disappoint her or disabuse her of her hasty preconceptions. And I had every intention of travelling north to Cap Haitien. It was the nearest town to Ile de la Tortue, the current name for Tortuga. But there was no need to volunteer this information. Better to appear an ill-informed twit.

"Thank you" I said. "I'll make sure I do. What is Le Cap?"

"Cap Haitien. It was the capital in the French days. And maybe you should go to Jacmel. You'll need a car." She turned and scrutinised me closely. "Do you drive?"

"Not much. I don't have a car in England. I'm not sure I should drive here."

"Get a driver" she suggested before swallowing the last of her fruit. "They drive like lunatics here." She stood. "See you later." Then she was gone as briskly as she'd arrived.

The quiet American had left a couple of minutes earlier. Time for me to do some work. I drained my coffee cup and vacated the table.

Down in the street, outside the gate, Jean-Pierre was waiting. In the glorious sunshine I could confirm my assessment of last night. Slim, probably in his early twenties, simply dressed in dark anonymous clothes, he looked very clean. He flashed me a diffident smile. Evidently he was keen to continue working as my guide.

"*Bonjour* Morkan."

"*Bonjour* Jean-Pierre. Today I look around Port-au-Prince. Tomorrow, maybe, I get car."

"Car? Auto? I can drive you." He wagged his finger. "You no drive. Not safe for you. I used to it."

Not a bad idea. Although I enjoy driving I was relatively inexperienced and, to be honest, I didn't fancy it here. They drive on the right for a start – officially anyway – and I certainly couldn't fathom their highway etiquette. If such a phrase could be used to describe the anarchy I'd already witnessed. But how could a poor person like Jean-Pierre have learned to drive?

"You have a licence?"

"*Ah oui* Morkan. Maybe we get car today?"

Why not? It would save some walking in this hot sun, not to mention taxi and *tap-tap* fares. And, even if it did cost more, having our own car would be more convenient. So we took a taxi to a rental company he recommended.

A small, single-storey, unpainted concrete building shared a large compound with around a dozen vehicles. Some were American compacts, others European. Minor accident damage blemished the shiny paintwork of a few. I quickly ascertained that the cheapest car was a Volkswagen Beetle. This boasted just two dents in its bright orange paintwork. I inspected it closely. According to the milometer this was a recent acquisition. It looked pretty new and in good condition apart from those dents. I strolled back to the concrete hut.

The manager was studying Jean-Pierre's licence with less than supreme confidence. Was it a forgery? Or his brother's? An interrogation session in Creole, during which Jean-Pierre seemed to be on the defensive, was in its final stages. Eventually the manager accepted the validity of the licence and passed me forms to sign. Being of a cautious nature, and wary now of Jean-Pierre's ability and experience, not to mention the general driving standards here, I accepted the recommended Collision Damage Waiver. Once my credit card was run through his machine the manager reluctantly handed over the keys. I passed them to Jean-Pierre as we strolled out into the yard.

He settled behind the wheel, adjusted his seat backwards and appeared to be familiarising himself with the controls. I sauntered over to the other side, tossed my red shoulder bag and camera in the back, wound down the window and slid into the passenger seat. I was just closing the door when the engine burst into life. The car shot forward with a jerk then stalled, throwing both me and my door first back then forwards. Ah. It had been parked in gear and Jean-Pierre hadn't checked.

Unperturbed he discovered neutral and tried again. The VW fired up a second time and ticked over happily with the unmistakable rattle of an air-cooled engine. Looking down he selected first gear and stabbed the accelerator. I was hurled backwards then forward again as the car fled the sanctuary of the compound in a series of kangaroo leaps. Fortunately I'd maintained a firm grip on the door. I pulled it shut just before we hurtled through the exit. Our good luck continued. There were no vehicles passing in the lane outside and Jean-Pierre had imposed a semblance of control over the Beetle by the time we reached the main road. He stopped – well almost – turned right into the traffic and headed into town. Our progress was still somewhat jerky, particularly as he moved through the gears, but at least the kangaroo in the back was resting.

I turned to Jean-Pierre. "You have driven a car before?"

"Yes of course" he answered calmly "I have a licence."

"Do you have to pass a driving test?"

"Yes, but I passed."

"What happens in this test?"

He hesitated slightly. "We go to the ministry."

"The Ministry of Transport?"

He paused before answering. "*Oui*. No. Maybe. We not call this office Transport. It is a government office." He flicked me a glance. Obviously I was expecting a fuller answer. He continued "They have a very *grande*, eh, large, eh, table with streets. Like in our capital, Port-au-Prince. They ave, eh, you know, little cars. I think you say models." Another quick glance in my direction. "They give orders and we push the cars."

"So you don't need to drive a car to get a licence?"

"Of course not! Only rich people have car! People like me not 'ave car. So we learn to drive little cars to get licence."

Good grief I thought. That explains a lot. And what am I letting myself in for?

The Oloffson was the highlight of the day's tour. It is simultaneously impressive and eccentric. Leaving Jean-Pierre to park the car I ascended a broad flight of steps at the top of which three smartly-uniformed butlers waited. Each wore a finely-tailored white jacket, neatly-pressed black trousers, matching mirror-shine shoes and a wide welcoming smile. I explained the purpose of my visit, offered a card and lingered whilst one of them strode smartly inside. Within two minutes he returned and led me into a spacious room. It was lavishly furnished with antiques and brightly-coloured rugs on a polished wooden floor. This was the office of the famous owner who was comfortably sitting behind a vast antique desk. Not the owner represented in the novel you understand, but the equally famous American who bought the hotel from him in the darkest days of Papa Doc's terror. Al Seitz.

Mr Seitz introduced me to a lady in her mid-thirties seated at the further end of his desk. An American journalist, he told me, here to interview him. Introductions completed I sat down to await my turn. First thing I noticed, among the books and papers casually strewn across the desktop, at the end closest to me, about an arm's length away, was a huge stack of dollar bills. Shouldn't they be in the safe? Or were they counterfeit? Of course with US currency notes all a uniform size and colour it was impossible to know how much was stacked there, but if they were all $1 bills – unlikely – then this pile would amount to a couple of hundred dollars.

I was overawed in the presence of this legendary figure. I'd never met a famous person before. I quickly decided that their interview could probably proceed more swiftly in my absence.

"It might be best" I ventured " if I just had a look around the hotel."

"Sure" smiled Mr Seitz. He raised an eyebrow to the butler, still in attendance.

The rooms are named after famous people – actors and actresses mainly -who have lodged there. I noted the Ann Bancroft Studio, John Gielgud Suite, Marlon Brando Cottage and the Graham Greene Room. This last was a surprise. Papa Doc was incensed at publication of *The Comedians*, producing his own riposte, *Graham Greene Finally Exposed*. If a room had been named after the author in his lifetime Duvalier Senior would have closed down the hotel or seized it and run the owner out of the country. Perhaps the suggestions that Jean-Claude was less repressive than his father were true.

I'd seen the movie of the novel. Although this was filmed outside Haiti, actually shot mainly in West Africa, the replica of the hotel – renamed the Trianon in the book and movie – was true to the original. So the intricate gingerbread work, the towers and turrets were familiar to me. The swimming pool is located exactly as in the film. Today though it was filled with water. There was no dead body slumped in his own blood in the deep end or anywhere to be seen.

Local guides are not welcomed in the capital's hotels so Jean-Pierre had waited with the car. Now we sped off on a scary journey through the congested streets. We hurtled through crowds of pedestrians and streams of anarchic traffic as Jean-Pierre exchanged curses with other drivers and forced heavily-laden women almost into the open sewers. I tried to moderate his behaviour but I could see it was pointless. After all, his driving was no worse than the other maniacs'. By the time we'd visited the essential sights and inspected a few hotels it was early evening. Jean-Pierre suggested we drive up to Petionville.

This is where the rich live. In spite of the excruciating poverty of the vast majority of Haitians there are many wealthy families who feel completely divorced from the teeming masses struggling for survival below. Some are entrepreneurs. Others will have benefited by skimming off the top of US aid. Up here with their fashionable nightclubs and excellent restaurants they inhabit another world. They breathe cooler hilltop air well above the smoggy fumes and malodorous stink of the town.

As we passed through the outskirts of the capital and began our ascent I was able to admire intricate fretwork in the French colonial style on many of the wooden buildings. Traffic formed into a snake as we entered Petionville itself and I glimpsed the mansions of the wealthy.

Suddenly my sightseeing was terminated by a screech of tyres, a hefty bang and a shouted curse from Jean-Pierre. I was thrown forward roughly in my seat. The snake of rush hour traffic had halted abruptly and my chauffeur was not paying attention. Our little Beetle slammed into the back of a Mercedes.

"Pull on the handbrake" I yelled as I thrust open the door

and leapt out. I rushed around to the front of the car to inspect the damage. The driver of the Mercedes, a smartly dressed mulatto, joined me. The bumpers of both cars were dented but there appeared to be no bodywork damage.

Presumably because I was a foreigner the mulatto waved his hand. "*No problème.*" He was returning to his seat when Jean-Pierre emerged and half-heartedly shouted abuse at him.

"Shut up" I yelled. "*We* drove into the back of *him*!"

Surprisingly, far from being offended at my riposte Jean-Pierre seemed relieved that he wasn't required to become involved in an acrimonious argument.

"Did you put the handbrake on?" I called as I strode back to the car. The snake had started moving again so I quickly regained my seat and we set off after the preceding vehicles encouraged by a volley of car horns from behind us.

It was now dark and it can get very dark in Haiti. I decided that a quick tour of Petionville then back to the guest house for bed was my wisest course of action. Jean-Pierre attempted to persuade me to accompany him on a visit to another nightspot.

"This better than yesterday. This one 'ave dancing."

He was not too insistent with his entreaties once he realised that I would let him keep the car overnight. He probably fancied the idea of racing around town without the burden of his responsibilities as guide and chauffeur. He can show off to his mates. With a bit of luck he would cruise around for two or three hours without hitting anything and learn the rudiments of driving.

Tomorrow we would undertake a long journey to the south coast on unfamiliar and probably very rough roads. Our chances of survival would be increased in proportion to Jean-Pierre's driving experience.

Chapter Twelve

"Lentement, Jean-Pierre, Lentement"

"I didn't introduce myself yesterday" she said. "I'm Colleen."

We were back at the breakfast table on the terrace of the Santos Pacot. I pushed my guide book aside, looked up and smiled.

"Call me Morgan" I said.

"You don't like Walter then." Colleen settled herself more comfortably. "Did you do what you wanted yesterday?"

"Yes thanks. I saw the places you suggested and checked out most of the hotels. We'll probably use the Oloffson as our main hotel."

"You have to really. And today?"

I finished buttering my toast and took a sip of coffee before answering. Let her wait a bit. And I need to be careful what I say.

"I'll probably drive down to Jacmel. I rented a car yesterday like you suggested."

"You're not driving yourself?" She seemed concerned. Maybe she doubted my ability.

"No. My guide, Jean-Pierre, has a licence. He's driving."

"I hope he's better than the rest of the locals."

I gave a short laugh. "He isn't. In fact I don't think he's ever driven a car before. But we survived yesterday so we'll probably survive today. And I've got CDW."

"Is he some kind of crazy speed maniac?"

"No. Well, I don't think so. Yesterday we didn't go anywhere you could drive fast. Too much traffic. Just around town, you know. He just seems to have trouble concentrating on the job in hand. He keeps talking to me, flapping his hands around and looking at me instead of the road. And his reactions seem a bit slow." I chewed a piece of toast before continuing. Now for the punch line. "We ran into the back of someone last night."

"Oh no! Anyone hurt?"

"No, just dented bumpers. The other guy didn't seem bothered about it." I picked up the last piece of toast. I briefly considered adding some jam then decided against. Before continuing I took a swig of coffee. "He should be here with the car in about half an hour. Do you want to come?"

"Love to. But you didn't let him keep the car last night?" Her tone suggested that the very idea would be preposterous.

"Why not? The alternative, which did occur to me, was to tell him to park it here and then take the keys from him. But, well, sometimes it's best to let people know you trust them."

"But he could have been driving around town all night!"

"He probably was. Showing off to his mates and picking up girls. I'm just hoping he hasn't pranged it. But sometimes you have to take risks in life."

Actually I was slightly concerned. Jean-Pierre had demonstrated an excitable side. But why worry about a damaged or missing car? If it happens, it happens. It was very unlikely that Jean-Pierre would steal it and any damage would be covered by the CDW.

I certainly didn't expect Jean-Pierre to do anything malicious. In Haiti the tourist was sacred. The avaricious government was always scheming to attract aid and investment. They understood that tourism is a major industry in The Caribbean. If tourists could be guaranteed protection from robbers and assured of their safety the public relations bonus would bring financial reward to Baby Doc's regime. Though his rule was less oppressive than his father's the population still lived in fear of the *Tontons Macoutes*. If any of the few tourists in Haiti were harmed the perpetrator could expect a slow and painful death.

Yesterday, when we were roaming the seedy streets near the Iron Market, we'd strolled through a game of football. Some kids were kicking a compacted bundle of rags around. It had obviously landed in the drains a few times as it was covered in a brown slime. A small lad gave it a hefty belt as we approached. It flew into the air but not in the direction of their makeshift goal. It hit me full on the middle of my chest then dropped to the ground leaving a nasty smudge on my white T-shirt. The kid was terrified. I've never seen fear like it.

"Don't worry!" I hastily assured him. "No problem! *Pas de problème!*"

Jean-Pierre rapidly reassured him in Creole. But that child would have suffered a week of sleepless nights awaiting a nocturnal knock on his door.

I finished my breakfast and Colleen, as usual, was speeding through hers.

"I'll see you by the gate in thirty minutes if you're coming" I said. "And, oh, you'd better bring an overnight bag just in case."

Colleen looked up sharply and shot me a suspicious glance. It was obvious that she wasn't interested in any romantic episode which, as far as I was concerned, was not on offer anyway. "Why a bag?" she asked. "You can drive to Jacmel and back in a day."

I shrugged that off. "Of course you can, in theory. But what if we have a breakdown or an accident?" I needed to be careful not to give away details of my assignment or my secret plans so I tossed in a red herring. "Also if we decide to go on to Les Cayes or along the coast we would need to stay somewhere overnight." Mustn't mention Ile-à-Vache. We could end up there 'on the spur of the moment' as it were.

About twenty minutes later we met by the gate. Jean-Pierre was waiting with the Beetle.

"*Bonjour* Morkan."

"*Bonjour* Jean-Pierre. This is Colleen. She is coming with us to Jacmel."

Colleen and Jean-Pierre exchanged small talk whilst I toured around the car. I halted at the offside rear wing. A new dent had been added.

"What's this Jean-Pierre?"

He shrugged innocently. "I not want leave car by my house. Very danger. So last night I bring back, leave here. I come this morning and, well, you see."

Yes, a likely story. As we made eye contact he became apprehensive. Did he expect me to bawl him out? Sack him from his role as driver and guide? I gazed at him sternly though I wasn't too bothered about an extra dent.

"OK, we go Jacmel."

Jean-Pierre seemed immensely relieved. At the least he must have expected me to be pissed off with him. Instead he was to drive me and this pretty lady to Jacmel. As I studied his face I could see another thought pushing itself to the forefront of his mind. Now would be a good time to ask.

"Morkan" he began. "My home not far from Jacmel."

"Yes?"

"I not see my family for many months. No, more than a year. Maybe we could visit?"

"Well, we will be pushed for time" I said, before realising the idiomatic English might be beyond him. "Not much time. If it is near Jacmel we can go there."

"Thank you Morkan, thank you."

Jean-Pierre slid behind the wheel whilst I tipped my seat forward to allow Colleen and our overnight bags into the back. This time Jean-Pierre fiddled with the gearstick to confirm it was in neutral and waited until we were seated comfortably, and our door shut, before starting the engine.

Once we were clear of town and headed out on the open road the traffic thinned out. The air became noticeably cleaner and the scenery increasingly pleasant. This road skirted the coast in a westerly direction with hills and mountains ascending to our left and often steep cliffs dropping away to our right. I wound down the window to better experience the pleasures of the drive and allowed my right arm to hang out. Jean-Pierre was controlling the car without difficulty. Perhaps last night, careering around town with his mates, he'd assimilated the rudiments of driving.

The nature of the road, winding and sometimes hilly, and the frequency of oncoming vehicles, prevented us from attempting much overtaking so our pace was somewhat sedate. No complaints from Colleen but it was not long before Jean-Pierre started showing signs of impatience. He would wave his left arm at a slower vehicle in front and even occasionally sound the horn.

"Jean-Pierre. Don't do that."

"He can go faster."

"We are not in hurry. And soon, maybe one hour, there will be not much traffic." I felt a bit foolish speaking in broken English.

Probably because he wasn't expected to prove his virility by overtaking everything he seemed to settle down and indeed relaxed. Colleen, who'd showed a little nervousness, accordingly also relaxed and settled back. I now surveyed my surroundings.

The area was still quite populous but the further we drove from Port-au-Prince the smaller the villages we passed. By now almost all the houses were very basic huts. Some were scattered in the hills in a more rural setting. Then we made our left turn and headed south. This road was much more mountainous with many more tight bends and much less traffic. The hills were more lush, not yet completely stripped of their timber. I was enjoying the ride when I felt a hand on my shoulder. Colleen was leaning forward on the edge of her seat, consternation drawing her face tight.

"He's driving too fast" she said.

Well, yes, now that she's mentioned it Jean-Pierre did seem to be motoring in Push-On Mode. The tyres had squealed a bit on one or two corners but I'd put that down to the hot road and possibly under-inflated tyres. Now that my attention had been drawn to the matter however I reflected that perhaps it wasn't wise to allow J-P to drive too fast. After all, it was likely that he'd never driven a car before this week.

"*Lentement* Jean-Pierre."

"*Pourquoi?*"

"You're going too fast."

"No. I good driver. Not too fast."

"Jean-Pierre" I said with some exasperation "you are not a good driver. You not have much experience."

"No. Is OK."

"Jean-Pierre. This is not a subject for debate. I am telling you. Slow down."

For a time J-P moderated his speed. Colleen relaxed back in her seat again and I made some mental notes. I would need to make a plan. Namely how to visit Ile-à-Vache without arousing Colleen's suspicions. With a bit of luck she might volunteer to stay behind in Jacmel while I push on to the west with Jean-Pierre. Maybe if she was a nervous passenger I could dissuade her from further adventure by telling her about the poor state of the roads. Indeed, as a Know-All she may already know about the appalling roads past Jacmel. This one we're on now is no great shakes, I thought, as we crashed through a pothole. I sensed unease behind me.

"He's going too fast again" called the voice from the back seat.

This is great. How did I manage to arrange this? Sandwiched between a boy racer and a backseat driver.

"*Lentement*, Jean-Pierre, *lentement*. Slow down. There's

potholes everywhere. Do you want to repair a puncture? Change the wheel?"

"OK, I can do that."

"And if you break the suspension. Can you fix that?"

This time I was rewarded with a sour expression. I wondered what sanctions I could impose if Jean-Pierre failed to comply with instructions. Perhaps I could deny him his family visit. Or maybe I could take over the driving. Better still...

I leant over into the back. "Do you have a driving licence?" I asked.

"Yes" she answered.

Presumably Jean-Pierre would understand this exchange.

I sat forward again and turned to my left. "Jean-Pierre" I began patiently. "I am very pleased to have you as guide and driver. But this is a very bad road and you have not driven on it before. Am I right?"

"I am good driver."

"Bearing in mind your lack of experience, perhaps you are. Nevertheless" I was beginning to lose patience with him "you don't know this road. This road very bad. Many corners. Because of mountains you cannot see road ahead. In front. There, see? What if car comes other way in middle of road? If we have crash you not see your family." Just a gentle hint.

"OK" said Jean-Pierre. He slowed the car noticeably and abandoned his 'racing driver' straight-armed driving position.

After a few more miles Colleen felt relaxed enough to start a conversation about Jacmel. "Do you know anything about the hotels in Jacmel?"

"No" I lied. "But there must be some."

"Why are you including Jacmel in your programme?"

"We're not necessarily including anything, except the Oloffson of course. That's why I have to check these places out. Why I went to Petionville and Boutilliers yesterday. Why I have to go to that Cap Haitien place you told me about."

This reply seemed satisfactory. We returned to individually admiring the scenery. J-P gradually increased his speed without Colleen noticing. Then we came up behind a slow-moving truck.

On a narrow, winding mountain road like this it would be sensible to slow slightly and change down a gear, if only to make sure the road ahead was clear, before beginning any manoeuvre. Any experienced driver would. Unfortunately that adjective did not apply to Jean-Pierre so without any reduction in speed we rapidly closed on the truck and then he pulled out to pass. We were approaching a bend to the left. He hadn't changed down so we pulled alongside the other vehicle at barely increased speed. This was a blind bend with an almost sheer rock face to our left and a vertiginous cliff on our right. I heard a sharp intake of breath from the rear seat. Inwardly I questioned the wisdom of the move too, there being insufficient clear road in front of the truck, but I considered it unwise to distract the driver by saying so.

Once we were slightly ahead and Jean-Pierre was cutting sharply in front of the truck in the finest Haitian fashion my tension was relieved slightly. There was nothing coming towards us. But we were travelling too fast. We were still in the middle of the road as we approached the bend and over to the right as we entered it. Normally that would have been fine but we were hurtling at speed and in the wrong gear. The tyres shrieked insanely, begging for mercy, as J-P hauled the wheel over to the left. The Beetle's body rolled over to the right. The rear wheels slid first right then left as he whipped the wheel round on opposite lock. Colleen and I were flung around in our seats. The left front wheel barely kissed the road. Then suddenly it gripped and flung the car over towards the cliff edge. I looked down on a near-vertical drop – quite dramatic on a normal outing but very scary in an out-of-control car. Jean-Pierre over-corrected and the VW slid back to the left side of the road heading for the rock face. He managed to avoid an impact by twisting the wheel viciously, threw the weight on to the Beetle's left side, and slalomed across the road. The car was rocking on its suspension and the rear wheels were scrabbling for grip. Controlling the rear in these conditions is always a problem with the heavy VW engine behind. Fortunately, perhaps instinctively, J-P had lifted his foot off the accelerator pedal and avoided the brakes. As we approached the next corner he crashed down through the gears, slowing us, and straightened up. He moved back into second gear then glanced across at me.

I was not impressed, though grateful. I looked into the back seat. Colleen had turned quite pale and was in no condition to take over the driving. I held up my hand to caution silence and turned back to Jean-Pierre. I hoped he'd learned a lesson. He did seem chastened.

"You don't listen do you Jean-Pierre? Can you imagine the pain to your mother if we'd gone over that cliff?"

"We're OK" he protested. "I control car. I drive slow now."

"Not now" I bellowed, as we were blasted by the horn of the truck we'd just passed and who was now up our arse. "Speed up now."

Jean-Pierre cast a glance at me then did as instructed. He moved smoothly through the gears and put some distance between us and the truck. Once I was sure we wouldn't be caught I spoke again.

"If another car had been coming" I pointed out "we wouldn't be here now. Your parents would be crying. Colleen's parents" I waved a hand at the back seat "would be crying."

That thought did seem to sink in but I was taking no chances.

"Listen carefully Jean-Pierre." I leaned towards him to emphasise the point. "If you start driving too fast again we will stop the car. You will get out. The girl" I vaguely waved to the back seat again "will drive." I hoped this reference to her sex would pose more of a threat to his machismo.

Jean-Pierre looked sick. Our near-death experience shocked him. He realised my threat was no bluff. I decided to rub it in.

"What will happen if you drive too fast again?" I asked.

Jean-Pierre glanced behind briefly. He hung his head. "The girl" he started. He decided to be respectful, to make sure I knew he understood. "Colleen will drive."

And, indeed, he drove quite well, and at a moderate pace, the rest of the way into Jacmel. He even paid full attention to the road and avoided most of the potholes.

Jacmel was like a ghost town. Beautiful old buildings in the French colonial style, reminiscent of the best of Guadeloupe or Martinique and blessed with the cast iron balconies normally associated with New Orleans. Probably brought over on French or American ships as ballast. Many of the buildings were painted or washed in attractive pastel colours. But there were very few people and hardly any vehicles. I seriously considered the possibility that there'd recently been a massacre or epidemic here. It provided a refreshing contrast to the homicidal traffic, frenzied turmoil, smog and filth of Port-au-Prince. Jacmel's few residents moved with a studied air and slow pace. Friendly too. They had time to smile at these *blancs*.

Jean-Pierre drove us to a café where we could all enjoy a drink and a light lunch but we'd barely left the car and sat down before three small children, aged between seven and ten, ran up to us and started chattering in Creole. They were making circular motions with the palms of their hands.

"They want to wash the car" Jean-Pierre said. "Let them." Apparently he thought that as the driver of the car, and on his home patch, he could give orders.

"That depends" I said. "How much do they want?"

He shrugged. "Maybe five gourd."

A dollar. That won't break the bank. "OK."

The kids enthusiastically set to work. Jean-Pierre stretched out, feeling important now.

After our refreshments we left the children to guard the nice clean car whilst we wandered the streets. I definitely like this place, though it offers little to attract tourists. The main hotel is a two-storey modern building on the very scrappy black sand beach. You certainly wouldn't come here to lie on that beach. Why build a hotel there? It was as empty as the town.

Dutifully we participated in the only known tourist activity, a visit to the coffee bean sorting warehouse. Even this was utilising only a small proportion of its capacity. The middle-aged ladies crouching amongst the beans treated us to very friendly smiles, but there was nothing else of interest.

"We visit my family now?"

"Good idea Jean-Pierre. Let's go."

We returned to the car and I handed the kids ten gourdes. "Five for guarding." All comfortably seated, off we drove on a road leading to the east of the town. Suddenly, after about two miles into the countryside, Jean-Pierre hauled the wheel over to the left and set off across a field. A muddy field.

"What's happening Jean-Pierre?"

"We go my family. Village this way."

"What was the point of having the car washed? Now it needs washing again."

He shrugged. "Is good for the children to have the money."

Soon a rough track appeared. We bounced along it until we spotted a lady, middle-aged but slim, strolling towards us. Jean-Pierre pulled up alongside her. They were obviously delighted to see each other. A longish conversation ensued, sometimes animated, with laughter on both sides. Eventually the lady waved goodbye to Colleen and me, J-P faced ahead and we continued.

"My schoolteacher" he explained. "She too much pleased I have good work as guide and chauffeur for tourist."

About a mile further on the track entered a forest, mainly of banana trees. Perhaps it was some sort of plantation. Very soon we saw scattered huts. Jean-Pierre pulled up outside one of them.

"We are here."

He led us inside the tiny thatched hut. I faced a couple, probably in their forties but they looked older. Most likely worn out by a lifetime's struggle. Both were thin and poorly dressed in very old faded and patched clothes. Jean-Pierre embraced them and there was excited chattering in Creole. I glanced around the hut. All it contained, apart from the five people now filling it, was a rough wooden table, a straight-backed chair made from wood and thatch and a basic bed constructed from the same materials.

Reunion complete, Jean-Pierre made the introductions. His mother motioned Colleen and me to sit on the only chair. I decided to take charge.

"Jean-Pierre. It is many months since you have seen your parents. We have not much time here. It is better for you to be with your parents. Colleen and I can take a walk."

Jean-Pierre communicated this to his parents. They nodded in agreement, then his father strode to the door and called. A small boy appeared.

"This my brother" said Jean-Pierre. "He will take you tour of the village."

The boy eagerly took instructions from his father, bowed to Colleen and me, then showed us the door. Puffing out his chest he led us on our excursion with a swaggering stride. Most of the huts were similar in design and construction – probably mud and wattle – to Jean-Pierre's family home. They were scattered apparently at random among the banana trees.

Our adventure had barely begun before we heard shouts of "*Blancs*" from several directions in the depths of the forest. As we approached the village store, which would have been a corner shop if there'd been a corner, small children appeared. A thin lady came out of the shop and stood in the doorway beaming. Our visit was a special occasion for the village, obviously a first and perhaps never to be repeated.

After indicating the shop and proudly explaining what it

was – as neither of us speak Creole we had to guess what the boy was telling us – J-P's brother led us into the thick of the banana forest. By now there were about eight children clustered excitedly around us. They chatted away to each other as they circled us and asked questions eagerly in Creole. I answered a couple in English, hoping they would understand that we didn't *sprechen* the lingo. Jean-Pierre's brother then addressed the other kids in a stern but friendly voice. This seemed to organise them into a crocodile behind us. More children joined until there were at least a dozen, all very excited but also very polite. Some of the braver ones approached us. "*Bonjour blancs*" were the only words we understood, but all the approaches were friendly and respectful. The bravest ones would touch us then pinch the skin of our wrists.

"What are they doing?" Colleen asked.

"They've never seen white people before" I said. "I've heard of this in Africa. The white skin is so strange to them they do this to confirm it's real or something. I'm not sure. We are the first white people they have ever seen."

"Have they heard of white people before?"

"I don't know, and I'm not sure we'll get a straight answer if we ask. But you heard them calling out "*Blancs*" and they addressed us as "*Bonjour blancs*" so presumably they know of the existence of white people."

"But there's no animosity. Don't they know their history?"

I laughed. "I doubt they know their history. I doubt they can read or write. They would have very little schooling. But you must have noticed that there is no animosity from the adults either. Haitians just don't have any resentment towards white people."

This certainly was a red letter day for the village. As the crocodile wound its way through the trees even adults could be seen at the doorways of their huts. Some waved. Jean-Pierre's little brother would be able to dine out on this for weeks. Metaphorically of course.

Chapter Thirteen

A Party From The Ministry

What was this staring at me? A face that was familiar but subtly changed. For the better. Not so long ago it had been pudgy and pale, nerdy even. But this relaxed self-confident person glowed with a light tan and seemed leaner.

Normally I'm not one for spending much time in front of the mirror. But I'd been on the road now for almost three weeks so I spent a few minutes inspecting myself. Hardly a radically changed man but, at least, a more experienced one. Travel broadens the mind, they say, but in my case it had also slimmed the body. With careful scrutiny, being as objective as possible, I could see the metamorphosis. The pinko-grey, chubby, bespectacled butt of the jokes at Sunstroke Holidays had disappeared somewhere. I stood sideways to catch my profile then turned back to full frontal mode.

I was no longer bespectacled. Of course, during the day in the almost constant bright sunlight I still wore my prescription sunglasses. But then most foreigners wore sunglasses so there was nothing remarkable about that and mine were aviator style – a timeless and neutral design. I don't remember why or when I stopped wearing my regular spectacles. It wasn't a conscious decision. They now seemed an encumbrance. My peripheral vision was improved without them and I always removed them for reading anyway. OK, distant objects might be blurred and my night vision is poor, but so what? I was more comfortable. And I still had the option of wearing them.

Now I stepped back three paces and studied my full-length form. I'd picked up some colour on the exposed parts of my body, hardened up my sinews slightly and lost weight. No sign of puppy fat now. Well, perhaps around the waist, but I always kept that covered. I'd also lost my pith helmet, either left behind at the Santos Pacot Guest House or forgotten in my panic to escape that whorehouse in Le Cap. This straw hat I'd purchased for a pittance in Port-au-Prince is slightly more appropriate for The Caribbean.

Mentally the changes felt more significant. My experiences in Jamaica – and more particularly Haiti – had already given me quite a different outlook on life. I felt more confident and outgoing. I was now not so sure I would enjoy the introverted life of a research student. Unless the research involved travelling in exotic countries. It may even be time for me to move away from home and find my own little pad, though I would need to get a better job in order to afford the rent. Maybe, if I looked around a bit, and now that I have some experience, I could find a travel company which would send me on more trips like this one.

All right. For starters I would stretch the time spent on this particular reconnaissance to the maximum I could get away with. I would need to watch the money though. Unsurprisingly my bosses had been parsimonious with their allocation of expenses. I was glad now that I'd conserved funds by staying in cheap guest houses and my four nights in Le Cap were particularly cheap thanks to Veronique's generosity.

Fortunately from now on my accommodation should be very cheap or even free. The company was known in these islands. It was extremely likely that I would be offered complimentary rooms.

In our fledgling Caribbean programme Sunstroke already featured Barbados, Saint Lucia, Tobago and Grenada. The first two are obvious choices. They are well-established major tourist destinations with regular scheduled flights and occasional charters. After much discussion the board had selected the other two precisely because few other companies offered holidays there. And here in Grenada the beaches were not lined with bland concrete multi-storey blocks teeming with regimented sun-worshippers. In fact there was only one hotel which broadly fitted that description and it wasn't multi-storey. Almost all the others were small – less than fifty rooms – and housed their guests in cottages or bungalows, usually on or very near the beach.

Of those four islands Barbados was the only one which retained any pirate connections so I decided not to bother visiting Tobago or Saint Lucia. And Grenada was only of interest to me because of the political situation. Officially I was checking that the country was still safe for tourists.

I remember the day I suggested Island Hopping holidays to Stuart Arrowsmith. Initially he wasn't keen. It sounded too much like hard work.

"Wally" he answered in his usual exasperated tone "you do realise that two-centre holidays mean twice as much work don't you?"

"Not really" I told him. "OK, two-centre is a lot more work than a single-centre, but four islands wouldn't involve much more work than two. And you keep complaining that we don't have a USP. This would give us an edge over the competition."

"What kind of punter wants to island-hop Wally?"

"People who want more than just the cheapest price" I told him. "People who want to do more than just lie on a beach. People who want a Caribbean experience."

"Can't they do that in Barbados?"

"All the islands are different. There's that smelly volcano in Saint Lucia and waterfalls with mountain hikes in Grenada. Some great sailing up The Grenadines. And nobody else is doing island hopping."

"There's probably a good reason for that. How are you

going to get them between the islands? Are there boats?"

"No. Only in The Grenadines. We would fly everyone into Barbados, like we do now, on Coconut Airways, then onwards with LIAT."

"LIAT?"

"It's the local Eastern Caribbean airline." Typical. He's supposed to be Operations Director and he's never heard of LIAT. I supplied the detail. "Their initials stand for 'Leave Island Any Time', 'Luggage In Another Terminal' or, my favourite, 'Late If A Tall'."

Arrowsmith glanced at me as if he suspected I was joking.

"OK" he said. "Put it in writing and I'll take it up with the board."

As I landed at Pearls Airport that afternoon I saw for myself why hardly any tour operators included Grenada in their brochures.

This tiny airport cannot cater for long range jets so that ruled out the major companies. Their customers like to board at Luton, Gatwick or Manchester and fly direct to their final destination. In addition there was a dearth of resort-style accommodation. Just the one beachfront hotel constructed of the familiar whitewashed concrete with a pool and entertainment facilities. Furthermore there was only a smattering of apartments suitable for self-catering customers. "Not enough beds" was the verdict of the big boys.

My arrival in Grenada almost equalled my first sight of Haiti. We droned through a bright afternoon without a cloud in the azure sky. Our flimsy LIAT aircraft fluttered low over the sea, passing a slumbering Carriacou in the distance to our right, then approached the airstrip from the east. It skirted the waterfront township and banked towards the brief runway. I couldn't be sure but on the final descent I thought I spotted anti-aircraft guns located on the periphery of the airport. I saw cattle grazing a few feet from the tarmac. Our plane touched down comfortably and taxied past a Cuban aircraft parked on the apron. As we came to a stop I noticed a group of soldiers in battledress flaunting Kalashnikov assault rifles. Ah. These would be members of the Grenadian People's Revolutionary Army.

The Immigration Officer was meticulous, polite and pretty speedy with me though not so friendly with many of the others. Customs were far more thorough. They rifled through my bags with the greatest care, paying extra attention to the side pockets and giving my camera a minute inspection. I was asked to remove the lens. Then they looked through it and inside the camera. What were they looking for? When I asked them one officer just glared at me whilst the other ignored me and continued searching. Guns, I found out later. OK, I know you can't hide a gun inside a camera, but there might have been a secret message hidden there. Or a dum-dum bullet. Apparently the authorities were concerned that mercenaries in the pay of 'counter-revolutionaries' might try to sneak in and depose the government by force. I thought then, and still believe now, they were overreacting. The PRA was a thousand strong, Cuban trained and armed, and there was also a volunteer militia stationed throughout the country.

I stepped outside the tiny terminal building, just a shack, into brilliant sunshine and one of the waiting taxis. I noticed a truck-bus, not dissimilar to a Haitian *tap-tap*, among the few parked vehicles. Yeah, there are parallels, I thought. Politically Grenada had been like a watered-down Haiti for many years.

The people of both nations suffered under the oppressive regime of a democratically-elected dictator. Grenada's equivalent of Papa Doc was Sir Eric Gairy. His Mongoose Gang of thugs was the local version of the *Tontons Macoutes*. But now there was one major difference. In 1979, whilst Gairy was away lecturing the United Nations on the subject of UFOs, the revolutionary socialist New Jewel Movement took command of his country.

Pearls Airport is on the east coast of Grenada near the small town of Grenville. That is the opposite side of the island from the capital, the best beaches and the tourist hotels. Very inconvenient. In between are the mountains.

My taxi driver rocketed along the narrow, twisting, hilly, potholed road like a demented rally driver. That doesn't mean that we were motoring at an international rally pace. The poor condition of Grenada's roads and the limitations of his vehicle restricted us to an absolute top speed of 40 mph – and then only on the relatively straight and flat or downhill stretches. He swerved and zigzagged to miss most of the potholes using the full width of the road and only retreated to the left when oncoming traffic forced him to. He wrenched the steering wheel from lock to lock and the suspension took a pummelling. Cars don't reach old age in Grenada.

"An hour just to drive across the island" I commented. "It's only about twelve miles wide."

"Twelve mile for de crow. At least twenny mile for we on dis road" said the driver. "And it tek our han' alf for de touris' dem. Dey get fright if I drive like dis. An our de record man. I de best driver."

Looking out I could see occasional small settlements and isolated houses, usually built close to the road. Frequently there were little children playing at the roadside, cocks strutting and hens pecking at the ground, all oblivious to our rapidly approaching vehicle. My driver made no attempt to moderate our speed. More than once we missed a child or a hen by a slim margin.

"Shouldn't we slow down in the villages?" I asked.

"Dis de road man. It for dem to look."

My question had no effect on his driving. Shortly afterwards we rapidly approached a mother hen leading a line of three tiny yellow chicks across our path. She *was* looking. She quickly scuttled across to the other side, her charges following in panic as we rocketed past.

The island was lush everywhere. I realised that most of the agriculture would be subsistence farming as it was too hilly for large scale cultivation. The people looked very poor and the dwellings humble. We passed a couple of large billboards brashly proclaiming Soviet-style propaganda. One featured a painted image of the Prime Minister, his clenched fist thrusting into the air, and a dreadlocked pistol-wielding militiaman, one saviour each side of the slogan 'IT TAKES A REVOLUTION TO MAKE A SOLUTION'. Whatever that was supposed to mean. Another promoted the message 'WOMEN EQUAL IN PRODUCTION AND DEFENCE' alongside a picture of a woman scissoring the air with her fists.

Eventually the taxi delivered me, without killing any children or hens, to Ross Point Inn. This was the smallest and least touristy hotel Sunstroke featured. It was renowned for the quality of its food. I was allocated a room with a great view of Saint George's, Grenada's picturesque capital. Actually the view was from the well-kept gardens outside the room but as I intended strolling through permanently-open French windows and down the three steps at every available opportunity I thought of them as my gardens and therefore part of my room. That was comfortably but simply furnished with largish twin beds, a dressing table and chair, plenty of wardrobe space and a very pleasant bathroom. Satisfactory accommodation for anyone, but sheer luxury compared to the hostelries I'd patronised in Haiti and Jamaica.

Four hours later, somewhat refreshed and satisfied with my reflection in the mirror, I set off for the restaurant. As I strolled over there I spotted the owner. He was standing on a terrace overlooking the impressive gates and the main road. I interrupted my journey and joined him.

"There's a party from the ministry coming for dinner tonight" Mr Hopkin informed me. He shifted a little uneasily.

"Which ministry?"

"The Finance Ministry."

"Oh, that'll be Bernard Coard then" I said. Bernard Coard was the Minister of Finance and Deputy Prime Minister. Mr Hopkin cast a sideways glance at me and suddenly seemed very nervous. Strange. He must know who the Minister is. How could the mere mention of the man's name cause such a reaction?

We chatted for a few minutes. After I'd expressed my satisfaction with the room I mentioned my transitory acquaintance with Mr Coard. Then three cars entered the drive at some speed. They pulled up sharply between the terrace and the bar. Seven armed men, four of them uniformed soldiers and the others dressed in civilian clothes, their opened jackets revealing holstered pistols, alighted from the first and last cars and looked around. Then Bernard Coard and two white people, a man and a woman, got out of the middle car and headed for the bar.

This dramatic arrival did nothing to quell Mr Hopkin's nervousness. We watched Mr Coard waddling over to the bar, flanked by his guests, ignoring his host for the evening. The plain clothes bodyguards accompanied the VIPs whilst the soldiers dispersed around the hotel.

The restaurant was empty except for a middle-aged couple to my right. I'd been seated for about thirty minutes and had just started eating when the VIP party arrived. They were ushered to the opposite side of the restaurant and took their seats with Bernard Coard in the middle. There was sufficient light for me to guess that the Minister's guests were Russian but I was too far away to hear any of their conversation. Judging by the body language and frequent outbursts of laughter there was probably nothing confidential discussed anyway. I remembered that Coard rather fancied himself as a raconteur and was fond of making heavy-handed jokes, the kind that Russians would appreciate. My mind flashed back to the episode in London.

I'd been nominated by Sunstroke Holidays to attend a seminar chaired by Bernard Coard and held in a

Knightsbridge hotel. Sunstroke's directors had guessed, correctly, that this would not be the usual type of cocktail party function hosted by tourist boards where the booze flows freely all evening. For a start this seminar would be held in the afternoon. Coffee, rather than rum punch, was likely to be the refreshment provided. Worse, the subjects under discussion were likely to be political. Boring. So send Wally.

I selected a seat close to the door and scanned the room. All the participants were suited businessmen of various ages except for two wearing tweed jackets and sporting red ties. I presumed those were directors of tour operators who specialised in holidays to communist countries. I discovered over coffee that I was right. Strangely they didn't sit together or speak to each other apart from a brief "Good Afternoon". One was a bluff Yorkshireman who was congenial enough to me. He was apparently under the impression that I shared his political stance. It didn't occur to him that I didn't have to be a communist – or even a socialist – to support the revolution.

All of the assembled three dozen or so represented companies who traded with Grenada. The largest group, perhaps six men, was from Plessey, the company engaged in providing electronic and other equipment for the new airport project at Point Salines.

Bernard Coard presented himself as a rather jolly fellow and had me completely fooled. He expounded his heavy-handed jokes in an expansive manner as if he assumed his audience was sympathetic.

"We are criticised for giving the people choice. 'At the supermarket in Grand Anse there are three kinds of jam' our critics claim. 'This is not what we expect in a socialist state'. I ask them why not? If capitalists can have three kinds of jam then socialists can too. Why not jam today? Why wait for tomorrow?"

He was at his most expansive on the subject of tourism. "I think everyone who comes to Grenada for a holiday should be given a medal" he began. "First they have a flight of nine or ten hours to Barbados or – even worse – to Trinidad. And that was probably delayed for a couple of hours." Pause for laughter. None came.

"They may need to overnight there, but let's say they don't. Say, by some miracle, their flight's on time and they can connect the same day. They have an uncomfortable flight for 45 minutes in a small propeller plane in the dark. Then they have a further hour and a half, in pitch darkness, being bounced over that dreadful mountain road to get to their hotel. By the time they arrive they need a holiday!"

Still no laughter but this time there were mutterings of agreement and a couple of nods. His audience knew exactly what he was talking about.

"That's why we need this new airport. We have people here from Plessey who can tell you that Reagan is talking crap." Some nods from the Plessey contingent. "We need an airport that can handle direct flights from the USA and Europe."

Somebody, not one of the travel industry representatives, asked him what sort of tourist they, the government of a communist state, were expecting to welcome when the new airport was functioning.

"I can tell you what we don't want." Misjudging completely the tour operator delegates present he continued "We don't want what I call 'The Cheese and Biscuits Brigade'. People who think they are helping the socialist revolution by coming here but don't spend any money. They come with their rucksacks, stay in the cheapest guest houses, never go to restaurants and enjoy our wonderful beaches and beautiful scenery without paying for it." He was warming up now. "We want the rich tourists. People who are going to stay in our top hotels – and we have many fine hotels, as you should know – eat in our best restaurants and book excursions with local tour companies."

Although surprised I could see what he was driving at. Sunstroke Holidays mainly featured mid-range properties but we did offer two of the island's top hotels. We didn't feature guest houses and had no plans to. There was no money in it. I assumed that the Red Ties didn't offer guest house accommodation either, but specialising as they did in communist countries they would obviously attract 'people who think they are helping the socialist revolution by coming here.' I couldn't quite see why Coard needed to labour that point.

Eventually questions were invited. One of the Plessey men asked "When are you going to hold elections?"

Mr Coard spread his arms. "You people are always asking this. Do you think elections will solve anything? We took over a country where the economy and agriculture were devastated by Gairy, quite apart from the money he stole. We have consistently improved the economy and the situation of the Grenadian people as even the capitalist banks agree." He was referring to The World Bank and The International Monetary Fund. "We will hold elections when the time is right."

I was reflecting on all of this as I finished my dinner and covertly watched the Finance Minister entertaining his guests. Why Russians? Surely they are getting all the help they need from Cuba?

I quit the restaurant whilst Coard was in full flow. Turning sharp left in the gardens to take the steps to my room in a short cut I stumbled over someone I hadn't seen sitting on the bottom step. A combination of the pitch black night, no lights and no spectacles. This person leapt up and saluted. It was one of the uniformed soldiers. "Goodnight sir" he said.

The next morning at breakfast Mr Hopkin strolled over to me. "Did you hear what they were talking about?" he asked.

"No, too far away. But they weren't talking business anyway. Coard was cracking jokes and the Russians seemed keen to laugh. Obviously they want something."

"They want something Bishop doesn't want to give them."

"So they think they can get it from Coard?"

"There's a split. A big power battle going on at the moment. The doctrinaire hardliners, led by Coard, who's staying in the background although everyone knows he's calling the shots, are trying to oust Bishop. Bishop is more moderate. People think he really cares about them. But no-one likes Coard and they all hate his wife, Phyllis." Mr Hopkin leant over and spoke quietly. "Some call her Syphilis."

"What's Bishop doing about it?"

"He's trying to fight back but Coard's group is too strong."

"Why isn't Coard talking to the Cubans then? They're supplying most of the aid and military hardware."

"Fidel Castro and Maurice Bishop are really close. They get on very well together. So Coard's been cosying up to the Russians and they think that Bishop's too soft. There's even been suggestions that Bishop wants to call elections!" Mr Hopkin accompanied that last statement with an expression of mock severity.

The Soviet leaders disapproved of multi-party elections. In 1983 the Soviet Union was governed by doctrinaire totalitarians who had no time for democracy. In addition they were aggressively imperialist.

"Another thing" I said. "Last night when I went back to my room I tripped over one of the soldiers. Why was he on my steps? To protect me from burglars?"

Mr Hopkin laughed. "No. From the steps to your room there's a really good view of the Prime Minister's residence. He was stationed there to see how long the lights were on in the office."

It appeared to me that the Prime Minister was under siege. I couldn't imagine our Chancellor of the Exchequer going to such lengths to depose Margaret Thatcher.

Chapter Fourteen

Dredged Out Of The Sea

An uneasiness, an unspoken fear, hovered over the island like an invisible mist. Perhaps there were hints of this on my arrival – the anti-aircraft battery I spotted at the airport and the patrolling Kalashnikov-equipped soldiers. The efficiency with which they searched my baggage. Quite a contrast with Haiti and Jamaica.

I don't recall seeing soldiers at Port-au-Prince airport on my arrival there. When I did see a pair loitering outside the Presidential Palace I noticed that they were armed with elderly bolt-action rifles and were ill-disciplined. One was leaning against the wall. Presumably they were on guard duty but that didn't prevent one of them summoning me. He smiled as I obediently sauntered across. Hauling himself almost erect he made a request.

"Take my picture."

"*Ne pas automatique*. Not Polaroid" I protested, apologetically waving my camera. In any event I wasn't sure whether photographing soldiers was considered an offence in this country. Perhaps this was a 'military installation'.

"OK. No problem. Take my picture."

The soldier was anxious to impress his colleague. I can speak English, he seemed to be saying. See how this tourist is taking my picture. His colleague did seem a little discomfited so I photographed him too, to cheer him up.

I don't imagine that pair would be much use in the event of an assault on the palace by well-trained commandos armed with modern automatic weapons. Perhaps their main duty was to ensure that everyone within sight of the Presidential Residence stood to attention at dusk.

I was photographing *Le Marron Inconnu*, the impressive statue of the freed slave blowing a call to arms through a conch shell, when I heard the sound of a bugle from the palace grounds. A soundtrack for the statue I reflected wryly. Jean-Pierre grabbed my arm, eased me upright and bade me be still. As I glanced around I noticed that all of the city within sight had come to a standstill. Pedestrians stopped dead in their tracks. Motorists ground to a halt and vacated their vehicles to stand ramrod-straight at attention alongside. Even the two sentries were attempting to emulate the guards outside Buckingham Palace. The whole effect was of a three-dimensional mural. The reason? It was dusk and the national flag was being lowered.

In all my time in Haiti this was the only occasion when the authorities were accorded any respect. Even when *Ebenezer* was halted at a road block shortly after leaving Cap Haitien the locals displayed no fear. Two police officers boarded the bus to inspect papers and possibly to search for known troublemakers. Initially they were jeered, but when they discovered a white teenager who protested, in apparently authentic Creole, that he was Haitian the laughter and good humour were general. The policemen left the vehicle without beating or arresting any of the passengers and in an atmosphere of universal friendliness. This, remember, was in the blood-soaked land of Voodoo and savage repression.

Quite a contrast here in Grenada, nominally a democratic member of The Commonwealth. I noticed a widespread uneasiness. People seemed cowed. There was none of the relaxed boisterousness of Jamaica or anarchy of Haiti. Nobody hustled me or even attempted to speak with me.

Whilst I hadn't yet seen elsewhere the fear that Mr Hopkin exhibited at the mere mention of the Deputy Prime Minister's name it was clear that dark clouds of foreboding loomed over this tiny nation. Even within the comfortable ambience of this restaurant sparse sentences spoken with caution replaced the optimistic speech rhythms and outbursts of laughter which I now associated with The Caribbean.

I'd called in to see Beryl at her office in town. Beryl was a slightly-built Canadian in her thirties who lived in Grenada and acted as the local representative for a number of tour companies including Sunstroke Holidays. She took me to Rudolf's, a nice little restaurant just off The Carenage popular with office staff and the middle classes. We were chatting over coffee.

"I've got a car for three days" I said "from Mr Lewis. He seems to be struggling a bit."

"He's a Gairy man. His son's still locked up I think."

"What for? They don't lock people up for political dissent do they?"

"Not officially. If they were in The Mongoose Gang, then some of them were jailed for the crimes they committed. Since then anyone who was destabilising the country – in their view – or otherwise causing trouble would be imprisoned. But now it's getting serious. They've just put Maurice Bishop under house arrest."

"The Prime Minister? How can they do that?"

Beryl was expressionless except for a stony stare. "The Party's been having meetings for days. It's a power struggle. Really it's Bernard Coard behind the scenes. He's a very clever man, but he stays out of all the discussions. Just turns up for crucial votes."

"I saw him a couple of days ago. At dinner. With two Russians."

Beryl nodded. "People don't like that. They don't like the Cubans much, though they are grateful for the new airport. But nobody likes the Russians."

We concentrated on our coffees and our thoughts for a minute. Then Beryl asked "How's the car?"

"Good. It's a Honda, nearly new. Only problem is the rear tyres are bald. Front tyres are brand new."

"He has to do that" Beryl informed me over her coffee cup. "Sometimes there are problems getting spares and tyres. So he's put two of the new tyres on one of his old cars."

"It'll be fine in the dry but in the wet the back'll be all over the place."

"Are you going up into the hills?"

"Probably."

"It always seems to be wet up there. Be careful."

I remembered my taxi ride from the airport. Brilliant sunshine at Pearls and for the first few miles, brilliant sunshine as we descended to town and Ross Point Inn. Drizzly with low-flying cloud in the mountains.

Beryl was studying me intently. Perhaps she was weighing me up, wondering whether I was up to the job. Or just concerned for my safety.

"Don't stay too long Morgan. Some bad things are going to be happening here. You don't want to get caught up in it."

But I did want to be caught up in it. History was my subject and politics my interest. I didn't want to miss out when history was being made. But I might need an excuse to stay longer.

"I'm going to Carriacou in a few days" I said. "Apparently it's very quiet there. Almost like a desert island. Some of our clients might like that."

"Good idea." Beryl finished her coffee. "You can see everything there in a day. Half a day even."

"Then I might take a look at the Grenadine islands."

"They belong to Saint Vincent of course, though you can almost swim over to Union from Carriacou. Maybe you could travel all the way up and fly to Barbados from Saint Vincent." I could read her mind. That will keep him out of harm's way.

A tallish, slim, Latino-looking man in his late twenties

glided over to our table. Beryl saw him coming. "This is Roberto. Roberto, meet Morgan. He's with Sunstroke Holidays."

"Pleased to meet you" we both said, almost in stereo. Roberto laughed. "What do you do there?" he asked.

"Currently I'm Section Leader for Greece, but I'm hoping that after this trip they'll transfer me to the Caribbean department."

"So why are you here, if you don't mind me asking" cooed Roberto. "This is not Greece."

"I got on the wrong plane" I answered, remembering someone who almost did that in Athens. "No, that's a joke. They needed someone to research a new type of programme we're planning to do and they thought I was the best person to send."

"Ooh, I say. Sounds exciting. What sort of programme?"

Theatrically I put my finger to my lips. "Sorry. That's hush-hush. Can't say. Beryl here might tell our competitors."

"You wouldn't do that would you Beryl?" Roberto asked teasingly.

"Well, you never know. Depends what's in it for me" she replied. She turned her attention back to me. "Roberto is with the Cubans."

"Oh" I said. "Are you Cuban then? You speak very good English."

"I'm the interpreter. Which is why I have to rush off. Just wanted to say Hi. Where are you staying?"

"Ross Point Inn."

"Very nice. Maybe I'll pop in and see you later. Bye bye. Bye Beryl."

As Roberto ambled towards the door I turned to Beryl. I leant forward and spoke quietly.

"He's, er, a bit camp isn't he?"

"He's gay" Beryl answered in a tone which terminated that subject of discussion.

I decided that I must see the new airport before the

political situation boiled over. I'd heard parts of US President Reagan's speech on the radio. Now I wanted to check it out myself. I let Beryl return to her office and set off in my nice new red Honda for Point Salines.

Earlier that year, March or April if I remember correctly, I'd also read the text of that infamous speech. According to Reagan's speechwriters the Cubans, for years the bogeymen of US propaganda, were building a military airport in the southwest corner of Grenada. It would have a 10,000 foot runway and it would be a 'staging post' for Cuban and/or Soviet aggression in the hemisphere. There would also be bunkers for long-range missiles secreted in the hills. All this was in addition to the large contingent of Cuban troops already stationed here. Allegedly. Now I would take this opportunity to see for myself.

After you pass through the Grand Anse area you come to the roundabout at the Sugar Mill. You turn right for the airport. There a group of four small children were waving frantically at me as I made the turn. I stopped.

"Airport?" the biggest one, presumably their leader, asked.

"Yes."

"We come?" asked a little girl excitedly.

"Sure. Get in."

Obviously they'd travelled in cars before. Hauling the door open and animatedly chattering they all clambered on to the rear seat. The last one in pulled the door shut using both hands. I checked to see that it was properly secured before proceeding.

As I drove towards Point Salines the road degenerated into a rough unsurfaced track, obviously churned up by the large trucks and construction vehicles being used by the Cuban workers. No sign of any airport but this had to be the right road. Then up ahead we saw the track was blocked by a bright yellow JCB-type excavator. I halted. Almost immediately a smiling middle-aged Latino man in a hard hat, which he lifted to acknowledge me, arrived and climbed up into the driving seat. Whilst I waited for him to remove his vehicle I turned around and chatted to the children.

"You been here before?"

"Ev'ry month. To see how de airport comin'" their spokesman, a child of ten or less, answered. The others were playfully pushing each other around, trying to get comfortable in the confined space. As the excavator backed off the track into a pile of dirt I waved to its driver, engaged gear and continued into the airport area. There was a small hillock, a vantage point, just a few hundred yards from the end of the runway. I stopped here and got out of the car.

"We not dere yet!" a little voice called out.

"I know. Hang on. I want to look from here."

The hillock gave a fair overview. There was the runway which looked completed. To its right was a large terminal building separated by an apron which I judged large enough for half a dozen passenger aircraft. The control tower was built into the side of a hill. There was a cluster of temporary buildings, probably workshops for the construction teams. I could see where the access road and parking would most likely be situated. What I couldn't see, because they didn't exist, were dispersal hardstands for military aircraft, semi-submerged bunkers or even hangars. There was no sign of anti-aircraft defences.

I wasn't surprised. With a US company involved at an early stage of the construction, and the British electronics firm Plessey still working there, it would have been impossible to hide any military intent. US intelligence agencies didn't need satellite surveillance. The British government could insert a spy amongst the Plessey staff and anyone could drive into the site just as I was doing now. I resumed my seat in the car, drove down to the terminal building and stopped outside. The rear doors were flung open and my passengers tumbled out with shouts and some playful pushing.

I engaged the handbrake, switched off the engine, stepped out of the car, closed all the doors and walked across to the building. Apart from some fitting to be done it looked finished. This end was quite obviously designed for Departures, then up here, walking along, this would be Arrivals. Peering through tinted glass picture windows I could see an area obviously intended to be the Customs Hall. I stood back to get an overall view. It appeared they were even making provision for a restaurant upstairs.

I strolled back to the car. Better have a drive around everywhere, make sure there's no hidden bunkers. Taking a close look at the nearby hill I could confirm that the control tower was the only structure there apart from some cabins, but those were evidently provided to house some of the Cuban workforce. Who were older than I expected. The majority were aged between 30 and 50 with more than half over 40. They seemed friendly too. A few waved at me and some called out. They didn't speak English so I had to fall back on my favourite Spanish phrase.

"*No hablo español*" I shouted.

Nobody seemed concerned that I was taking pictures. Eventually I ended up near the other end of the runway, down by the sea, which lapped aggressively at the rocks as if resentful of this human intrusion. I spotted a black guy wearing a different uniform so perhaps, I thought, this chap is Grenadian, a government employee. I left the car and ambled over to him.

"It's a long enough runway" I said.

"9,000 feet."

"Slightly shorter than Reagan was claiming."

A disgusted grunt. "Dat all lies man. Dem Yankees, dey not like what Maurice doin' for we."

"It looks like you've had to build it partly on reclaimed land."

"Dat right man. We haveta mek up de lan' wid stuff we tek outa de sea." As he said this the man swivelled his body and indicated the runway with his right arm. Some of his words were stolen by the breeze and this theft, combined with the heavy accent, made his answer barely comprehensible. I repeated the question.

"I see. So part of this is reclaimed land?"

"Yeh man. Dey level off wid de tractor over dere, see, and use dat, but still dem need more from de water dere. But not all dem can use. See dat big heap dere?" he asked, pointing to a pile of mixed rubble about a hundred yards away. "Dey can't use any dat. Jus' garbage."

"So what will they do with it?"

The man shrugged. "I guess dey jus' trow it back in de sea."

The pile of rubble dredged out of the sea was an easy walk away so I strolled over there. Most of it appeared to be soil and pebbles that for some reason unknown to me was unsuitable but the rest was assorted debris. Bits of dead trees and planks of wood, maybe rotting ship's timbers. One long rounded piece could have been part of a mast. Another fragment looked suspiciously like part of a bowsprit bearing a vessel's name.

The researcher and historian in me was immediately interested so I reached over and pulled it out. A chunk broke off in my hand but I got it close enough to read. This was not easy as lumps had rotted and broken off. The lettering was damaged. The original paint was long gone. First I took a photograph, just in case. Then I crouched next to it. Eventually I deciphered the words. *Nuestra Señora de las Nueces Variadas*. That name was familiar to me but I couldn't place the context.

I turned around and saw that the Grenadian official was still within earshot. "Excuse me" I yelled. "Can I have this?"

The man raised his hands. "It all trash. Tek anyting you want."

"Thank you" I yelled back.

Problem was, it appeared to be too long to fit into the boot of my little Honda. I started to pull it out anyway but the wood was so rotten it broke up. Problem solved. I would load it in pieces. Three journeys were sufficient to carry most of it to the car. Yep, I'll admit it. I'm a bit of a tosser. If I was intelligent I would have driven the car to the rubbish pile. That occurred to me as I was completing the final journey.

Chapter Fifteen

Two Could Play

Ross Point Inn, as my hotel was known until the Americans acquired it, is situated on a bluff half a mile north of Grand Anse in a great strategic position with fine views of picturesque St George's. It was blessed with pleasant gardens of large lawns, well-tended flower beds and tropical trees. The rooms were comfortable and the food excellent. There was only one problem.

It is not on the beach. There is a steep and twisty path down to the sea, but the scrappy little stretch of sand there was not to my taste. I fancied a spell of relaxation on the famous mile-long Grand Anse beach, preceded by some gentle sea bathing. Accordingly I'd packed my swimming trunks, towel and Hawaiian Tropic in a bag which rested on the front passenger seat of the Honda.

So, as planned, on my return from the new airport development I stopped by The Flamboyant Cottages. I parked by the office and entered. The receptionist buzzed through to Jim Needham, the owner, who lived slightly higher up the hill. Jim came to the front of his balcony and called down.

"Morgan! Come on up. I'm just having drinks with some people here."

He met me at the door. Jim was a big man, American, a large frame, slightly desiccated like most expats but still obviously strong and fit in spite of his age, which must have been over 70. He favoured a crewcut but his head was not quite shorn like the Marines. I was reminded of the Green Berets. Apparently the hunting, fishing, hard-drinking type. I fondly imagined that he would have been a good companion for Ernest Hemingway.

"These are some people staying on the island came to look at my place" he announced as he ushered me inside.

Jim's home was built to the same common design as the rest of his cottages. Bedrooms with *en suite* bathrooms were situated at both ends. These sandwiched a substantial living and dining space, including an open-plan kitchen. A broad balcony facing Grand Anse Beach and the sea ran the length of the cottage. St George's was just about visible in the distance.

I strode straight through the living/dining room to the balcony where three people were relaxing. I nodded to them as I stepped up to the handrail. The view was inspiring. A foreground of variegated green, the grassy tree-covered hill sloping down to the beach, a shimmering turquoise sea, a pristine ribbon of white sand shaded by gently swaying palms. The distant capital cosseted by heat haze.

"This is where they take the pictures from" I said.

"Yeah, people are always coming up here" drawled Jim. "Let me introduce you. This is George and Mildred." He indicated a seated elderly couple. "They're fixing to retire here. And this is Sean who's – well I don't know what he's doing. I'll let him tell you himself. What are you drinking?"

"Oh, just a cold beer thanks Jim."

I bent down to shake hands with the oldtimers then straightened up and faced the other guest. Sean was a fit-looking man of medium height and build in his late twenties, probably British or Irish. He was casually yet smartly dressed in beige tailored shorts and white polo shirt. He flashed me a smile as we shook hands.

"So what are you doing here?" he asked. No trace of an accent.

"Obviously Jim hasn't told you" I began. I was

interrupted by my host returning with the beer. He chipped in with "I thought I'd leave that to you. Sean's a bit secretive about his business so I don't tell him anyone else's."

We both stood and appraised Sean, beers in hand.

"Maybe I'm a spy" Sean suggested.

"Mebbe you are" agreed Jim. "There's sure plenny of 'em around these days. D'you know who you're spying for?"

Sean laughed. "I said maybe."

It was Jim's turn to laugh. "You know what they say bout women? They rarely say Yes. When they say No they mean Mebbe and when they say Mebbe they mean Yes."

Everyone laughed. It must have been the effect of the beer. George had a question. "What about those who do say yes?"

"They're jus' nymphomaniacs" said Jim.

George chuckled at this, whilst Mildred snorted into her drink – whether out of amusement or disgust wasn't clear.

"It's the opposite with the Japanese apparently" I said. "They never say No. When they say Yes they mean Maybe and when they say Maybe they mean No."

Nobody laughed. They sipped their beers and ruminated. Then Sean returned to his questioning. "You still haven't told us what you are doing here."

I told him.

"But what about you?" I asked. I sensed the three Americans were listening keenly for an answer.

"In a way" Sean said "I'm doing the same as you. Research."

Obvious next question. "What kind of research?"

"I work for a chemical company – one of the smaller ones, you won't have heard of it – and we've been asked to quote for supplying Grenada. You know, fertilizers, growth-inducing products and so on. So they've sent me here to check the soil, other agricultural conditions, the types of farms, you know, private smallholdings, co-ops and the like, crops they grow and, of course, the political situation. Which doesn't look too good at the moment, frankly."

That's right. Blind us with science and irrelevant detail.

"What will you be reporting to your company?" I asked.

"Don't know yet" replied Sean. "It depends how things pan out."

"I meant regarding agricultural conditions, types of crops etc."

"Oh, that's coming along. I'm about two-thirds of the way through that."

So maybe Jim's assessment of this character wasn't too wide of the mark. I took a swig of my beer then turned to the elderly couple. George was dressed in khaki long pants, sandals and a check short-sleeved shirt. He was balancing his beer on a generous midriff, hand loosely guarding it. Mildred favoured brightly-coloured polyester garments, or maybe they were Crimplene.

"So you're staying here?" I asked them.

"No, we're down the road there at Blue Horizons" said George. "We've just come up here to see Jim."

Mildred leaned forward. "We're thinking of buying one of the cottages."

I turned to Jim. "I thought you were looking to sell the whole place Jim?"

"Sure, though folks ain't exactly standin' in line to buy hotels in Grenada right now." He addressed the couple. "I wanna get back to The States and get some hunten' done before I get too old furrit." He leant back and laughed as if he believed the day he was too old for it he'd be dead. "But you know Morgan, I've already sold a coupla cottages privately to people who wanna live here."

I nodded. I knew that Beryl lived in one. I turned back to George and Mildred. "So you're thinking of retiring here."

"We're already retired" said Mildred "but we don't like how things are back home and the climate's better here."

"We'd prefer Cuba" George pronounced, as if proudly presenting his credentials "but they won't pay our pensions there."

Wow! I expect that news went down like a lead balloon with Jim, who's bound to be a Reaganite. I tried to check out of the corner of my eye for a reaction from that direction. None. Obviously Jim already knew. And he could afford to be diplomatic if he might get a sale at the end of it. On the other hand, wasn't Hemingway fond of Cuba? He lived there for a couple of years after the revolution. Friendly with Fidel Castro too, allegedly.

Then again it was precisely his presumed Reaganite sympathies which would account for Jim's forbearance. At that time listening was more productive than speaking. I'd already heard from several sources that Grenada and the surrounding islands had been crawling with spies for some time. Every country with interests here wanted to know how the internecine battles within the ruling New Jewel Movement were progressing.

Few people know that Cuba and The Soviet Union sometimes disagreed over foreign policy. For example, the Russians objected to Cuba's military involvement in Angola. But it suited both those countries, and even more so The United States, to pretend that Cuba and The Soviet Union were inextricably linked in brotherhood. If The White House and its tame media could declare Cuba to be a client state of the USSR then the American public could be frightened into believing that the oppressive military power of The Soviet Union was loitering on their doorstep.

What intelligence might this Sean be hoping to gather?

I was soon to discover that during the last few days Maurice Bishop had been judged guilty, by a majority of the Central Committee, of being too populist, insufficiently committed to Marxist-Leninism, seeking too much power and 'Suspicious that other members of The Party may be trying to seize power from him'. He'd been stripped of his official positions and placed under House Arrest with his girlfriend, the Education Minister, and other members of The Party had seized power from him.

This much all the spies, and presumably most Grenadians and expats, knew today. But that was no reason to stop using unofficial information gatherers like Jim who might pick up the odd snippet at a drinks party.

At this point we decided it was time for a swim. We could continue to chat in the water. We strolled down the slope to the beach where Jim maintained changing rooms. This part of the beach, the southwest extremity, is in many ways the best. Most tourists don't venture this far and the water is calm. It is deep enough for swimming yet shallow enough for me to stay within my depth. In addition there is no underfoot coral, just a smooth bottom of fine sand.

After about twenty minutes we all came out of the water together. I turned around to say something to Sean but he'd disappeared. Hang on. Where was he? I couldn't see him anywhere along the beach, he wasn't hurrying through the palm trees to the changing rooms, he wasn't toiling up the slope to Flamboyant and he wasn't in the sea. Unless he was underwater. He'd just disappeared. Obviously he was a spy.

I arrived back at my hotel in the late afternoon. There were no messages for me but I detected an extremely tense atmosphere around the premises for some reason. Well, I knew the reason. Beryl had told me. Their popular Prime Minister had been arrested by the faction which struck fear into the people. Although the staff were pleasant to me, as usual, they were afraid and seemed distracted.

Possibly this is why they failed to phone through to advise me that a visitor had arrived. I'd just emerged from the shower, wearing only a towel around my waist whilst I briskly dried my hair with another, when I heard a voice calling outside.

"Cooeee. Morgan" it called.

I glanced towards the open French windows and saw Roberto jauntily ascending the steps.

"Are you home?" he called.

This I found hard to believe. Were the hotel staff in the

habit of directing strangers to guests' rooms without warning? And Roberto must have thought Christmas was early this year. A semi-naked Morgan standing right in front of him. His eyes nearly popped straight out of his head. I acted quickly and decisively.

"Roberto. Wait there" I instructed, lifting my right hand. "Better still, take a seat just over there. I'll be right back." I slipped into the bedroom, closed the door, then re-emerged three minutes later fully clothed apart from my feet.

"This is a surprise" I said.

"Well, I did say I might pop by later. I've got the rest of the day off, although with all these things going on they might need me. But they will have to find me first" he lowered his voice "and they don't know I'm here" he added conspiratorily.

"What things going on?"

"Well, you know. Political things. With the Grenada government. Nothing to do with us. You're English and I'm Cuban."

"Would you like a drink Roberto? We could go to the bar."

It had occurred to me that if Roberto stayed too long people might put two and two together and make five.

"Oh no. People might see us in the bar. Then they would know I'm here and call me away. Besides, this is a lovely room they've given you. You must be important."

Flattery. He must know the real reason, namely that the hotel was almost completely bereft of guests like most of Grenada's hotels. Tourism was suffering badly and, anyway, it was still Low Season.

"I quite fancy a drink though."

"They must do room service Morgan. I'll have a beer."

I got on the phone and placed the order for two Caribs. "Tell you what" I said, returning to Roberto "let's compromise. As you say it's a lovely garden so we could sit out there. Look at the view. A shame to waste this lovely sunshine. We hardly see the sun in England and I'll be going back there soon."

"When will that be?"

"Oh, in about a week or so."

I strolled past him, down the steps into the garden and selected two sun loungers which were side by side and separated only by a small table. Roberto bent over and began to remove the table.

"No, leave it" I said. "We'll need it for the drinks."

Presently the beers arrived and we continued our chat. The conversation was innocuous enough but I decided it might be a good idea to turn the subject around to Cuba. I knew very little about the country and it might direct Roberto's mind away from other matters.

"Are you from Havana?" I asked.

"I live there now, well most of the time, but I'm from Camagüey." Suddenly he sat up and grinned at me mockingly. "You should know it as one of your relatives visited us."

"My relatives? As far as I know none of my family have ever been to Cuba." And if they had, how would Roberto know?

"Silly me. Not relatives. One of your ancestors."

"I didn't know. Who exactly?"

"Henry Morgan. Although in those days the town was called Puerto Príncipe. We had to rebuild it and change the name after he left. A very violent man."

Of course, it was the pronunciation. If I'd seen it written I would have known straightaway. Roberto was pulling my leg. Well, two could play at that game.

"How did you find out? I was hoping to keep that secret."

Roberto had relaxed, smirking to himself, after his brief explanation. Now he sat up sharply again. "So you *are* related. How exciting. Is that why you're here?"

I put my finger to my lips and made a great show of looking around.

"Before I tell you anything" I whispered "you'll have to

promise to keep it secret. And I think we should order another beer now. So, once we've got it, they won't come back whilst I'm telling you."

I returned to my room and telephoned the bar. Then I deposited the towel in the bathroom – my hair was almost dry now – and strolled back out to my sun lounger. I could see that Roberto was impatient for me to continue the story so I put my finger to my lips.

"We must wait."

Those beers were a long time coming. Caribbean Time. We admired the gardens and the panorama whilst we waited. We were relaxing on the lawned promontory surrounded by the few scattered trees and a host of flowering shrubs. Through the trees and across the harbour we could see the tiered streets of stone and brick buildings rising up the rim of the extinct volcano.

Eventually a waiter appeared bearing a silver tray on which sat two bottles of Carib and two fresh glasses. Once he'd deposited them and left Roberto was impatient to hear my story.

"So you're related and that's why you're here?"

I looked up as I carefully poured my beer. "Promise."

"Yes, I promise. I won't tell anyone. But Morgan never came to Grenada."

"Of course not. The pirates didn't come here. But this is a cover, so that people don't guess what I'm really doing."

"This is exciting. What are you really doing?"

"Looking for his hidden treasure. My mother found a diary and a map with some old things in her grandmother's house. Just in a trunk. Handed down. Nobody realised what it was."

"Do you think you'll find it?"

"I have found it. Where nobody would think to look."

Roberto stared earnestly at me. "Where?"

"Promise you'll keep it secret?"

"Yes of course." I detected a trace of impatience.

I took a sip of beer, glanced over at Roberto and set my glass down on the table. "It's very important you don't tell anyone."

"Yes of course. Where is it?"

I spilt the beans, as it were. "In his grave at Gallows Point near Port Royal in Jamaica. It is part of the peninsular which didn't collapse into the sea during the earthquake. It's still there."

Roberto wasn't convinced. "How could he bury it in his own grave?"

"He was a very mean man, besides being horrid and violent. He had them make a special coffin with a false bottom. So that nobody would inherit his wealth he hid the most valuable items – jewels and gold – there. So when they buried him they buried much of his loot. He must have thought that a great joke."

Roberto wanted to believe me. He was enthralled by the story. But his brain was still calculating quickly.

"What a mean and horrible man" he said. "So you found it and moved it. Where to?"

"I didn't move it. I put the coffin back exactly as it was. It's all still there." I took another sip of my beer, then put the glass down and lay back in my sun lounger.

Roberto glanced at me then took a generous swig of his beer whilst he evaluated this information. After a couple of minutes he had another question.

"What if somebody else finds it?"

"How? Why would anyone else look? It's been there for nearly three hundred years. Only you and I know it's there and you've promised not to tell anyone."

Now I sat up straight on my sun lounger and finished my beer. The night was creeping up on us. I could feel that this would be one of those deliciously cool evenings. With a secret smile I surmised that even now Roberto would be calculating how to get to Jamaica. Not easy from Cuba if you're a Cuban. As in all Workers' Paradises the ungrateful masses are kept in to enjoy the fruits of Socialism. That gave me a thought.

"Roberto" I asked "aren't your government concerned that you might flee the country? There's nothing to stop you just leaving Grenada."

"Well, I haven't got my passport. That's at the embassy. And they watch the airport of course. But what if I did get away, in a boat perhaps, at night. Where would I go? My friends are in Cuba, and my family. And we're not badly off."

"How so?"

"It's not like Russia. They didn't take everything from the middle classes. We have a house in Camagüey, an apartment in Havana and a beach cabana. We have a car too, a Lada, which gets us around. We also have one of those wonderful old American cars, a '55 Chevrolet, but we don't use it much because sometimes gas is expensive or difficult to get. Petrol, sorry. So it stays in the garage. Morgan" Roberto sat up. "You're taking the mickey aren't you? About finding that treasure?"

"Of course" I laughed. "But you started it. Pretending you thought I was related to the old rogue."

Roberto laughed too. "But tell me one thing. Is there a Gallows Point, and is Henry Morgan buried there?"

"Oh yes. That part is true. But tell me about Cuba. I don't know anything about Cuba. When I get back."

"Where are you going?"

"To the bar. To get two more beers. I fancy the walk." And to reinforce my innocence.

I returned and plonked the beers down on the table. "Tell me about Havana."

"It's a beautiful old town Morgan, but sadly falling down. They can't afford the maintenance. The old part of the city – which was going to be demolished and rebuilt in modern American style by the Batista government – is crammed full with poor families. Every year dozens of buildings collapse. Because people were starving to death in the countryside Fidel concentrated on helping them first.

Then they invested heavily in health and education so there was no money left for improving or repairing Havana. Most of the hotels, the ones built by the Mafia, could do with renovation. The older hotels too, like the Sevilla and the Inglaterra, but it doesn't matter so much with them."

"Why not?"

"People don't mind if old hotels look old. But newer, flashy ones look terrible if they're not maintained properly."

"Is there any nightlife?"

"Oh yes. We have the Tropicana. Probably the best nightclub in the world. Fantastic shows, lovely, sexy girls – you'd like that Morgan – big bands. Salsa bands. The roof opens up on nights like this and you can see the stars. When you come to Cuba I will take you."

We both gazed up at the stars in the clear night sky, each lost in his own thoughts for a few minutes. Suddenly Roberto leaned over towards me.

"May I kiss you Morgan?"

I was horrified at the suggestion. The terror probably showed on my face. "No" I replied quickly.

"Why not?"

I needed to think fast. "Because I'm English. We don't do that in England."

"What do you do?" Roberto mischievously enquired.

"Well, we shake hands."

"Don't you like men Morgan?"

"Oh, they're OK I suppose. One or two of my best friends are men. But yes, I prefer women."

"Don't you have a boyfriend then?"

"Good God no" I said, beginning to recover my composure now that I realised Roberto would not force himself on me. I'd twigged that this was largely a game. "We don't do things like that in England."

"Surely some people do. I have met English men who do. In Cuba."

"Well there's probably a few. But I don't know any. I think

they stick together, you know, go to the same pubs and clubs."

"You're sure you don't want to try it? You might like it."

I laughed. "The last time someone said that to me was at a party. He was offering me cocaine."

Chapter Sixteen

"If Ye Be So Featly With These Galleons"

Well, yesterday had been busy. Events kicked off with a visit to Beryl and concluded with a visit from Roberto. In between I slotted in a short refreshment stop at The Flamboyant and, more importantly, I discovered vital evidence at the airport construction site. Namely scraps of wreckage. That ship's name was familiar and should be checked.

I still don't know why I brought all my research data with me. The decision was made on instinct, a gut feeling.

Before leaving home I'd compiled a list of all the ships which had been connected in any way to the Caribbean freebooters. Now I withdrew the file from the bottom of my bag. Turning to the section which listed the Spanish galleons which had been attacked, sunk, captured or otherwise interfered with by pirates I found quite a few *Nuestra Señoras* – which translates as Our Lady, presumably a reference to The Virgin Mary – and noticed that there were two named *Nuestra Señora del Rosaria*. Presumably the second was christened after the demise of the first. I came across a *Nuestra Señora de la Esperanza* and a *Nuestra Señora de Loreto*. At last I found it – *Nuestra Señora de las Nueces Variadas*. It was one of the galleons Henry Morgan's cutthroats commandeered when they departed San Lorenzo and Chagres in 1671. This couldn't be right, surely? I turned to my notes on that Panama raid.

I discovered that this vessel was judged barely seaworthy. It should have been abandoned or scuttled but because many of Morgan's ships had been damaged in the crossing he decided to keep it. Apparently he reasoned that as it was designed specifically to transport plunder it would suit his needs. If it was repairable.

I found a reference to the ambitious crew who'd tried to repair the galleon disabled by the Spanish in the harbour at Panama. They were in disgrace. As a punishment for exercising their initiative they were forced to escort the mules burdened with barrels of pitch on the overland trek back to The Caribbean. It seems that there was no pitch or, anyway, insufficient, stored at San Lorenzo to repair ships battered on the journey from Ile-à-Vache and Santa Catalina.

When the barrels were delivered few were found to be more than half full, a strange but interesting detail in the records. The escorting pirates claimed that some of the contents had been spilled when the mules carrying the barrels slipped and fell on the mountainous and muddy jungle track. In addition, according to them, some of the remaining pitch was jettisoned to lighten the load.

Henry Morgan was not convinced. Other pirates told him that at least some of the barrels were full on arrival at San Lorenzo but then suddenly, overnight, their contents was depleted. But he had more pressing matters to attend to, such as how to cheat his men and get away with it, so he decreed a light punishment. With the taunt "If ye be so featly with these galleons" he allocated *Nuestra Señora de las Nueces Variadas* to the miscreant crew. They were to make this ship seaworthy by the time the fleet was ready to leave and then sail it back to Port Royal, presumably via Ile-à-Vache.

They never arrived. The returning fleet ran into a severe tropical storm two days after leaving San Lorenzo. Waves and winds of near hurricane-force tossed the fragile wooden vessels helplessly like a baby's bathtime plastic duck. Decks were flooded and water penetrated below. Several of the ships were blown miles away from the main body. Nevertheless most of the fleet eventually made landfall at Port Royal, Tortuga or Ile-à-Vache. This *Nuestra Señora* was not one of them. It was never seen or heard of again. It was presumed lost with all hands and a substantial cargo of plunder. Those were the facts. So how did parts of it get to Grenada?

The political crisis was evidently hotting up so I was anxious to remain here as long as possible. I needed to make maximum use of the car whilst simultaneously extending my stay. Today I would visit some hotels and tomorrow I would tour the island. Sunday could be a day of rest. Monday I would review the situation and act accordingly.

Shortly after breakfast I received a phone call from Beryl that offered me the perfect excuse to drag my feet.

When she'd visited Sunstroke's clients she let it slip that an executive from the London office was on the island. Some of these clients were aware of the political turmoil, knew about the arrest of the Prime Minister and had seen small groups of people talking excitedly. They needed reassurance. Beryl promised that I would call in to see them. Oddly enough, she told me, it was the clients due to leave tomorrow who were most afraid. The couple staying at Blue Horizons for a further two weeks were totally unconcerned.

I decided to visit them last. First I drove to Horseshoe Bay where a middle-aged couple were vacationing. When I arrived they were sunbathing down by the small beach. Once I'd assured them that LIAT services to and from Grenada were operating as normal and that Beryl was on top of all their arrangements, including the taxi, they seemed happy. Especially when they realised that Sunstroke Holidays had sent someone from head office specifically to take care of this very problem. The family occupying a cottage at Flamboyant were worried about the children. I set them at ease.

The Blue Horizons couple were enjoying an island excursion and were due back at four. Fine. I was glad to relax with a beer at the poolside bar for half an hour until their return. They were a cheery northern couple.

"Oh yes, we've 'ad a smashin' day thanks. Bin t' waterfall and reservoir – what they call it luv?"

"Grand Etang."

"Also that Carrier's Leap in t' north."

When I asked whether they were concerned about the political situation they were dismissive.

"No, nowt t' worry about. It don't concern us, do it?" said the husband. "It's their country, it's up to theyselves who they ave in govament."

I wish we had more clients like these. I left them to enjoy their holiday after telling them to contact Beryl if they had any problems and advising them that I was off to Carriacou in a few days to visit our clients there. Actually we didn't have any but who's to know? Now I would return to Ross Point Inn and make sure they understood that nobody, absolutely nobody, should be shown to my room. Then an early dinner and an early night.

I didn't get to sleep immediately of course. Too much on my mind. Besides the job and my secret agenda I needed to evaluate the political situation here. How it would affect me, President Reagan and the Grenadian people.

It was clear that The Party had forfeited the support of The Masses. Right from my arrival I noticed that citizens were afraid to discuss the political situation. The tension was palpable. I remembered Mr Hopkin's nervousness when I mentioned Bernard Coard.

It wasn't always like that.

The 1979 revolution was popular with a majority of the populace. They were glad to see the end of Gairy, his corruption and his Mongoose Gang. There was dancing in the streets and Maurice Bishop was a very popular leader. His political ideology didn't seem important as few Grenadians understood Marxist-Leninism or what it stood for. Granted, they were cautious about the involvement of

Cuba. They knew it was a Communist country. But what, actually, were the Cubans doing? They were building an airport capable of handling intercontinental jets. Most Grenadians wanted that and it was essential if Grenada was to progress economically. In addition the Cubans were providing doctors and helping with agricultural development.

Unfortunately they were also training and equipping an army and militia. Ostensibly this was for defence of the nation but educated Grenadians realised it could be used against the people. A sort of legalised Mongoose Gang armed with Heavy Duty weaponry. Ominous signs were apparent. Some of the more indoctrinated youth flocked to join the militia and a few of the soldiers were intoxicated with their power, displaying arrogance and expecting preferential service in the shops.

Following the revolution the economic situation was favourably reviewed by The World Bank and The International Monetary Fund as Bernard Coard claimed. People could see things were better. But within four years disappointment with the slow rate of improvement in living conditions was becoming widespread. Most of the roads were still appalling. There were regular power cuts.

Grenadians could see that a doctrinaire wing of The Party led by the Coards was trying to take power. Ordinary people wanted elections like they used to have and like they have in England and America. They didn't want Grenada to become a Communist country like Cuba or Russia where eventually they wouldn't be allowed to leave. But with an army one thousand strong, a countrywide militia and informers everywhere they were afraid to express their views.

This is what I discovered when I arrived but by the Saturday, with Bishop under house arrest, that fear was turning to anger.

I decided to drive anti-clockwise around the island. That way I would arrive at Pearls Airport before the LIAT flight departed for Barbados. Then I planned to continue north to Sauteurs and Carib's Leap and return down the west coast road via St George's. I might be rewarded with some beautiful sunset views.

This time at the Sugar Mill roundabout I turned left and took the badly-signposted route for Westerhall and St David's. The roads were dreadful, as I expected, with nothing of outstanding interest to be seen. Similar surroundings to those I'd witnessed on my taxi ride from Pearls. Hillsides of lush and verdant forest interspersed with plots of farmed land reaching down to the roadside, small villages and isolated houses. There were no signs of tourism on this southeastern coast. Apart from Pearls airport all the infrastructure needed for a tourist industry – beaches, hotels, restaurants, banks and supermarkets – were crowded into the southwest corner along with the capital.

Occasionally during my drive I saw small groups of people in earnest discussion. Mainly agricultural workers. I learned later they were being organised for a demonstration in support of Maurice Bishop on the instructions of the President of the Agricultural and General Workers Union.

I passed through St David's and eventually arrived at Grenville, a bustling little town, probably thriving as a result of its proximity to the airport. Nothing there of interest to the tourist and I could see why there were no holiday hotels in the area. Where the road passed close to the shoreline the only beaches I could see were scrappy with unattractive beige sand. And this is the windward coast so the currents would probably be dangerous.

Small groups of people were discussing the political situation here too. And there were more travellers on the road to the airport than I would have expected. Some were in cars, some in trucks and minibuses and some were walking. Were they meeting friends and relatives on the incoming flight? Were they leaving the country? If so, why walk?

A group of four oversized blokes flagged me down. Are

you going to the airport? Certainly. Jump in. Three crammed themselves in the back whilst the largest man sat in the front. He carried my red Moroccan leather bag and camera, which normally lived on that seat, on his lap, sitting stone-still, staring ahead impassively, his knees rubbing the underside of the glove box.

The purr of the Honda's eager engine was the only sound. My passengers didn't want to discuss anything on the short journey. After I pulled over and parked at the terminal building they thanked me, disembarked and went to join a group being harangued by an excitable man about fifty yards away. A few soldiers of the PRA armed with AK47s loitered on the fringe of this group but they were quite relaxed. Other soldiers were in evidence, mainly strolling in pairs.

There were more people here than I would have expected. Most were engaged in earnest discussion in small groups whilst some were obviously here to meet relatives and others were leaving the country. The Cuban plane was loading women and children, apparently for a minor evacuation.

Our clients were all checked in. Beryl came over to me as soon as I'd locked the car. We wandered into the terminal shack.

"LIAT are bound to be overbooked today" she said. I noticed that The Flamboyant family's children were getting fractious in the heat, as kids do, with their parents doing their best to cope.

The Horseshoe Bay couple strode over to me. "I still can't understand why we had to get here so early" the man said. "We've got confirmed seats haven't we?"

"Of course" I answered. "You can see that from your tickets. If you check the 'Status' box you'll see 'OK' written there. But LIAT always overbook and with the political situation here a lot of people – look, you can see – will be trying to get away. It's first come, first served with LIAT."

"What's the political situation got to do with it?"

This from the guy who was extremely nervous yesterday. Perhaps he feels safe now. Ridiculous. I could barely believe what I was hearing.

"Look around you" I said, waving my arm. "You can see that the situation is unstable."

"So what are Sunstroke Holidays playing at then" the man demanded, thrusting his chin forward and very full of himself, "sending people to unstable countries? And don't say you didn't know" warming to his theme now "because you should have known it was a communist dictatorship." He stood back and cast an appropriate glance to his meek, mouse-like wife who clutched his arm. That's telling them.

Was he angling for compensation? That's all the rage now. You tripped over a paving stone? Sue the council. The government of the country where you're holidaying is toppled in a coup? Sue the tour operator. I've no patience with that type.

"Half the countries in the world are unstable or totalitarian" I informed him. With the index finger of my right hand I counted off the fingers on my left. "Cyprus could break out in civil war at any moment, they have constant wars in the Middle East, there was that coup in Greece, even Northern Ireland isn't safe. As for totalitarian countries" I could see that the guy was trying to butt in but I wouldn't let him "as for totalitarian countries, you've got the whole Soviet bloc, most of Latin America, South Africa . . ."

"OK, OK, what's your point?" Our valued client was a little less sure of himself now but still truculent.

"Half the world is unstable or under totalitarian government. If people were stopped from going there then there wouldn't be much left would there?" Half the world actually, but this guy won't pick up on that.

"Well, you must have known this would happen here. They had a revolution you know."

"They had a military coup in Greece but nobody predicted that they would invade Cyprus. And our government seemed surprised when the Argies invaded The Falklands last year."

"You could have told us about the revolution before we booked. So we could make our own minds up."

Ha, got him now. "It's mentioned in the brochure."

A minute's silence whilst the couple exchanged looks. They turned to go, but hubby needed to fire a parting shot. This would be the last word. "Well, we're not happy" he spat over his shoulder as he hustled his wife away. "I'm going to write to your Managing Director."

"Good idea" I called after him. "You do that." And best of luck mate. I've seen what they do with letters of complaint.

Beryl had remained within earshot but some distance away during the wrangling. As soon as the couple had passed from sight inside the tiny Departures room she approached me wearing a wide grin.

"If I spoke like that to clients I'd be sacked" she said.

I shrugged. Frankly, I didn't give a damn. "He won't write. Tell you what though Beryl, if you spoke like that to him and you were black then he would write. He's that type."

"What if he does write?"

"In the first instance he'll lie to strengthen his case. He's a prat. Then nobody in London will believe him because they all think I'm a wimp."

"Why do they think that?"

I laughed. "Because I was before I came out here."

That last reply was almost drowned by the roar of twin turboprop Rolls Royce engines as a Hawker Siddeley 748, pride of LIAT (1974) Ltd's fleet, touched down. The cows chewing the cud twenty yards away looked up then went back to their meal. Within fifteen minutes the passengers and baggage were loaded and the plane taxied away for take-off. I made a point of waving to our clients as they ascended the steps.

"I have to go into Grenville" Beryl said.

We strolled back to our cars. I decided that, in order to get back before dark, I would cut short my island tour and head for town on the cross-island road I'd experienced as a passenger when I arrived. Let's see if I could do it in an hour. I'll go up to Sauteurs some other time. Give me an excuse to prolong my stay.

After a couple of days with the car I was beginning to get the hang of driving Grenadian-style. Like the taxi driver I didn't bother driving on the left except round blind corners or when there was oncoming traffic, but unlike him I did moderate my pace through the settlements and whenever I saw, or expected, children and livestock. This precaution hardly slowed me. What did impede my progress was the need to steer round potholes. There were so many that it was impossible to avoid all of them by swerving across the road. Sometimes there were potholes inside potholes.

I was enjoying my stint as an amateur rally driver until I reached the middle of the island where the hills are highest and the road was wet. Sometimes just patches, sometimes completely sodden. Here I found the rear of the car reluctant to follow the front. Those bald rear tyres offered no grip and, though I could sometimes use this to my advantage, sliding the car round at impossible angles to miss potholes, it did cause my heart to beat faster. Well, race actually.

Suddenly my fun was curtailed by a nasty shock. Recklessly speeding on a rare completely dry stretch of open road, a section almost bereft of potholes, steep hillsides to my right and a sheer drop on the nearside, I hurtled through a left hand bend and hit an invisible stream. I could see it as I slid on it but it was invisible to any driver approaching that corner. Water dribbling down from the mountains and streaming across the road on its way to the precipice. I was doing 40 at least. And, of course, I was turning. The rear wheels lost all grip. My little Honda aquaplaned and slid sideways across the road. A shattered wooden fence ahead of me inefficiently guarded the sheer drop. Obviously a previous driver had encountered the same problem, stamped on his brake pedal and plummeted through it and over the edge. My front wheels, the driving wheels, retained their grip and were determined to fling me into the abyss too.

I don't deserve any credit for my survival. My reactions saved me.

I didn't brake. Instead I floored the accelerator and hauled the wheel over to the right. Those front tyres bit into the road as they started to turn but I doubt if that alone would have saved me. Fortunately those bald rears slid left as I wrenched the wheel to the right. Within a split second the car was pointing in the right direction again. Briefly. My Honda and I fishtailed up the hill to the next corner straightening out as I eased off the gas.

That was a close one. I'm as bad as Jean-Pierre. No, not really. I don't have two passengers in the car, one a woman. If I had plummeted over the cliff it would have been my funeral only, no-one else's. Literally. If, that is, they ever extricated my body from the tangled wreckage. I wonder what happened to the other guy? Is he dead? Did he have passengers? Maybe his vehicle is still down there.

I moderated my pace as I drove away from the scene. Idly I wondered how recently that fence was breached. The shallow stream of water seemed to be a permanent hazard, rainwater draining from the hills above. Surely locals would know about it. So presumably the unfortunate bugger who'd mashed his brakes and crashed through the fence was a stranger or, at least, a Grenadian who hadn't used this road before. Surely not a tourist. Those few tourists who rent cars tend to drive sedately. They chat and stare at the scenery. The Americans in particular drive very slowly. Their cars back home are automatics so a 'stick shift' presents them with a minor challenge.

Shortly before the corner I'd shot past a group of four youths loitering by the roadside. Now I suspect that watching unwary drivers negotiate that hazard, or fail to, was an entertainment for them. In that scary split second as the car slithered broadside, about to plummet, I saw them looking at me. A fraction later with the car straightening itself I heard a "whhhoooooaaaaa" escaping from their direction. Maybe they were lookouts. When a vehicle goes over the edge they can report it and assist the occupants if they feel so inclined.

The temporary shock encouraged me to take more care whilst the road was still wet. After all, it was not absolutely crucial that I beat the taxi driver's record. Now my driving was smoother. I had difficulty maintaining my concentration. Once back in the sunshine with a dry road on the descent to town I was able to increase my speed again until I hit traffic. Entering St George's I glanced up at a clock. One hour ten minutes. Not bad for a first attempt.

There were an awful lot of hyperactive schoolchildren roaming the streets in large groups. Some wielded placards but I couldn't read the slogans as they weren't parading with them. Some kids were dragging them along and others were lugging theirs tucked under their arms. Looks like something has been happening here. Maybe some kind of demonstration. Then I saw Roberto. I hit the horn and pulled over.

"Do you fancy going to The Nutmeg for a drink and a bite to eat Roberto?"

"Oh, you're still talking to me then."

"Don't be daft."

"Well, I thought the way you hustled me out of your room I'd upset you."

"It wasn't my room, it was the garden. And it was getting late. I'll park over there and we can go up to The Nutmeg."

It was full today. Fortunately two men were just leaving so we grabbed their vacated table. All around us discussion of the crisis was lively. One or two diners glanced at Roberto as we entered but without malice or much curiosity. They knew who he was and his irrelevance.

"I saw a lot of schoolchildren just now" I said as we sat. "What was that about?"

"Oh yes, they were parading earlier. Where have you been all day?"

"I drove around the south of the island then went up to Pearls to see my clients off. What happened with the kids?"

"Just demonstrating. Supporting Bishop and insulting Coard. I do hope that works out all right. Fidel is very fond of Maurice you know."

"Yes, and the Russians are fond of Bernard."

Roberto leaned forward. "I don't like those Russians you know. I don't trust them."

"Who does. But I thought, Roberto, that you Cubans were supposed to be here in some force."

"What do you mean?"

"There's supposed to be hundreds of Cuban soldiers here but I haven't seen one yet. All I've seen so far is construction workers at the airport and you."

Roberto wagged his finger. "Morgan, you've been listening to that naughty Mr Reagan haven't you?"

"Well, he is naughty, and I have been listening to him, but there's also what I read."

"Morgan! An intelligent man like you believing what he reads in the newspapers!"

"Well? Where are they? Confined to barracks?"

Roberto leaned back in his chair. "You're asking the right person. As interpreter I know these things. There are 784 Cubans here in total, including embassy staff. Some of those left today – well, wives and children. 43 of the total are military personnel, here to train the Grenadian People's Revolutionary Army. There are 636 construction workers at the new airport."

"So they'll be leaving then?"

"Most are scheduled to leave very soon. When the airport's finished all the workers are due to return home. I'm due back there in a month."

"Why were wives and children being evacuated?"

"In case the Americans invade."

"You really think that's likely?"

"Morgan, yes. They've been waiting for an excuse for months. They even had a practice one or two years ago near Puerto Rico."

"Yes, I heard about that."

"This crisis in the government could be their excuse. They could claim instability."

I thought about this for a few minutes. I didn't think it likely as things stood, but if the situation worsened . . . . . . Well, you never know. We finished our meal in silence.

Roberto was glad of a lift to the Cuban Embassy. "Oh, I rather like this red bag Morgan. Can I have it?"

I laughed. "Sorry, no. It has sentimental value."

I never saw him again.

Chapter Seventeen

"Lor! Dem Shootin' De Chillun!"

I stepped out of the shower refreshed. Now to do some planning. Years ago I'd read that famous account of the 1917 Bolshevik revolution, '*Ten Days That Shook The World*', and I could see the parallels. In both cases the established order was overthrown in a popular revolt. Here, as in Russia, a moderate reforming administration was displaced by a hardline faction. Of course this was on a much smaller scale. A tiny Caribbean nation with a population of less than 120,000 could hardly compare with the vast rambling Russian empire, the world's largest territory with a population numbering hundreds of millions. In Grenada millions would not be starved or slaughtered in decades of civil war, famine and purges. But there might be foreign intervention. There would be interesting developments. So I wanted to remain here as long as possible before moving on to Carriacou, but I needed an excuse.

I was entitled to a day off and Sunday was an appropriate day to take it. Obviously I couldn't pester hotel owners and managers on a Sunday could I? That would be my story and I would stick to it. Then tomorrow and possibly Tuesday I could revisit our hotels with the explanation that I wanted to see how they were faring in the deteriorating political situation.

But I couldn't think of any justifiable reason to stay longer. I would have to leave for Carriacou on Wednesday and if I wanted to delay going on to Barbados then maybe I could visit The Grenadines.

I decided to walk to Grand Anse. As I sauntered in the hot sun I passed groups of people engrossed in urgent discussion. Something was brewing. Occasionally cars slowed down then stopped. Their drivers and passengers called out to pedestrians.

The beach was lively. Of course, today is Sunday, the day of rest when locals and expatriates come down here, weather permitting, to relax, swim and picnic. They prefer the shady part of the beach where my stroll began. Those expats had lost their northern hemisphere pallor years ago. Now they sought to protect themselves from the curse of the melanoma and sunburn with wide-brimmed hats and loose cottons. They usually kept clear of the island's few tourists who preferred the broader sun-soaked expanse of the beach at its centre, in front of The Grenada Beach Hotel, formerly a Holiday Inn. Some guests frolicked in the sea or tossed a ball but most just sprawled in their multicoloured beachwear on sun loungers or towels.

The locals were scattered randomly in clusters so I just meandered amongst them *en route* to my favourite spot. Today they were more numerous than normal and they were all discussing the crisis. Complete families from teenagers to the very elderly were angrily criticising the government and formulating a response. There was a major demonstration planned, probably for Tuesday. So maybe I should go into town on Tuesday. As I ambled slowly past them pretending to be a dopey tourist I kept my ears wide open.

"Adolphus say Coard resign" was one snippet. The response was sharp enough for me to catch too.

"Doan' trust it man! Coard behind dis whole ting."

Someone in another group stated the obvious. "Dey got Maurice lock away."

"Maurice de only one we can trust. We got free 'im."

"How we know Maurice still living?"

All the comments were pro-Bishop and anti-Coard. There was a consensus – Bishop would allow them a form of democracy, although socialist, and probably elections, but under Coard they could only expect a totalitarian communist future.

Finally I arrived at my favourite spot, about a hundred yards past Spice Island Inn. There were no tourists or expats or animated discussions here, just two off-duty soldiers lounging under sea grape trees. As I got closer I identified them as Cubans from the unadorned olive drab of their uniforms, their lighter skin and Latino features, their ages – they appeared to be in their thirties – and their totally relaxed attitude. Also they were unarmed and without webbing belts. The only strange thing was their attire. Don't they have casual clothes and swimming trunks for their days off?

They called me over when they spied me approaching. "*Amigo!*"

I waved to them "*No hablo español!*" I shouted.

One continued beckoning to me and yelled something I didn't understand whilst the other reached behind and rummaged in a bag. His hand emerged flourishing a bottle of beer. "*Cerveza*" he offered.

As I came abreast of them they invited me to sit and handed me the beer. "*Gracias*" I said. I knew that much at least, but so that I wouldn't be drinking their beer under false pretences I repeated "*No hablo español*". I didn't catch their response but it was obviously friendly so I sat with them, raised the bottle in salutation then pressed it to my lips.

These guys sensibly restricted themselves to using key words so we conversed at a simple level. One sat up straight and with his right hand made a broad sweep of the beach and sea. "*Bueno*" he said.

I nodded. "*Si*" I replied, showing them my beach togs.

They were most interested in my Hawaiian Tropic. They passed the bottle between them, trying to read the print.

"*Estados Unidos*" one said.

"*Si*" I confirmed. "*Americano*. For *sol*." I pointed to the sun.

He handed it back. "*Usted Americano?*"

"What?"

The other guy pointed to me. "*Usted Americano?*"

"Me? No. English. *Inglisi. Inglaterra.*"

"Ah, *bueno.*"

Around about now we all realised that we couldn't hold a proper conversation so the Cubans lay back and relaxed again. I decided to finish my beer and have a swim. These chaps would keep an eye on my stuff.

I took a Dollar Bus into St George's on Tuesday.

I'd already heard that the Central Committee was pushing forward Hudson Austin, the army commander, hero of the revolution and hitherto staunch Maurice Bishop supporter, as their spokesman. *Radio Free Grenada* broadcast a speech late on Sunday night in which he condemned Bishop's actions whilst claiming "No-one loves Comrade Bishop more than the members of our own party."

Yeah, right. That reminds me of Oscar Wilde – '*And all men kill the thing they love*'.

Few people were fooled by this speech and I sensed that Bishop's supporters were active throughout the country organising something. By Tuesday afternoon they were out in force. The schoolchildren had previously been protesting sporadically both in Grenada and Carriacou but now the farm workers and other adults helped them fill the streets of St George's. The Prime Minister's supporters, who included union leaders and politicians who had been members of the government until very recently, organised buses and trucks to ferry demonstrators into the capital from all over the island. Some protestors marched with crude banners proclaiming 'C FOR COARD, C FOR COMMUNISM' as if they were condemning a type of plague. Theoretically Maurice Bishop was also a Marxist-Leninist so obviously the Central Committee and the Coard faction were not the only people doubting his commitment to a communist dictatorship. Other placards simply stated 'WE WANT MAURICE BISHOP' or 'WE WANT DEMOCRACY'.

I estimated that the demonstrators numbered at least two thousand. Although vocal the protests were peaceful. The police stood outside their headquarters watching whilst members of the PRA patrolled quietly. It was obvious that the government, whether led by Bernard Coard or Hudson Austin, was not ready for a clash with the nation just yet.

After a few hours the crowd dispersed but I knew this wouldn't be the end of it. I would still take the boat to Carriacou tomorrow but perhaps I wouldn't miss anything. I would need to return to Grenada anyway for my flight to Barbados. If necessary I could cut short my stay in Carriacou. Probably the situation here wouldn't change much for a day or two.

On Wednesday, the day which was to become the most notorious in the history of Grenada, I decided to arrive early at the ferry. The political crisis was increasingly incendiary and talk around the hotel suggested that the schoolchildren were organising a critical initiative. They felt, as did many adults, that the army would not fire on schoolchildren. So to be sure of getting a taxi I was packed and ready to go by 10 o'clock. At 10.15 the taxi arrived.

"You're my last this mornin' man" said the driver.

"Oh, why's that?"

"They going Mount Royal for get Maurice. I go too after I lef' you."

"Who's going?"

"The chillun go fust, we follow. De army not shoot de chillun."

I reflected on this. Hopefully he was right. But what would the government do if the children were successful and managed to release Bishop? If Bishop was free, and had the power of the people behind him, the army might split. They had been taught that they were the servants of the people. And whatever their commander might order, and no matter what was decreed by those who'd seized control, many soldiers would still feel loyalty towards The Prime Minister. He was their Commander-in-Chief. I expected many of their families would put pressure on them to disobey orders too. Unfortunately Hudson Austin, the Coards and their acolytes were unlikely to give in without a fight. In their view Bishop's return to power would mean the end of the revolution. Democracy and *vox populi* did not feature in their plans. The only outcome I could foresee was a bitter civil war.

By leaving for Carriacou today I feared that I would miss history in the making. I stood uncertainly on The Carenage and watched my taxi disappear up the hill towards The Prime Minister's Residence. Before transferring myself and my baggage to the ferry I spent a few minutes thinking about it. I considered postponing this trip.

Eventually I decided to continue as planned. OK, I would miss today's events. But if the schoolchildren were successful in releasing the PM the most likely outcome would be a standoff for a day or two. There might be no conflict anyway, especially if a majority of the army decided to back the Prime Minister. By the time anything significant happened I would probably have returned from Carriacou. If I was really lucky all LIAT services would be cancelled for a few days and I would be forced to stay in Grenada. So, all in all, better to stick with Plan A.

I dumped my bags on the ferry and found a seat by the gunwale. The boat was filling up as departure time approached. The passengers chattered as they settled themselves for the journey. Some were travelling to Carriacou because of the crisis and others in spite of it. Most of them were apparently natives of Carriacou. Talk centred on the courageous plans of the schoolchildren. I lost track of time as I concentrated on my eavesdropping.

Suddenly I heard the crackle of machine-gun fire from

the direction my taxi had taken. One long burst. I might also have heard some shouts and screams. Conversation amongst my fellow passengers ceased abruptly as everyone turned to look up the hill towards The Prime Minister's Residence. The silence was broken by an exclamation from a fat middle-aged woman dressed entirely in blue.

"Lor! Dem shootin' de chillun!"

Next I heard muffled crowd noises, punctuated by random shouting, drifting down from the hillside. This hubbub continued for some minutes but these were not the panicking sounds of a crowd in retreat. There were no more gunshots. A frisson of excitement rippled through my fellow passengers. They scented success. Then I heard cheering from distant streets. Car horns joined in and presently I could hear a crowd of people and vehicles moving, apparently, towards me.

The ferry was filling up nicely now but disorder was affecting the passengers. Some, who feared danger rapidly approaching, wanted the captain to leave early, like this very minute. Others wanted him to delay whilst they ascertained what was going on up there. A few were inclined to disembark and join the crowd.

Round about ten to twelve, as I later calculated based on the ferry's scheduled departure time of midday, it was obvious to us all that Bishop had been released. Groups of people were running up from The Carenage towards Market Square shouting. Then I heard the rumble of vehicle engines. It sounded like a convoy of cars and trucks was motoring through the town. "Church Street" somebody said. We were all staring up the hill although our view was obstructed by the tiers of stone and brick buildings which muffled the excited shouting and singing of the PM's rescuers. Then, through a narrow gap, I caught sight of a celebratory procession.

"Dey heading for de fort!"

My fellow passengers were more familiar than I with the

layout of St George's. I knew the location of Fort Rupert – as Fort George had been renamed after the revolution in honour of Maurice Bishop's father, murdered by the Mongoose Gang – but not the best route there. As the crew were casting off more passengers decided they wanted to postpone their journey so they could join the throng swarming towards the fort. The captain decided to let them. The ferry was tied up for ten minutes while excited people, mainly men and teenage boys, leapt ashore and rushed along The Carenage.

"Dis your last chance. If you want off, then be off now. I not stappen again."

I clicked the 300 mm telephoto lens on to my camera. By looking up Young Street and between gaps I could catch a glimpse of events around the fort. The garrison had apparently joined with the crowd. Spontaneous arrangements for defence were being put into effect. Those on foot had caught up with the vehicles and were also pouring into the fort.

Our crew cast off for the last time and now we were finally bound for Carriacou. We left the harbour, rounded Fort George Point and headed north. The fort was now to our right and slightly behind us. Passengers were pointing towards it and shouting so I aimed my telescopic camera in that direction.

I heard the thunder of heavy vehicles before I saw anything. They were rumbling through the town at speed. I hoped any stragglers in the crowd were alert enough to jump out of their way. Suddenly I glimpsed three armoured personnel carriers and a truck tearing up the incline into the fort. Friend or foe? They ground to a halt together. Soldiers leapt out of the truck and rushed forward. Then the three APCs started up again. The first two fired into the crowd. Pandemonium broke loose. Passengers on the boat screamed and shouted as the crowd in the fort scattered, running in all directions to escape bullets, some people even jumping over the walls on to the rocks below. I felt sick. If this was history being made I didn't want to see it.

A man crushed next to me asked to use the camera. I handed it to him. Even without it I could see that the crowd was now dispersed and the APCs with their accompanying infantry were moving out of our sight into the fort itself.

On the boat an initial silence of disbelief erupted into a maelstrom of noise. Angry shouting and fearful clamouring. Screams from some of the women. What about those who'd disembarked to join the crowd? Their friends and relatives were obviously terrified. Some asked the captain to turn back. Others were fearful for their own safety. If Hudson Austin could order the army to massacre ordinary Grenadians and the army was prepared to execute those orders then nobody was safe.

The captain summed up the situation. He could see his passengers were evenly split between those who wanted to return and those who wanted to get away as quickly as possible. He announced a compromise.

"I cain't go back. Dose tanks, maybe dey shoot we outa de water."

This reinforced the shouts of those who wanted to get to Carriacou as quickly as possible.

"I stop at Gouyave. Dem dat want off can get off dere."

By now the fort and St George's were out of sight. But muffled sounds escaped over the water to us. Then I clearly heard two more bursts of machine-gun fire. More gasps, and faces sank into hands.

Now I was glad to be on this boat. There was no way of knowing what would happen next in Grenada. Coard's hardliners obviously commanded the support of the heavily-equipped army but not the majority of the populace.

An elderly slim man, who may have been a minister, started organising prayers. Most of the men keen to return passed around opened bottles of rum and Jackiron.

Normally I would have enjoyed gazing at the rugged and

verdant coastline but today I was too shocked to appreciate the beauty. I reclaimed my camera and now used it to study the coast road on those stretches visible from the ferry.

"See anyting man?" the fellow next to me asked.

"Just normal traffic, both directions. Well, maybe more than normal, but no military vehicles."

"Lemme look man."

I handed over the camera again. This man and the two with him took turns to peer through it then passed it back. They agreed that there was no abnormal activity ashore.

"Mebbe dey not know yet."

Now I took time to glance around the boat. These men next to me, and some others, were angry but calm. They seemed to think they could disembark at Gouyave before any military arrived. Probably the PRA would have no need to go there.

"The militia man" one, less gung-ho, said.

"Coard an' Austin doan' trust 'em" another suggested. "Dey tek dere guns las' week."

This group decided to land and face the consequences.

In the middle of the boat a religious service was being conducted by the elderly slim man. Most of his congregation were women with a few men and children amongst them. The rest of the passengers had formed into small groups arguing furiously, the men and a few of the women reinforced by swigs of the rum bottles. Some passengers tried to listen to transistor radios but they were of little help. *Radio Free Grenada* was silent so everybody was tuned into stations broadcasting from Barbados, Trinidad or Saint Vincent. According to them shots had been heard from Fort Rupert and smoke had been seen. That was all. Everyone on the ferry knew that much already.

As we headed towards the quay at Gouyave I saw people rushing through the streets to meet us. Those on the boat who wanted to get away from Grenada as quickly as possible became even more anxious, but they were put more at ease by others who pointed out that there were no uniforms or weapons among the crowd. The captain announced that he would only pull alongside if he was certain the situation was safe.

By the time we reached the quayside it was obvious that this crowd was not hostile. They just wanted information on the shooting.

Most of those who wanted to disembark did so. Some took their baggage with them, others left their possessions behind. A few people from the town had decided to leave when they saw the boat approaching. They rushed onto the quay clutching hastily-packed bags. There was now total confusion as some, all men, hastened to get off the boat and a few others, women and children, pushed to get on. All the time questions from the crowd ashore were fired at the passengers and crew. They received miscellaneous answers. Some reported what they'd seen, others told what they thought they'd seen, and a few offered their opinions of what happened afterwards and what would happen next.

It was odd that *Radio Free Grenada* was still off the air. Some passengers suggested that Coard and Austin were deciding what lies they would instruct the staff to broadcast. It was also considered likely that the staff there were split. Many, perhaps the majority, would be supporters of Maurice Bishop. Not only that. If anything bad happened to him then only hardened Coard supporters would be prepared to peddle the official line. Just last week, after Bishop's house arrest, the staff of the government newspaper, *The Free West Indian*, chased a member of the Central Committee off the premises when he attempted to explain the political crisis by blaming the Prime Minister.

We were docked in Gouyave for less than ten minutes. Apart from the normal rough ride over Kick-em-Jenny, the often turbulent sea above a simmering volcano, the rest of the voyage was uneventful. The passengers quietened down. We all knew the ferry wouldn't stop again until it reached

Hillsborough. Some passengers tuned in to foreign radio stations and were listening intently, others were discussing the plight of the nation, while a number were lost in their own thoughts. Of course I was one of these so the coast of Carriacou took me by surprise when it appeared. I could see beautiful sandy beaches. As we turned to enter the small dock at Hillsborough I spotted an idyllic reef-fringed island formed entirely of shimmering white sand and studded with palm trees about a mile offshore.

The dockside was thronged with worried people but this time I saw two uniformed PRA soldiers, who were apparently armed, among them. As we pulled alongside anxious questions were flung at us. My shipmates, glad to be home safely but struggling to disembark with their baggage, answered tersely. I stepped off as soon as the boat was fully flush and as the ropes were flung ashore. As I pushed my way through the crowd one of the soldiers stepped forward and halted me.

"Wha' appen down dere man?"

I told him. The soldier turned to his colleague. "Man, dem use de army against de people!"

By this time everyone had some idea of the slaughter in the capital. There was a continuous question and answer session in the mêlée and soon no-one was interested in me. I forced my way through the crowds to the street. For once I was not harassed by touts or taxi drivers but I didn't need a taxi. I knew there were only two hotels here, The Mermaid Inn right there in the village, and White Sands Beach Hotel just outside to the north. I decided White Sands would probably be quieter and commenced my three hundred yards stroll.

I saw more revolutionary slogans in this 300 yards of village than I'd seen in the whole of Grenada. At least it seemed so. As well as hoardings and peeling posters there were graffiti scrawled over the walls of buildings. The barracks of The People's Revolutionary Army was the focus of radical fervour. Did that mean the PRA here would strictly enforce the edicts of Hudson Austin and the Coards? If so, they too would be in the minority. I sensed already that the populace of Carriacou strongly supported Maurice Bishop. I just hoped there wouldn't be too much shooting in Carriacou.

Accommodation at White Sands was housed in self-catering bungalows set in scrubby gardens behind the restaurant and bar which were right on the beach. Whilst this hotel was not in the class of Ross Point Inn, to put it politely, it suited me perfectly. The management were happy to charge me $15 a day including breakfast and I wouldn't be tied to meal times if I had my own kitchen. Some premonition warned me that I would be staying in Carriacou longer than I'd planned.

I'll have a drink then I'll go for a swim.

I strolled over to the bar shortly after 5.30 and found it in a ferment. Everyone was talking at once so it was difficult to hear what the newscaster on the radio was telling us. *Radio Free Grenada* was still off the air so it was tuned to the Barbados station.

I located an empty stool at one end of the bar and ordered a Rum and Coke. The barman indicated the radio with his left hand as he placed the drink in front of me with his right.

"Dey sayin' Maurice bin shot" he said.

"Who?"

"*CBC.*"

I strained to listen to the radio above the clamour as I sipped my Cuba Libre. The newsreader retracted the station's claim concerning the shooting of the Prime Minister. Previously they'd announced his death but now stated that the allegation was an unfounded rumour. The revised statement was met with much, but not unanimous, relief. Some people felt that *CBC's* initial claim might have been accurate judging by some of the reports they'd heard from the ferry's passengers who were eyewitnesses. The barman turned to me.

"You was on dat boat man."

"Yes."

"What you see?"

I told him. As I described the events I'd witnessed I became the centre of attention. People seemed to think that a foreigner, and an Englishman to boot, would be a reliable witness.

A woman asked me "Yo' sure you hear shooting after de boat go outa sight?"

I nodded gravely. "Yes. Two bursts."

"Like I say" a man at the other end of the bar interjected. "Dey got it right de fust time."

"If Maurice dead man" someone added "we in de hand of de communist."

All this depressed me. I didn't fancy that swim now, so I returned to my room and took a shower instead.

Chapter Eighteen

What Killed Them?

I awoke around 7, realised where I was and recalled the previous day's events. I decided to take an early morning swim before I spoke to anybody or sat down to breakfast. A few early minutes in the sun would be congenial. Don't wait until the harmful rays penetrate later in the day.

I slid the door of my cottage shut and strolled through the deserted restaurant out on to the beach wearing just my sandals, swimming trunks and a T-shirt, a towel slung over my shoulder and clutching my Hawaiian Tropic. Selecting a spot at random on the virgin soft white sand I flicked off the sandals, deposited the towel and HT, pulled the T-shirt over my head, dropped it on the heap and stood for a few minutes admiring the view.

Out almost on the horizon to my left, beyond the alternating ribbons of turquoise and blue sea, Sandy Island held my gaze. This is the name of the idyllic isle I'd spotted from the ferry. It's a low sandbar supporting two groves of palm trees and fringed by a coral reef. The desert island of the adventurous tourists' dreams. If I have time I'll hire a boat to take me out there. Half a day snorkelling over that reef would be a tantalising excursion for our clients, especially as there's little else to do in Carriacou. For now I'll just have a short swim and then perhaps twenty minutes sunbathing.

The beach shelves gently into a calm, pleasantly tepid, reef-protected shallow sea. After splashing around for a few minutes I found that a short spell of sun was sufficient to dry myself completely. That was an agreeable start to the day. Now I fancied a leisurely stroll along the beach. A few hundred yards ahead I could see a bluff so I decided to wander up to that then turn round and stroll back for breakfast.

I didn't walk in a straight line. I preferred to meander haphazardly at the water's edge so that I could alternate the tactile pleasures of the powdery sand under my feet with the cooling seawater as the ripples swirled up to my ankles.

Just before I reached the bluff something caught my eye. A shape regular and grey, apparently man-made, lurking in the scrub adjoining the beach. Without my glasses I couldn't be sure but it looked like a gravestone. Mildly curious I wandered over there and discovered that yes, indeed it was. The inscription was too worn to be readable but I noticed more of the same further into the bushes.

Very interesting. Why bury people on a beach and then erect proper headstones? Should I investigate? In my practically naked state I was loath to venture further into the untamed undergrowth carpeting the copse of casuarina and manchineel trees. Not that I was afraid of snakes or biting insects. Just that it would be more sensible to get properly attired first.

The historian in me overcame my natural caution. I pushed the low branches aside, ducked under the higher ones and forced my way through the scrub for a closer look, immediately wishing I'd retrieved my sandals to protect my tender city dweller's feet from the sharp detritus on the ground. Stones, twigs and thorns but thankfully no broken glass. I hardly noticed the scratches I was rapidly accumulating on my legs and torso.

On two of these further headstones dates were still

readable. Very strange. They were both adult males who died in June 1692. I knew that date. It was in June 1692 that Port Royal was devastated by an earthquake. Jamaica is a thousand miles away so these two couldn't be earthquake victims.

Those first few headstones were just a hint of what I would find. Peering into the wilderness I could see more slabs of weather-beaten grey stone peeping out from the greens, browns and beiges. Some were still upright but most had subsided to rest at oblique angles. Hardly surprising after almost 300 years. I moved further into the thicket. Now I noticed the black scars of fires and some mysterious holes in the sand adjacent to many of the gravestones. At first I thought I was seeing evidence of some voodoo ceremony, then I realised the holes were probably burrowed by land crabs. The residue of fires was odd though, particularly as they must have been fairly recent. Strange place for a picnic so was this an indication of something more sinister? I'd heard, or maybe read somewhere, that the rituals of a voodoo-type cult were still practised on Carriacou. But here? Surely black magic ceremonies would be performed in a remote spot in the hills, not so close to a tourist hotel and the island's main settlement.

After breakfast I would return armed with pen and paper and properly dressed. Some of these names were familiar.

Look at this. Samuel Kydd, born 1641. So he would have been 51 when he died. Quite a respectable age in those days. But I know that name. What will I find when I check my files? If he was one of those pirates why was he buried here?

Grenada and Carriacou were unveiling all kinds of surprises. First ruthless political brutality and now an historical conundrum.

As I wandered back down the beach I became increasingly excited. I pulled on my T-shirt, scooped up my towel and HT, shuffled into my sandals and wandered into the open-sided restaurant. They won't mind me eating breakfast dressed like this. They're as casual as you can get.

The waitress came over straightaway. The brevity of my attire was not uppermost in her mind.

"You hear de news las' night?" she asked.

"No" I replied. "I went to bed early."

"Austin come on de radio. He say de army tekkin' over de country. Gonna be a curfu" she continued. "Anybody out, dem gonna be shot."

"What, all night?"

"No man, all day too."

"So no-one can go out unless they want to be shot? For how long?"

She shrugged. "Dem saying four days but who know for sure?"

"So nobody can go out" I mused.

"Dat so. How can mudders feed dere lickle chillun? An' de farmer need to tend to his animal too."

A thought suddenly occurred to me. "So how could you come to work then? Do you live here? In the hotel?"

"Dis Carrycou. No curfu here yet. De army people, dem discuss right now."

I thought back to my arrival yesterday and the multitude of revolutionary slogans I saw plastering the barracks. Those did not auger well. On the other hand the two soldiers who questioned me were horrified to hear that the APCs had opened fire on the crowd. It would be interesting to see which sentiment carried the day.

"You know what you havin' for breakfast?"

"Oh yeah. Can you do scrambled eggs?"

The waitress spread her arms. "Sure. Anyting."

"OK. With toast, coffee and orange juice."

As she was turning to depart another thought occurred to me. "Er, hang on" I said. "What about Maurice Bishop?"

"Oh. Like you say yesterday, in de bar. Maurice dead."

I was sure I hadn't said any such thing. This is just another example of how quickly rumours turn into hard facts around here, and in this case there was the authority of a foreigner to boost it. Now the word would circulate how the Englishman who came here on the ferry, how he, with his special camera, had witnessed the whole episode.

After breakfast I returned to my room and checked my notes. Samuel Kydd was one of the sailors missing on the *Nuestra Señora de las Nueces Variadas*. So why didn't that surprise me? Presumably the galleon had survived the tropical storm. For some reason the crew had sailed it to Grenada. Why? Were they trying to escape Henry Morgan or intending to sail around the coast of South America into the Pacific? Then off Point Salines the ship had been wrecked, probably on uncharted rocks.

In 1671 Grenada was occupied by French colonists. They massacred the native Caribs and fought off all new arrivals so this shipload of pirates had plenty of incentive to flee from Grenada and no doubt Carriacou was quiet then. Well, it's quiet now, so back then it was probably barely populated if anyone lived here at all.

I was just picking up my pen and paper prior to revisiting the graveyard when I heard a sharp rap on the glass door. I strode over there and slid it open. To my surprise I was staring at two members of the People's Revolutionary Army. The porch was dominated by a huge, bulging sergeant, well over six feet tall, extremely broad and boasting a waistline which was normally a sign of a comfortable lifestyle. It's a good job these are sliding doors. This chap would have trouble squeezing through a normal doorway. The other man was tiny. Shorter even than me, he was very slim, sharp-featured – I would say rat-faced – and sported a small moustache, steel-rimmed glasses and an officious air reminiscent of a parking warden. There was no insignia on his uniform.

"We need to speak wid you man" the sergeant said.

My heart sank. This looked like some sort of trouble.

"Sure, come in" I replied, sliding the door fully open and standing back to allow them past. "I'm afraid I can't offer you a drink as I only arrived yesterday." A bit cheeky that, but a good icebreaker.

"Dat OK man" said the sergeant as he carefully sat down on one of the kitchen chairs. The other man remained standing. His head was barely above the sergeant's even then.

"We just need to know what you seed yesterday" began the big man, spreading his legs as he settled himself. Possibly his subconscious mind doubted the strength of the chair.

Unsure of their intent and ignorant of the conclusion the meeting of the PRA had reached I decided it was unwise to tell them everything I knew immediately. So I told them briefly what I'd seen from the ferry, beginning with events in town before we cast off and continuing with the glimpses of action in the fort as we rounded the point. The men exchanged glances and nodded. Presumably my recollections were in accord with the accounts they found most trustworthy.

"What appen nex' man?"

"I heard two bursts of gunfire coming from that direction."

"Automatic weapon fire? From de fort?"

"Yes. Probably from the fort, but we were out of sight by then. From that part of St George's anyway."

The soldiers exchanged looks again then the sergeant leaned forward,

"Dis very important man. Tell us exactly what you see from when de soldiers arrive dere."

"There were three, I would call them, armoured personnel carriers. They're like armoured cars but they can carry a few soldiers." My guests nodded. The shorter one pulled up a chair and sat himself down now. "Behind them there was a truck full of soldiers" I continued. "They all stopped then the soldiers in the truck jumped out and ran forward, but to the side. Then the armoured cars drove forward and the first two opened fire with their machine guns into the crowd."

"Jus' the fust two? You sure?"

I spread my arms. "That's what I saw. Maybe the third one couldn't get a clear shot."

"Or mebbe de tird one not wanta shoot de people" the second soldier suggested.

"Sure" I agreed. "That's quite possible. After all, the soldiers in the fort sided with Bishop and the crowd."

This seemed to satisfy them. They both stood, ready to leave. I gained the impression that Hudson Austin could not necessarily count on the support of his troops in Carriacou. The soldiers moved towards the door.

"One thing" I said "before you go. What about the curfew?"

The men stopped and turned around.

"Dere ain't no curfew in Carrycou man" said the sergeant. "Dis a small place. All of us in de PRA got neighbours, brudders, sisters, farders, mudders, chillun mostly too. You tink we gonna shoot dey if we see dem on de street?"

"Haven't you had orders from Grenada?"

"Sure we 'ave orders. Tree time Austin send order. But also we get call by frens in Grenada, some in d'army. What dey tellin' us we not follow dem orders. Maurice de Commander-in-Chief de army and you tellin' us dey kill im. No curfew here man."

As they left the second man paused at the door and delivered a final pronouncement. "De army de servant de people. We not kill Carrycou people."

Well that's good. Now I can go back up the beach without being shot.

I collected my pen and paper and strolled up there. First I returned to Samuel Kydd's headstone. Clearing away moss and three centuries of grot I discovered that there were two bodies buried under it. Lower down I uncovered an inscription for a Francis Kydd, born in 1674. Aha, probably his son, buried with him. So there must have been some women in the community too. Francis was born after the Panama raid and died at the same time as his presumed father.

I spent the next two hours conducting a thorough and systematic search of the area. A few tombstones were chipped, a couple were cracked and some were lying flat, almost completely hidden by the undergrowth. Altogether I counted twenty three headstones. Over half were weathered to the point of being indecipherable, some even worn smooth. On others I could read a few letters and dates, or parts of dates, but it would be a time-consuming and onerous task to find complete names. I decided to concentrate on the four which were still, miraculously, legible. Perhaps the angle of the stones had protected them from the worst of the elements or maybe the mason had incised deeper. I'd noticed on my early morning visit that these were all men who'd died in 1692. Now as I carefully scraped away the moss, lichen and other grot I was able to read their full names and dates of birth. I carefully recorded this information then returned to my chalet and my files.

Taking fresh sheets of paper from my bag I listed their details methodically:

Samuel Kydd, born 1641, died June 1692;
Francis Kydd, born 1674, died June 1692;
Pierre L'Onnois, date of birth unclear but could be 1640, died June 1692;
Henry Vane, born 1645, died June 1692;
Juan Perez, no date of birth shown, died June 1692.

All of these men except Francis Kydd left Chagres on board the *Nuestra Señora de las Nueces Variadas* in March 1671 bound for Port Royal. Why did they all die at the same time? Was it a massacre, or some disease like plague or yellow fever? And was there any significance in the fact that they died at the same time as their fellow terrorists in Port Royal?

Various questions and theories had been roaming around in my head for some time now. This new intelligence added a further dimension. It was time to put it all down on paper in a logical format. I started writing.

Why did Henry Morgan prevent these men repairing the damaged galleon they boarded in the harbour at Panama?

Surely he could have allowed them to sail away if they forfeited their share of the loot? He didn't need the additional manpower now that his forces had soundly defeated the Spanish and he would hardly have objected to them terrorizing Spaniards in the Pacific. Maybe he was afraid that too many others might choose to go with them.

Why did Henry Morgan march 600 hostages from Panama across the isthmus to Chagres and then, eventually, release them?

He had threatened to kill them or transport them to Jamaica to be sold as slaves if they wouldn't tell him where their wealth was hidden. The journey across the mountains and through the jungle would take at least a week in each direction so how would it help him if they revealed the burial places of their valuables only when they reached San Lorenzo or Chagres? Morgan and his men – and the hostages – would then need to spend over two weeks, more like three weeks, going back to Panama, digging up the treasures, then returning to the Caribbean coast with the loot. Crazy. So why would he do it? No historian to my knowledge has yet answered – or even asked – that question. I suspected that the answer held the key to Henry's enrichment.

Why did Morgan insist that every man, including himself, be searched at Venta de Cruces?

This was the settlement where they re-embarked in their boats to return downstream. Officially the search was conducted so that no man carried hidden booty and all would receive equal shares at San Lorenzo. Yet Morgan was accused both at the time and since of cheating his men.

Where did his extra loot come from?

What was the significance of the half-empty barrels of pitch? The explanations offered by Samuel Kydd and his shipmates were reasonable. But why did someone report to Morgan that some of the barrels were full on arrival yet only half-full when distributed amongst the ships?

Why, if he was suspicious, did Morgan order a light punishment? Was he hoping that the repaired galleon would sink so he could claim that these men had secreted much of the booty on board?

Why had they sailed this ship to Grenada?

Perhaps it had been dismasted in the storm and carried here on the currents. Or perhaps the crew still clung to their plan of piracy in the Pacific and intended to sail there by the perilous route around Cape Horn, perhaps attacking settlements in Portuguese Brasil on the way.

Why had these men settled in Carriacou?

Presumably they could have returned to a life of piracy. Maybe they did have more than their fair share of loot on the ship. Which suggests that they kept it so they had no need to continue their lives as outlaws.

Finally, what killed them?

I realised that my thinking was slightly muddled. Also there would be supplementary questions. The answers might well be hidden here in Carriacou. The obvious first place to begin my investigations was by talking to the hotel's owners, a married couple, Canadian.

Chapter Nineteen

Descendants Of The Pirates

I collected a Rum & Coke at the bar and popped into the office. The female half of the married owners was sitting behind her desk poring over the reservations board laid flat on top. There were ominously few strips of coloured tape affixed to it. She looked up as I entered.

"Good afternoon Morgan. Won't you sit down?" With a resigned flutter of her right hand she indicated a wooden armchair facing the desk then continued without waiting for my reply "You've heard the news then?"

"About Maurice Bishop being shot and the curfew? Yes. And two chaps from the PRA dropped by to ask me questions." I sat and reached for a coaster on the desk. Sliding it over I placed my drink on it.

She smiled. "People think you're the oracle around here with that fancy camera you've got."

"I didn't actually take any pictures. I was using it as a telescope."

"Pity. They would make you a rich man."

"I was stunned, frankly. And I felt a bit sick." I sipped at my Cuba Libre. "Tell me about the graveyard."

She started. "Graveyard?" Concern suddenly showed in her eyes, although she made a valiant attempt to smooth over the question. "Oh, you mean the cemetery. It's in town. Anyone can show you where it is. You interested in that kind of thing then?"

"No, not really. I don't mean the cemetery, though I might need to go there as well. I mean the graveyard."

"There isn't another one, not as far as I know anyway." She was calm now. But wary.

"I'm talking about the one a few hundred yards up the beach there" I said, waving with my free arm in the general direction.

"Oh no, I don't know who told you that. There isn't one up the beach."

"But there is" I persisted. Why was she denying it?

"People talk about a graveyard on the beach because they think it adds mystique to the place but it's just an old wives' tale."

I took another sip of Cuba Libre, replaced the glass on the coaster then leant back in my chair. "It was there this morning" I informed her. "I've been up to it twice today."

"Oh that graveyard" she said, as if it had slipped her mind. "It isn't really a graveyard you know Morgan, just a few headstones by the beach."

"Twenty-three. There are twenty-three at least. I counted them. Most are worn smooth but some are still readable."

She rose from behind her desk, strode over to the office door and closed it. She returned to her seat and motioned me to pull my chair close. Leaning forward she explained quietly.

"Those graves have been there a very long time. They spook the locals. When this hotel was being built they found skeletons which must have been washed down here over the centuries. Local people think they have connections with black magic or voodoo."

"Is that why they have fires there?"

"I don't know anything about any fires. Just don't tell anyone about the graveyard. There's nothing interesting about it and it might put people off coming to the hotel."

I smiled inwardly. I certainly had no intention of telling anybody. Coupled with my discovery in Grenada I now knew something nobody else in the world knew. I intended to keep it that way. My secret and mine alone. But I needed more information.

"Most of the gravestones are worn smooth" I said "but a few are readable. They were all men who died at the same time. Why was that?"

She spread her hands and leaned back. "Who knows? The original settlement on Carriacou was over the other side, where the boatbuilding is now. Windwardside. The rumour I heard is that they had an outbreak of yellow fever or perhaps plague or cholera and many of them died. In those days it was normal to bury plague victims far away from where people lived. Like they did in London in the 17th Century. They threw them in plague pits in Kent and those sorts of places and covered them with lime. The British government knows where the plague pits are and they still don't allow building there."

I shuddered. "Thank God. But this isn't a pit. They are all buried separately, apart from a father and son."

"Yes. It suggests there were a sufficient number of healthy survivors doesn't it? And maybe they were quite rich. Maybe they built good boats."

"If ye be so featly with these galleons." That was Henry Morgan's taunt to the men who eventually settled on Carriacou. It seems that their featliness, if that is a word, has been passed down through the generations. For 300 years boat building has been the trade, in a small way, of these pirates and their descendants though nowadays, with virtually no demand for traditional island schooners, it is a skill in danger of dying out. Nevertheless a small community remains on the eastern side of Carriacou. I realised that I would have to travel across the island to find answers to my outstanding questions. Over that side, maybe, there would be descendants of these men who could tell me more.

First let's see what I can find out within easy walking distance of the hotel. As promised there was no curfew here and the village streets were buzzing with activity. Well, relatively buzzing. If it had a horse Hillsborough would be a one-horse town but in those days it wasn't even that and, as in most tropical countries, people didn't feel a need to rush around. The only unusual activity was the sight of small groups discussing the crisis. I spotted two or three soldiers but none were armed. People seemed to agree that The Revolutionary Military Council, the gang of murderers ostensibly headed by Hudson Austin and allegedly running the country, were seeking to impose totalitarian communist government and nobody wanted that. Ironically, in view (literally) of the revolutionary slogans plastered and scrawled all over town, everybody supported and mourned the revisionist Maurice Bishop and his 'boojwa' allies. Talk was now moving on to the possibility of a military invasion by the USA and what, if anything, should be done about it.

My first stop was the cemetery. This was too recently established to contain the graves of Kydd's colleagues, unless they were beneath the really worn stones where nothing was legible, but I did see names of people who could have been descendants of the pirates. I wasn't disappointed as this is what I expected to find. I was just 'eliminating it from my enquiries' as the police would say. Next I tried the small library. The records there were sufficient for those – tourists and amateur historians – with more than just a transitory interest in the island but hopeless for treasure hunters. Fortunately I could find nothing there at all which connected the island with Henry Morgan's assault on Panama.

I had plenty of time at my disposal so the next day I slogged over to Windwardside. As I strolled along the beach I studied a small ship on the stocks in an early stage of construction. It would be one of the island schooners when completed. There was still some local trading up and down the Grenadine chain and these sailing vessels were adequate for the job when time was not pressing. Some, such as *Scaramouche* and *Friendship Rose,* became popular with tourists for day cruises in The

Grenadines. I'd seen a couple of schooners moored at the Carenage in St George's but it would be only a few short years before the world passed them by.

This was reflected in the community there. The houses were mainly wooden, a sturdily-constructed mixture of bungalows and two-storey dwellings. None of them could be accused of pretentiousness. Those that were still inhabited showed signs of proper maintenance but the few abandoned houses I saw were evidence of a community in decline. More than half the buildings were formed into a small hamlet with the remainder scattered randomly. Some were down by the beach and sea, others further back amongst scrub. A number of the men in the community obviously earned their living from fishing nowadays judging by the half dozen boats I saw on the beach.

On this first trip I saw few residents but nevertheless I was encouraged. There was a fisherman mending his nets, another painting his boat and two more having trouble with a recalcitrant outboard motor. I exchanged the time of day or brief words with them. The time for serious questions would come when I was more familiar with the lie of the land.

I decided to stroll through the hamlet. I was further encouraged by what I saw, which confirmed my suspicions. The ethnic mix was more varied. Certainly the predominant type was Afro-Caribbean but there were other mixtures evident. European blood obviously but also I sensed some Indian, as in Native American. That was a surprise. Possibly descended from the Caribs who, allegedly, had been wiped out by the French or committed suicide in Grenada at Caribs' Leap near Sauteurs. I also spotted some who would be classified as White though quite different to the whites softened by city life. These were tanned with tough, weatherbeaten and wrinkled skin. Some had a sort of inbred look to them. I thought I saw a flash of red hair in a darkened doorway.

On leaving the far side of the hamlet I spotted a broken-down building off slightly to the right set in abandoned land

and surrounded by weeds, gorse and trees. Apparently the structure was only kept upright by a tree growing from one corner *inside* it and penetrating the roof. I strolled over there.

Sure enough this was a building of some antiquity but well made. The wood might have been treated with something to prevent it rotting, and to deter termites, as there was no other reason to explain its survival. I stepped carefully through the undergrowth and peered inside. The floor was completely overgrown. Brambles, grasses and even tree roots had forced their way through tiny cracks. I decided to return another day to complete further investigations. This trip is just to get my face known.

As I edged my way clear of the building and turned a corner a butterfly fluttered by.

"Oh, damnation, you've scared it" a man's voice exclaimed sharply. He sounded annoyed. I halted in surprise as a middle-aged white couple rose up from the undergrowth.

"Oh hello. I was just trying to get a picture of that" said the man. He lifted his hat, which was a deerstalker, to introduce himself. That, I thought, is about as appropriate for The Caribbean as my pith helmet.

"I'm Cavendish, Simon Cavendish, and this is my wife Edith."

"Hohw do you doo?" she said.

"Hello. I'm Morgan Fairchild. Sorry to have frightened your butterfly. Are you an enthusiast?"

"Ooh no, not rearlly, we're Twitchers" said Edith.

"That's birdwatchers" Simon explained.

The deerstalker was not the only eccentric part of his attire. He wore shorts, hardly appropriate if he was intending to forage in prickly undergrowth as I had found to my cost when I went crashing through the beachside graveyard in my swimming trunks. I collected a fair number of cuts and scratches which needed a good wash and an application of Savlon. In fact I could see that this man did have scratches on his legs. And he should have been covered up elsewhere too.

Although he wore a short-sleeved cotton shirt which was appropriate for the climate the parts of him which were exposed to the sun had been rendered a bright pink. Obviously he was unaware of the benefits of Hawaiian Tropic or any other protective formulation. Around his neck was slung a Japanese SLR camera with a zoom lens attached, a Konica if I remember correctly, and on his back he carried a small knapsack. Both of them were kitted out in strong brogues and thick socks. Edith wore a lightweight full length cotton dress in a floral pattern and a wide-brimmed straw hat embellished with a powder blue ribbon. A canvas shoulder bag dangled across her shoulder like a child's school satchel.

"Is Carriacou good for bird watching then?" I asked. Maybe this could be another untapped market for Sunstroke to exploit.

"Yes" Simon answered. "The bird life here is remarkably undisturbed. No tourists you see."

Excuse me? So what are you then if not tourists?

"Oh, urr, urrm, why are you heyar?" Edith asked.

"Research" I told her. "I'm a travel agent." They wouldn't understand what a tour operator does.

"Oho no, you're not gohing to send thousands of tourists heyar, are you?"

That made me laugh. "There's not much chance of that is there? With war about to break out."

"War? Heyar? What doo you mean?"

"Either there will be civil war or the Americans will invade. Perhaps both."

Simon says "Do you mean the political squabbling in Grenada?"

"It's a bit more than squabbling. They've murdered the Prime Minister and, if the latest rumours are true, some of his political allies. I myself saw them massacre a crowd of people. Listen to the Barbados station, *CBC*."

"Well I'm afraid we've rather lost touch out here old boy" said Simon.

"Where are you staying?"

"Mermaid Inn."

Good God, that's right in the middle of town. How could they possibly have failed to realise what's going on? They must be pretty dedicated to their birdwatching.

"*CBC* from Barbados" I repeated. "I don't know the frequency because I haven't brought a radio, but people will tell you. Or you could just ask people what's happening."

Edith leaned towards me and spoke quietly. "You know, Morgan, sometimes we have difficulty understanding just whhat they are sahying."

I shrugged. "*BBC World Service*?"

"Oh rearlly? Will it be on the *BBC*?"

"It will be if the Americans invade."

Simon now made a big show of scrutinising his watch. "Look at the time dear! We must be getting back. Nice to have met you Morgan, hope to see you again."

Edith and I exchanged waves as the Twitchers departed, disturbing more butterflies as they went.

Back at my hotel I luxuriated in a long shower then collapsed on the bed. Walking both ways was probably not a good idea. However the adrenalin kept me awake so I made my way to the bar and ordered a beer. The radio was still tuned to *CBC* who had established a special team to deal with the crisis full time. Leaders from the region were unanimous in their condemnation of the murders and the previous day's Cuban government statement was repeated. A particularly telling passage, which made it quite clear that The Revolutionary Military Council could expect no help from them, stated "No internal division can justify atrocious acts such as the physical elimination of Bishop and the prominent group of honest and worthy leaders who died yesterday. The death of Bishop and his comrades must be cleared up. If they were executed in cold blood the guilty should receive exemplary punishment."

A few heads nodded at this even though most had heard it yesterday.

"Dem Cuban, dem not like dis a tall."

"Maurice and Castro, dey close man."

"Yeah, dem good frens."

"If de Yankee dem come dey Cuban dem no gonna help Coard an' Austin."

I turned to the barman. "Anything else happen in Grenada?"

"Well you know" he answered, absently mopping the bar counter, "we hear dey drivin' around in de curfu rrestin' people." He glanced around to make sure nobody there minded him imparting this information to the Englishman. Reassured he continued "Dey lookin' for dem people who ornagise de demastrations an' free Maurice."

"Any news on the Americans?"

"Nuttin' yet man. We was hopin' you could tell us."

I nodded into my beer. "I don't know any more than you. But if you want my opinion" I began, then hesitated. Silence and a couple of nods suggested that my opinion was precisely what they wanted. "I think the Americans will come."

This started a lively debate. Most agreed with The Oracle's assessment but there were several theories of what form this intervention would take.

"Yeah, dem gotta come. Dey bin waitin' on dis chance."

"Dey'll bomb de whole place flat man."

"Dem cain't do dat. Too many of dem own people dere."

"Who gonna stop dey comin'? De militia not gonna fight for Coard, nor some of de soldiers neither."

I left them to it. Moving to the restaurant I demolished a brief dinner and retired to my cottage. Tomorrow I would put myself about at Windwardside again.

Chapter Twenty

One With Red Hair

I felt a strong sense that I was being watched. Good. Although yesterday nobody seemed perturbed as I toured Windwardside I hoped that questions were being asked. Hopefully someone made enquiries last night and now knew something about this tubby fellow. If they'd discovered where I was staying they may know my name. They may even have discovered the name of my employer. They would wonder why a tour operator representative would bother traipsing over to this side of the island and be even more interested in my subsequent visit.

I spotted a group of youths loitering about a hundred yards from the bus stop. Three detached themselves and shambled, chattering in patois, a short interval behind me as I strolled along the beach road. They stopped and watched from a discreet distance as I conducted a brief conversation with the fisherman who was applying a final coat of orange paint to his boat. Then they resumed their shamble as I turned left into the settlement and sauntered through. I paused outside the church and studied it as if interested in its architecture or history. Out of the corner of my eye I saw them engage in some teenage horseplay. I continued slowly, apparently taking note of the rum shop in particular.

Once through the hamlet I left the road and headed for the abandoned building. Where, yesterday, I'd encountered

Mr and Mrs Cavendish. The three lads didn't follow me across the wasteland but stopped behind a tree directly in line with the decrepit structure. This would obstruct my view of them. Shortly before I reached the ruin I picked up a stout stick and began thrashing at the undergrowth. I made a preliminary circuit, randomly beating at bushes, then started to trudge in increasingly larger circles around the building, continually striking loose bushes and weeds as I proceeded. These were not geometric circles you understand. Trees and bushes caused many diversions from a strict spiral. Sometimes I would stop by a tree or large bush and study the base intently. Eventually, when I was about fifty yards from the structure and approximately in line with the door, I strode, as directly as the encroaching scrub and copse would allow, inside.

Now it would be difficult for them to watch me without breaking their cover. They would need to peer through the doorway, one of the two windows or a crack in the walls and there was a considerable risk of discovery. From my vantage point inside this oversized shed I would easily spot any movement in the wilderness outside. But I never spotted faces peering in. They evidently decided to hold station until I came out then presumably one of them would look inside once I was clear of the area.

After ten minutes I forsook the shed and set off back to the village. I sauntered slowly through until I came to the rum shop. I strode up to the counter.

"Have you got a cold beer?"

"Carib?"

"Sure."

Between swigs I asked questions and received brusque answers. How long has the village been here? Long time. Why have people left? Many reasons. Work. I was tempted to ask about smuggling but thought it wiser to avoid that topic.

I'd almost finished my beer by the time the three youths

joined me. Two were black, one with red hair, and the third brown. The red hair looked so incongruous that at first I thought it must be dyed. I nodded to them.

"Morning" I said.

They looked me in the eye. "What you after man?"

I smiled again. Ha. The beater had flushed out the tigers. It was obvious that these guys were interested in my actions which was why I put on that pantomime with the derelict building. I swigged the last of the beer.

"History" I answered. "I'm having another beer. Would you chaps like one?"

"Dat all tree hundred year before man. Why cain't you let it be?"

"What was?"

"Yo' name Morgan, right?" asked Red Hair.

"That's it, Morgan Fairchild." I took a mouthful of beer from my second bottle. "You sure you don't want to join me?"

"So your famly send you to deal with we families. How you find we man?"

What? Now I genuinely had no idea what they were talking about. "I don't understand what you mean. My family doesn't know I'm here."

"You Morgan right? Famly of Henry Morgan."

Now I understood. I laughed and briefly set my beer on the counter.

"I'm not related to Henry Morgan. Morgan is my middle name, like Christian name. Like, er, Henry or Samuel or Maurice." Those were the first three names which came to mind. "My family name is Fairchild. I'm nothing to do with Henry Morgan."

The youths discussed this in patois whilst I retrieved my beer, took a swig and watched them. Then Red Hair, who seemed to be the leader, turned back to me. "So why you here?"

"I work for a travel company in England, Sunstroke

Holidays. We want to arrange Caribbean holidays with a pirate theme. You know, stories of buccaneers and where they went."

"So why you come Carrycou?"

"My company already does holidays to Grenada. I was down at the new airport when I saw some wreckage of a ship." Another swig of beer. "The name was *Nuestra Señora de las Nueces Variadas*. That ship was thought to have sunk in a storm back in 1671 when leaving after the raid on Panama." I spread my palms, almost spilling some of the beer. "So how could it have got to Grenada?"

The three youths again exchanged a few words. Red Hair turned back to me. "So what you sayin' man, was jus' chance."

"Well, double chance. I'm staying at White Sands Beach Hotel."

Red Hair nodded.

I continued "On Thursday morning I was walking up the beach when I saw the graveyard. You can still read some of the names and when I checked I found most were on that ship."

"What names?"

"Oh, if I can remember. Samuel Kydd and someone who was probably his son. L'Onnois, Pierre I think. Henry Vane and a Spanish name."

Red Hair nodded again. He held up his hand and spoke to the others. Turning back to me he asked "What you want now?"

I considered this question carefully. I wasn't going to tell them exactly what I wanted, what I dreamed I might find, but I could shoot them the 'official' line.

"If there's a connection with Grenada and Carriacou it would be good for our programme. People would come to Carriacou on holiday."

"What do we get?"

I pondered. What indeed? Normally natives of the host nations would be employed in hotels, restaurants and night clubs. Sometimes as workers on infrastructural development. Taxi drivers. I couldn't see much scope for any of that here, on the 'wrong' side of the island.

"Well, if there's someone in the village who knows the history, maybe you could have a little shop or museum" I suggested. "You know, sell things to the tourists."

Red Hair gave his attention to the others. They appeared to be waiting on him. He turned back to me. "It not up to us man. We need to speak with people. Come back here tomorrow. Morning."

On Sundays there is no bus so I splashed out on a taxi. I was sitting down by the beach just after 1030, contentedly puffing my pipe and listening to the monotonous tinny klang . . . . klang . . . . klang . . . . klang . . . . klang . . . . klang . . . . klang of the bell on the little church when they found me. Today it was just Red Hair and the brown guy.

"Come wid us man."

We strolled along the beachfront road until we reached a little shack, not much bigger than a shed. Red Hair indicated a crude wooden bench outside. "Wait here man."

The two youths entered the house and emerged carrying a wooden rocking chair which they placed in a shady and breezy spot by the side of the shack. Back they went inside and came out supporting a very old man. His remaining hair and wispy beard were white, but I thought I detected touches of red. He was obviously frail. Carefully they settled him in the rocking chair. At this stage Red Hair considered it proper to introduce himself.

"I Courtney James. Dis my grandfarder, Duncan Selkirk. Well, de farder of my grandmudder." That makes him great-grandfather. I wonder if he is related to Alexander Selkirk, the model for Daniel Defoe's *Robinson Crusoe*?

"Wow, he must be old."

"Nobody know how old him be. But he remember Queen Victoria."

223

At this the old man smiled. Obviously not deaf then.

"De problem, him not speak English like you and me. Not all de time. But he want to tell you de tale. He tinkin' to die soon. He de only one know de story. Many year before, he say, he been told a man would come from England dere. Dis man would want to know de story an' he shoul' tell it. But when him not speakin' clear I de only one understand what im say."

"Thank you" I said. "Can I take notes?" The old man nodded.

Where to start? There were so many questions and probably this man wouldn't know all the answers anyway. And if the tale had been handed down over the centuries the result might be corrupted as in Chinese Whispers.

Start at the beginning. I leaned forward and spoke as clearly and slowly as my impatience would allow. "Why did they try to repair that galleon in Panama?"

The old man's eyes lit up. He cackled with laughter, pointed shakily at me and said something I couldn't understand.

Courtney James translated. "He say dat question prove you are de man he expexing."

"And the answer?"

The old man leaned forward and took a deep breath. "Dey" another breath "dey find sumting hid."

"Gold?"

The old man coughed and nodded.

"An altar?"

Now he got excited, pointed at me again and cackle-coughed.

Interesting. I had already worked out, more or less, what really happened with that altar, but I didn't realise they'd stumbled on it so early.

The brown guy, who for some reason was never introduced, was despatched for some beers with funds I was pleased to contribute. The old man was given a drink of water before questioning resumed. Well, would have resumed, but as I was about to speak he held up a hand to stop me. He called Courtney close and croaked out a long tale, incomprehensible to me, then made sure he had been understood. The beers arrived so Courtney sat back with his and translated.

"Dis altar was in de church. Solid gold man. De priest paint it black, tinking to fool de pirates. But Henry Morgan see it an' when he tink nobody see, im scratch de paint in a part outa sight. But Vane, dat Henry Vane, see im. So when Morgan lef' de church Vane go an' check an' him see gold shine dere. He tells de udders and dey gets a carpenter to mek a copy outa de mahogany wood. Dey find some gold paint an' paint it. Den, when it dry, dey paint it black. When it dry again dey mek a scratch where Morgan scratch. Den dey get de luck. Morgan tell dem dey ave to tek de mules wid de tar. So dem break up de real altar an' put it in de pitch barrels. Now de funny part." He took a swig of his beer before delivering the punch line. It's the way you tell 'em.

"Jus' before dem all leaving Morgan come back for tek dis altar. De priest dere. Course he don't know dat de real altar gone. So he tell Morgan, No, dis altar not gold. It wood, painted gold. So Morgan find his scratch mark, he tink, cut deeper and find it wood like de priest him say. So he leave it. De Spanish, dem tink de priest save dis gold altar but it just painted wood an' Morgan never know dat dere was a solid gold one."

We sat back and assimilated this. Duncan Selkirk, the star of the show, beamed. I calculated. OK, that answers the question of the half-empty pitch barrels. Or does it?

"Did they put anything else in the pitch barrels?" I asked.

Selkirk almost choked on his beer. I should have waited until the guy was lying back rocking gently in his chair, not starting to sample his Carib, but I could barely control my impatience. I was really getting somewhere now. After a brief splutter Selkirk was again pointing at me shakily and giggling.

"Jewels" he said.

"Jewels?"

"Dimons. Emrals. Jewels."

Courtney was becoming engrossed in the story too. Probably he realised that it was a fascinating tale which it would be tragic to lose when the old man died. Maybe he could work with me on this one to our mutual benefit.

We both realised that Duncan needed another break so we supped our beers for a few minutes. I suddenly noticed that my bottle was empty and reached for another. I'm becoming an alcoholic I mused. I resumed my questioning.

"The prisoners Henry Morgan took back to San Lorenzo with him. They weren't from Panama were they?" I caught the glint in Selkirk's eyes and continued. "They were from San Lorenzo and Chagres, evacuated when the Spanish knew Morgan's armada was coming. So they buried their valuables near their homes on the Caribbean side before leaving for Panama. Is that right?"

Duncan Selkirk nodded with his broadest grin yet. He'd obviously decided to pace himself now. He summoned Courtney and spoke to him quietly and slowly then sat back.

Courtney turned to me. "Jus' Morgan an' a few frens know dis. Dey tell de 'ostages if dem tell anyone else dey 'ave dere troat cut." He made the sign with his finger. "So after a night of de pirates drinking plenty an' gamblin', when Henry Morgan ships ready to leave, dem mek dese people dig up dey valables. Den dem load up all dis stuff in de middle of de night and lef' fo' Jamaica. Henry Vane him see all dis appen because Morgan friendly wid im. Morgan tink he got Vane spying on Kydd an' de udders but really Vane spyin' on Morgan."

Obviously I had a lot more questions but I could see that all this storytelling was inflicting a strain on Duncan Selkirk. I didn't want the old chap to die just yet.

"Maybe we should take a break" I suggested. "I could come back tomorrow morning."

Duncan nodded. "Nine" he said, and pointed at me in a way which meant Don't Be Late.

Chapter Twenty One

With The Help Of The Tree Root

I was losing touch with news from the outside world. I mean Grenada of course. Investigating the wanderings of Samuel Kydd and his shipmates was becoming an obsession. I'm as bad as The Twitchers, although hopefully my investigations should be more profitable than theirs. So with my research activities on hold until the morrow I decided to seek out the latest news on the crisis.

As soon as I arrived back at White Sands I showered, dressed in a change of clothes and ambled over to the bar. From speaking to the barman and his customers, combined with what I was hearing over the radio – still tuned to *CBC* – I quickly ascertained that most countries with interests in Grenada had condemned the massacre and the murder of the Prime Minister. Caribbean nations were particularly incensed. The exception, unsurprisingly, was the Soviet Union, but they were about to become an irrelevance.

A substantial US carrier fleet was steaming towards Grenada. Officially they were coming to evacuate foreign nationals, particularly hundreds of medical students who were studying here because they had been unable to secure college places in the USA. The US government claimed that counting all these students, retirees, nationals working here and tourists their citizens in Grenada totalled more than 1,000. That's a laugh I thought. Now they're admitting that their own citizens outnumber the Cubans!

Of course no-one believed that this task force was hurrying here for the purpose of evacuation. Hudson Austin's Revolutionary Military Council was not preventing any foreign nationals from leaving and instead – in order to forestall an invasion – they were trying to assist wherever possible. Any medical students who wanted to leave could do so and those who feared for their safety were flown from the island on four charter flights. Quite a number remained, but only because they chose to. LIAT flights were suspended on the orders of the airline's shareholding governments but Pearls airport was still open and in use.

Radio bulletins were biased and repetitive as is usual when the media report 'breaking news'. Whether this was due to incompetence, ignorance or the result of journalists believing the briefings fed to them was irrelevant to me. I just knew that the Carriacouan man in the street was a more reliable source of information. So I took to the streets.

It was going to be another of those deliciously cool evenings. A gentle stroll through Hillsborough was very calming. People seemed strangely relaxed, apart from those with relatives in Grenada. There would be no curfew here and the local PRA troops were standing firm with the citizens. From talk in the bar and eavesdropping around town I was able to discover the Cuban government's position.

Apparently the RMC had been begging Fidel Castro to send troops and weapons but the Cubans had steadfastly refused. If there was an invasion, they insisted, Cuban nationals would restrict themselves to self defence within their workplaces. They would not attack the Americans and neither would they co-operate with the Grenadian forces in any way. The message was straightforward – "You've made your bed so lie in it." They would give no support to the RMC until the murders of Maurice Bishop and his closest allies were properly investigated and the perpetrators punished. It occurred to me that there was insufficient time for such an investigation to be conducted before the US task force arrived. So quite obviously the Cubans would be keeping their distance.

I stuck my head through the door of a bar popular with members of the People's Revolutionary Army. There, sitting with a group playing dominoes, was the sergeant who'd visited me. I strolled in and stood nearby watching the game. At a suitable break in the proceedings I addressed him.

"The Americans are coming then."

"Yeah man." The sergeant didn't deem it necessary to look up.

"I suppose the RMC want you chaps to go down to Grenada to help."

"Yeah man." Still his eyes remained on the cluster of dominoes being shuffled around the table.

"So are you going?"

Now the sergeant twisted around in his chair and faced me. "No-one ain't goin' man. You tink we goin' down dere to help dey Bishop murderers? Tink agen man."

The game resumed.

So, I surmised, if nobody was travelling down from Carriacou, the Grenadian militia couldn't be counted on for support, the Cubans had made it clear that they wouldn't help and there were bound to be more desertions from the PRA, then there would be very few nuts for the Yankee sledgehammer to crack. I concluded my intelligence-gathering foray and returned to the hotel.

I awoke with a strong sense that today would be an important day in my life. Quite the opposite of a normal Monday Morning feeling.

I arrived at Duncan Selkirk's shack at five minutes to nine to see the old man somnolent in his rocking chair. I feared for a moment that he'd died. I leant over and could just hear gentle breathing so I sat on the bench and waited. Sure enough Courtney soon ambled into view and within a few minutes was sitting between us. He placed his hand on the old man's left arm and Duncan opened his eyes. We got down to business.

"So they smuggled the golden altar and the jewels aboard the ship they were allocated. Did they take them out the barrels first, or did they carry the barrels on board?" I asked.

The old man knew his end was near. He'd evidently decided to pace himself today. He explained the pirates' actions slowly and patiently to Courtney. After fully five minutes Courtney turned to me.

"Like my grandfarder say yesterday, dem ave to tek de mules wid de tar barrel. Morgan ave all de men search at Venta Cruz, imself also, but dey expek dat from Henry Vane spyin'. So everyting dey got dey put in de barrel. Dey see dat some of de barrel got red cross on dem. Dey know from Vane dat dem ones got stuff which Henry Morgan hidden usin' de same trick as dey."

I judged it inadvisable to be drinking beer so early in the day so I'd brought some cold Cokes with me this morning. We opened the first three. Courtney resumed.

"When Morgan tekken his loot outa dey barrel dose barrel now 'alf full only. So Kydd and dem tek out de jewels but leave de gold. Dem tek de barrel wid de gold on to de ship, which need pitch for de repair."

He took a long swig of Coke before continuing. "Some of de udder pirate suspicious dem when they see de 'alf full barrel so dey speak to Morgan. He tink they mean him barrel, dem wid red cross, and he know why dem 'alf full. But Morgan gotta do something, so he shout at Kydd and de udders. Dey tell dat de tar escape from de barrel when de mule fallin', so Morgan tell de udder pirate dis. But one man say some of dey barrel full when dey arrive. Kydd say Yes, of course, we took dose for repair dis wreck ship you give us. Morgan happy wid dis because no-one suspek him."

I was amazed at the wealth of detail Duncan Selkirk

remembered. He was telling a story which had been handed down by word of mouth over three centuries. Perhaps each custodian of the story impressed upon his successor the paramount importance of accuracy. I would have liked to ask about the veracity of the evidence, how sure Duncan was that the tale had been passed down unchanged. But better not put too much strain on a dying man. I decided to concentrate on drawing out the facts I needed first.

I moved on to the pirates' departure. "Two days after they left there was a storm. Some of the ships became separated from the fleet, but they all got back to Port Royal or Tortuga except *Nuestra Señora de las Nueces Variadas*. How did they end up in Grenada?"

I could tell from watching Selkirk's face that this would be a very long answer. I relaxed whilst Courtney bent close to hear clearly. There were two breaks in the account where both Courtney and Duncan took refreshment. Finally Courtney was ready to spill the beans.

"Wha' happen, dey was lost in de storm. When de storm finish dem see no ships. So dem say Why go Port Royal? We cain't spend dis stuff dere. Iffen we go east an' change de name of dis ship den Morgan tink we lost. So dey go Barbados and find a lickle bay wid no people livin' near. But soon dem find dat Morgan was known in Barbados. So dey take fright an' bring de ship to Carrycou where no people livin'. No white people. Dem sail down Grenada but find de French control dere." He looked at the old man to confirm that he was telling the tale correctly. Duncan nodded.

"Dey tink better not change dis ship because people know it anyway. So dey build pinnaces and udder small boat. Dem mash up de ship at Point Salines dere and sail up to Carrycou in de lickle boats."

OK, so far it all fits. But what happened to the loot? They would have been rich so why pursue a humble life boatbuilding? And what killed so many of them in June 1692? I patiently put these questions to the old man who nodded but asked us to wait. I took a second Coke and wandered down to the beach.

The regular rhythm of the incoming waves lapping the sand was conducive to pensive brainwork. If, I mused, the altar was solid gold they could melt it down. Obviously it was not formed as one piece or they wouldn't have been able to fit it into the pitch barrels. Probably interlocking sections. The jewels would be negotiable. Both melting down the gold and flogging the jewels were activities best performed in Barbados. The island attracted settlers only from 1627 but it was developing rapidly. So probably they returned from Barbados as wealthy men, if they'd tarried there long enough. Perhaps they decided that retirement in a backwater was safer than a continued life of crime and the risk of being traced by Morgan.

They may also have heard about the Jamaican Governor's recall to London and his imprisonment in The Tower. This was his punishment for allowing the assault on Panama. The infamous raid had been launched in spite of a peace agreement signed by England and Spain so all hostilities should have ceased. As the perpetrator of Panama's destruction Henry Morgan was also brought to London and charged but his glib tongue and heroic status with the populace got him off the hook. He was knighted and sent back to Jamaica as Deputy Governor.

Now there would be no more commissions to raid Spanish settlements and capture their galleons. Pirates would be hunted down by the Royal Navy and executed unless they desisted. The risks now were so much increased that only desperate men and psychopaths would continue to terrorize the Spanish. Of course, some of Kydd's men may just have been tired of the pirate lifestyle with the attendant risks of being killed or maimed in action, maybe dying of malaria, yellow fever or a host of other diseases. It was a rough existence alleviated only by whoring, drinking and gambling. What was a pirate's life expectancy? Dead before 30?

I wandered back up to the shack and resumed my seat. In my absence Duncan had finished telling the tale to Courtney. He was ready to repeat it.

"My granfarder not too sure what appen to de gold an' jewels. He tinking dey exchange some for land. Mebbe here, mebbe Barbados. But dem hafta leave Barbados sudden. Some stay here but some of dem catch a French ship and sail for de southern ocean dem call it. De people here never hear from dose men again. Now de sickness. Dat very strange."

He shook his head in wonderment then took a swig of Coke. He glanced at his great-grandfather who seemed alert still, but less so. His spirit wouldn't keep his body alive much longer.

Courtney settled back. "Dere was about eighty people here den. Forty eight men and de rest women an' chillun." He leaned forward. "De strange ting, exactly half de men, twenty four, die of de sickness. An' even more strange" he wagged his finger "it happen de same time Port Royal fall into de sea. De same year, de same month, mebbe de same day!" He slapped the bench three times, forcefully, on year, month and day.

"What were the symptoms?"

"Not plague. Not yellow fever. Not quite malaria. Just shakin', tremblin', very hot den very cold. Den in two or tree days dem dead." He looked me straight in the eye then slapped the palm of his hand firmly on the bench again to emphasise the point. Clearly he was already familiar with that part of the tale. Its hint of supernatural forces would go down well in Carriacou.

"Divine retribution perhaps?" I suggested.

"You say it man!" Courtney responded excitedly. "After dat appen, de ones still doin' a little piratin', dey stap also. Now jus' boatbuilding', fishin' an' smugglin'. Some start a lickle farmin', growin' a lickle an have some stock."

Well, I don't think I have any more questions. From what I've been told I can work out the rest myself. I think I'll just go and let the old man die in peace. I stood up, ready to thank them and leave, but was stopped by Duncan Selkirk. He grabbed my arm roughly and with more strength than I would expect in a very old and dying man. He pulled me close.

"The kirk" he said. He pointed with a wavering arm. "The kirk."

He made a sign to Courtney that may have meant "Show him" or "Help him." Then he sank back in his chair exhausted. We looked at him, gently rocking, and decided that he wasn't about to die just yet.

Courtney and I stepped out of the shade and strolled into the sun. "Thank you for all your help" I said. "The problem is, I feel like I've killed your grandfather."

"Doan' worry yourself bout dat man. Everybody got to die some day. You hear him say, he just waitin' on you to come. He very old, mebbe a undred. He cain't do tings. We haveta look after de house, cook for him, cleanin', sometimes dress him. We don't mind, but him do. He just wanting to die in peace and him can now for he tell you what dem say he must."

We pondered this for a few minutes. Then I asked "What was that about a kirk?"

"You already knows about dat man. We seen you dere, walkin' round wid de stick de udder day."

"That old abandoned building outside the village? What did Mr Selkirk mean?"

Courtney shrugged. "Me not know man. You better jus' go an' look. Harder dis time."

I strolled through the village up to the kirk. Part of the reason for my pantomime with the stick was precisely because I suspected it was a disused church and I was looking for the graveyard. I hadn't discovered any signs of one so maybe I should concentrate my efforts on the ruin itself. I entered.

Presumably I was supposed to be looking for something. Either something valuable or further evidence of Kydd's sojourn here. First I checked the walls. They did appear to be too thin to have any hidden panels but nevertheless I probed around them, carefully searching for anything unusual. As I stumbled through the undergrowth and over brambles I was glad I'd come in sensible shoes.

It took me a good hour to scout all around the walls as far as I could reach, just above head height. I found nothing. I decided to try the floor next. If I drew a blank there and needed to investigate the roof and upper sections of the walls I could come back later, or another day, borrow a ladder and climb up.

Some of the floorboards were intact though covered in creepers, grasses and moss which had obviously been growing for a long time. Other parts of the floor had been pushed upwards by hardy shrubs forcing their way up in search of light. I checked those first. Those shrubs must be stronger than me because I couldn't budge those planks. I found my stick where I'd left it on my previous visit and forced that into some of the cracks but still made no progress. After a time I gave up. Tired and sweaty I gazed around the ruin's interior. The region most damaged was the corner where the tree was growing so I did the intelligent thing and crossed over there. Perhaps a floorboard had been loosened three centuries ago. I reasoned that if anything had been secreted under there then that part of the flooring would have been most easily dislodged.

Sure enough it appeared that some planks had been forced out of position by a force stronger than the rusty nails which held them. On close inspection it looked like this tree, when a sapling, had pushed itself through a gap between boards. Over time it had forced those boards up. They were good hardwood too. I selected one which was very loose, pulled it free and used it to lever up the adjacent planks. It was a tricky and lengthy job. Sometimes the tree's roots were in the way, sometimes they aided me in my search by providing a fulcrum. Eventually, breathing heavily and by now covered in sweat, I stood upright and surveyed the result of my efforts. I'd created a space under the floor large enough to reach an arm beneath but not of a size to permit a man to climb under. Even allowing for one or two centuries of growth since the kirk was abandoned I estimated that even at construction the gap between the floorboards and the earth would have been too tight.

If only I'd brought a torch or, even better, a chainsaw. With a chainsaw I would have been able to cut through the undergrowth, the bushes and roots which impeded me, if not the floorboards. Choosing my spot carefully I lay down as comfortably as I could and felt around in the gap I'd made. There was nothing there on the ground.

It now occurred to me that if the pirates had hidden anything they might have attached it to the underside of the floorboards. I felt around. Still nothing until I came up against the tree's roots again.

There I felt something man-made wedged between the root and the underside of the floorboard. I ran my hand around it as far as I could. I felt straight edges. It could be rectangular, and parts of it felt metallic. I withdrew my hand, sat up and examined that floorboard from above. It was already raised a little from its original position and, unless the tree died, it would be forced away completely within the next fifty years so exposing its secret.

I couldn't wait that long. I reached to the side and reclaimed my handy plank. With the help of the tree root I began prising away at the underside of the offending board. Eventually I wrenched it up to reveal a very old bible. This was a shock. I didn't think pirates had any use for bibles. I eased it out with minimal damage to its mouldy binding and turned it over in my hands.

Because of the ornate nature of the metalwork, which I suspected was brass beneath the corrosion, I concluded that it was probably Spanish. I speculated as to whether the text was printed, or written, in Spanish or Latin. Actually, I decided, if it was of 17th century vintage it would be Latin. Unless it was an English King James bible.

It was held firmly shut by a metal clasp which would have been a secure fixing when the item was produced. Now, with centuries of corrosion sealing it, I couldn't get it to budge. I realised that modern tools would be needed to prise it open. So I will take this away to inspect minutely and then, depending on what it reveals, perhaps I will return to complete my search. First I need to report to Courtney James.

I emerged from the kirk to see the sun sinking low in the west behind the hills. Good God, I've been at this for over half a day. No wonder I'm hungry – and thirsty. I'll pop down to the rum shop for a beer and then find Courtney.

I was in luck. Courtney was in the rum shop surrounded by eight or so men of varying ages listening intently to him. He spotted me approaching but presumably didn't recognise me immediately. He looked away, then sharply back at me and laughed. "Man! Yo' sure been lookin' *hard*."

I scrutinized myself as well as I could without a mirror. I was covered in muck from chest to ankle with cuts and scrapes on my arms and legs. I'd again made the mistake of wearing shorts. My shirt was torn. I chuckled and ordered a Carib.

"I'm looking for you" I told Courtney. "I found this."

"Keep it. My granfarder want you ave it man. You eard he dis morning. Tomorrow I tell him dat you find it den him die in peace."

He waved a hand towards his attentive listeners. "I bin telling de story man. Without you come my grandfarder die unhappy an' de story gone too." A couple of the men nodded as if grateful.

"I would like to take this back to my hotel if I could."

Courtney flicked his left wrist. "Take it man. It yours now."

One of the group was a taxi driver so once I was refreshed and partially rested I engaged him for the trip back to White Sands. Courtney had included me in his talk while I knocked back a couple of beers and the taxi driver extracted further details on the run back to the hotel. I reckon I'll be remembered in Carriacou.

Back at the hotel some journalists had arrived. They seemed a bit sniffy about the standard of accommodation on offer but I caught enough of their conversation to discover their interest here. They were anxious to get to Grenada as quickly as possible, preferably before the commencement of hostilities. They were already established at the bar of course. If any of them noticed this exhausted and bedraggled fellow tumble out of the taxi they would have assumed I was just a twitcher having a bad day.

Chapter Twenty Two

The Assorted Hacks

I lingered under the shower. Then, with time at a premium, I dried myself and dressed promptly. I hadn't eaten since breakfast, there was dirt under my fingernails and one was broken. It was probably around 7 now and I would need to be in the restaurant no later than 8 if I wanted dinner. I felt occasional rumblings from my stomach, urgent messages muttering Hey, Don't wait until 8, what if there's no food left?

But I was excited by this mildewed grot-encrusted bible. Sure, there was a possibility that the pirates had turned to religion. Half the men in the settlement had died from a mysterious illness within days of each other so it was quite likely that many of the survivors would have become religious. Certainly once they heard, probably within a year, that Port Royal had been devastated by an earthquake in that same month they may have suspected a supernatural hand. The biblical legend of the destruction of Sodom and Gomorrah would emerge from a half-forgotten childhood memory to the forefront of their minds. It was quite likely, as Duncan Selkirk said, that those survivors still engaged in piracy would stop immediately. A church would be built if one didn't already exist. A bible would be found. If not a King James translation then one in Latin would do.

But there was a chance that this bible wasn't used for religious purposes.

Fortunately I'd brought a copy of the *Free West Indian* newspaper. I opened it out at its centre pages and laid it on the kitchen table. I placed the bible in the middle and started rummaging in the kitchen drawers for utensils that might prise open the brass clasp.

First I scratched and probed the metalwork with the combination can and bottle opener in an attempt to force a gap but only succeeded in scraping off chunks of corrosion. There was no movement at all in the clasp. OK, I did realise that this artefact could be a valuable archaeological treasure, but the fact that I'd discovered it hidden under floorboards suggested that it had a secular use. It might contain some secret. The greedy fortune hunter overcame the historian. Why hide a bible in a church? If it was of great value in its day it would have been hidden somewhere else, not stuffed under the floorboards. If it was purely a bible, used regularly for religious purposes, then you might keep it in the church but you wouldn't hide it.

My hesitation was brief. After another fifteen minutes of determined scraping the good news was that I hadn't damaged a precious antique. The bad news was that I'd removed most of the corrosion but the clasp was still locked solid.

I sat back, picked up the bible and turned it over in my hands. It was bound in a thick brown leather which was mildewed over most of its surface area. There was even a risk, after maybe three centuries of exposure to a humid climate, that the pages were glued together so that if I did manage to unlock the clasp I might still have difficulty opening it. That could be a major problem if there was a secret message written on a sheet of paper inserted between two pages. Or, worse, if something had been inscribed in invisible ink. Did they have invisible ink in those days?

I returned to the kitchen drawers again but none of the implements there looked suitable. One or two of the knives might eventually force the pages apart if time was not pressing. If, for example, I was just starting a ten year prison sentence. However I would like to eat tonight and preferably after I had revealed this bible's secrets. I needed tools.

Stopping briefly at the bar to grab another beer I called next at the manager's office. Tonight the husband was on duty. He glanced up from his desk as I entered.

"Hi Morgan. I saw you get back earlier. You looked as if you'd been down to Hell and back. Been prospecting in graveyards again?" Obviously his wife had told him about my trek up the beach the other day.

"Sort of. Do you have some tools I can borrow?"

"Anything specific?"

"Well, probably a pair of pliers and a file would do." I thought perhaps a chisel would be useful too but as this was likely to be returned with its cutting edge damaged I thought it best not to mention that.

He pointed to a corner. "In that cupboard there. A toolbox. Use anything you want but be sure to bring everything back."

I gave him a mock salute. "Yes sir. Thank you sir." I retrieved the tool box and took it back to my room.

Ten minutes work with the pliers and file was all I needed to force the clasp open but, as I'd feared, the pages were stuck together. To find out if it was a Spanish bible, and to ascertain which language it was printed in, I would need to separate the first two or three pages. But some intuition told me not to bother about that right now. Instead I rummaged through the tool box searching for a sharp knife. Ah, great. There was a Stanley knife. I took that and carefully inserted it about one third of the way into the book.

Painstakingly, starting in the middle of the longest side, I eased a gap between two pages. I slid the knife all along that side and then down both edges as deep as the blade would reach. It was only about an inch but it was a clean separation. Then I returned to the kitchen drawer and selected a broad-bladed kitchen knife that seemed reasonably sharp. I eased that in further all round. Now the pages were opening up. Printed type began to appear but I didn't stop to decipher it. The bond created by centuries of tropical humidity was slowly surrendering.

Suddenly I met no resistance. I was able to slice the remainder of the way through to the spine and completely separate those pages. Now I could check which language the divine message was recorded in. And I hadn't really damaged anything. I put the knife down and opened the book. Latin? English?

Who cares?

What I saw banished any historical curiosity. And any feelings of guilt I was suffering for assaulting a precious artefact. I was staring at a crudely cut rectangular hole. Well, not just that. An oilskin package reposed there.

I pulled it out carefully and unwrapped it. Inside, in pristine condition, was a rolled sheet of parchment. Now I was beginning to get excited. My first instincts were correct – the pirates had no use for religion. This parchment scroll, hidden in a bible concealed in a church, must provide a clue to buried treasure.

I unrolled the parchment to find another, slightly smaller, sheet tucked inside. I unrolled that. Now I held two maps drawn in pen, or quill, and ink. Black ink. The first was headed 'Barbadoes' and consisted mainly of a serrated line twisting a tortuous route from the bottom left of the sheet to the top right. It was uneven with occasional indentations and the odd spike. Were it a sales graph in the offices of Sunstroke Holidays the MD would be very pleased.

Evidently it was a coastline. On the right, or the underside, of the line the sea was depicted by a couple of squiggly lines. A fish surfaced for air through a couple more waves and a galleon had been crudely drawn. No mermaids though. If the arrow in the top right corner indicated north then I must be looking at a sketch of the southeast coast. A sloppily-scrawled circle isolated a patch of this coast.

Perusing the other map I decided that it represented a detailed close-up of the circled area. Apparently it indicated the location of something. The letter Z lay halfway along two twisting equidistant dotted lines. Apart from the titling on the first map there was no writing on either, front or back, except for that Z on the second. Presumably the finder of these was expected to know their significance and, probably, also what awaited discovery at the Z.

Was someone having a little joke here? Why a Z instead of an X? Was this whole thing a hoax? Also I'd heard, or read somewhere, that the pirates habitually booby-trapped their buried booty. If these chaps had fled Barbados for Carriacou I could see no reason to leave anything behind. Perhaps this was a trap for Henry Morgan, his associates or descendants should they trace the Kydd gang to Carriacou. Well, I thought, tough. I've come this far so I'm not going to chicken out now. This is my secret agenda. My dream. I'm off to Barbados ASAP.

But first I was off to the manager's office and restaurant to return the tools and get some dinner. With a brief nod and a Thank You to the manager I returned the toolbox and headed for the restaurant.

The journalists – there were seven of different nationalities – were already seated and enjoying a lobster dinner with ample liquid refreshment. I selected the table nearest to theirs so that I would be within earshot. Noticing, by observing their relaxed demeanour and other clues from their body language, that the assorted hacks were not intending to scoff their food quickly before retiring for an early night, I took my time to order and then consumed my meal at an even more leisurely pace than normal. This gave me plenty of time to learn how they'd arrived here, when and by what means they intended to continue to Grenada, and also to find out the latest intelligence on the impending war.

Apparently the Barbados government had banned all flights to Grenada and Carriacou. Not just the LIAT scheduled flights, but also charters – except those arranged to evacuate the medical students – were *verboten*. When one of these reporters asked the Prime Minister, Tom Adams, to lift the ban so as to permit journalists to report on the political crisis he received an evasive response. So the group assumed that the Barbados authorities, and therefore presumably also the US government, intended to keep reporters out of Grenada.

Now why would they want to do that? Obviously because they were preparing an invasion. These journos had therefore determined to get to Grenada as quickly as humanly possible.

So they chartered a small plane to fly them from Barbados to the tiny Union Island. This is the nearest nugget of Vincentian territory. It's just three or four miles away and within sight of Carriacou. They then employed a fisherman to bring them over in an open boat. There should have been eight of them but apparently another reporter failed to make the rendezvous in Barbados.

The US task force had arrived and was anchored on the horizon off the southwest coast of Grenada. I also learnt that over the previous few days there'd been a flurry of meetings between the leaders of those Eastern Caribbean nations that were former British colonies and are now members of the Commonwealth. Allegedly Eugenia Charles of Dominica and Tom Adams of Barbados were to the fore. The reporters seemed to think that these politicians were trying to agree a formula under which an American invasion could be passed off as legal. They also believed that the British government was not in favour of an invasion and, furthermore, it was telling questioners that an invasion was unlikely.

Unlikely? Very few people here believed that. The journalists expressed different opinions to explain the UK's official position. Two thought the Thatcher administration really believed it and blamed the incompetence of the intelligence services, others thought they were being misled by Reagan's officials whilst a couple expressed the view that they were lying as usual.

Now this is the bit I wanted to hear. These chaps have chartered a boat to take them into St. George's early tomorrow morning. Maybe I can get myself on it. I waited for a lull in their conversation then leaned over.

"Excuse me. I'm Morgan Fairchild. I'm a travel agent staying here. I couldn't help overhearing some of what you were saying. Are you all journalists trying to reach Grenada?"

They were in good humour. Pleased with themselves for outwitting the Barbados Prime Minister, relieved that they had managed to slip away from Saint Vincent's Grenadines before the authorities banned reporters heading for Grenada, happy that they had been received cordially by the Carriacou administrator and replete after a pleasant meal, they were prepared to talk to me. They introduced themselves.

After a few minutes of inconsequential chat I cut to the chase.

"I heard you say you've chartered a boat to take you to Grenada tomorrow morning."

Two or three exchanged looks.

The ringleader answered. "Yes. We're sure the Americans will invade and we want to get there before they do. Also, of course, we want to report on the situation there as we find it. We don't expect it to be as relaxed as here."

"It won't be" I said. "It was starting to get nasty when I left."

"When was that?"

"Wednesday."

"The day of the massacre? When Bishop was killed? Did you fly up?"

At this point the whole group was starting to become interested. This fellow might have some newsworthy information.

"No. I came up by boat. I was wondering if I could go back the same way, tomorrow, with you chaps. I'll pay my share of the charter of course."

Now the journos were sitting upright. Some were anxious to discover how much I knew, others seemed dubious about the wisdom of allowing me to join them. Four spoke at once.

"Are you the guy with the camera we heard about?"

"Not a good idea for you to come with us. It's dangerous."

"Did you see it all happen?"

"What did you see?"

I decided to play it cool. I held up my hand to arrest the flow of questions and took a sip of my Tia Maria. If I could get the majority on my side they would let me join them. What would they want? Mainly an eye-witness account and also, perhaps, an exclusive interview.

"First" I responded "the danger. If it's dangerous for me then it's dangerous for you. So maybe you shouldn't go either."

"We're used to it. We're journalists. You're a travel agent."

I ignored that. "Secondly, I've been in the country almost two weeks now. I arrived in Grenada a couple of days before they arrested Bishop. I was there for over a week so I saw the demonstrations. I spoke to people, listened to people, drove around the island. I've met Bernard Coard" – a slight exaggeration, but never mind. "I also have a good English-speaking contact among the Cubans."

I paused to let that sink in and note the reaction. These chaps did seem very pleased with themselves so I reckoned they would let me accompany them if they could get an interview with an eye-witness. I finished my pitch.

"I can tell you a lot about what's been going on there, but it's getting late so there's no time tonight if we have to make an early start tomorrow. The trip will take four or five hours so I can tell you all on the boat."

They discussed this proposition. It was late and they did need to be up early. They'd eaten well and drunk their fill so most of them didn't fancy an exhausting interrogative session right now. Some of them, of course, had secret plans –

specifically, how to get me alone for an exclusive interview. At the moment the majority seemed to be in my favour but eventually they decided to make a final decision in the morning.

"We'll be leaving at about 7. Let's see the situation then. We'll let you know."

"Fine. No problem. I'm going anyway tomorrow, so it's just a question of whether I go with you or by myself. I'd prefer to go with you because it will be cheaper."

Favouring them with my best smile I rose and stepped over to their table. Pulling out my wallet I handed each a business card then after a "Goodnight" sauntered to the bar to settle my bill. Within ten minutes I was back in my cottage and packing. I tucked the maps safely inside their oilskin bag and returned the package to its centuries-old home. Carefully I wrapped the bible in clean pages from the *Free West Indian* idly wondering, as I did so, whether any of Grenada's totalitarian Marxist-Leninists had read George Orwell's *1984*. That newspaper's readers certainly weren't free. Maybe the *Free* just meant you didn't have to pay for it.

I was already asleep when the first one tapped on the window. A very discreet tap, but obviously enough to wake me.

"Errr uh" I said through my daze.

"I want to talk to you" a voice whispered.

I'm sure you do I thought. And if you get the information you seek you'll be voting me off the boat in the morning. I groaned "Whaaaat?"

"I need to talk to you."

"Have you seen the time?" I had no idea of the time but it's what people say in movies in these situations. "We'll talk in the morning."

"My paper would pay well for an exclusive."

"Tomorrow. Goodnight."

There was further whispering but I pulled the sheet over my head and ignored all entreaties.

Twice more I was awakened, once by a rap at the door and again by tapping on the window. This time I ignored the whispering and knocking. Hopefully these three would now be in favour of me joining them tomorrow.

Chapter Twenty Three

A Legitimate Target

At 06.50 I slid the door shut for the last time, leaving the key in the lock, and wandered with my bags over to where four journalists, also packed and ready to go, stood talking. They were listening to a radio.

"It's started" said one.

An officious male voice issuing from the radio was instructing 'The People' to defend their homeland.

"*Radio Free Grenada*?" I asked, again conscious of the unintentional Orwellian reference.

"Yes. They're claiming that US Marines have been landed in force by helicopters at Pearls. Also Point Salines has been attacked. They're not sure whether they were paratroopers or not there."

That reminded me. "I heard someone say they were going to block the runway at Point Salines with trucks and oil drums" I told them. "So that planes couldn't land."

Now the whole group was assembled and taxis were waiting, although the dock was just a short distance away. Obviously too far for journos to walk.

"You'd better come with us" one of them suggested. Nobody dissented.

My journey back to St. George's was a lot less comfortable than the trip north. We all clambered into a 15 foot open boat powered by an outboard motor. It boasted a crew of two, Captain Albert and his mate. Mind you, an open boat has its advantages in a war zone – the warring parties can both see that none of their enemies were on board.

We set off at about 07.30 and the journalists sensibly started quizzing me on my experiences as soon as we were under way. From their baggage they produced an assortment of tape recorders and dictating machines. One guy was also taking notes, an intelligent precaution. He would still have something if the authorities confiscated their machines and tapes. One of the group was a photographer. He took a few shots of me. It's a shame I didn't still have my pith helmet. That would give him the kind of picture newspaper editors love.

"I just know him as Roberto. I don't know his second name. He gave me precise figures for the Cuban personnel there." I repeated these, as accurately as I remembered. One of them suggested that the airport workers were possibly soldiers in disguise.

"I doubt it" I responded with a laugh. "The ones I saw were middle-aged."

I recited a comprehensive description of Point Salines, emphasising the civilian facilities in the course of construction and the total lack of any military infrastructure.

"What about the runway? It's 10,000 feet according to the Reagan administration."

"9,000 apparently. But they need that for the big jets. They'll want to get 747s and DC10s in."

Another chap was interested in the two Russians.

"A man and a woman" I told him. "Probably in their 40s. Maybe 50s."

"Describe them."

"I only saw them twice and I wasn't wearing my glasses. The first time was when they arrived. It was dark. The second time they sat at the far side of the restaurant."

"Well? Were they tall, short? Fat, thin?"

"Average. They just looked like, well, Russians."

"So. Were they wearing fur hats?"

We all laughed at that. Of course most of the questioning was aimed at discovering as much as possible about the events of that tragic Wednesday. I repeated slowly, in detail, the events as I had witnessed them.

After we passed the northern tip of Grenada and were stuttering down the coast we saw the first signs of war. A column of smoke ascended skywards from the vicinity of Victoria. Helicopters flitted around on the horizon down south. Some of the group watched and remarked on this whilst others continued interviewing me. Obviously that's when we were spotted.

The interview was rudely and suddenly terminated as two US jets screamed past us. They turned, circled back, slowed and buzzed us. They came close enough to check that there were no uniforms or weapons aboard and may even have taken photographs. I realised they were not going to attack us. We were not yet a threat to their invasion plans. If we were a small group hostile to their forces – perhaps the PRA members from Carriacou hurrying south – we were neutralised as long as we were chugging along in the open sea. It was not necessary to blow us out of the water just yet.

Some of the reporters waved their arms and shouted to the planes in what they judged to be a friendly manner. It's a pity they don't have a Stars & Stripes with them I thought. Someone suggested waving a white shirt but another guy pointed out that was a signal of truce or surrender. Hardly appropriate as we were noncombatants. The jets roared out of sight, presumably back to their carrier, and we continued to chug southwards.

Well before this event *Radio Free Grenada* had gone off the air. Possibly the transmitter at Morne Rouge had been taken out or maybe US troops had captured the radio station. Then again perhaps today's temporary staff, presumably diehard Coard and Austin supporters and members of the militia if not the PRA, had grabbed their weapons and were fighting the invaders. The journalists now tuned their radio to a *Voice of America*-style station, *Radio 1580*, which was pumping out pro-American propaganda and reports – not of course strictly truthful – on the situation in Grenada.

Half an hour after the military jets left two helicopters appeared. They were out at sea but heading towards us. As they clattered closer I could see machine guns protruding from both sides. Gunships? They approached rapidly then hovered about a hundred yards away. Then they circled round behind us and stationed themselves between the land and our little boat. Southeast of us. The sun behind them. I had to shield my eyes to make out what they were doing. I assumed they were taking pictures, both still and video footage. Probably right now images of the boat with its captain, mate and eight passengers were being studied back at the flagship, *USS Guam*.

Captain Albert and a couple of the journalists were nervous. The captain, who was probably regretting his decision to accept this charter, only continued south because he wouldn't be paid until he delivered us to St. George's. I'll admit that I was a little trepidacious too, although I calculated that we wouldn't be fired upon unless Rear-Admiral Joseph Metcalf III was sure we were a threat to his plans. Fortunately Reagan's administration were aware that their invasion would be heavily criticised around the world so they would make sure that 'collateral damage' was restricted to the minimum. Blowing a boat carrying a contingent of international journalists out of the water would not be clever. Thus I reasoned. But then I had my own agenda, one more exciting to me than the attentions of a couple of helicopter gunships. I was anxious to get ashore and then on the first plane to Barbados.

After half an hour the helicopters headed off to the southwest.

St. George's was definitely a war zone. Before the town

came into sight we heard the very faint popping of automatic gunfire punctuated by an occasional explosion and the howl of jet aircraft engines. I also imagined I could hear the whaap whaap whaap whaap of helicopters. Were they landing assault troops near the town?

The captain was not keen to continue and some of the reporters expressed concern too, although all of them were anxious to arrive. I was also keen to have dry land under my feet although I preferred to keep well away from any battles which might be raging.

Once St. George's appeared we studied Fort Rupert. I clicked my 300 millimetre lens on to the camera but even without it I could see that the fort had suffered bomb damage. The green roof of the citadel was fractured and a gaping hole was clearly visible. Looking through the lens I expected to see frenzied military activity but all appeared quiet. Deserted. An odd contrast to the murder of innocents I witnessed when I last passed.

We rounded the tip of the peninsular. In contrast to the desolation of Fort Rupert I saw people rushing in and out of the hospital on the point. Also at sea level, or just above, but much further away to the east on the far side of the harbour at Tanteen Field, I glimpsed the frantic movement of military vehicles. There was obviously an anti-aircraft battery situated near to it. I heard repeated thuds from that direction and saw flashes and occasional whiffs of smoke. Further away still, up on and beyond Richmond Hill, I could see black fumes rising in a writhing column. The prison was in that direction and also a couple of forts if I remembered correctly.

Captain Albert headed as quickly as possible for the safest landing place on The Carenage. He slithered our exposed craft against the harbour wall on the far side by the fire station. It was not quite the nearest dock, but he must have judged it the quickest and easiest to reach. The reporters scrambled ashore as soon as the boat was brushing the wharf. I did too, throwing my bags on to the quayside then leaping after them. Just as the last man was ashore two jets blasted overhead on a strafing run. Anti-aircraft and small arms fire from the defenders spat into the sky. Most of us hit the deck but a couple ran into the fire station.

Almost immediately a Land Rover screeched to a halt and four PRA soldiers leapt out. Shakily we all stood up, brushed ourselves down and accompanied the soldiers into the nearby building. They checked our documents and found them to be in order. We were then instructed to remain there whilst the American bombardment and Grenadian defence continued. Some of the reporters wanted to roam around to discover evidence of damage and casualties but initially they were kept inside for their own safety. Without doubt it was dangerous out there. We'd already seen the damage inflicted on Fort Rupert and the PRA men told us that Butler House was being continually strafed. Interesting that the Yanks hadn't bombed that.

The first targets the aircraft aimed for were all the command and control centres. Nowadays that's standard military practice. Their intelligence suggested that the RMC and PRA were co-ordinating their operations from Fort Frederick. So blitz it. Very unfortunately their information was faulty. They confused Fort Frederick with Fort Matthew nearby so that was the first objective. But Fort Matthew is – was – the mental hospital. Denizens of The Crazy House, as it was known locally, were already wandering around the streets of St. George's unable to comprehend what was happening to them. Maybe they were the lucky ones. By the time digging in the wreckage was completed, a week later, dozens of bodies were unearthed.

My major concern was to keep my holdall safe from prying eyes. At any time an officious member of the PRA might call in and decide to search us and our belongings. My best plan, I decided, would be to tell any official that I'd drawn the maps myself for the purpose of these theme holidays that Sunstroke were planning to organise. Obviously, if we were to offer holidays based on the legends of buccaneers the company would need to sponsor some sort of treasure hunt as part of the fun. But better hope we wouldn't be searched because they might confiscate the maps and then I would never find my way to the site.

Whilst the thunderous barrage of bombing and strafing attacks, defensive anti-aircraft guns and even the popping of Kalashnikovs continued to reverberate around the town I sat and thought. The Revolutionary Military Council was short of friends. To be precise, outside Grenada they had just one, The Soviet Union. Well, maybe places like North Korea in addition but the point was – they must be feeling isolated. They may even know that their enemies were trying to prevent journalists reporting the invasion accurately. This could be why we were being treated courteously after our unconventional arrival and were now being protected. So, maybe, if I could persuade these soldiers that there was an even safer place for me they might allow me to go there. Even better, they might take me. So where would I be safer?

Somewhere a fair distance from the military targets but still close to, or in, St. George's. South of town would be best as an assault force was most likely to attack from the north. Radio reports suggested that their snatch squad of navy Seals, tasked to extract and protect the Governor-General, had infiltrated from the north in the early hours. Also both sides were anxious to keep hostilities away from the Grand Anse area because most of the medical students were holed up there.

I would need somewhere to sleep so a guest house or hotel to the south of town would be perfect. And there could be nowhere better than Ross Point Inn. I could prove that I'd stayed there prior to departing for Carriacou from my bills. Also, because of the hotel's strategic position, the PRA might have someone there to watch the capital as they did the night Bernard Coard came to dinner. So I would still be supervised.

After we'd been cowering in the fire station for a couple of hours an officer arrived in a Land Rover. Again he was courteous to us and promised that as soon as it was safe we would be taken to a hotel in the town and provided with facilities to communicate with our newspapers. This wouldn't be until the evening, he regretfully told us, as any movement in St. George's during the day was being targeted by US planes and helicopters. The officer was sure that the aggressors would have monitored our arrival, would know we were journalists, and would therefore have made the fire station off-limits to their air forces. Therefore, he said, you must stay here until the evening. A corporal would be sent later to give us any assistance we might need.

I realised that this was my opportunity to speak up. It was like being back at school. Please sir.

"Excuse me sir" I said. "I don't need to be in town at all. I'm not a reporter."

The officer turned to face me then glanced at a list of names and professions attached to a clipboard he held in his left hand. "You must be Fairchild."

"Yes. When I was here a week ago I stayed at Ross Point Inn. That's south of town, before Grand Anse."

The officer stared at me in amazement. Is this guy, a foreigner, telling me about my own country?

"I know where it is" he said.

"Maybe I could go there."

"And how you tink you get dere?"

"It's less than two miles from here. I could walk. My bag's not heavy. If the Americans see me they'll think I'm one of their students or mad."

The officer gave me a withering examination. Maybe he agreed with my assessment of the Americans' potential judgement. But then he seemed to concede that moving me somewhere distant from the fighting could be a good idea.

"OK. Dat your bag? Take it. Come."

I squeezed into the back of the Land Rover alongside two

soldiers, my bags on my lap. The driver engaged first, hurled the vehicle round in a tight 180° turn and set off for the south at speed. Almost immediately we hurtled past Tanteen Field, which I could see was indeed a major centre of defensive operations. Military and commandeered civilian vehicles were hurtling into the compound or departing hastily and armed figures in military uniform were rushing around. There was a ring of anti-aircraft emplacements spurting fire and metal into the sky.

As we approached a bend in the road I heard the clatter of an American helicopter. From the cramped confines of the Land Rover it was difficult to see it but by craning my neck and leaning against the window I caught the occasional glimpse. It swooped low and turned, apparently about to wipe us out. To the north and east buildings provided some cover and prevented a clear field of fire so the pilot, perhaps wishing to avoid collateral damage, decided to sweep in from over the expanse of Tanteen Field. He could tuck in behind us and chase us down Tanteen Road. I presume that was his plan of attack.

That was also his fatal mistake. As he banked hard over and prepared to blast us out of this world anti-aircraft guns and Kalashnikovs poured hundreds of rounds into his machine. Not a sitting duck but certainly a cumbersome and slow-moving one. Ignoring the danger its crew fired at the Land Rover just as we swerved to avoid a crashed motorcycle and its injured or deceased driver, separated and prostrate in the road, slaloming between them. The bike was partly on the sidewalk, almost inverted, its rear wheel still rotating furiously. The rider was inert. The soldiers and I were thrown against each other as our driver slewed the vehicle between the two and accelerated away. Then the helicopter was hit, obviously by something more powerful than AK47 bullets. It bucked, the rotors feathered, then it turned on its side, twisted back in the direction of its attack, plummeted into Tanteen Field and exploded in a ball of orange flame. The soldiers cheered. The officer turned around to me.

"See what I mean man?"

I adopted a suitably chastened expression and nodded. I was more than a little frightened. Up to now I'd been excited in the same way that war correspondents would be. Sure, I was surrounded by people trying to kill each other, but nobody was trying to kill me. Now that had changed. As far as the Yankees were concerned anything moving on the streets of St. George's was a legitimate target. And it was over a mile to my hotel.

It was the possibility of more helicopters with aggressive intent that worried me. I was sure that the jets would leave us alone as the Land Rover was a swiftly moving objective hurtling along narrow winding roads bordered by civilian buildings. Bad PR for the invaders if too many houses were blown up by their jets. Worse if they killed more innocent Grenadians. Perhaps realizing this the driver avoided the coastal Lagoon Road, where traffic would be completely exposed to an attack from the sea, and took the winding and hilly street through the suburb of Paddock. Without slowing he screeched into the right fork on to Belmont Main Road, again twisty and bordered by tall trees and tiny houses. The soldiers in the back and I craned our necks, peering as best we could into the sky. The driver and the officer concentrated on the road ahead.

We hurtled round another right hander into Belmont and within a few minutes we were pulling into the driveway at Ross Point Inn. The officer was out of the vehicle before it had stopped moving and headed for Reception. He spoke briefly to someone then rushed back indicating to me to get out.

"Dey got no electric but you here now so you stayin'."

"Thank you" I said as I rapidly ejected myself and my baggage from the Land Rover. I could live without electricity. The words were barely out of my mouth before the officer was back in his seat and they were rocketing out of the driveway. That's decent of them I thought. They don't want to make the hotel a target.

Chapter Twenty Four

Confusion And Accidents

Sir Paul Scoon was the Governor-General of Grenada, the Queen's representative and therefore the acting Head Of State.

As part of their spurious cloak of legitimacy the US Administration devised a spiffing wheeze. This scheme would make their invasion legal. They would sneak a detachment of Special Forces personnel into Grenada, snatch Sir Paul and ferry him out to their flagship. Awaiting him was a document typed up and ready for his signature. This was an invitation for the USA to invade Grenada to save the people from the murdering bunch of thugs who styled themselves The Revolutionary Military Council. As soon as Sir Paul had the pen in his hand the invasion would begin.

In the dark wee wee hours of Tuesday 25 October Navy Seals were dropped north of St. George's. They made their way quickly to Government House, located Sir Paul and prepared to extricate him. Unfortunately they were spotted and the alarm raised. Grenadian forces surrounded them and kept them pinned down with small arms fire. Oh dear. The invasion will have to go ahead without the Governor-General's signature then.

In fact it will have to commence immediately in order to rescue the Seals.

At dawn helicopters landed an assault force from the 22nd Marine Amphibious Unit at Pearls Airport. The anti-aircraft battery I'd noticed on my arrival knocked out one of the helicopters but failed to prevent the Marines from quickly securing the airport. This was just a foothold of course. Large aircraft can't land here and Pearls is the opposite side of the island to the capital. But it would serve as a staging post for helicopter-borne troops.

Simultaneously 500 Rangers parachuted out of ten C-130 Hercules aircraft above Point Salines. As they hit the ground a firefight ensued with soldiers of the PRA and idealogically-committed militiamen. Around an hour later the Rangers had cleared the trucks and barricades from the runway and formed a defensive perimeter. Now the first wave of what eventually became 5,000 troops of the 82nd Airborne could be flown in.

All this noise awakened the Cuban construction workers. Although there were just a few military men among them, and this wasn't their fight in any case, they must have been prescient. The weapons stores were opened and small arms distributed. Castro later claimed that "there were not enough to go round" which is probably why a number of unarmed Cubans were taken prisoner by the invaders. Using these prisoners as a human shield in emulation of Henry Morgan's tactic at Portobelo the 82nd Airborne attacked the construction workers.

This was a mistake. Presumably they assumed that assaulting dispersed groups of a few hundred half-trained middle-aged men stiffened by a handful of soldiers would be a walkover. Instead they found themselves pinned down. Then they were attacked from their rear as the PRA forces were reinforced by militiamen from other parts of Grenada. The Grenadians knew the lie of the land. The invaders didn't. As evening approached control of Point Salines was still in dispute. US forces held the runway and surrounding area, which allowed them to bring in further troops of the 82nd Airborne, but they couldn't break out. Or overcome the Cuban construction workers.

OK, Plan B. At 1800 hours the US representative in

Havana handed the Cuban government a note, seemingly, of apology. It expressed regret for the assault on the construction workers and blamed "confusion and accidents". The Cubans fell for it. The note and a lull in the fighting suggested that now they would be left alone. If only.

Of course I didn't witness any of that. I arrived at Ross Point Inn late in the afternoon. I was allocated my previous room and found a partial solution to the problem of cold showers and warm beer caused by the electricity supply cuts. I bought a few beers, filled a basin with cold water and left them lying in it. So they were slightly chilled at least.

From my strategic location I observed the continuing air strikes. Pairs of jets screamed in from the sea on low-level strafing runs. I learned that Fort Rupert had been bombed and rocketed during the morning whilst we were still chugging south from Carriacou. The PRA soldiers and anti-aircraft crews had abandoned the position as indefensible which is why it was both damaged and deserted when we passed. The defenders were also afraid that the hospital would suffer collateral damage. Now the planes were bombarding targets above the town, probably Fort Frederick and Richmond Hill prison I reckoned. It seemed though, to me, that they were taking care to pound only military objectives. The great majority of the town was spared. This gives the lie, I thought, to the myth that when the Yanks launch an attack they flatten everything in sight.

Helicopter gunships occasionally clattered into view from all directions. They targeted anti-aircraft emplacements, the frenzied military movements at Tanteen Field and the PRA units still racing around town in Land Rovers and commandeered civilian pickups.

The defenders blasted their ordnance skywards in hope. Obviously they lacked radar-guided weapons. If they had Surface-to-Air Missiles they weren't using them. Maybe such sophisticated weaponry was under the control of the Cubans. Who were hoping to stay out of the conflict.

On that first day I saw no sign of American ground forces. Probably, as Grenada has no air force and PRA anti-aircraft fire was both inaccurate and feeble, the US plan was to knock the stuffing out of the defenders before putting boots on the ground.

Tuesday night I took stock in the garden looking towards St. George's. The aerial bombardment ceased at nightfall. Now the main event was Butler House blazing away. Occasionally aircraft screamed overhead but they kept well out of range. Must be some form of reconnaissance. Again I relaxed on a sun lounger and again I had company.

This time it was two soldiers of the PRA sitting a few feet away. They were celebrating a stalemate.

"We still got most of de new airport" one told me. "Dem Cuban workers holdin' off de Yankees and de PRA still got Calivigny. All de Yankees got is Pearls an' Grenville."

I found out later that this assessment was largely correct though a slight exaggeration. I hoped the two Cuban soldiers I met on Grand Anse Beach were OK. Roberto is probably inside the embassy so he'll be fine.

The apology delivered to the Cuban government was insincere. It was just a ploy to buy a breathing space. During the night further planeloads of the 82nd Airborne were flown in so that by dawn they had a significant force of 3,000 well-trained and heavily-armed professional soldiers to overcome the Cuban workers. Which they did during Wednesday. Twenty four Cubans died in an invasion which had nothing to do with them. Collateral damage?

Also on the Wednesday morning the situation changed in St. George's. Still in Ross Point Inn's garden, and with my 300 mm lens locked on to the camera, I saw US Marines arriving in town from the northern suburbs. From time to time the two PRA men would borrow my equipment for a closer look at certain locations in the town. Listening to their squawking radios and eavesdropping on the occasional visits from their colleagues I picked up scattered news of the conflict.

They were elated when they heard of an action on Grand Anse Beach. I don't know if this incident actually occurred as I have never heard it corroborated, but at one point a soldier rushed to them in the garden. The excitement was obvious but I couldn't understand their euphoric exchanges. As soon as the messenger departed I asked what he'd told them.

"Dey shoot down a Yankee helicopter man."

"Where?"

"At Grand Anse" the second man answered. "Dem ave a missile launcher at Spice Islan' Inn."

An hour later their euphoria turned to despondency. A radio report claimed that a US jet had destroyed the cottage along with the missile launcher and its crew. Further reports increased their despondency. Point Salines airport and the surrounding area had been completely overrun by the 82nd Airborne. The Cuban workers had surrendered and were now prisoners. The final centre of resistance was the PRA's Calivigny Barracks and that was surrounded and under attack from overwhelming force. As we saw US troops investing the capital with very little opposition the two soldiers moved away from me and discussed the situation in a huddle. About half an hour later they departed with a slightly sheepish goodbye. I was now in sole command of Ross Point Inn's garden.

It was all over by Thursday morning. US forces had overrun the Point Salines area including the airport and the Cuban compound as I'd been told. They located and then surrounded the medical students with a protective cordon, quickly took control of St. George's and captured the Calivigny Barracks. Most members of the Grenadian People's Revolutionary Army and the militia abandoned their vehicles, their weapons and their uniforms then disappeared. Over time they would reappear as civilians. Now, judging from the radio broadcasts I heard in the hotel lounge and the relief expressed by the staff, I decided it was safe to wander the streets again.

Nevertheless I thought it wise to wait until the afternoon just to be sure. After all, I am Walter Morgan Fairchild the travel clerk not some Rambo-style hero. So after lunch, during which I remembered that there were still two Sunstroke Holidays clients on the island, I set off walking to Blue Horizons.

This was the same route I'd taken that Sunday, my official day off, nearly two weeks ago now. But this time there were no cruising cars or groups of citizens anxiously discussing the political crisis. Just an eerily empty road and an air of calm like you get when a storm has passed. Turning a corner I encountered a platoon of the 82nd Airborne.

"Hi" I said.

"OK" they answered, apparently glad of an excuse to stop walking.

"You guys see any action?" I asked.

"No" one replied mournfully "only when the Marines was firing at us."

Another asked me "Are you a journalist?"

"No, I'm a tour operator. That's like a travel agent. Sunstroke Holidays."

"Sunstroke!" a third exclaimed. "That's the outfit that crazy couple said they was with."

"What crazy couple?" I asked.

"Down there on the beach" he answered, waving his arm whilst reaching for his Luckies with his free hand.

"About an hour ago" said the first soldier. "We seen this couple lyin' on the beach. Leo here thought it was a trap. We'd be ambushed by Cubans, you know. So we went in real careful, checked the trees, checked for booby traps, you know, the usual, got to the beach an' it was just this limey – sorry, I mean Briddish – couple."

"We said 'Come on. Let's go, we'll get you out'. They refused."

"I said 'There's a war on, didn't you know? We have to evacuate you'."

264

The soldiers seemed to enjoy telling this tale. Some were now smoking, a couple were sitting on their packs, others leaning on their assault rifles. M16s.

"Yeah, they're real comedians. The guy says 'Call this a war?' Turns out they was in some place one time where Greeks and Turks was shootin' each other."

"Cyprus" I suggested.

"Yeah, I think that was it. Guy says 'We've paid for us 'oliday so we're gonna enjoy it'."

"The guy's nuts. Says they had no news for a week, no English newspapers and nuthin' about England on the radio. Asks me do I know the English soccer scores from the weekend."

"I think I know who they are. I'll go and talk to them" I offered. "They're due to leave on Saturday so if LIAT aren't flying by then you'll have to evacuate them anyway."

"You think you can talk some sense into them?"

I laughed. "I doubt it. They'll probably invite me back to their hotel for a beer."

"It'll be a warm beer with these power cuts."

"They won't mind that. They're from the north of England. They'll be used to it."

As I left them I heard one say "That limey's nuts as well. Wanderin' about like that. What's he gonna do if he gets caught or shot by Cubans?"

I agreed. The Walter Morgan Fairchild of a few weeks ago would have left for Barbados as soon as trouble started brewing. He certainly wouldn't have joined a small group of journalists on a tiny chartered boat heading for a war zone.

Sure enough my clients were down on the beach preparing to head back to Blue Horizons. Sure enough they invited me to join them for a drink. Sure enough, the beer was warm.

"I'm gonna complain to my travel agent about this" said Ted with a wink.

"About the invasion or the warm beer?" I asked.

"T' beer of course. You southerners think we like it warm up north. Not so. Not lager any road."

"Why did you decide to come to Grenada?" I asked, just to make polite conversation.

"Well, some year ago, when they won the Miss World, I said to Mabel – didn't I Mabel? – she's luvly. We'll 'ave to have us 'oliday there one year."

"Then it were on one of they 'oliday shows on telly" Mabel contributed. "An' Ted says 'We'll try that'."

Ted winked again. "Though she'll be a lot older now."

Mabel nudged him with her elbow. "Ged off wi' yer. No, Morgan" she continued "none o' t' neighbours had heard o' place an' no-one in t' street has been. So we thought we'd be first."

Chapter Twenty Five

Little England

I needed to get to Barbados as quickly as possible. Just my excitement of course. If there truly was a hoard of antique treasure buried on the coast then an extra couple of days here wouldn't make much difference. It had remained hidden for three hundred years so how could someone else beat me to it now? I would wait patiently for LIAT flights to recommence.

I spent Friday mooching around St. George's and the Grand Anse area inspecting collateral damage. Thankfully there was hardly any. I already knew about Tanteen Field, Fort Rupert, Butler House and 'The Crazy House'. The waterfront of The Carenage had survived remarkably intact. Those tiers of Georgian buildings rising up the hillside in that comforting semicircle were still a photographer's delight. There were a couple of hotels – The Grenada Beach Hotel and Secret Harbour spring to mind – where US troops smashed through unlocked doors in a fruitless search for non-existent Cuban soldiers but vandalism was thankfully rare.

As I wandered the streets I noticed graffiti sprayed and painted on walls throughout St. George's Parish. I never witnessed anybody writing it but I assumed grateful Grenadians were the perpetrators. I further presumed it was a spontaneous outpouring of gratitude to the USA. The message was always the same – 'GOD BLESS AMERICA'. Only a cynic would suggest that the Psychological Operations Battalion of the US Army, landed as soon as fighting permitted, had a hand in this expression of thanks for deliverance from evil.

Certainly everyone I saw and spoke to was relieved and happy to welcome the US occupying forces, in spite of minor inconveniences such as roadside vehicle checks. The children were excited to see all these military jeeps and trucks and hordes of gum-chewing Yankee soldiers. They loved the constant flow of helicopters. The adults were glad to have been delivered from Communism and totalitarian rule. Many refused to describe recent events as an invasion.

"No Morgan, it's not an invasion, it's an intervention" was the most common riposte when I spoke in plain English. Some went so far as to describe the US action as "a rescue mission".

Whatever the terminology employed I agreed that this state of affairs was the best result for the country. I remembered the fear that the hardline Marxists had inflicted on the mass of the population. The willingness of the Coard faction to murder indiscriminately. There was no doubt that the Grenadians' welcome of the invaders was genuine.

Unlike the lies broadcast by the US Administration. The Cubans were not building a military airfield, a staging post for Communist aggression in the region. Their soldiers were not encamped on the island in large numbers. And they certainly had no involvement in the wholesale killing of Grenadian civilians.

Of course the Americans had no real desire to help Grenada's people. They had intervened purely in their own interests. To them the invasion was just a cleaning job, sweeping a nest of Marxist-Leninists out of their back yard, an intervention in line with previous escapades in The Caribbean and Latin America. Enforcement of The Monroe Doctrine. Their attempts to legitimise it by flaunting a handful of soldiers and policemen sent by tiny Eastern Caribbean states – and claims that the Governor General had requested their help – fooled very few informed international observers. Their assault on the cabins of the Cuban construction workers in a pathetic attempt to claim an easy victory over illusory Cuban military forces did delude many ordinary people – principally their own citizens back home and most of the fighting men – but that propaganda success was short-lived outside the USA. A United Nations Security Council motion condemning the invasion was only scuppered by a US veto. Britain abstained.

Many Grenadians I spoke to felt let down by Britain, in particular by Margaret Thatcher. It was only the previous year that the UK had sent a large naval task force to the Southern Atlantic to restore British rule to The Falkland Islands.

"Why didn't Margaret Thatcher help us Morgan?" I was frequently asked. "Is it because we're black?"

How to answer that one truthfully?

"She wasn't ready for it" I usually explained. "The Americans had their troops ready and they'd been practising for months. Thatcher's mistake was not supporting Reagan. 'Ronnie told me he wouldn't do this' is not good enough."

"Right man" a smile and a slap of hands was the usual response to that.

Why am I defending Thatcher? I thought. I must be mad.

Now, at last, the new airport at Point Salines had become a military base. But it was controlled by the US military, not the Cuban/Soviet variety threatened by Reagan. Now it was out of bounds to civilians. Thank God I went down there when I did. The Yanks have probably tossed that pile of rubbish back into the sea by now. Without the evidence of that scuttled ship I wouldn't have been so thorough in my researches in Carriacou.

LIAT were allowed to resume services to Grenada just in time for Beryl and me to get Ted and Mabel on their previously booked flight to Barbados. I flew with them. As I made my departure the Americans were negotiating a lease on Ross Point Inn, which was to become their embassy. So I was the last person to stay there as a hotel guest. I left my wooden bowsprit behind, idly wondering what the new tenants would make of a rotting piece of a ship's timber. They'll probably chuck it out with the trash and never know its significance.

There was still a military presence at Pearls Airport but now there were different accents, different uniforms and different assault rifles. M16s instead of AK47s. The twin-engined Cuban aircraft, which they had been using to ferry their officials back and forth, was still parked there. I suspected that it wouldn't fly again.

Departing Grenadians were being scrutinised closely. Members of the Coard faction were being rounded up all over the island and interned whilst they awaited trial but there was no interest in a couple of tourists and their travel agent.

Now we were sitting in the upstairs restaurant in the new Departures Terminal at Barbados airport, chatting and occasionally glancing out through the picture windows.

"You spoilt our fun there Morgan" Ted said. "I were lookin' forrard to flyin' in one o' them Yank army planes."

I laughed. "You blew it Ted. You had your chance on Thursday when the 82nd Airborne tried to evacuate you."

"Oh no, we still 'ad two days of our 'oliday left."

"Don't mind him love" Mabel said. "He'd rather have the comfort of a proper flight really. He jus' wants summat to tell his mates down t' pub."

"I would have thought he's got plenty to tell his mates" I said, turning to her with a smile. "He won't have to buy a drink for weeks. This will have been on the news back home every day."

We'd noticed parked US military aircraft as our LIAT flight landed. Taxiing to the terminal we saw a cluster of vehicles and stacks of stores at the old terminal building with men loading and unloading at a leisurely pace. Obviously the government here had reopened the facility and handed it over temporarily to the Americans. Presumably ordnance and supplies were being shipped to and from Grenada. But here at the new building all action was overtly civilian. Ted and Mabel's Coconut Airways DC10 was being cleaned and fuelled ready for the flight to London. Ted was gazing out at the aircraft.

"It don't say Coconut Airways on it" he observed. "It's British Caledonian."

"Well" I replied "everything out there is not what it appears to be. They never had any planes. Originally they were run by Laker and you know what happened to him. You see those two Pan Am jets there?"

"What of it?"

"Why two? One, at the most, is their scheduled service. The other will have something to do with this invasion."

Once I'd seen Ted and Mabel off I could concentrate on my own plans. First a hotel, preferably one featured in Sunstroke Holidays' programme, then buy a decent map of Barbados, next a little reconnaissance trip to the appropriate stretch of the southeast coast. If, indeed, that proved to be the part of the coastline depicted on the maps.

I checked into Casuarinas Beach Club, a fairly new apartment hotel built among casuarina and palm trees on the beach at Saint Lawrence.

This enclave became popular in the 70s with British holidaymakers of enterprising tastes but limited means. It was, relatively, a haven of tranquillity. The main route from the airport to Bridgetown follows the coast for much of its journey from the fishing village of Oistins. As it reaches Maxwell Highway 7 shies away from the sea, taking a more direct route to Graeme Hall. Just fine if you want to get from the airport to town quickly, but you will have bypassed some lovely beaches. To see those you would need to abandon the traditional route. Turn left at Dover. The minor road takes you past Luigi's Italian restaurant to Casuarinas Beach Club.

Drive past and swing right and you have a slow, easy cruise for about a mile, meandering among unpretentious apartment hotels, bars, Caribbean-style restaurants and even a pub. Then this access road rejoins Highway 7 just before Worthing police station.

You'll have to go north of the capital, to the west coast, for the posh hotels and fancy villas. They're principally in the parish of St. James, the traditional haven of the rich. Here beautiful beaches stretch forever and the sea is calm. Perfect for waterskiing and posing.

Hotel development along the south coast, mainly in the zone stretching from Rockley to Worthing, began in the sixties but really accelerated in the following decade. The catalyst was Coconut Airways which was established and operated by Freddie Laker on behalf of the Barbados government. Now adventurous younger people, pre-yuppie middle-class professionals, could afford to discover the Caribbean dream. Backpackers bound for or returning from South America found friendly Barbados to be a convenient and civilized stopover. In the gorgeously hot UK summer of 1975 the mock-calypso pop tune 'Barbados' hit Number One in the charts.

Saint Lawrence Gap was the perfect resort for this new generation of tourists. Self-catering apartments proliferated. Then by 1981 tourists arrived with bigger budgets and the south coast began to ease itself upmarket. Over Christmas that year Casuarinas Beach Club opened.

In the beginning there were 64 rooms in a three-storey block constructed among the casuarina and palm trees. 400 feet of white sand beach adjoined the hotel grounds and facilities included tennis courts and a large swimming pool. Guests were accommodated in roomy studio apartments cooled by large ceiling fans and air-conditioning. A comfortable environment for me though quite a contrast to Ross Point Inn and the small, basic guest houses where I'd lodged in Jamaica and Haiti.

I spent that Sunday relaxing and wandering around Saint Lawrence Gap. Now, on Monday, I returned to my treasure hunting. I had a car delivered after breakfast and drove into Bridgetown where, following a brief search and a few enquiries, I bought an Ordnance Survey map of Barbados. This was now spread out on the table in front of me.

Obviously the sketch map headed 'Barbadoes' was not as accurate as this modern OS version. Some of the pirates had made valuable contributions to contemporary cartographic knowledge but they didn't have the resources available today. And this was just a sketch map. Not even that really. Just a serrated line twisting a tortuous route from the bottom left of the parchment to the top right. It was unevenly drawn with occasional indentations and the odd spike.

It was evidently a coastline. Probably the southeast coast. But first I should eliminate all other possibilities. 'Never assume anything' is a good rule and I would have been kicking myself if I spent days on a fruitless search in the wrong part of the island.

With my OS map flat on the table I turned the sketch map upside down and sideways to make my comparisons. First I checked the west coast. This is the leeward side of Barbados and where the first English settlers landed in 1627. Samuel Kydd and his accomplices arrived less than fifty years later. Presumably most settlements were in this area back then.

No. There was no similarity. I then checked the southwest coast and the eastern side of the island. Not really. Whilst not impossible there were significant differences. I concluded that my original assumption, that the arrow indicated North, was correct. So my target area would be the rugged southeast coastline. Or, at least, I would try there first.

The sketch map showed no scale but comparing it with my OS map I decided that the distance from the bottom left of the squiggly line to the top right was around eight to ten miles. Somewhere along that coast was a cache of buried loot. Careful study of the OS map and systematic further elimination should direct me straight to it. If it was still there.

I found paper and pen and set about making notes. First, the relatively straight edge running at an angle of 60° from the bottom of the sketch probably represented Long Bay. If that was so then the southern extremity would be Inch Marlowe Point. Remembering that this was just a crude sketch map, and lacking a scale, I assumed for the time being that the northern extremity would be either Palmetto Bay or Kitridge Point. My search area therefore should be between Salt Cave and Sam Lord's Castle, around four or five miles of coast. Now, perhaps, the other sketch map would help me pinpoint precise spots to reconnoitre.

A series of bold downward strokes, so close together that sometimes they touched, probably represented cliffs. A crescent-shaped area separated from the sea by a thin line was obviously meant to indicate a beach. And the crooked, double broken lines? The odds are that must be a cave. Frankly I didn't fancy abseiling down a cliff face to a cave entrance but, well, I'll worry about that later. First find a location within these eight miles of coastline where there might be cliffs, a beach and a cave.

There were four, perhaps five, sites which appeared to satisfy the criteria. Two of them, which featured both beaches and cliffs according to the OS map, had already been exploited by hotel developers.

The Crane Beach Hotel was already famed for its spectacular setting and wide white sand beach. It is very photogenic. I knew that glossy magazines eulogised over its dramatic cliff top position and fashion shoots frequently monopolised the pool area. Even the Barbados Board of Tourism featured a striking shot on the cover of its hotel directory. Holidaymakers staying on the west or south coasts came here on day trips, though the hotel's owners struggled to attract package tour guests because of the isolated location.

I decided that if the loot had been buried here my search would be fruitless. It would have been unearthed years ago.

The second hotel was Sam Lord's Castle, named after a notorious wrecker who'd allegedly become rich through luring ships on to the rocks then looting their cargoes. This was more of a conventional tourist hotel. Its isolation would perhaps make it an ideal all-inclusive resort. It is situated right on the very edge of my search area so I decided to leave it to last. First I would drive down to Crane Beach and have a good look around, then Beachy Head, backtrack to Salt Cave and Oliver's Cave and finally – probably, by then, in desperation – try Shark's Hole and Sam Lord's Castle.

Chapter Twenty Six

"You Get Tru Man?"

"When we say car" we used to tell the reps "we mean Moke." That's what most of our clients expected. This was their only opportunity to savour the joys of 'wind in the hair' motoring. And cruising the Caribbean countryside behind the wheel of a Moke is nothing like racing a roadster through Britain's bracing climate. No freezing fog or piercing rainstorms here. Guaranteed warmth, gentle breezes and glorious sunshine most of the day, most days, make alfresco motoring one of the pleasures of a Barbados holiday. But the Moke wasn't quite right for me. I didn't need a roof, or doors either, but I did need a lockable boot and the Moke doesn't have one. Or didn't then. So I was fortunate to be allocated a Caribbean Cub. With its open glass-fibre body built on a Reliant Kitten chassis it was like a Moke but with added security and rear wheel drive.

Compared to both Grenada and Haiti Barbados is blessed with excellent roads so I reached Crane Beach Hotel in 25 minutes. First I drove along Highway 7 through Maxwell and Oistins then took the left fork, heading inland. Once through Oistins all tourist development petered out – logically because that road traverses areas far from the beaches – and once I'd passed the airport I noticed the district was very thinly populated. Even before the road entered Saint Philip parish it gave up all pretence of being a highway. Mind you, it was still adequate for the volume of traffic it would be expected to carry. For a few miles I drove between sugar cane fields, their crop towering above my low-slung vehicle, and the narrow road wound past three quarries.

The hotel is well signposted so I reached it without difficulty. I pulled into the capacious car park, switched off the engine, slid out and headed for the gate. Here a uniformed lady relieved me of five dollars, the entrance fee to the hotel grounds. She handed me a ticket which could be used as part-payment for food and beverages. Not a bad idea. I feel a bit peckish. Spotting the cliff-top café I headed for a vacant table overlooking the beach and sat down. A waiter promptly appeared with a menu.

I ordered a beer, a hamburger and French fries then transferred my gaze to the view. A broad expanse of soft white sand was swept at its outer edge by clear turquoise waves and white breakers. There was no-one in the water today. Very advisable as the currents here are notorious for their vicious undertow. Only good swimmers venture into the sea on this beach so it is only good swimmers who are sucked far out into the ocean and drowned. The beach was deserted – almost. In the soft sand above the high water mark a couple were lounging on beach towels chatting. No-one else was in sight.

That would make a good picture. A double page spread in the brochure, perhaps overprinted with copy. I could do it with the standard lens too. Empty sand filling most of the frame with the wild sea in the top right hand corner and that couple slightly off-centre to the left. Honeymooners perhaps. I leant down, rummaged in my bag and dragged out my camera. I was leaning over the rail, framing my shot and focussing when another figure strode into the composition. He was very black, presumably a local, with a fine physic clothed only in a pair of shorts. He looked sharply up at me.

"Hey man!" he shouted. "Don't take my fuckin' picture."

Why would I want to take his fuckin' picture? He's

ruining the whole point of the shot, namely a honeymooning couple with the beach to themselves.

"I'm not" I shouted down. "It's the view I want."

"Jus' don't take my picture" was bellowed back up to me. Mr Aggressive strode out of the frame. It would have been uncool to stand and argue.

Although a little rattled now I took a couple of shots. I hoped I hadn't been put off by the intervention. The real subjects of the photo seemed unconcerned.

I spotted rickety but presumably safe wooden steps zigzagging down the cliffside to the beach. After I'd eaten I settled up and cautiously descended. The staircase did creak a bit, and wobbled at times, and their fixings to the cliff face were eaten by rust, but I made it down to sea level without drama. I strolled a little way along the beach, past the sunbathing couple, then turned and looked back. It's certainly a dramatic setting. Imposing, rugged, weatherbeaten cliffs topped by the majestic hotel of white hewn coralstone ascend skywards from the beach.

I scanned those cliffs for any sign of caves. None. Nothing in the face ahead of me and nothing to my right either. Of course where the cliffs on my left curve out of sight – 'The Horse' and 'Cobbler's Rock' according to the map – there could be caves. But there's no beach there. They would only be visible from the sea. I turned and strolled slowly along the sand, away from the hotel, scrutinising the cliff now on my left. Still nothing. But that was good news. Any caves this close to the hotel would have been thoroughly explored.

The beach narrowed as the cliffs advanced towards the sea then broadened again. Now I was alone. The hotel was out of sight and no guests or daytrippers had ventured this far. I stopped walking and sat on the sand gazing out to sea.

After perhaps five minutes a figure appeared round the headland coming from the direction of the hotel. It was Mr Aggressive. As he strode along the firmer sand close to the breakers he gave me a cursory glance but said nothing.

Presumably because no camera was to hand. I watched him continue to the end of the beach then clamber lithely over the rocks with the agility of a mountain goat. It was low tide. I need to go up there, I decided, and before the tide comes in. I got to my feet and followed.

My progress across the rocks was less elegant. Sometimes I would step on an apparently stable stone only to find it tipping under my feet. But then I wasn't negotiating these boulders on a daily basis. Eventually I crested the rockfall to find my progress rewarded with the sight of another empty beach. Again I scanned the cliffs but saw no sign of a cave. At the end of this deserted stretch of sand was Beachy Head, number two on my list. Beyond it, according to the map which I now studied, were six more bays guarded by steep cliffs as far as Shark's Hole. Any one of them could be the home of the treasure I sought but it would be hazardous to continue along the coast at sea level. I hadn't checked the times of the tides.

There was no sign of Mr Aggressive but I could see an easy route to the top of the cliffs. According to the map there were some buildings up there, probably houses. Perhaps Mr Aggressive lived in one. Best therefore to climb up there and make a decision up top. No point in wandering along this new beach to the headland. I turned to my left and clambered up the rockfall at the expense of some deep breathing. I glanced around then consulted the OS map again.

In one direction, almost a mile away, was my parked car. In the other over a mile of curving hilltop would lead me to Shark's Hole. But I wouldn't be able to spot a cave from the top of the cliff. Also I noted that many of the houses were built close to the edge so if I was to stroll along the rim hoping for a view of a suitable cave I would need to trespass through residents' yards and gardens. Possibly excusable if I knew for a fact that the riches I sought were definitely secreted along there but not advisable just on the off-chance. And at the end of my search I would be two miles from my car. Better to return to the car and drive up there.

I studied the sketch maps again. Even allowing for their cartographic inaccuracy it was unlikely that the loot was buried this far up the coast. It was more likely to be in the area of Oliver's Cave or Foul Bay. So best to retrieve the car and drive to that area. There would probably be enough daylight left to search those cliffs and if I was unsuccessful I could continue tomorrow. Perhaps rent a boat and scan the cliffs from the sea. I strolled the leisurely mile back to Crane Beach Hotel, reclaimed my car, checked the map again and set off for Oliver's Cave.

A short and easy drive. Follow the road round to the right, first left, then left again, then 400 yards past another right bend. The cliffs and the cave should be about 200 yards from the road.

I found it easily enough but I didn't like what I saw as I arrived. I parked and double-checked my maps. Unfortunately this was the correct spot.

Between the road and the beach, covering what I'd expected would be abandoned wasteland, were piles of broken limestone and coral. Heaps of earth. Bad enough, but what really disturbed me were the mechanical diggers, earthmoving equipment, an assortment of cars and small trucks and a scattering of men wearing hard hats. If this was the location featured on the maps I feared that they were about to find what I was searching for or – worse – maybe they'd found it already.

I started the car, drove across there and parked again. I slid out and approached a man who might have been an engineer or surveyor.

"Hi" I said, as casually as my concern allowed. "What are you chaps building here?"

The man looked up from the plans he was studying. "Jus' a hotel. Who are you?"

"Morgan Fairchild from Sunstroke Holidays. It's an unusual spot for a hotel isn't it? I thought the sea was too rough on this side. What's the beach like?"

The man shrugged. "I jus' paid to see to de building. The beach is good, an' dey got a grotto from up here down to the beach."

"A grotto?"

"It like a cave man. You can walk from up here down tru to de beach. Dey plannin' to make a attraction of it."

"Can I take a look?"

"Sure. See dat rock dere? The entrance just de udder side."

"Thanks."

Beyond the rock was an irregularly-shaped hole, obviously formed naturally, which was partly illuminated from above. There was enough light to reveal primitive steps leading down to a sandy bottom. At some time man had cut crude shelves into the sides of a sloping aperture presumably formed by water. Perhaps this part of the coast had once been under the sea. I clambered down with little difficulty and glanced around.

When I examined the passage ahead I was faced with almost total darkness. I waited a couple of minutes to allow my eyes to adjust. There was enough light reflected off the limestone to suggest that this tunnel curved to the left. I meandered through keeping to that side, feeling as much as seeing my way. After that left bend the passage then bent to the right then as I rounded that obstacle I was rewarded with daylight seeping in from the sea. I continued my cautious exploration and almost immediately emerged onto a fine beach. The waves were a little more vigorous than I like, and I suspected that there could be a vicious undertow, but it was certainly picturesque. I ducked back just inside, where there was still sufficient light to read, and unfurled my sketch maps. I scrutinised the one which showed the close-up of the circled area marked on the first. Sure enough those dotted lines accurately represented the twisting confines of this grotto. I needed to restrain my excitement. This must be the place.

I'd brought a powerful torch I purchased that morning

in Bridgetown. Venturing back inside the cave I stopped at the point marked by the 'Z' on the map. Of course this was near the bend, the only really dark section. I shone the torch across and up both rock faces to my left and right. Nothing of any interest on the left. The wall on my right did seem to have a fissure, though I couldn't be sure. It was above head height, around seven feet from the ground, just below the roof. I couldn't tell whether it was sculpted naturally or man-made but I suspected that any cache of treasure would be in there. If this is the right cave. If someone hasn't beaten me to it. I'll need to climb up there.

I heard a shout from above. "You get tru man?" Damn.

"Yes, sure. Just coming." I turned off the torch and replaced it with the maps in my red Moroccan leather shoulder bag. Hogging the wall I felt my way back through the tunnel to where sunlight illuminated the landside aperture. I clambered up the crude steps and emerged into the bright glare of the building site.

"That's a nice grotto" I observed, panting a bit. "And a great way to get down to the beach. Might be a bit of a struggle for some of the older guests though. What are they planning to do with it?"

"Dey say dey gonna put some wooden steps down, make it easy for the touris', and a ice cream stand."

"An ice cream stand?"

"Well, accordin' to what I seen dey gonna put a cart down there."

"Nice. Have they got a name yet?"

"The name of dis place is Ginger Bay so mebbe dey call it so."

"Good name. Thanks for your help." We shook hands and I strolled back to my car.

Chapter Twenty Seven

Out Of The Line Of Fire

I decided to return at the dead of night. I set off around eight, calculating that the construction crew would have finished work several hours earlier and the site would be dark enough for me to sneak into the cave unseen. Unfortunately after dark one cane field looks like any other. I'd been driving for almost forty minutes before I realised that I was lost.

The roads are good in Barbados. The problem is that there are so many of them but few signposts in the sparsely inhabited districts. Even the Bajans get lost. To us it's a small island – around 21 miles by 14 at its widest – but everything is relative. A local guy will be familiar with his own neighbourhood but frequently know nothing about other parishes. I discovered that it is quite normal for the native to drive into Bridgetown then out again on the appropriate main highways rather than travel cross-country on the minor roads, even if that doubles the length of his journey.

Tonight I was approaching Oliver's Cave from the opposite direction to this afternoon's route. Then I'd been returning from Crane Beach. I pulled over to the roadside, unfolded my OS map, shone the torch on it and tried to work out where I was.

I must have taken the correct road as far as the parish boundary. I'd driven past the airport but had I then turned right at Rock Hall? No. I'd probably blazed straight past that turning. I didn't recall seeing the quarries but then I probably wouldn't have noticed them in the dark anyway. Those houses I've just passed. If that was the settlement of St. Martins then I should have seen a church. I should have turned right just past it.

In fact I don't think I've turned right anywhere. I'm halfway to the middle of the island by now, four miles from the sea. Well, not quite so far. Somewhere like Sunbury, Harrow or Chapel. No, not that far. I couldn't have missed the intersection of Six Cross Roads. Or even the village at Four Roads.

Tracing my finger back along the red-and-white broken lines – 'secondary roads' according to the key – I decided that I mistook the second right for the Rock Hall turning. I'd probably turned right there. I was on my way to Sandy Hill.

I executed a 23-point turn in the narrow lane and headed back the way I'd come, towards the sea. Probably. I drove very slowly in the hope that my headlights might illuminate a direction sign or place name. All buildings of any importance were marked on the map and even the location of a church would give me a clue.

Eventually I spotted a turning I recognised. Having overshot my objective I was now heading towards it from the same direction I'd taken earlier in the day. I remembered the profusion of scattered houses. Soon I saw the building site approaching on my left. I slowed right down intending to turn in then changed my mind and drove past.

My lights had flashed over two parked cars and a small group of people standing around chatting. What were they doing there? I cruised slowly for a few hundred yards then saw a gate guarding a field. That'll do. There was a gap just long enough to accommodate my Cub. I parked there then slipped out and strolled quietly back towards the building site.

It was a pleasant evening for a stroll. Temperature in the

mid 70s cooled by the constant easterly breeze. A blend of scents from the tropical flowers, herbs and spices of paradise wafted through the air around me. Once within earshot of the construction site I stopped behind a tree and waited.

Caramel voices rose and fell in the melodious Bajan rhythms I enjoyed listening to. I could pick out occasional phrases which punctuated the constant chirping of the cicadas and tree frogs. There were about four or five people in the group chatting, obviously all in good humour. Occasionally there was a short burst of laughter. This was presumably a late night picnic or perhaps a mild drinking session but why here? Maybe the cars had been travelling in opposite directions and the occupants recognised each other.

Quite obviously there was no way I could circumvent these folks to descend unseen into the grotto. Of course I could clamber down the cliff further along and try to gain access along the beach but where was the sense in that?

After twenty minutes or so I strolled back to my car. On the way I noticed another parking slot on the opposite side of the road but within earshot of the picnic. Luckily the engine started up immediately without the telltale stutter of the starter motor. This time a three-point turn was just possible. I swung the Cub into the new bay, switched off the engine and listened.

The party broke up suddenly. Maybe there was a late night movie on TV they all wanted to see. One car drove past me, the occupants still chatting happily and oblivious to my parked vehicle. The other drove away in the opposite direction. After two minutes, once I was certain that I was alone, I started the car and slowly, still with my lights off, drove to the building site. A swift glance was sufficient to confirm that it was now deserted. I turned in and parked behind an earthmoving vehicle which hid me from the road. I sat quite still and waited for another five minutes then slid out and silently trudged the few yards to the grotto entrance.

Fortunately there was sufficient moonlight to illuminate

the contours but I still eased myself carefully down nature's crude stairwell feeling the rock with my hands and feet. As I reached the sandy bottom I switched on the torch. Hopefully its light would be absorbed by the twisting confines of the tunnel. I didn't want stray flashes broadcasting my activities. As I reached the midway point of the cave I shone the light up to locate the fissure then down to ground level checking for handholds and footholds. I didn't much fancy the climb but the irregular surface did seem to have enough bumps and hollows for my needs. I clambered up without dislodging too much of the loose surface, steadied myself with my head cocked flat against the roof and shone the torch into the crevice.

There was something stashed there. It looked like a small trunk with a leather handle on its short side, the one facing me. It was just out of my reach. This fissure ran quite deep into the rock but it was barely more than a slit. I needed both legs and one arm to keep me anchored to the rock face so I would have to manage without light. I switched off the torch and tossed it gently down, hoping that the flick of my wrist would guide it in a gentle loop to a soft landing.

Now I forced my head completely sideways to avoid striking it on the roof and squeezed as much as possible of my upper body into the crevice. I paused for breath and to make sure that my feet and left hand held me securely. Then I reached in with my right hand and scrabbled around until I felt the trunk. I located the handle, grabbed it and urged it a few inches forward.

It came easily so obviously it was not too heavy and hadn't been wedged into the gap or secured in place. It was waiting to be found. Unless there was some kind of spring-loaded booby trap behind it. I didn't fear any sort of explosive device because I doubted that the detonator would still be effective after three centuries. But a mechanical booby trap might still work. A sword blade primed to decapitate the unwary.

I am always suspicious when things seem too easy. I pulled it very gently close to the edge of the fissure, quickly retracted my hand and waited. Nothing untoward. Just a small trunk scraping along a rock fissure. Well, I thought, OK. This was left here to be found by fellow adventurers who would be privy to its history and the reason it was hidden. They could only find it with the maps, which they themselves had hidden. On another island. It can't be booby trapped.

I carefully manoeuvred my body to the side, out of the line of fire, then gave the trunk a strong jerk and whipped my arm away. It scraped unevenly along the rough surface for eight inches or so but nothing else happened. Now its leading edge was overhanging the gap. Swinging my body back I grasped the handle again and pulled hard in a wide arc which I calculated would haul the trunk completely out of its hiding place. As I let go it crashed down on the sand next to the torch. No booby trap then, but what if there was something else hidden in the crevice? I climbed down tentatively, feeling my way in the enveloping blackness, rescued the torch, switched it back on and clambered back up. I shone the light into the crevice. It ended just beyond where the trunk had been. There was nothing there now.

I jumped down and brushed myself off. I picked up the trunk in my left hand. It was very light. Obviously not full of solid gold bars or pieces of eight. What if it's empty? Well I'm not going to check right now. I can do that back at the hotel. Best get out of here. Using the torch I groped my way back to the entrance. Now I wanted to get away as quickly as possible.

I briefly shone the light on the roughly-hewn steps and memorised the route up. I turned off the torch and returned it to my shoulder bag which I looped around my neck. Gripping the trunk in my left hand I made the short ascent with some difficulty and looked around cautiously as my head reached the night air. I eased myself and my baggage out, lay prone on the ground and allowed my eyes to become accustomed to the moonlit scene. Ghostly diggers and bulldozers, just identifiable as yellow hulks, heaps of spoil. But nothing moving. I listened carefully. The only sounds were my own heavy breathing, some chirping tree frogs in the distance, the electrical hum of thousands of crickets and the rustle of the wind through some nearby palm fronds. I stood up slowly and sauntered back to the car, eyes to the ground so I didn't trip over anything. I reached the boot, about to open it, when I heard a car and saw headlights approaching. I froze.

Instead of continuing past, as I would have liked, this car slowed, turned into the building site, lurched over a bump and parked the other side of my cover. The lights were extinguished. Then I heard voices, one male and one female, as the doors opened and closed. I didn't move. I didn't look. The voices started walking off towards the cliff, although if they were heading for the beach I knew the grotto was the best route down there. It suddenly occurred to me that this grotto could be the local equivalent of Lovers' Lane.

Thank God, that's just what it was. The girl was giggling nervously and the male voice was offering reassurance and promise. They made for the opening. I could hear him helping his lady down the clumsy steps. Then their voices echoed and faded.

I gave them ten minutes to become engrossed in whatever they were doing then quietly opened the boot. I slipped in the chest, eased it closed with the slightest click, stepped round to the driver's side and slid behind the wheel. That Reliant engine fired up without the telltale starter rattle again but I didn't hang around. I quickly whacked it into reverse and swept around in a wide arc onto the road just missing the lovers' car. Simultaneously I put it into first, switched on the lights and stamped on the accelerator pedal. I sped away from there as fast as safely possible only slowing down after five minutes.

Back at the hotel I parked, slung my shoulder bag around my neck again, retrieved the chest from the boot and set off smartly for my room. I wanted to avoid curious eyes. I'd kept my key so I didn't need to pass through Reception. I was strolling through the trees and not far from my ground floor room when a shadow stepped out in front of me.

"What you 'ave dere man?"

It was the night security guard.

"Oh hi. You startled me. I'm Morgan Fairchild. Sunstroke Holidays. I'm staying here." I fished my key out of my pocket, flashed it briefly to the guard, returned it, then brandished the trunk. "We're going to organise a treasure hunt for our clients."

"You hafta do dis at night?"

"We bury it at night, yes. So nobody can see us. I've just retrieved it from last time. I'm going to put some stuff in now. You know, T-shirts, souvenirs, that sort of thing."

The watchman shone his torch on the trunk. "It look like de real ting man."

"Yes. Good isn't it?" I replied enthusiastically. "But don't tell anyone you've seen me or they'll sneak out at night and try to follow me. Good night."

I reached my room, dropped the trunk just inside the door and switched on the lights. I'd drawn the curtains before I left but now I had a sudden thought. What if they're not totally opaque? I didn't want anybody to see me fiddling with this box, particularly not that security guard. He might still be curious. He might check and discover that Sunstroke doesn't have any clients staying here at the moment. I glanced at my new watch, the last of my purchases in Bridgetown. It was only a $10 plastic digital model, but now that I was returning to the real world – the bustle of Bridgetown and its immediate environs felt to me like London with palm trees – precise timekeeping might be necessary.

Eleven minutes past twelve. Better leave it until the morning.

I slid the chest under the bed, visited the bathroom, then hit the sack.

Chapter Twenty Eight

Forty Named Persons

Very strange.

Back in London I'd yearned for a chance to break away from my humdrum and dreary life. Then I was selected to conduct the research for these themed holidays. From the start I'd dreamed the impossible dream – or, at least, the extremely unlikely. The chance that I would discover buried pirate treasure, sudden untraceable wealth that would release me from my daily grind. Before I even left London I'd investigated the locations of all the known buccaneer bases in the Caribbean islands. Some, such as Isla de Providencia, a speck 150 miles from the coast of Central America, would definitely be off-limits. I would not be able to justify a visit there. I did talk Arrowsmith into allowing me to visit Haiti but I found I was two centuries too late. Jamaica also. So I gave up my dream and travelled to Grenada and Carriacou more interested in the current political turmoil. Then fate intervened and directed me back towards my original goal. Now I was in possession of a hidden trunk which may contain the answer to my dreams and what did I do? I fell asleep.

And I overslept.

Possessed by pent-up excitement I shouldn't have fallen asleep so easily and I should have woken up at dawn. But when I eventually opened my eyes to greet the new day, the first day of the rest of my life, I found my room flooded with subdued light. I peered at my new watch and saw that it was past 9. Quickly I hopped out of bed, showered, shaved and dressed. I decided to skip a hotel breakfast. I fastened the 'Do Not Disturb' sign on the door and wandered over to the kitchenette. I switched on the kettle, spooned some instant coffee into a cup, poured some orange juice and broke off a banana from the bunch. Then I returned to the bed.

I pulled out the chest. It was about 15 inches long, 10 inches wide, 8 inches high and fashioned by a skilled carpenter from a polished dark wood, probably mahogany. The top – which was flat, not curved like the illustrations in romantic fictional tales of buccaneering derring-do – was secured by two leather straps with brass buckles. Easier to stack I suppose and more sensible in the cramped confines of a pirate ship.

The kettle was starting to boil. I caught it just in time and added water to the coffee. I knocked back the orange juice in a single draught and unpeeled the banana.

Careful. First, make sure no-one can see me. I glanced towards the windows. Though the curtains were still drawn there was enough light penetrating for my purposes so I was right when I got back last night. My silhouette, and therefore my movements, could easily have been observed through the curtains. Second, be wary of booby traps.

I studied the chest as I slowly chomped through my banana. I must be very careful. This loot had been surprisingly easy to find – if there was loot stashed inside. It hadn't been buried and although its hiding place was well above head height, and the chest had been pushed right to the back of the fissure, it could well have been discovered by accident. Possibly its owners were being pursued and needed to hide it rapidly. Or maybe it was equipped with a device to kill or maim any unsuspecting fellow unaware of its contents. I decided to open it from behind so that I would benefit from partial protection from the lid if there was some terrible device fitted inside.

It was surprisingly easy to unfasten. As I fed each strap through the metal buckles I held the top down firmly, just in case it was sprung. There was no pressure so I eased my hands free. I adjusted my feet so that I was squatting comfortably on my haunches. Now, grabbing a strap in each hand, I jerked the top open and deliberately fell flat on my back. Nothing happened.

I stood up and strode round to the front of the trunk. Inside I could see an oilskin package which almost filled the available space. I lifted it out carefully and laid it on the table. Lying in the bottom of the chest was a sheet of parchment loosely rolled and secured with a red silk ribbon. Two leather purses sat beside the scroll. They were made from soft glove leather and kept closed with a drawstring around the neck. I lifted them out and placed them on the table which they met with a reassuring clunk and an unseen shuffle. Finally I removed the parchment scroll. Before making my examination of these artefacts I checked that the trunk was now empty and had no false bottom. Satisfied, I sat down and poured a cup of coffee. Now to analyse my discoveries.

I slipped the ribbon off the parchment scroll and unfurled it. I spread it carefully on the table. I was rewarded with the sight of several lines of neat handwriting, in a centuries-old style, apparently in black ink, and a sketch map.

For years I'd hoped that a degree in Mediaeval History might one day prove useful. Today was that day. The information on the parchment sheet was intended for the finder and written in late 17th century English, when spelling was optional. So it fell between my two areas of knowledge, namely early English and 20th century usage. It was very easy therefore for me to understand what was inscribed. Much was in the style of 'Ye Olde Englishe Tea Shoppe'.

The document stated that gold and precious stones had been traded with the notorious Sam Lord for parcels of land in Barbados. The deeds were inside the oilskin package. The sketch map showed the location of the land. The means by which the gold and jewels had been obtained was specified – it was loot from Henry Morgan's sack of Panama as I had deduced – and the rightful owners named. There was no mention of the two leather purses though. Perhaps these contained some of the precious stones mentioned by Duncan Selkirk. I presumed they'd expected to sell these before they left Barbados, but why not take the purses with them? They were portable and surely untraceable plunder.

I sat back, savoured my coffee and thought about it. Well well well. Sam Lord had allegedly enriched himself working as a wrecker, luring unwary ships on to the rocks with lanterns and then plundering them. According to this he was really a fence, exchanging stolen property for land. Although, of course, he could have followed both professions.

Now I unwrapped the oilskin package. Rolled up together were six deeds to land on the coast of Barbados. The west coast in fact, as shown on the sketch map. A strip of beachfront land centred on Discovery Bay, present day Holetown, extending north and south of it and divided into six portions. Land worth next to nothing three hundred years ago but now more valuable than a gold mine. Each deed listed forty named persons who I knew would be the men reported lost on the *Nuestra Señora de las Nueces Variadas*. I searched for, and found, the names of those whose tombstones I'd discovered by the beach on Carriacou. There was also a Selkirk.

Each deed made it clear that those forty men were the legal owners of the land and after their demise it would pass on to their descendants if proof were provided of such descent. *If proof were provided of such descent.* That phrase screamed at me. It was followed by an even more interesting paragraph. If no descendants could be traced with proven descent then the deeds, and therefore the land to which they assigned title, would belong to the bearer. Quite an incentive for someone to murder those forty men and eliminate their issue if these deeds had been unearthed three hundred years ago. Obviously this is why the Barbados sketch maps were hidden in a cutaway bible which itself was secreted under floorboards. Those in the know were just waiting for the chance to return to Barbados and claim their land. Why didn't they? Possibly because in those days beachfront land was only useful for boatbuilding or as a parking lot for fishing boats. They'd found an excellent alternative beach in Carriacou so why bother returning to Barbados?

I wondered why this part of the story hadn't been passed down to Duncan Selkirk. Perhaps it had been but he'd forgotten. He did know there was something to be discovered in the derelict kirk. Or maybe those who knew the complete story had died without divulging the full details.

Finally I opened the two purses. The first contained beautiful green stones which I assumed were emeralds. The second was filled with cut diamonds. Of course I'm no expert and they could have been glass copies – 'paste' – for all I knew, but if that was the case then this was all a fantastic practical joke. I needed to have a good long think about this.

I slipped the deeds and letter back into the oilskin wrapping and the whole package, along with the purses, into my holdall in the wardrobe. I slid the chest back under the bed. There was no problem if the maid found an empty chest when she was cleaning the room. That security guard would probably talk anyway.

Time had rather run away without me noticing and it was midday already. Possibly I'd taken too long checking that the names were all exactly the same on all six deeds and then speculating on their nationalities. Then I'd started to create scenarios, weaving my factual researches together with adventure stories. I shouldn't be doing that. I should be calculating exactly how I could convert this lucky find into personal wealth. Perhaps an early lunch and a stiff drink would inspire me.

The hotel restaurant extended from the bar area towards the swimming pool. I chose a table with more sun than shade and ordered. I'd barely started on my Chicken-in-a-Basket and Piña Colada when I heard someone call my name. I looked up and saw, the other side of the pool, one of the staff pointing me out to a beautiful, slim, young black woman. She was neatly dressed in an emerald green uniform enlivened with pink highlights. She strolled towards me, elegantly weaving her way through the rows of overweight lobsters grilling themselves on sun loungers.

"Morgan Fairchild?" she enquired with a sweet smile.

"That's me. Won't you sit down?" I said, indicating the chair opposite.

She sat. "I'm Wendy-Ann, Sunstroke's rep here in Barbados. I've got you listed as Wally Fairchild but Jonathon says you prefer to be called Morgan. I thought he was joking at first for obvious reasons."

Jonathon Morgan was the hotel manager. I laughed. "That's right. It's my middle name, just co-incidence really. Pleased to meet you" I continued, returning her smile. I was too. She was lovely. "Anything wrong?"

"Not really. We've just received a telex from the London office. They're wondering what's happened to you."

"Did you tell them there was a war in Grenada?"

Wendy-Ann grinned. Obviously she shared my views on the awareness and competence of the London staff. "They knew. They had a telephone call yesterday about you from one of the Grenada clients."

Oh yes, I thought. That prat who was going to write to the Managing Director I suppose. I took a sip of Piña Colada. "What did he say?"

Wendy-Ann consulted a handwritten note. "It was a Mr Bartlam. He phoned to say it was the best holiday he'd ever had and how fantastic that Sunstroke Holidays should send someone to Grenada to make sure everyone was OK. He says you even flew with them here."

"Great clients Wendy-Ann. You'd love them" I said, a little relieved. "If London know I arrived here with them why do they say they don't know what's happening with me?"

She leaned forward. "They like reports Morgan. They say you don't send them reports."

I swallowed a mouthful of chicken and considered my answer. I would only need a few days to do what I needed.

"They never asked me to send reports" I said. "In fact I suspect they only sent me out here to get me away from the office. Most of them don't like me very much." I took another sip of my drink and sneaked a glance at Wendy-Ann over the lip of the glass before continuing. "Maybe they're missing me." I grinned to suggest that I might be joking. Wendy-Ann smiled briefly.

"Tell them I can send a report if they're desperate for one but it's about thirty pages long already. To post that would be crazy. How long will it take to get to London? I'll be back long before anything arrives. Unless I telex them. That'll cost a bomb for thirty pages. And you must know, Wendy-Ann, how tight they are when it comes to spending money." I glanced across at her and received another smile. "What I've written so far will be very expensive in telex time. And they probably won't read it anyway. Better to wait until next week, tell them, when I can present it nicely typed up." I waited whilst she made a note.

"Tell them I've almost finished my research and I'll be on Saturday's plane or, at the latest, next Wednesday's. Not tomorrow. I need to check out the west coast hotels, historical societies, libraries, some of the plantation houses and Codrington College. I should get over to the east coast too. They tell me Bathsheba is a compulsory excursion."

Wendy-Ann made another note then looked up. "Codrington College is over on the east side too" she said. "Maybe you could visit there on the Bathsheba trip. Anything I can do for you?"

"Not that I can think of right now, but I've got your number. I'll give you a call if I get a problem."

"OK". She got up. "I'll see you later then."

Chapter Twenty Nine

The Significance Of The Z

Now I settled down to scoff my bar snack and ruminate. First, the deeds. The pirates had been cheated. Back in 1671, a mere forty-odd years after English settlers arrived and claimed the island in the name of King Charles I, sugar was the white gold. The forests that covered the island were being felled and land cleared for planting by the newcomers and their slaves. Flattish acres inland were the most valuable. Sugar and shorelines were incompatible. In those days the tropics were condemned as unhealthy and sun seeker holidays were unknown so beachfront land was next to useless and cheap. Just garage space for fishing boats. Did those pirates think they could establish a boatbuilding industry on these shores or was this the only land Sam Lord had available?

Presumably they'd intended settling here so their plans changed suddenly. Duncan Selkirk suggested one possible reason – they learned of Henry Morgan's involuntary sojourn on the island as an indentured labourer. Probably clearing land for sugar plantations. Maybe he still cultivated contacts here. Whatever the reason they quickly fled, abandoning their useless strip of coastline but leaving the deeds tucked away in a cave.

Today the situation is reversed. Their land is now the most valuable in Barbados – perhaps in the whole Caribbean. These deeds together comprise a continuous narrow strip bordering the beach of the 'Gold Coast' from Paynes Bay up through Holetown almost as far as Gibbs Beach. Nearly all of the prime real estate in the parish of Saint James. The island's top hotels – including Sandy Lane, Sandpiper, Treasure Beach, Coral Reef and Colony Club – now dominate this coast. Think of the rents I could demand!

I was already considering the question of ownership. These deeds properly belonged to Duncan Selkirk and the other descendants. But how could they prove it? And it would be naïve to assume that all the descendants of those forty men live in Carriacou. By now they were probably spread all over the world. There would be hundreds of them, possibly thousands, mostly untraceable. So what would happen if the proceeds from the sale of this land were shared out among those that could be traced – residents of Carriacou and others recently emigrated – but then additional claimants came forward later? And there would be bogus claims too.

OK, let's say somehow this could all be sorted. Place most of the money in a trust fund maybe. But what would happen if the impoverished people of Carriacou suddenly inherited wealth beyond their wildest imaginings? It would ruin their lives. Like pools winners in England. Spending would be profligate, greed would rear its ugly head and they would probably end up fighting each other.

I ordered another drink but even before I finished it I realised two things. First it was unlikely that anyone would be able to prove legitimate descent as there were probably no birth records kept in Carriacou in the early 18th century. Secondly it would be much better for today's residents if I claimed this land and then gave some of the income to the inhabitants of Windwardside.

So why didn't Duncan Selkirk know all this? The location of the cave and its secret stash of loot? Maybe he did and is a wise old man. Maybe he felt he had to pass on the responsibility of his knowledge to one person who would be able to manage it. Someone who could devise an equitable solution.

There was, however, one major snag.

There was no chance that the Barbados government would willingly hand over the country's prime real estate to some foreigner who just turns up with bearer deeds. Those hotel owners would be one hell of a pressure group. Most of them probably had friends or relatives in the government. Maybe some were members of parliament themselves. Actually, on reflection, probably not. Barbados has a black government and the hotel owners would be rich whites. Some of the hotels could be owned by overseas companies. Sandy Lane for example. I knew that hotel was the flagship of an international chain.

Power and wealth are interlinked. As all these thoughts competed for space in my brain I remembered that this current government was supportive of big business. They had allegedly been helped into power by local capitalists.

If I was going to claim such a prime chunk of real estate I should drive up there and inspect it. Perhaps something would inspire me to formulate a cunning plan.

The jewels were a different matter. No-one need know about those. I could get their authenticity checked and then, once they were proved genuine, I could sell them and bank the proceeds, possibly offshore. Then I would decide what to do about the money. It would be probably be a considerable sum. Quite a few of the stones were an impressive size.

I paid my bill, returned to my room and phoned Wendy-Ann's number. It was picked up after three rings.

"Bajan Hosts, Robert speaking, how can I help you?"

"This is Morgan Fairchild from Sunstroke Holidays."

"Wally Fairchild?"

"Call me Morgan. Is Wendy-Ann there?"

"She not back yet. Can I help?"

"I need a photocopier. Do you have one, or do you know the best place for one that can copy A3?"

"What's A3?"

"Twice A4."

"We've got a photocopier. You're welcome to use it. Come on over, but remember that we close the office at four."

"Thanks. I'll see you in about an hour."

Now for the jewels. I retrieved my holdall from the wardrobe, dropped it on the bed and took out the two leather purses. I opened the one containing the diamonds. Then I rescued my camera from where I'd dumped it among my clean socks and underwear and unscrewed the lens. I slipped my finger behind the mirror, flicked it up, pushed one of the largest rocks behind it and let it slip back into place. Then I replaced the lens, stepped outside on to the patio and snapped a picture of the hotel's grounds.

Everything worked though the resulting snapshot, I mused, wouldn't be up to much. I closed and locked the patio door, made sure the curtains were completely drawn and returned to my task.

First I wound the film back into its canister, opened the back of the camera, plucked it out and stashed it with the rest of my exposed film. Then I selected three large diamonds which together exactly fitted and shoved them into the space just vacated by the film canister. I snapped the back of the camera shut and with a few clicks of the lever wind registered a few exposures on the missing film. What next?

Talcum powder. Fortunately this tin had a removable top. It was about one third full but I couldn't hide many stones in there as the increased weight would give me away. I wet two medium-sized stones, dropped them to the bottom, replaced the top and shook it. I removed the top again and checked. All I could see was talcum powder.

There were a lot of small stones of the type that nowadays would be set around the rim of an expensive watch. Back then they were probably used to decorate brooches and rings. I unscrewed the cap from my toothpaste tube and pushed these, one by one, into the goo using a metal skewer I found in a kitchen drawer. Probably intended for kebabs. This left me with three medium-sized diamonds.

My medicated shampoo bottle was fitted with a dual use top. You could snap it open and squeeze or you could unscrew it and pour. I unscrewed it and dropped in the last of the diamonds.

Now only the emeralds remained. I would worry about those later. If I was unable to devise an alternative plan I would take them through as they were. I knew that Barbados has many shops where you can buy Colombian emeralds. Possibly even Cave Shepherd sell them. Next time I was in town I would pick up a brochure or two. Possibly I could bribe someone – there must be a dodgy dealer somewhere on the island – to sell me a false receipt.

Satisfied with my work I returned the holdall to the wardrobe and set off for town, removing the 'Do Not Disturb' tag from the doorknob before I quit the room.

In those days to get from Saint Lawrence to the west coast you needed to drive through Bridgetown. No problem for me as I needed to conclude my business there by four anyway. That would leave me a little over two hours of good daylight to survey my new beachfront empire.

I finished my business in town by 3.30. As I headed north I found driving through the capital surprisingly easy. Once past the cricket ground of Kensington Oval there was little traffic. The road met the coast shortly after the university campus and then I entered Saint James parish at Batts Rock. Almost immediately the coast road took me through Prospect, shortly before the extensive strip of real estate which I now regarded as mine. Prospect is primarily residential and not part of the 'Gold Coast'.

The first posh hotel I reached was Coconut Creek. That's perched above a photogenic spread of beach just before a sharp left turn which heralds a short stretch where the road runs right alongside the beach. Then Paynes Bay, home to Tamarind Cove and Treasure Beach, before a meandering mile bordered by walls overflowing with tropical plants. Behind the walls lay the very exclusive Sandy Lane.

Holetown is not exclusive. A great beach hosting a clutch of top hotel yes, but accommodation for budget tourists too. Across the road from the bustling beachside restaurants and bars, chaperoned by a handy police station, was the sprawling Sunset Crest Resort. By Barbados standards it's about as downmarket as you can get but as it wasn't built on my land that doesn't bother me. There again, that's one of the pleasures of Barbados. Everything mixed up together. Because the population is densely spread and includes a substantial middle class there was no room for tourist apartheid.

This mingling of natives and visitors is most noticeable on the south coast. They dine in the same restaurants and shop in the same stores. Visitors, especially those from the UK, have always found it easy to make enduring friendships with the locals. This is one of the main reasons Barbados enjoys a high percentage of repeat tourism. But I'd also noticed this potpourri as I drove through Prospect. Hotels and holiday apartments there are built among and alongside local houses.

I continued driving up the coast mentally noting all the luxury hotels built on my land without my permission until I crossed the border at Gibbs Beach. I was now in the parish of Saint Peter. Passing Cobblers Cove Hotel which, unfortunately, was north of my property, I proceeded to Speightstown. This is officially the country's second city but it's little more than a bustling village. Here I turned and retraced my route.

Immediately I entered my room I noticed that the maid had been in. Good. I pulled out the trunk from under the bed and put five of the deeds, rolled up inside the oilskin, back inside. I shoved the other deed and the maps into one of the drawers in the dressing table. Then I strolled over to the wardrobe carrying the sports bag I'd purchased in Bridgetown. This contained the photocopies. I transferred the emeralds to it and dumped it on an empty shelf.

Two important points had occurred to me during my afternoon tour. Firstly I realised that my chances of a successful claim would be enhanced if I presented just one of the deeds. If I could pull that off then I would present the other deeds over a number of years, one by one. A precedent would be set and each successive claim would be easier to pursue. And if I could discover the political affiliations of the current landowners I could make my move when their party was in opposition.

My second thought concerned the significance of the Z. Normally 'X marks the spot'. You get a spade and you dig. My subconscious mind must have suggested that a Z means you look for a crevice. That mental process may not be common to everyone, especially someone who hadn't searched as rigorously as I, so I'd bought a spade in Bridgetown. Now I would just treat myself to a *siesta* before tackling dinner and embarking on my night's task.

Chapter Thirty

A Proper Receipt

Restaurants in Barbados stopped serving at eight. I knew that. So unless I was prepared to drive to Baxter's Road I should eat now.

I decided to dine at the hotel. Most importantly, even more important than eating, I needed to think this thing through. Tackling an indifferent fish dinner without haste in an idyllic alfresco setting would avert stress and prevent over-excitement. Electrical impulses could interact with my grey cells without the distractions of worrying about the time or my taste buds savouring the cuisine. I needed to calculate my strategy like a chess player, evaluating the probable response to every move I made. I needed to be managing the situation, manipulating unknown adversaries – really two ways of describing the same process.

What was I trying to achieve here? I was trying to attain great wealth, to get rich quick. Not just to acquire my 'Drop Dead Money' but also to avoid the cost of doing so. There would be dozens of people, all of them more powerful than I, conspiring to stop me. There was one lesson I'd learnt when studying world affairs and specifically inter-community conflicts – those who possessed power and wealth were determined to hold on to it. Whether the fighting was ostensibly over race, religion or 'class struggle' it always seemed to be triggered by the same cause. Those deprived of power and wealth wanted some and those calling the shots were determined to keep the status quo.

Of course, I was assuming that my find was genuine. Maybe it wasn't. Though the trunk was battered and covered with a fine dust when I located it the contents were pristine. The deeds – admittedly protected by their oilskin wrapping – were not in a condition I would expect if they'd been hidden there for three hundred years. The ink had not faded much and there was no significant yellowing of the paper. OK, maybe the chest had been airtight. But what if the genuine loot had been discovered and removed by someone else? Somebody who'd accidentally found what was really secreted there, removed it then replaced it with apparently genuine 17th century artefacts?

After all, this stuff hadn't been buried on a remote desert island or in the impenetrable vastness of a South American jungle. I found it very easily in a spot frequented by young lovers and where a hotel was now being built. Did I really believe that nobody, in three hundred years, had satisfied his curiosity and climbed up to peer, or feel, into that fissure?

Well you never know. It's quite possible that nobody had seen the fissure. It is above head height. Even during the day it is pitch black at that bend in the grotto and the lovers would presumably come at night. They would have other matters on their minds too. It was only with the aid of the map and torch that I'd located it. And I had a fair idea what I was looking for.

There again, I thought as I tossed it around in my mind, if someone had found it why would they bother replacing the trunk? Why would they bother forging documents? Leaving fake jewels? They wouldn't leave real ones would they?

At least I could check the authenticity of some of the items. Tomorrow, or maybe Thursday, I would compile a list of all the dealers in Colombian emeralds and visit them. Then I would select a couple and on Friday revisit them with a few of the green stones and request a valuation. If they proved to be genuine then I would assume the diamonds are too. My only problems then would be sneaking them through UK Customs and, once safely home, finding a way of selling them for the best price without drawing attention to myself. There might even be a possibility of selling the emeralds to dealers here. You never know.

The tricky part was the deeds. First verifying their authenticity, then staking my claim, finally maximising their value. There must be a land registry office even if it went by some other name. I would call in there and inspect their records. Would their files verify that my west coast real estate once belonged to Sam Lord? If not, what was the earliest date ownership was registered? Names, too, would be useful.

If I decided that the deeds were probably genuine I would present one, just one, to the relevant government department and stake my claim.

All those moves would be played out in the days, weeks and months ahead. Tonight I had a job to do. Whether or not I was in possession of a trunk which had been hidden in a cave during the reign of King Charles II I decided that it must be returned there. This was the first move in my imaginary chess game. Unfortunately the flow of traffic at that building site was like Piccadilly Circus on a Friday night. Hopefully I could get down into that grotto and away again without being seen, but it was a chance I had to take.

I'd no idea what was the best time to go – for all I knew lovers could still be arriving at 3 in the morning – so I left when I was ready. That was around 9.30. With the sports bag slung over my shoulder and carrying the trunk in my left hand I strolled through the trees to my car hoping that the security guard would see me. I dropped both items into the boot and set off for the airport.

Grantley Adams was much calmer at this hour of a Tuesday night than it had been when I arrived with the Bartlams in the turmoil of a Saturday afternoon. There were no more flights expected and just two snaking lines of luggage-laden passengers at the check-in counters. LIAT must have been on time today. Weary staff were leaving for home and there were just two surly porters resting on their trolleys and chatting. Taxis were departing full but the line was not being replenished.

Two minutes would be plenty of time. I parked illegally at the kerbside by Departures, slid out, strode around to the boot, extracted the sports bag and sauntered over to the infamous yellow Left Luggage lockers hoping to find one vacant. Allegedly, so I was told, the airport cleaners routinely commandeered all the lockers for their personal storage. But then I don't always believe everything I'm told. There were three empty in fact. In less than two minutes I'd shoved the bag into one, pocketed the key and was back behind the wheel. A policeman had spotted me and was ambling over. I ruined his evening by driving away smartly.

Tonight I found my way to the construction site without any trouble. I drove at a more sedate pace, alert for the dimly-lit landmarks. I cruised slowly past, scanning the assorted vehicles and piles of rubble for signs of life, then turned around, drove back and stopped on the road just before the site. I turned off the engine and lights and waited for five minutes listening keenly. Once my eyes were fully accustomed to the dark I made sure no cars were parked there, just JCBs and CATs, then started the engine and drove across. Again I parked behind the earthmover, though that was not in exactly the same position. Taking the chest, spade and torch from the boot I crept silently to the entrance of the grotto then stopped. I sat down and listened intently.

For ten minutes I was lulled by the nocturnal sounds of paradise. Tree frogs or maybe cicadas chirping, the rustle of palm fronds in the breeze, the gentle murmur of waves breaking on the beach below. Mankind's only intrusion was the hum and swish of a car passing on the road behind me. I couldn't hear any giggling, whispering or heavy breathing. I was alone.

I dropped the chest and spade through the entrance to the sand below and clambered cautiously down with the torch in my left hand. I switched it on, picked up the spade and walked to the bend guided by the beam. I stopped just below the crevice and tested the sand with my foot. Very soft indeed. Lovely. Let's hope it's really deep.

It was. Within fifteen minutes I'd dug a hole big enough to accommodate the pirate chest. It was also deep enough to be credible as the original hiding place. I'd scooped the sand over to the seaward side so that I could easily stroll back to the entrance and collect the trunk. I dropped it into the hole and quickly covered it, spreading the excess sand evenly through that part of the cave. Then I spent another fifteen minutes stomping backwards and forwards to tramp the sand down consistently.

Next I shone my torch up the cave wall. Was there any evidence that someone had been clambering up there? I decided there wasn't but, anyway, it might only mean that someone had searched. Ah, but. I climbed up again with the torch in my pocket. I pulled it out and flashed it across the crevice. There were marks in the surface dust where I'd dragged out the trunk. I spent a few minutes clearing the sand then slithered back down to ground level. I checked the wall one last time. OK. I stamped the loose sand into the floor. To the casual eye nothing was amiss. Only a trained person who knew what he was expecting to find would suspect that something had been buried recently.

Now I took the same precautions as on my previous visit. I listened carefully before clambering up and out of the cave and waited up top whilst my breathing subsided. Then I tiptoed back to the car. This time I made a small diversion. I dug the spade in the dirt a couple of times to clean it of any clinging sand then abandoned it near a JCB. Hopefully the finder would assume that a sloppy workman had mislaid it. I drove slowly back to the hotel looking forward to a good night's sleep.

I would need to be alert tomorrow.

They kept me waiting for almost an hour, ostensibly because I hadn't made an appointment. Of course, they said, if I was prepared to be attended by a junior official, one of the regular clerks, I wouldn't need to wait at all. I politely insisted that this matter was of such importance that it needed the attention of their top man. I could wait all day if necessary. Eventually a smart lady in a lightweight suit showed me into an air-conditioned office. A trim man aged about fifty wearing a shirt-jac was standing with his hand outstretched. I shook it.

"I'm Julius Alleyne, the Chief Registrar" the man said, indicating that I should sit. "How can I be of service?"

"Morgan Fairchild of Sunstroke Holidays. Pleased to meet you."

"It says Walter on your card."

"That's my first name, but I don't really use it" I said as I sat down. I smiled and continued "I have recently come into possession of some property deeds which seem to indicate that I own some very valuable land in Barbados." I opened the briefcase which I'd bought on my way here, took out a title deed, and handed it across the desk.

Mr Alleyne had an assistant with him. Together they studied the document whilst I relaxed. They appeared to be experiencing some difficulty with the antique writing style and use of English even though Bajans would understand that more readily than the average Brit. Some words and phrases which have fallen into disuse in the UK still pepper speech in Barbados. Measurements too. When giving directions they are still likely to describe distances in chains (a chain is the distance between the wickets).

After ten minutes Mr Alleyne looked up.

"Would you like some coffee? Or we could do tea."

"Coffee would be fine thanks."

Mr Alleyne flicked a switch and requested coffee for

three. He turned back to me. "We'll need some time with this. This deed is over 300 years old."

I nodded. "I've got a degree in Mediaeval History so I'm used to antique English." I let that sink in before proceeding. "Basically it says that the land belongs to those forty men in equal shares, but after their death becomes the property of their descendants if descent can be proven. Probably it would be impossible to prove. It then stipulates that in that case the land belongs to the bearer, which is me."

The coffee arrived. "Sugar? Milk?"

"One of each please."

That brought an amused expression to Mr Alleyne's face.

We all sat back with our coffees and gazed at each other. Julius Alleyne eventually broke the spell.

"You probably know that Barbados wasn't settled until 1627 and these deeds were issued in 1671, only forty four years later. And the land they refer to is just slightly north of the original landing site, close to Holetown. Where Discovery Bay and Settlers Beach hotels are now."

I nodded.

Mr Alleyne continued "We will need to carry out some thorough research on this. First, of course, we will check our records. They may show a continuous chain of ownership from 1627 to the present day. If that is the case then these deeds" he shook them with a flick of his wrist "will probably be a forgery."

I was quite unperturbed and let it show. "I've checked the public records and they're not clear. Recent title is emphatically shown, but if you go back a hundred years you'll notice that it becomes a bit ambiguous."

Julius Alleyne appraised me again. He realised that I was very serious if I'd checked the records already. Conceding the point that the public records could be ambiguous he continued "Probably we will need to contact the British government. They were the former colonial power as you know. Even if this proves to be genuine, these men's descendants" he tapped the unwound scroll, which crackled reassuringly "have first claim."

"I know what happened to the forty men" I said.

This did surprise them. Mr Alleyne and his assistant exchanged glances.

"I've met people who must be their descendants but there will be no way of proving it. Unlikely anyway." The two men were looking at me now with anticipation. "They settled in Carriacou. I was there last week, talking to them. They know the story and I have their blessing but unless there are records of births in the late 17th century and early 18th, and later, in Carriacou it can't be proven. If it can't be proven I am the legal owner. If I am the legal owner I can make sure that the benefits go to those people in Carriacou who I believe are descended from these men."

Julius Alleyne and his assistant were gazing at me as if they doubted my altruism. Anyway, that was irrelevant. First the document needed to be acknowledged as genuine. All other questions could be investigated later. They had one immediate question however.

"How did this come into your possession?" Mr Alleyne asked, waving the document again.

"Indirectly" I answered "from the descendants of those forty men." I nodded towards the deeds. "They told me where to find it. I can't say any more for obvious reasons."

Julius Alleyne and his assistant exchanged knowing glances again. Obviously they were aware of the problems which would be caused as a result of this document's sudden appearance. If genuine it would have significant ramifications for the Barbados government as well as the current occupiers of the land. They knew that, I knew that. I expected them to check with London. But what else would they do?

"We'll have to keep this of course" said Mr Alleyne.

"Why? Couldn't you just make a photocopy?"

"No. The paper will have to be tested for age and whether this type of paper, or parchment, existed at that time. Of course my staff will make exhaustive searches in the land registry records, which will include some documents which you, or other members of the public, will not have had access to, and we'll let you know what we find. When are you leaving Barbados?"

"Next Wednesday, a week today." 'Exhaustive searches' take a long time. I knew they would make sure of that. "Could you give me the photocopy then?" I asked.

"I don't think that would be appropriate. You see" Julius Alleyne sat quite upright in his chair "if this document is genuine then it is very old. The light from a photocopying machine might damage it."

I leant back and smiled. "You don't really expect me to leave those deeds with you and leave here empty handed do you?"

"Of course not! Mr Fairchild!" He gave a little chuckle of reassurance. "My assistant here will prepare a proper receipt."

Back at the Casuarinas Beach Club car park I granted myself a private grin as I slid out of my Caribbean Cub. The receipt merely acknowledged delivery of a document. No clue as to its importance or subject matter. Of course I kicked up a bit of a fuss. They would have been very suspicious if I'd parted with such a valuable item too easily, but Mr Alleyne was always ready with a convenient official riposte to any objections I raised. "Trust me" was his favourite comforting phrase. Of course you never trust anyone who says "Trust me".

Now I was hoping that Mr Alleyne, who was, of course, the current bearer of the deeds and therefore technically the owner of that chunk of real estate, would claim it. The hotel owners would fight hard to retain their rights and if necessary they would take the battle to court. Well, it would definitely go to court. Possibly claims would also be expected from Carriacou.

I need do nothing. Let these other people fight over it and foot the legal bills. Then, if Julius Alleyne won, a precedent would be set. I would capitalise on it.

Chapter Thirty One

Sound, Loyal, Competent and Frugal

As part of their comprehensive civil service reforms nineteenth century politicians and architects invested a fortune designing and erecting a complex of government offices flanking Whitehall. At the heart of their physical declaration of Britain's worldwide pre-eminence stands that elegant Victorian monument to imperial grandeur, The Foreign and Commonwealth Office.

The empire was ruled from these auspicious premises sited between King Charles Street and Downing Street. The building boasts commodious chambers with ultra-high ceilings, fine wood panelling, majestic staircases and delicate pastel shades. The State Staircase, overlaid with a crimson carpet and flanked by marble balustrades, winds graciously up to a gilded balcony lined with marvellous murals. The three-storey Durbar Court is coolly relaxing. Its muted marble in beiges, greys and off-white is lit through a shimmering glass roof.

The many grand public rooms suitable for international conferences are supplemented by a range of offices of various sizes and with a variety of functions. Typists' shared quarters contrast with mandarins' salubrious suites.

Sir Denis Skeene-Flinte's domain was not perhaps the finest, but he enjoyed the view over the courtyard. As the senior man he could choose whichever sanctum he liked but he felt comfortable here. He hadn't called in the decorators after his promotion even though in his exalted position he was entitled to commission extensive and expensive redecoration at the taxpayers' expense. He was rather fond of the wood panelling and ample bookshelves and those antique yet sturdy furnishings were very much the sort of thing he would have chosen anyway.

And why spend money unnecessarily? Sir Denis was rather proud of his reputation as a man who led by example, so he hoped that his budgetary circumspection would provide a good practical demonstration to his juniors – even though none had emulated his sartorial choices. Which were, shall we say, dated. At first sight his ascetic appearance – slightly emaciated, head barely crowned with sparse grey hair – suggested a vague similarity to Neville Chamberlain. A character from a bygone age. One would almost expect him to wear a wing collar and swallow-tailed coat. But no. That, to his mind, would be eccentric behaviour and that would never do. Instead he dressed in a good quality double-breasted all-wool grey pinstripe suit, one of two tailored many years ago. White cotton shirt of course, marginally enlivened by his club tie. His extreme conservatism in his choice of attire and his prudence when disbursing his own or taxpayers' money earned him the semi-affectionate nickname of 'Old Skinflint'.

Today, Thursday, he was sitting at his desk mulling over a fax he had received from Barbados. This photocopy of a property deed they had sent overnight, along with their explanatory letter, was a little worrying. There shouldn't be one. There should be six. And together those six deeds assign title to the most valuable real estate on the island.

Last week Sir Denis was the only man alive who knew of the existence of those deeds. Not even the government of Barbados was aware of them. On independence it had been deemed unwise by the powers on high to trouble the civil service of the new sovereign state with a whole raft of matters.

315

They would have plenty of problems to deal with. Don't bother them with issues which may never see the light of day. So certain secrets dating from colonial times were known only to the top mandarin in the UK although, of course, precautions were in place should he suffer an untimely death. Were he to die in harness the next two officials below him were told of the location of a strong room. This contained a large safe which could only be opened by two different keys inserted simultaneously. Each of those senior subordinates had one of these. Once a week Sir Denis would collect both keys and be driven by a specially-cleared chauffeur to the secret location. He would open the vaults and satisfy himself that no-one else had visited recently.

The Bajan Registrar was obviously aware of the gravity of this discovery. He had been astute enough to fax this document directly to the senior UK official's private office. Therefore so far Sir Denis and his private secretary were the only people in the UK who knew of its unexpected appearance. In Barbados it was just the Chief Registrar and his assistant, according to their letter. And, of course, the young British chap who'd approached them. Who else? Hopefully nobody. Even five people was four too many. If this matter became public knowledge it would open a can of worms which could lead to major problems in Barbados and might even spread discontent to other Caribbean Commonwealth countries. Grenada and Carriacou obviously, but fortune hunters might start snooping around elsewhere too.

In the final years of the colonial period attempts were made to clarify property ownership throughout Barbados. During the centuries of British rule land had been traded and plots all over the island claimed under squatter's rights, particularly after emancipation. Large tracts still belonged to the crown of course. British administrators had attempted to finalise remaining areas of doubt before independence but there were inevitably some loose ends. It was acknowledged both by Britain and the civil service of the new nation that ownership issues concerning much of the most valuable real estate were fuzzy. Perusal of ancient records, and in particular some dubious documents allegedly from the estate of Sam Lord, had traced a number of names to Carriacou.

So Sir Denis discovered, shortly after he rose to his current position, that a number of people resident in another country could be the rightful owners of some prime property in Barbados. But it was very unlikely that those people would have any knowledge of their legacy. So the sensible course of action would be to destroy the evidence.

Sir Denis took the appropriate steps without delay. He sent someone to Carriacou to find and destroy any records that might exist of births in the late 17th and early 18th centuries. He calculated that if lineage could not be irrefutably traced back to those years then there could be no successful claim. Posing as an amateur historian his agent gained access to official and church records and, for good measure, toured the cemeteries. As hoped there were no records of births during that period and therefore no need to eradicate them. Sir Denis was therefore confident that no challenge to the current owners of the 'Gold Coast' would come from that island. Or, at least, he had been very confident before he arrived in his office this morning.

The Barbados Registrar had been presented with this document just yesterday and sent his fax overnight so presumably he did not intend to stake a claim. Of course if he did then that would place him squarely in the same position as the young British chap and he would need to be dealt with in the same manner. Not ideal in his case and so a situation best avoided. Perhaps some sort of reward could be arranged.

As Sir Denis viewed it there were two problems here. First, all six deeds must be recovered, delivered to him and then destroyed. Secondly that travel agent fellow should be neutralised.

Sir Denis had phoned Russell at M10 and invited him to attend these offices at 1100 hours. He was now awaiting the reedy squawk from his intercom which would announce the man's arrival. It came five minutes early.

Good, German Time, thought Sir Denis. "Show him in."

Russell strode into the room, shook hands and sat down. The two men swapped a couple of phrases of small talk then tea arrived. Neither had exceptionally sophisticated tastes so the tea was Earl Grey, but as both were men of discernment it was served properly. As he sipped his Sir Denis observed Russell.

A big man, captain of both his rugby and cricket teams at school and still active in sports and outdoor pursuits in late middle age, Russell liked to wear a tweed sports jacket and flannels whenever he thought he could get away with it. He was doing so today as the men were well acquainted and enjoyed a mutual respect. Sir Denis got down to business.

"A document has turned up in Barbados" he began "that we need here."

"What sort of document?"

Sir Denis paused, eyeing his guest over the partially raised teacup before answering. "I think Russell, it would be best for everyone, particularly yourself, if we keep this on a need-to-know basis. I can tell you that this matter concerns property deeds. Our problem is that the document which has suddenly appeared is just one of a group of six. We do not know the whereabouts of the other five. But we need the complete set."

"So you need a trustworthy and loyal operative."

"Correct. And fully competent of course."

Russell smiled. "All my operatives are fully competent."

"Lucky you." Sir Denis smiled briefly. "I wish I could say the same about all my staff. Now, we have to be careful here. This is something of a rum do." He took a sip of tea whilst Russell waited. He considered his next words carefully. One cliché would be enough for Russell.

"The document, a copy of which we have received, is being held by the Barbados authorities. They contacted me direct, presumably because they appreciate the gravity of the matter. It was presented to them by a British subject who intended to retain possession. We suspect that this chap knows the whereabouts of the other five but will not willingly disclose their location."

"The tea's good today. Why do you think that?"

"He must have found them. Probably just luck, but then, you never know, do you? He may be working with one or more others." That comment signalled to Russell that perhaps Sir Denis was preparing the ground for possible conspiracy charges.

"I am fairly confident that all six documents would have been kept together" Sir Denis continued. "I think he presented himself at the appropriate office in Barbados with just one to test the water, so to speak."

Russell took another sip of tea before asking "Do you have a file on this fellow?"

"Obviously we're assembling one now. The fax arrived overnight so I've only been aware of the problem since seven this morning. He gave a name and address and details of his employer. They're a travel company apparently. Not one of the important ones. At the moment I'm proceeding in the belief that the information is correct. We'll soon find out if he's lying. Enquiries are in hand but obviously far from complete. I need to balance the urgency of this matter against the need for discretion." Sir Denis drank a little of his tea whilst he considered what additional information to offer. Russell waited. Sir Denis tossed him a couple of meaty scraps.

"He has no criminal record and no history of subversive activities or connections with dissident groups. No evidence of marriage has been discovered."

"Would you want anything done about this chappie once we have recovered all the documents?" Russell asked. There seemed a good chance that few people would miss this fellow.

Sir Denis remained impassive. "He would need to be silenced by whatever means were deemed appropriate."

Both men reflected on this answer. Perhaps an accident could be arranged. But between now and the unsuspecting fellow's probable demise as much information as possible would need to be unearthed so that the ramifications could be assessed.

Russell spoke first. "Should I send 007?"

Sir Denis Skeene-Flinte laughed, a reaction very rarely witnessed. "007? He's a bit long in the tooth isn't he? I'm surprised Ten are still using him. I would have thought by now you'd have transferred him to Six."

Suddenly a thought occurred to him. "And you do know, of course, that there are no casinos in Barbados. They tried to introduce them about two years ago but the local churches soon put a stop to that. Without a little flutter to augment those frightfully mean wages you pay him 007 would never be able to afford his high living." They both laughed at 007's expense.

"So who would you like?" Russell asked. "019?"

"Is he available?"

"He's available. I'll send him to you to be briefed. Rather a favourite of yours isn't he?"

"He's sound, loyal, competent and frugal" commented Sir Denis.

Chapter Thirty Two

All Too Easy

Operative 019, who cannot be identified or described for obvious reasons, was comfortably ensconced in a window seat in the Club Class section of a British Airways 747. He'd deposited his briefcase and a couple of magazines on the adjacent seat and was apparently listening to music, through headphones, from a Sony Walkman lying casually on top of them. In fact the tape was the one handed to him three minutes before he passed through passport control.

Yesterday, Thursday, he'd been briefed by Sir Denis Skeene-Flinte. A situation had arisen that needed to be resolved rapidly and with the utmost discretion. In outline his task was simple. Without giving cause for suspicion he was instructed to locate and, if necessary, contact a British subject. As quickly as possible he needed to acquire five documents in the possession of this character and another one held by officials in a Barbados government department. He would check these for authenticity based on an analysis of factors divulged to him in confidence at the briefing. Then, using all the information available at the time and exercising his own best judgement, he had to decide whether to take any further action. If security was likely to be compromised then termination might be necessary. Only as a last resort of course.

This crisis had developed so suddenly that detailed intelligence on The Target had not been available yesterday. Now, almost 24 hours later, he'd been handed a fuller brief. But not a written one. Operative 019 disliked written briefs.

In his view a paper trail frequently led to trouble. In fact, as far as he could ascertain, it was the discovery of written evidence which had led to this current crisis. He preferred intelligence information to be held inside his head. And the best means of transferring a brief to that safe place was by means of tape recordings – which were, additionally, quicker to create than a typed brief. For added security this rapidly-assembled taped dossier on The Target would be erased once memorised.

Walter Morgan Fairchild was 25 years old, lived in Gravesend with his widowed mother, had no brothers or sisters, was unmarried and lacked a steady girlfriend. He preferred to be addressed by his middle name, perhaps no surprise given the disrespect accorded to the sobriquet 'Wally'. Apparently he had no close friends at his workplace, a minor tour operator called Sunstroke Holidays. As far as was known he had no regular contact with his university friends. He voted regularly but had never been a member of a political party. He took *The Guardian* six days a week and *The Observer* on Sundays. Subscriber to *History Today* and occasional purchaser of *Amateur Photographer*. Height five seven, weight around 160 pounds.

Some specifics of his Caribbean travels were sketchy. The date in late September on which he arrived in Montego Bay, Jamaica, was known, as were the flight numbers and dates of his journey through the islands. He'd left Jamaica by air from Kingston so presumably he'd crossed the country by some form of surface transportation, but his exact route and details of his accommodation were yet to be discovered. His stay in Haiti had been of such duration that it was likely he had taken excursions to various parts of the country. Similarly Grenada. In fact he'd spent such a considerable time there that it was thought highly likely that he'd visited the sister island of Carriacou – unless he'd been trapped on Grenada by the political uncertainties and subsequent invasion. Maybe he'd gone into hiding. Enquiries were continuing. (A hastily-added comment at the end of the tape furnished one result of these enquiries. The Chief Registrar in Barbados recalled that Fairchild had volunteered the information that people he'd met in Carriacou had 'told him where to find' the deed he'd presented.) Hopefully by tomorrow the names of the hotels he'd patronised on his trip would be known. In Barbados he was staying at the Casuarinas Beach Club in Saint Lawrence, in the parish of Christchurch.

019 checked in to that hotel in the early evening of Friday 4th November. As the receptionist handed him his room key he asked "Is Mr Fairchild about? He's a colleague of mine."

He watched carefully as she checked the keys hanging behind her. She seemed to be looking for 126. She turned back to him.

"His key's not here so he may be in his room, but sometimes he takes it with him when he goes out."

"I think he said he's in room 126. Is that correct?"

"Yes." She leant over the counter to her left and peered in the direction of the restaurant. "That looks like him in the bar."

"Thank you. Can you ask someone to take this bag to my room whilst I say hello to Mr Fairchild?" He put the key on the counter.

"Of course sir."

019 strode into the bar. At the second table sat a tubby fellow in his twenties reading a book with the help of a Cuba Libre. Adjacent to the beverage lay a pair of sunglasses and the key to room 126.

"May I join you?"

"Sure" said The Target, indicating a chair with his right hand.

"I say, you have a terrific suntan. Been here long? On holiday?"

"Just a few days in Barbados. But I've been in The Caribbean for some weeks. Grenada, Haiti, Jamaica. I'm

Morgan Fairchild, Sunstroke Holidays."

"Pleased to meet you. I'm Thompson. Grenada you say! I hope you didn't get caught up in that frightful mess last week."

"I'm afraid I was. I saw the invasion and the massacre."

A waitress appeared at their table. "Oh, a Banks for me" said 019. "I've only just arrived." He turned back to The Target. "Weren't you frightened?"

"Oddly enough no. That surprised me" The Target replied. "It wasn't really dangerous for visitors, although at one point I was nearly blown up by an American helicopter."

"What happened?"

"The Grenadians shot it down." He polished off the rest of his Cuba Libre. "I'm afraid you'll have to excuse me. I've got a dinner date with a lovely lady and I don't want to be late for the pre-prandial drinks."

"Of course old boy, don't mind me. Staying here long?"

The Target shot him a suspicious glance as if wondering why this new arrival would interested in having that information. "Until next Wednesday. See ya later." He stood up, collected a red leather shoulder bag he had hooked over the chair back, dropped his book in it and departed.

019's eyes followed him through Reception and their owner noted that he handed his room key to the girl. Good. He left the table and strolled through the trees to a position which gave him a clear view of the car park. The Target slid into a white Caribbean Cub. He mentally noted the registration number then returned to his drink. Almost immediately the bellboy appeared.

"Your key sir. I've left your bag in the room. If you need me to show you anything please ask."

"No, that's fine. This is for you. Thank you."

Five minutes late 019 paid for his beer, strolled to his room, unpacked and took a shower. He waited another 40 minutes before wandering, apparently aimlessly, back to the bar.

Darkness had descended. The restaurant and pool area were illuminated with oases of light which barely penetrated the gardens. But Reception and the bar blazed a bright welcome, lit like the stage in a West End theatre. Operative 019 stationed himself in the shadow of a palm tree in a spot where he could observe the action in Reception without being seen. Good. Very good. As he'd hoped, a new girl was on duty now and she seemed new to the job. A small group arrived and she became flustered as she dealt with them.

He slipped stealthily through the gardens to the car park then breezed confidently into Reception from that direction. He caught the receptionist's eye, smiled and said "126 please." She reached behind, detached the key and gave it to him whilst returning his smile. She resumed her work with the group.

He let himself into the room, switched on the light and checked that the curtains were drawn. They were. This is all too easy he thought. But then he wasn't dealing with a fellow professional was he? Just some twerp of a travel clerk. Who reads books in a bar.

First he went to the dresser and tried the drawers, opening them from the bottom and working upwards as burglars do. He saw nothing of interest until he pulled out the top drawer. There his eager eyes spotted an Ordnance Survey map of Barbados, similar to the one with which he'd been supplied, folded incorrectly. Very out of character for The Target if what I've been told is right. Then he realised why it was folded like that. A stretch of the southeast coastline had been clearly isolated with a scrawled pencil line and peppered with a series of small crosses. Obviously that was the only part of the island of interest to The Target. He examined it more closely. Those crosses marked Salt Cave, Oliver's Cave, Crane Beach, Shark's Hole, Beachy Head and Sam Lord's Castle. This must be The Target's search area. There was a tiny red dot beside the cross at Oliver's Cave, almost as if he needed a discreet reminder. Is this where he found the document?

That suggests that he hadn't found anything in Carriacou. Information from his contacts there must have led him to Barbados.

Now where would he hide anything?

019 closed the drawers, stood up straight and idly surveyed the room. Quite a few possibilities but first I'll try the bathroom. He strode in there and gazed around. Toilet cistern? Cabinet? He carefully lifted the top of the cistern and revealed the flush mechanism and clean water. He replaced the cover then checked that nothing was taped behind or underneath it. Opening the cabinet door he saw a sparse range of toiletries. Toothpaste, toothbrush, shaving foam, razor, a spare blade, talcum powder, shampoo. Just the basic necessities. No aftershave, deodorant or cologne. No room behind them for parchment deeds and no space behind the cabinet, which was screwed flush to the wall.

He closed the cabinet door and scanned the bathroom again. There was no other possible hiding place. He left the bathroom and quickly checked the clothes in the closet. Most were folded on shelves with just a lonely shirt on a hanger. The holdall was empty with no secret compartments. Returning to the bedroom he stood and surveyed the furniture for a few minutes. This guy is not a professional so maybe he has hidden the deeds somewhere obvious.

The bed. An SLR camera, an East German Praktica, lay on top where it had been tossed. Hmmm, just a little bit too casual. Carefully, memorizing its exact position, he picked it up and laid it on the table. Then he grabbed the end of the mattress and heaved that up with a jerk. Oh, what a surprise! There were two sheets of parchment hidden there. Supporting the mattress with his right hand he reached down with his left, withdrew those items, then let the mattress fall back. He replaced the camera then studied his find.

He was holding two maps. A quick glance suggested that one, headed 'Barbadoes', identified the patch of coastline revealed on the clumsily-folded OS map. The other was probably an enlargement of the area circled on the 'Barbadoes' map. Then his trained ear picked up a slight sound from the corridor. He froze.

Happy voices, one male, one female, were entering from the gardens. They sounded youngish and they were heading this way. Maybe chummy had concluded his pre-prandial drinks session and he was bringing his 'lovely lady' here for dinner. The Target didn't look much of a ladies' man but then you never know. 019 soundlessly killed the lights then stepped between the curtain and the sliding glass patio doors. Those he unlocked in case he needed to escape at speed.

The voices moved along the corridor and had almost reached 126. They were chattering loudly in English, both somewhat excitable. Maybe they'd been drinking heavily. Then they suddenly stopped. The man produced a key which he inserted into the lock of the room next door. They went inside, shutting the door after them.

Operative 019 relocked the patio exit and emerged from behind the curtain. He rolled up the maps and secured them with a rubber band. Stepping cautiously to the door and ignoring the lights he halted with his hand on the knob for a few seconds and listened with his ear flat against the door. Nothing. He opened the door silently and checked the corridor. Nobody. He slipped out and closed it behind him. Working quickly he pulled out his skeleton keys and tried a number until he found one which would unfasten that lock. Still nobody coming. He detached that from the loop which held it and its siblings and slipped it on to the ring which held his own room key. He checked that the door was locked then returned to his room.

All he needed there was his own OS map. Having memorised the location from The Target's copy he could probably have driven there without it but better to be sure. Anyway, although Oliver's Cave was the most likely site of this travel agent's discovery – as indicated by the tiny red dot – there was no guarantee of that.

The receptionist was assisting a couple who were hoping to rent a car tomorrow. Or trying to. For some reason she was having difficulty. He dropped the key to 126 on the counter with a smile and sauntered out to the car park.

They'd told him the make, colour and registration number. A blue Toyota Corolla. He strolled casually along the line of cars until he reached it. He stopped at the rear and glanced around nonchalantly. Then the maps slipped from under his arm to the ground. As he bent down to pick them up he quickly felt inside the exhaust pipe, located and withdrew the car keys and opened the boot to reveal an aluminium briefcase, a shovel and a sports bag. He wasn't about to check the contents of the briefcase right now but he knew what it should contain. This model was designed specifically for rapid assembly and even quicker disassembly. He would need to adjust the sights but he could do that later tonight in a quiet part of the island using the image-intensifier 'scope. He opened the sports bag, checked that all his requested tools and implements were there, put the parchment sketch maps inside, zipped it up and closed the boot. He strode round to the front, unlocked the door and sat. Once he had adjusted the seat and mirrors he slotted the key into the ignition, reversed out and set off for the southeast coast.

Tonight there was a full moon so there was sufficient light to illuminate piles of rubble and heavy construction equipment at the location marked with a pencilled cross and a red dot on The Target's OS map. 019 drove on another 150 yards, pulled off the road to his left and parked by a gate at the entrance to a field. He killed the engine and headlights and waited. Nothing happened for ten minutes.

Then he opened the driver's door. Good. They'd taped up the interior light switch. He closed the door silently, locked it, retrieved the sports bag from the boot, forced the shovel inside it and then waited another five minutes. He'd dressed as he assumed a British tourist in his age group holidaying on the south coast would dress. Reeboks, fake designer jeans and T-shirt. With his close-cropped hair he could be mistaken for an English football hooligan. He would have no problem faking drunkenness and if necessary he could dump the sports bag.

He strode confidently up the road and then, as if by magic, disappeared behind a JCB. Back at the hotel he'd decided that those dotted lines represented a cave of some sort. Now he suspected and hoped that there was an opening above it so that he wouldn't need to shin down the cliff face. He didn't think The tubby Target would have done so.

He almost stumbled into the hole. The full moon saved him. It also provided enough illumination to reveal roughly-hewn steps and a soft sandy bottom. He skipped easily down half the distance and jumped the rest. He switched on his torch and flashed it ahead of him along the ground and lower parts of the cave walls. He soon reached the bend in the tunnel, about halfway, where the 'Z' on the second map suggested something might be discovered. He could only speculate on the reason the cartographer had drawn a Z and not an X. Possibly 'X' only exists in fictional tales. Also, in the times when illiteracy was the norm a man's signature would be represented by an X. Or the explanation could be simpler. The 'Z' could be a code, something which signified precisely what was hidden to those privy to the secret.

He swept his torchlight along the ground. The beam lit up packed sand at this point but it appeared, to his eye, to be recently and deliberately packed. As if somebody had stomped it down. He selected the absolutely central point and started digging. He decided to excavate six feet here and then, if unsuccessful, he would try either side. Again, it proved all too easy. He'd barely cleared three feet before he struck something solid. It felt like wood. Quickly he cleared the top and sides and realised that he was looking at a trunk or chest. He pulled it up out of the hole, laid it on the sand, unbuckled it and opened the lid.

Inside was an oilskin package almost the size of the chest. He reached in and extracted it. Quickly he checked that there was no false bottom to the trunk then opened the package. These were either the five missing deeds or clever forgeries. He wasn't about to check that right now. If they were forgeries then clearly the originals would not be here and The Target was a lot smarter than he appeared to be. But would a clever person return the deeds and the trunk to their original hiding place? A place so clearly marked on a map left lying in a drawer? Of course not. A clever person would find another secluded spot and dump the evidence there.

019 shoved the deeds back into their oilskin home and dropped that into his sports bag.

During the fifteen minutes or so that he'd been underground his sensitive ear had remained alert to any unusual sound. Two cars had swished past on the road but now he heard one slow down, pull off and park on the construction site above. He stopped stock-still and concentrated. Soon he heard voices, one male and one female, approaching. This was becoming annoyingly recurrent. These two also sounded as if they'd been drinking, though something about the timbre of their voices and their speech patterns suggested they were locals.

They're coming here. Probably for a lovers' tryst. Shit. They may stay above ground, but that wasn't very likely was it? This cave has probably attracted lovers for over a hundred years. People have probably been conceived here for generations. Maybe including these two. And tonight, with the full moon, they'll be able to see clearly down the hole. Full moon. That gave him an idea.

As the voices approached the cave entrance he cupped his hands together around his mouth and let out a wail that he hoped might emulate a werewolf. That caused some consternation.

"I don't like it Caesar."

"Jus' a wile dog girl."

That first attempt sounded more like a sick banshee so he now let out a full-throated howl that he hoped sounded like The Hound Of The Baskervilles on the hunt for his next meal. He followed that with some panting and grunts then scraped the wooden handle of the shovel on the rock face. The girl screamed. She rushed away from the entrance shouting "I not goin' down dere Caesar." He heard the man run after her.

019 stilled himself and listened. It sounded like the couple had stopped by their car. The girl was threatening to get into it and continuing to screech loudly, though not hysterically now, whilst her man was trying to calm her. Soon he would volunteer to descend alone and scare away that 'wile dog'. 019 reckoned he had a two minute window.

Good. Quickly he turned his torch back on. He flashed it up the cave wall. First to his left, up to the top and down. Nothing. Then as far as the beam reached, both ways along that side. Still nothing. Then he tried the wall on his right. To seaward it was undulating though unpromising but right here, where he was standing, there was a black spot right at the top. Just above head height, just under the roof, there was a crevice which might be big enough to hold the chest. He quickly closed and rebuckled it. Holding it in his right hand and scaling the rock face he swung it into the gap and pushed it back as far as it would go. He jumped down and roughly dumped sand into the hole. That would do. It might look as if a wild dog had been searching for a bone. He listened again to the courting couple.

They were speaking quietly but intently. The girl was determined to get away from here and appeared to be winning the argument. He thought he heard her say "Tek me home Caesar" a couple of times. Maybe they wouldn't venture down here tonight after all. Later, perhaps tomorrow, their friends might come looking for evidence to substantiate an unlikely story centred around terrifying howls issuing from an empty cave.

He shoved his spade back into the sports bag and strolled

through the rest of the grotto to the beach. He didn't worry about disguising his footprints. He wasn't expecting a visit from police forensic scientists and once a few excited people ventured down here in daylight there would be dozens of feet trampling over his spoor.

Neat. The tide was out. He could stroll along in the direction of his parked car whilst he searched for a suitable place to climb the cliff. He stayed close to the water so that the incoming waves would obliterate his footprints. After a hundred yards or so he spotted a slope and noiselessly gained the cliff top. He sat there and waited ten minutes, listening intently. Nothing untoward. Rising slowly he walked casually to the road and stopped in the shadow of the last tree. He could see his car almost opposite. No lights, no human sounds, no movement, so after another two minutes he strolled over to his car, opened the boot and deposited the bag.

He strode straight to the driver's door, opened up, started the car, flashed on the headlights and drove a little way until he found a place where he could execute a three point turn. Retracing his route at a moderate pace he had time to spare a glance at the construction site as he passed. The girl was standing between the open passenger door and the seat of a black Japanese hatchback, her left hand on the doorframe and right arm across the roof. The guy was pacing towards the cave.

As he continued to drive towards Saint Lawrence 019 speculated on the lovers' situation. Would that guy get his just desserts tonight? After a mile or two, at a point he'd spotted on his journey to the grotto, between fields of waving sugar cane in an area totally devoid of houses, there was a track leading off to the right. He turned into it, switched off his headlights and proceeded slowly.

Almost a quarter mile from the road he discerned a tree about a hundred yards distant. He stopped the car, took a piece of paper and a drawing pin and strolled up to it. He pinned up the piece of paper and returned to the car.

Assembling the rifle and scope he loaded it, sighted the target and, using the bonnet for stability, fired. It took three attempts, punctuated by subtle corrections to the nightsight, before he was satisfied. Then he rambled over to the tree, removed the paper and pin and returned to his car. Hopefully, if anyone heard those shots and reported them tomorrow, people would assume it was someone taking pot shots at that 'wile dog'.

By the time he arrived back at the hotel it was quite late. So no dinner tonight. The Target's Caribbean Cub was not in the car park and the key to room 126 was on its hook. He made his way there, opened up, returned the maps to their temporary home under the mattress, closed and locked the door and retired to his own room. A thorough inspection of his discovery assured him that these deeds were almost certainly genuine.

He lay back on his bed with his hands clasped behind his head. He would take extra care tomorrow. Today everything had been all too easy.

For some reason he couldn't sleep. Something was troubling him. What? He was in possession of the deeds – well, five of them, and the sixth was in a safe place – so it couldn't be that. It must be the security aspects of this operation. Sir Denis had expressed concern that too many people knew of the existence of these deeds. They cast doubt on the ownership of some very valuable real estate and were best destroyed. But would that be enough to resolve the problem? What if somebody talked, creating a rumour, and that led to a perusal of the public records? Apparently the records were incomplete and ambiguous so it was imperative that this recent discovery was hushed up.

Sir Denis and his private secretary would say nothing. He himself could be trusted to hold his tongue. For the time being they would trust the Barbados officials to stay silent. But what about this travel clerk? How would he react when the Bajans tell him that the deed he'd left with them was invalid and that, furthermore, as it was a forgery it wouldn't be returned to him? He would probably return to that cave with a spade. Once he found that the chest was no longer buried under three feet of sand he would realise his foolishness in replacing it there. Of course he would have a good look around the cave and might find the trunk. And find it empty. He would very likely cause a fuss. Maybe go to the newspapers. Write a book. So something should be done about him.

As with the other actors in this drama there were two choices. Either (a) acquaint him with all the details and persuade him to be a loyal citizen or (b) terminate him. Operative 019 wasn't authorized to conduct option (a).

But that wasn't the problem that was troubling him. If the termination was to be executed in Barbados there was ample time to arrange an accident. Between now and Wednesday in fact. So what was it?

Suddenly he realized. The 'lovely lady'. Sir Denis had suggested the possibility of an accomplice but actually that was unlikely. Anyway, should the deeds disappear and Fairchild meet with an accident an accomplice would be smart enough to take the hint. But what about this 'lovely lady'? Fairchild might tell her of his discovery soon in order to get inside her knickers. "I own the most valuable strip of land in Barbados" would be a good line. Time could be of the essence here.

019 rose from his bed and sauntered over to the balcony window. He drew the curtains and allowed the pale moonlight into the room. Then he stepped back two paces and stood quite still, waiting. For a few minutes he gazed at the gardens basking in the subdued light. A zephyr wafted through the grounds gently rustling the palm fronds and stirring the feathery casuarina leaves. Shadows quivered gently for some minutes. Then he saw what he was waiting for. A shadow detached itself from a tree and slowly moved across his field of vision. A night security guard. So stay clear of the gardens.

He dressed and glanced at his watch. 3.16. Going to his suitcase he felt his way to the bottom and withdrew a Walther PPK. Not a weapon popular nowadays with the department but still his preferred pistol for close work. OK, the magazine capacity was small by today's standards and its 9mm short round a little feeble but that didn't matter. The 'K' stood for *Kurz*, German for short, and that was its advantage. The PPK's compact nature made it ideal as a concealed weapon. He was just as handy with the semi-automatic Colt .45 or a Magnum when he needed the stopping power but on this assignment, he'd decided, stopping power was not required. It wouldn't take much to stop one unarmed chubby travel clerk.

The Walther was loaded but not cocked. His hand dived into the suitcase again and this time emerged grasping a silencer.

Of course he wasn't planning to terminate The Target right here right now. A travel agent discovered shot in the head in his bed would not only attract the full resources of the Barbados police. It would also be front page news in the tabloid press back in the UK. And what if he'd scored with his date and brought her back with him? Unlikely, but why risk being seen by a witness? No. He was attempting to formulate some plan whereby he could neutralise the threat as discreetly as possible. Maybe he could persuade The Target to accompany him to some remote spot on the island. There he could question him. Did he have an accomplice? Who else had he told of his discovery?

Operative 019 slumped back on his bed. He tossed the handgun and silencer back into the suitcase. He was not being realistic. If he persuaded The Target to accompany him from the hotel there was a risk they would be spotted. Even in the middle of the night. Then, should The Target not return or be found dead, 019 would be identified as the last person to be seen with him. Also, whose car would they use? If 019 used his own vehicle then the police would want to know how Fairchild reached the place where his body was discovered. If, on the other hand, they took the Caribbean Cub and he left it near the body then how would he, 019, get back? Not to mention that receptionist. She might remember him asking after The Target when he arrived. I'll need to give this some thought.

Actually what it amounted to was very simple. This chappie had got under his skin. Rubbed him up the wrong way. There was something a bit creepy about him and a hint of smugness. Or it could just be chemistry. Some people are just naturally repelled by others.

The Target hadn't actually done anything wrong yet had he? He'd found, or been given, some property deeds which declared, in the absence of alternative proof or ownership, that the bearer owned some very valuable land. He had delivered one of them to the appropriate authorities. He wasn't involved in any act which was unpatriotic, subversive or illegal. He'd only done what anyone in his position would be expected to do. It wasn't his fault that his actions had precipitated a crisis.

019 cooled his head and thought dispassionately. Tomorrow he would collect the final deed and make absolutely sure he possessed a matching set. He would report that success to Sir Denis. Then he would follow The Target, at a distance, over the weekend and arrange an accident at a suitable opportunity. If an accomplice should emerge at a later date there would be no evidence to support his wild claims, particularly if the rather vague receipt Fairchild had been given by the Registrar was also recovered.

019 undressed and slid under the sheet. His mind at rest he now enjoyed a good night's sleep.

Chapter Thirty Three

Then, Finally, Silence

"Well, hallo again old boy. Mind if I join you?"

"Sure."

This was at breakfast, next morning.

"Planning anything special today?"

"No. I'll just check out some of the hotels we feature."

The Target had got hold of a recent copy of the *FT* and was studying the share prices. Thinking of investing profits from land sales was he? He needn't waste his time.

A waiter approached and 019 ordered a Continental. Really he fancied something more substantial like a genuine Full English with kidneys and lashings of mushrooms, especially as he'd skipped dinner last night, but let's get this job to bed first. And a little hunger often gave him an edge. Maybe he could treat himself to lunch once he'd collected that final document. He returned his attention to The Target, who'd just requested his bill.

"It's Saturday old boy. Surely they don't make you work on Saturdays?"

"I'm only here until Wednesday" Fairchild replied. He finished his coffee. "What I usually do" he continued "is have Sunday off. I can't really pester hotel managers and owners on a Sunday."

If I have my way you certainly won't be pestering anyone tomorrow. Or ever again, come to that. What a twerp.

Like yesterday, The Target didn't seem interested in a protracted conversation. He paid his bill, which arrived with 019's breakfast, picked up his pink paper and that red shoulder bag and mooched off to his room with a "Cheerio" tossed over his shoulder.

019 watched him go as he rapidly demolished his own breakfast. He could just see The Target's room from here. After a few minutes the curtains, which for some reason had been permanently drawn, were opened and The Target appeared. He sat on his patio with that *FT* and a banana.

Her Majesty's loyal operative left a few dollars under his plate, stood, picked up his magazine, felt for the transmitter in his pocket and strolled out to the car park. He saw The Target's Caribbean Cub almost directly in front of him. There was a small problem with that car. It's based on a Reliant. Unlike the Robin – which used the same 850 cc engine – it had four wheels, but like all Reliants the body was moulded from fibreglass. A magnet won't stick to that. Just a minor irritation though. The chassis is metal.

As he passed the vehicle 019 stumbled clumsily, dropped his magazine, stared back with an accusing glance at the ridge of tarmac which had tripped him, then picked up the magazine and attached the transmitter in one deft movement.

He walked on to the boot of his own car. Surreptitiously he removed the shovel from the sports bag and silently laid it flat. Then he grasped the sports bag, slammed the boot shut, unlocked the door and sat in the driving seat. He placed the sports bag on the front passenger seat. Any passing casual observer would see him rooting in there for something but in fact he was peering at a small screen on a battery-powered receiver. It showed a map of Barbados with a tiny green blip blinking in the Saint Lawrence district.

This is a great piece of kit. I can track that vehicle anywhere on the island without moving from my seat but the best part, brilliant in fact, is the extent to which each sector can be enlarged. If necessary I can detect the precise location of that car, in any part of the island from any part of the island, by its proximity to the closest building. I just need to cross-reference the amplified co-ordinates with my OS map. There is no need to follow him by keeping his car in sight. If the Caribbean Cub remains in the car park at Casuarinas Beach Club then the odds are that The Target will be there too.

The accident would happen elsewhere, preferably in a remote spot, so deal with the urgent business first and just wait until that blip leaves the hotel. He zipped up the bag and started the car.

Julius Alleyne was his usual courteous self. He offered tea but his guest declined on the grounds that the meeting would be brief. They both had better things to do this weekend. The operative remained standing whilst the Registrar smiled and opened a desk drawer. Presumably he'd unlocked the safe and transferred the cause of the crisis in anticipation of the British man's arrival. He withdrew the deed and handed it over.

019 carefully studied it, first feeling the quality of the paper. It certainly seemed to match the other five.

"Did you give Mr Fairchild a photocopy?" he asked.

Mr Alleyne smiled. "I told him photocopying might damage it. I gave him a vague receipt which didn't specify what he'd presented."

"He was happy with that?"

"No, certainly not. He kicked up a fuss. Very vex' in fac', specially with the wording." Remembering the tension of the argument Mr Alleyne had briefly abandoned his normally cultured enunciation. He recovered his articulacy. "The receipt was just for delivery of a document."

019 nodded. That just confirmed what he already knew. "Could you give me the photocopy, a sheet of blank paper and a pen?"

"Photocopy?"

"The copy you made to fax Sir Denis. I assume you didn't pass this valuable document through the fax machine."

Mr Alleyne's smile was rueful this time. "Certainly."

He reached back into the drawer and pulled out four photocopied sheets. Then from another drawer he produced a pen and a sheet of paper. 019 reached across and scribbled something on the paper, signed and dated it, laid down the pen and scooped up the photocopies. Mr Alleyne picked up the paper, read it and laughed.

"A receipt for five documents. Signed by you when we both know Thompson is not your real name."

019 looked Mr Alleyne straight in the eye. "Unfortunately your government and the people of Barbados will never know what a great service you have performed for them by your prompt action. Your honesty has also been noted. I am assured by my government that your contribution to stability will be rewarded but that the benefits will be delayed, very vague and have no obvious connection with these events." He held out his hand. "Good day to you sir."

The operative returned to his car, dropped the sports bag on the passenger seat, leaned over it and peered at the receiver again. The blip had moved. He glanced around him. As you would expect on a Saturday there were few cars parked here. Just his and three others, one of which presumably belonged to the Registrar. There were no people in sight. He enlarged the sector to which the blip had travelled, noted the co-ordinates, reduced the picture to its default size and zipped up the bag. Taking his OS map from the glove box he checked the co-ordinates. Hmm. Wildey. That's a residential district on the outskirts of Bridgetown. No hotels there. He sat back and thought for a few minutes.

Chummy was very late back last night. Maybe he had scored with his 'lovely lady' – though looking at him that seems unlikely. Perhaps she lives in Wildey. It's quite possible that he didn't really intend to waste a Saturday inspecting hotels. No reason why he should tell a stranger his plans for the day.

019 started the engine. Before he did anything else he needed to drive to the Secure Communications Centre to check if there were any further intelligence reports concerning The Target or revised instructions. He needed to report the success of phase one to Sir Denis too.

The new intelligence was all negative. Which was good. The details of Fairchild's movements and accommodation during his Caribbean travels were still sparse, which suggested that he'd kept a low profile. Probably he'd travelled on local buses so there would be no records and few recollections. No new information had emerged of hotel accommodation in Haiti although it was now verified that he had lodged in a cheap hotel in Carriacou for a few days. News from the UK was negative too. He was not a member of any club or society except for his local library and apparently he enjoyed no close friendships. There was no-one who would make waves if he met with an accident. Only his mother would miss him.

At 1131, before leaving the SCC, 019 checked his receiving equipment again. The blip had moved. It was now on the west coast, in the Paynes Bay area. He enlarged it then checked the co-ordinates with his OS map. Apparently the Caribbean Cub had found its way to Treasure Beach Hotel. So chummy was doing some work then.

As he watched the blip it started to move. Let's see where he goes. 019 zipped up the bag, strode out to his car, tossed in the bag and sat in the driving seat. The sports bag now seemed to have staked a permanent claim to the front passenger seat. He unzipped it and sat hunched over it for a few minutes. He decided to see where the blip was going before starting his own car and following.

The blip travelled down the west coast road towards Bridgetown, occasionally halting, sometimes for up to a minute, but that was just probably the effect of traffic and parked vehicles. Though this was the grandly-named Highway 1 by UK standards it was just a B road. He stopped again briefly on the outskirts of the capital then continued towards the city centre. Past the University of the West Indies and the hospital at Belfield. He took a right turn which would eventually bring him into the centre of town so presumably he was following the well-signposted route. There were the few inevitable stops and starts before he reached the eastern end of Broad Street, a short distance before Trafalgar Square. Here he stopped again. Two minutes passed and the blip didn't move. Were there traffic lights there? Operative 019 couldn't remember. After five minutes he decided that The Target must have found a parking spot in an impossible place.

He started the engine and joined Highway 1. Once he reached the capital he was carried along like a wind-blown autumn leaf in the stream of traffic meandering through the busy streets until he reached the main artery, the one-way Broad Street. Why would his man park here? Sightseeing? Shopping in Cave Shepherd? Taking photographs of the Nelson Monument and The Careenage for the company's brochures?

Sure enough, The Target had achieved the impossible. There was the Caribbean Cub parked in a prime position at the end of Broad Street. But no sign of its driver. Operative 019 cruised slowly past in the river of traffic and onwards into Trafalgar Square casting around for a sight of Fairchild as he drove. There were a few tourists to be seen mooching about but as today was a Saturday the sidewalks were overflowing with hundreds – nay thousands – of Bajans who'd come into town for their weekend shopping. Over there a tourist was photographing his girl friend in front of the Nelson Monument. The celebrated Admiral was staring towards The Target's Cub, daring anyone to interfere with it.

019 continued cruising with the traffic like a piece of flotsam. He turned right, then right again and finally parked up near the bridge. No sign of The Target so why not take the opportunity to sample a well deserved lunch at The Waterfront Café, the current 'In' spot?

Obviously he selected a table which gave him an excellent view of other patrons and passing pedestrians, but there was no sign of his man so after a good meal and a couple of beers he ambled back to his car. He retrieved the sports bag from the boot, plonked it on the passenger seat and unzipped it. If he hunched over it no passerby would see what he was really doing.

The blip had moved again. Presumably The Target had completed his business in Bridgetown and was leaving the capital. He was now in the northeast suburbs near Waterford. The enlarged sector showed that he was driving along Highway 3, the normal route to take for the east coast. Surely Sunstroke Holidays didn't feature either of the hotels over at Bathsheba? Quite apart from the fact that the beaches on that side were pebbled or, at best, wave-lashed coarse sand, swimming was notoriously dangerous. Only surfers ventured into those Atlantic rollers. And, according to his information, neither hotel was appropriate for a package holiday programme. Maybe he was just driving over there to admire the view.

019 set off in pursuit. Once he had closed the gap somewhat he kept a distance of some two miles between them until he noticed that the blip had halted again. Now he was in the middle of sugar cane country. There was not a soul to be seen in any direction so he pulled over and stopped.

This could be his chance. It's quiet around here. He ran through the procedure again. Note co-ordinates, cross-reference with OS map. According to the contours The Target had halted on a hilltop which would permit fine views of the Bathsheba coastline. Maybe he was taking pictures.

He restarted the car and drove on towards the coast until he saw, parked just off the road about 400 yards ahead, a white Caribbean Cub. There was nobody in it or near it. He pulled over and parked, slipped some tools from the bag into his pocket, zipped up the bag, got out and locked the car. He strolled casually up the hill. Yes, it was the same vehicle all right. As he reached it he stopped to admire the view. He swivelled around, breathing the sea air in deeply. Exhilarating. The strong breeze of the Trade Winds which bent the trees double, fierce waves crashing on to the pebble beach, itself picturesquely host to half a dozen brightly-painted traditional fishing boats. Surprising, really, that there weren't more people up here to enjoy this. He could see nobody in fact.

Nobody would have seen him slip under the car and only the ants would have watched him making a few snips and 'adjustments'. He was soon upright again, pocketing the transmitter as he re-emerged. He was so quick in fact that if anyone had seen his brief disappearance they would be convinced they'd imagined it. Stretching out his arms, as one does sometimes when appreciating the wonders of nature, he ambled back to his car. There he sat and waited.

After some time, 34 minutes according to his watch, he saw a couple emerge from the other side of the hill and get in the Cub. He couldn't make them out easily from this distance but the passenger did seem to be a female. So maybe chummy did score last night. Maybe they'd been having some more nooky just now. Well, why begrudge the little twerp that? After all it's really the equivalent of – though better than – the condemned man enjoying a last cigarette before the firing squad fill him full of holes. Though why he should need to come out here for it when he has a perfectly good hotel room available is strange. Maybe he enjoys alfresco sex. Whatever, presumably he has his reasons.

The Caribbean Cub pulled slowly back on to the road, over the brow of the hill and commenced its run down the steep and twisty descent towards the seafront. Operative 019 started his engine and followed. As he'd already discovered, about half an hour ago, the top of that hill provides an excellent view of the coast.

He stopped at the brow and pulled over to park in the spot recently vacated by the other vehicle. He got out of the car. He was just in time.

That Caribbean Cub was careering down the narrow winding road at a pace well in excess of the speed commensurate with safety. It weaved across the road, jerking the occupants from side to side as the driver attempted to lose momentum. Its female passenger gripped the dashboard with both hands to avoid being flung into the road. They were a few yards from a tight right hand bend. At that speed there seemed little chance that they would negotiate it safely. They didn't. The driver attempted to turn but couldn't control the centrifugal forces. The car slid then tipped. It clipped the low wall on the outside of the corner which acted as a pivot, launching the vehicle into a series of barrel rolls before contact with a tree stump catapulted it over the cliff and towards the sea. At the zenith of its flight the Cub was completely inverted. The spinning wheels found no grip in the air. Loose baggage dropped seaward. Obviously neither driver or passenger were wearing their seat belts. They were flung clumsily into the air and followed their vehicle into The Deep.

This electrifying view was accompanied by the soundtrack of a screaming Reliant engine, a crashing of gears as the driver had tried to engage reverse, the scraping of fibreglass against coral stone and a screeching female. Then splashes as the Cub and its powerless occupants hit the water.

Then, finally, silence.

Postscript

Sunday morning at Gatwick Airport. The overnight flight from Barbados had just arrived, slightly late as usual. All work completed. Report tomorrow. Baggage hauled off the carousel and dumped on the trolley. Just push through the Green Channel. Customs officers standing in pairs behind empty tables alert for likely suspects. Almost through the sparse, brightly lit, twisting but broad passage then two gimlet-eyed officers beckoned.

"Where have you just come from sir?"

"Barbados". Just reach down to the trolley here. Feign eagerness to lift baggage onto their table.

"Not just yet sir. Do you have anything to declare?"

That's a stupid question. What's the Red Channel for then?

"No. Just a bottle of rum. Mount Gay."

"Have you visited Barbados before sir?"

"No. My first time."

"Business or pleasure?"

"Both, actually."

They stared for a good twenty seconds without saying anything. Why worry? They could search the baggage if they want to.

"Thank you sir. You may proceed." The one on the left indicated the exit with a sweep of his right arm.

A gentle stroll past the barriers restraining hordes of friends, family and, presumably, taxi drivers or chauffeurs.

Some brandished placards bearing handwritten names. Follow the signs for British Rail. Ticket bought, trolley abandoned at the head of the stairs, holdall shouldered and then the gentle trot down to the waiting Gatwick Express. Stow bag in the capacious cubby-holes provided and select a comfortable seat, preferably one facing the direction of travel.

Once I was settled and the train started to move I relaxed completely. My thoughts turned to yesterday and recent events.

I felt guilty about lying to Wendy-Ann at dinner on Friday night. It was important that she believed I would be leaving on Wednesday. I took a chance with the hotel, but otherwise that was the story I told everybody. I was trying to buy time. Hopefully she would forgive me after I explained to her, last night at the airport, that I'd been forced to revise my plans again.

I made somebody's day though. When I phoned the rental company after breakfast to tell them that they could collect the car immediately they were overjoyed. Someone had let them down. Apparently they had a rental booked by some guests at Treasure Beach that day and the vehicle they'd allocated hadn't been returned by the guy who'd hired it. They said I'd got them out of a hole.

All in all it had been a fascinating, enjoyable and – hopefully – profitable trip.

Thank you for reading *Only The Whores Wore Watches*. As a reward here is a sneak preview of my next book, *Tiger Beef Crying.*

THE 39TH DAY

Grumps opened the door. Toting his flip-flops in his right hand he stepped out stealthily into the pre-dawn silence, easing the doorknob soundlessly back home with his left. He disappeared into the dark envelope of the night along the shrub-bordered sandy path that led to the beach 30 yards away. Once well clear of the bungalow, almost at the beach, he shuffled his feet into his sandals. To his right he found the steps to the Eutopia Bar and Restaurant. He selected the third one up from the sand and sat there looking out to sea.

This was the third time Grumps had followed this routine and it was to be the last. On each occasion he'd been as quiet as a mouse in order not to wake me and each time I had regained consciousness as he slipped out of the room. Perhaps if he'd blundered around in the darkness like a drunken elephant, kicked my bed a few times, dropped a couple of heavy objects and then finally slammed the door I would have slept through it. I frequently sleep through thunderstorms.

I decided to follow him. Slipping out of bed I selected the famous Hong Kong T-shirt and a pair of jeans, picked up my camera bag and sauntered quietly down to the beach. I could see Grumps silhouetted against the brightening sky to the east staring out to sea at the dark mass of Ko Pha

Ngan. A long-tail boat, its helmsman relaxed at the stern, headed home, its wake furrowing the placid sea and its unsilenced engine throbbing steadily.

Grumps and the fisherman – if that's what he was – were the only people abroad at this early hour. The two mile sweep of Mae Nam beach witnessed only the constant thrumming of his passing engine, the whispering of the breeze rippling through the palm fronds and a gentle murmuring of the waves as they caressed the sand.

Moving silently so as not to advertise my presence I ascended the side steps to the bar, placed my shoulder bag noiselessly on a table and released my camera from its cool confinement. I hoped that Grumps wouldn't hear the gentle rasping of the zip. With an almost inaudible click I changed lenses.

As the sun began to force its way up behind the horizon one of the staff appeared, quietly but not silently, ready to commence her 14 hour shift.

"That's typical" Grumps muttered. "I just come out here for a bit of peace and the whole bloody island decides to turn up."